Dope Tits

Bix Skahill

Thicke & Vaney Press

What follows is some legally binding and serious shit:

THICKE & VANEY PRESS
876 7th Street W. #126
Saint Paul, MN 55102
Thickeandvaneybooks.com

ISBN: 9780998150406
LCCN: 2016916728
T&V# 1515

Art by Spot
Editted by Reginald Thicke

This is a work of fiction. Names, characters, pales, and incidents are either products of the author's imagination or are used fictitiously, and any resemblance to actual events or persons, living, dead, or undead, is entirely coincidental.

Printed in the United States of America. God save the Queen.

To Deborah
who has a pair

… stand up for the stupid and crazy…

■ Walt Whitman

But if when you hear my love call ring clear
Oooooooo, oooooooo
And I hear your answering echo so dear
Oooooooo, oooooooo

■ Slim Whitman

Part One:
Purple Hayes

As if they were common beasts of the field, Rusty Slump and CoCo McArdle rutted into one another, grinding their privates together, sweating, swearing.

It was disgusting.

Connie Pendleton moved closer to get a better look.

She was hidden among the pines that surrounded the Rutherford B. Hayes Memorial Rock Quarry, observing the couple offend the Lord perilously close to the edge of the pit.

Finding CoCo, a girl widely known as a shameless slut, in such a wanton activity was no revelation to Connie, though watching Rusty thrust into her was an unpleasant surprise. Certainly, he'd had his run-ins with Police Chief Pendleton, Connie's father, over his disgusting hobby of public defecation, but he wasn't a bad boy. At least, not in Connie's eyes. He had a nice smile, the most brilliant blue eyes, and he didn't treat her like a leper like the other kids at Rutherford B. Hayes Memorial High School.

Regrettably, she'd noticed a change in him recently, since he'd begun dating CoCo. He'd begun chewing gum, skipping classes, and listening to heavy metal. Even bought a black leather jacket emblazoned with the logo - the cross Jesus died on for our sins entering a human anus - of his favorite band, Satan's Butt Buddies. It was upon this abomination Rusty and CoCo lay as they fornicated. Gasping, grunting.

Edging closer, Connie found herself at the tree line. She could move no nearer for fear of exposing herself. But this was close enough for her purpose, the gathering of evidence.

Closing her eyes, she took a mental picture of the debauchery, which she could refer back to later. Whenever she needed.

As Rusty's bare bottom became permanently etched in her mind's eye, Connie felt her stomach flutter.

Once again, the young woman had to convince herself it was perfectly Christian to spy upon these two heathens, for she was doing God's work. Connie was assisting her father, the chief of the Fremont Police Society, even though he was unaware of her assistance. Sneaking out of her home in the middle of a chilly October night, the young woman had walked out to the quarry to attend an illegal high school party. Standing at the periphery, pretending to sip from a red Solo cup of suds, Connie memorized names and deeds, detailing all stripes of criminal acts. But when Rusty and CoCo had snuck off, hand in hand, into the shadows, she followed and struck gold, crime-wise, though it sickened her to do so. This was a true Christ-like sacrifice, bearing witness to Rusty Slump's monstrous scrotum, which hung between his legs as if constructed by wasps.

"Oh God, oh God, oh God," blasphemed CoCo, "I love it when your giant nutsack *fwaps* against my ass!"

Rusty cleared his throat. "You do remember, Sugar Lips, that my scrotum is enflamed due to condition called orchitis, which I got thanks to a case of chlamydia given to me. By you, I might add."

"Oh yes, ram your diseased dick into me and shut the flock up!"

Taking another bite of her father's famous hardtack, Connie settled in and watched as this illicit display of impiety gained momentum. Though disgusting, the sexual congress was, admittedly, informative. Despite being a senior at Rutherford B. Hayes Memorial High School, Connie had never even kissed a boy, and here, right out in the open, two of her classmates were doing things to each other that she could only imagine.

As her father pulled her out of school every time Health Class descended into the immoral abyss that was Sex Ed, everything she knew about the act of love came from the Bible: Onan spilling his seed on the ground and being struck down by the Lord, the wicked cities of Sodom and Gomorrah getting the deserved double whammy of fire and brimstone, and God smiting the bejesus out of 24,000 Israelites for being sexually immoral with Moabite women.

In God's world, sex was dangerous business. Even thinking about it.

Fear that the Lord might happen by and smite them was certainly not impeding Rusty and CoCo as they writhed on the ground. Quite the opposite, they seemed to be having more fun than Connie had ever experienced. Even on her birthday when she was released from chores and received a present, which was always a new sackcloth dress. CoCo was groaning, her eyes closed and her head lolling, while Rusty, his dirty jeans down around his dirty knees, had a smile slicing his face from ear to ear as he did the dirty deed.

Connie was surprised to find she too was smiling. Probably because she knew the ever-crackling flames of hell awaited these sinners.

A feeling of righteousness swelled in her breast as she licked some sweat from her lip. Connie wondered if her soul could stand much more of this savagery. Reminding herself that she was doing this for her beloved father, Connie stayed. In fact, she edged a mite closer, out of the safety of the trees, and tried to regulate her breathing. Apparently she was still winded from her long hike out to the quarry. Funny, though, that it seemed harder and harder to breath as time passed.

But she stopped breathing altogether when she noticed Rusty

was no longer looking at his partner as he hammered his hips. He was staring straight at her. Seeing into her soul.

Connie fell backward into the woods as Rusty came to a finish. One final thrust, a visage that looked pained, and a guttural grunt which, fortunately, covered Connie's own loud gasp.

As if they had not just shared the most intimate act, CoCo pushed her boyfriend off her and said, "Well, that was adequate. Now, let's have some Purple Hayes!"

If she'd not already fallen back onto her haunches, the young detective would have fallen back onto her haunches.

Purple Hayes, she whispered to herself, incredulous.

His attention now focused back on the whore of Fremont, Rusty smiled as he reached into his pocket and retrieved a vial of lilac colored powder. "Now go easy, Sugar Mouth, we've already talked about this. Our supply is running low."

As if she hadn't heard him, CoCo grabbed the vial and poured a heaping helping of the powder onto her thumb. She inhaled it into oblivion, a human vacuum.

That's Purple Hayes, Connie told herself, unable to believe her luck, encountering both underage sexual congress and dangerous drugs on her first teenage stakeout. Her father would be rapturous.

Time and time again Police Chief Pendleton had warned his daughter about the dangers of Purple Hayes. Although it had been around for only a short period, Purple Hayes was now the drug of choice for the numerous ne'er-do-wells of Fremont. It was more addictive than crack, pantaloon stew, or bullshit burgers. It was a higher high than cocaine, choo-choo boner, or devil's doorknob. It was more deadly than crank, globballs, or cheese brickenstein.

"If you're ever in a social situation," Police Chief Pendleton had counseled his daughter, "and some cussed idiot pulls out some light purple powder, avoid it like the devil himself. It makes people act all goofy, seeing things that ain't there and ignoring the laws of the Creator. I haven't found out yet what blamed fool is bringing that crud into my city, but when I do, with God as my witness, I will smite them with malice aforethought."

Seeing as she was rarely in social situations, Connie feared she'd never get a chance to see the evil purple powder, much less run away from it.

But here it was, just twenty feet away, being ingested by her classmates.

Rusty gently removed the vial from CoCo's hand. "Hey Sugar Knees, go easy. When our supply is gone, you know I can't produce no more."

Connie's breath caught in her throat. Rusty Slump, the boy with the angelic smile, was not only hooked on Purple Hayes, he was the mysterious supplier of the drug! Imagining the look of glorious jubilation on her father's face when she brought him this news, Connie's heart soared.

All her life she'd tried to please her father and had usually failed miserably.

When she was just a babe, Connie's mother, a garden-variety harlot, had run off with the boy who mowed their lawn, and Connie had been raised by her father. Throughout her life, the girl had overheard other parents accuse Police Chief Pendleton of being too strict, but they didn't understand he was just a simple, God-fearing man who would rather kill his daughter than have her follow in her mother's whorish footsteps.

If one spared the rod, one spoiled the child. Her father had said that many times as he reached for his belt.

Oblivious to Rusty's admonishments, CoCo was already rolling on the ground, acting goofy, just as Police Chief Pendleton had promised. Talking to people who weren't there, reaching for imaginary objects, yukking it up.

With a shrug, Rusty joined her by snorting a small mound of

the drug. Soon, he too was rolling on the ground, completely out of his mind. He howled at the moon, which was quickly being obscured by clouds.

Saddened by Rusty's weakness of will and new station in life as both CoCo McArdle's sexual congress partner and a drug kingpin, Connie got to her feet, unafraid of being heard by the obliterated lovers, and walked away stridently.

As she strode back toward town, Connie's sour mood was slowly replaced by a giddiness, as she reflected on her successful teenage stakeout. She had garnered enough evidence to put Rusty Slump behind bars for the rest of his earthly life, which would be for his own good.

Overhead, lightning flashed.

Watching the storm sweep over Fremont from the safety of his living room, Police Chief Pendleton folded his arms in prayer. An act made difficult by the massive Savage 1861 Navy revolver, a double-action firearm used widely in the War Between the States, he was clutching. The handgun was unwieldy and the second trigger, used for cocking the weapon, was a pain, but, as it had sent many a Confederate Soldier to their grave, Pendleton had made it the official weapon of the Fremont Police Society.

In a low voice, the cop said a quick prayer for his daughter. Beseeching the Good Lord to condemn Connie to a life of suffering. Amen.

That harlot, he thought, *she's just like her mother.* Out in the middle of the night, carousing. When she gets home, I'll-.

A crack of lightning veined the sky and unlinked his chain of thought.

A few hours before, Pendleton had woken with a start, his police senses tingling. He'd heard something, the shutting of a door perhaps, maybe footsteps, coming from somewhere in his home.

Grabbing the Savage 1861 Navy revolver from his nightstand, where it shared space with a well-thumbed Bible, the Police Chief smiled to himself. Hope burned in his heart that he'd get to blow away some drug-addled intruder.

Scampered down the hall to Connie's room. His beloved progeny. Pendleton had to be sure the interloper was not foisting his festering manhood upon his virginal daughter. Flicking on her light, he saw that everything was normal. Connie's wall was plastered with posters of the Sweet Baby G, all her sackcloth dresses were hung carefully in the closet, her bed was made perfectly.

No intruder, but no Connie either. At midnight.

Pendleton's heart clutched, stuck in his chest, his throat, his mouth.

Connie had obviously snuck out sometime after he'd gone to bed, breaking his rules and, probably, a handful of commandments.

Just like her mother, a garden-variety harlot who was a scourge upon the land.

He took up the role of sentinel at his bay window, wearing only his sackcloth underwear.

As he stood watch, he prayed and fashioned a plan.

When Connie tired of her carousing and returned home, she'd receive the beating of her life. After this punishment was administered, Pendleton would wipe away his daughter's tears and inform her, yet again and in great detail, how the ever-crackling flames of hell awaited those females who drank alcohol and rode in fast cars with fast boys.

But there was a special place in hell for anyone who dabbled in the devil's candy: drugs. Especially Purple Hayes.

Hitting the bay window with the butt of his Savage 1861 Navy revolver, making it vibrate, Pendleton cursed himself for not telling Connie the whole truth about Purple Hayes. Not only was it a deadly drug, the manner in which it was manufactured was ungodly beyond imagination. That's the part that he'd kept from Connie, had kept from everyone.

A few weeks prior, the Fremont Police Society had busted Rob Allen, an inveterate cactus-fucker, for breaking the restraining order acquired by the Rutherford B. Hayes Memorial Greenhouse. In his pocket, the cops found a tiny baggie of lavender powder. Purple Hayes. Which, until then, had been just a rumor, a myth, a lilac ghost.

Pendleton sent a sample of the drug up to Toledo for analysis. When the results came back he was nearly shocked out of his knee-flap boots. The powder was made from one quarter grape flavored Jell-O, one quarter molly (for the ladies), one quarter talcum powder (for cutting), and one quarter 'organic material'. In the notes at the bottom of the page, it detailed this 'organic material' was human flesh. Specifically, the penis flesh of a man who'd lived during the nineteenth century.

As if this info were not unsettling enough, the Police Chief had a sneaking suspicion he knew the identity of the former owner of the penis flesh.

Just a month before, some dastardly rapscallion had perpetuated a crime so heinous, so odious that the Police Chief not only kept it out of the papers, he forbade the entirety of the Fremont Police Society, all two officers, from mentioning to anyone, certain that if this malefaction became known, it would cause widespread panic. Pendleton feared riots in the streets, the collapse of the stock market, and, possibly, the end of Western Civilization as we know it.

Scaling the fence of the Rutherford B. Hayes Memorial Cemetery, this dastardly rapscallion had, using a blowtorch, cut his way into the crypt of the cemetery's namesake and absconded with the body of the nineteenth president of the United States of America.

When Pendleton received the results from Toledo, the depths of human degradation were revealed. Some hell-bound ne'er-do-well had used the penis flesh of native Fremontonian and greatest American ever, Rutherford B. Hayes, and turned it into a powerful hallucinogen.

Again, Pendleton hit the by window with the butt of his weapon and cried out, "Dear Lord, please bring my daughter home safely. That is, unless she's been tainted by the touch of a man, then smite her as you smote her mother!"

As if reflecting his mood, the rain picked up, coming down in black sheets, obscuring the night. By squinting, the Police Chief spied something moving at the edge of his lawn.

Her hair plastered, her sackcloth dress clinging, Connie stepped out of the darkness. A ghost, a dream, a drenched girl. Without lifting her head, she shuffled toward the front door. Pendleton didn't move, his feet frozen with anger.

When she entered the house, her father didn't bother looking at her, didn't offer a salutation. Just thundered at her to stay on the rug. "I don't want you sullying my blessed home."

"Daddy, I have the most amazing news," she cried, her voice electric with excitement.

"So do I, you're about the receive the beating of your life."

Then he moved. Like an ibex, Pendleton was on his daughter, raising his un-gunned hand in anger.

Connie screamed, attempting to dart away, but her father was too quick. The first strike caught her across the cheek. The cop smiled when he heard the sickening *fwap* of flesh meeting flesh for he was doing the Lord's work and he was doing it well. She turned away. Ecstasy raced down his spine when he delivered his second blow across her back. She jumped, yelped. This only added to his pleasure.

"Daddy, please stop! I have some important news concerning Purple Hayes!"

These words fought through his bliss and arrived on the shores of his brain. Pendleton stopped, put down his hands.

Catching his breath, he asked her what in the tarnation she was talking about.

Tears streaming, Connie turned on him. "I snuck out to the rock quarry tonight because I overheard at school that there was going to be a big party. I thought I could spy on my classmates for you. I assumed I would catch some of them drinking or smoking the devil's cigarettes, but it was so much worse than that. I saw Purple Hayes, Daddy, I saw it with my very own eyes. Some kids were snorting it and they were acting all goofy."

Pendleton grabbed his daughter, pulled her close, shook her. He demanded to know which kids, their names.

"It was Rusty Slump and not only did he have a bunch of Purple Hayes, he's the main supplier for Fremont. He's a rotten apple, Daddy, he cheats when we play crab ball in gym."

Letting go of his daughter, the Police Chief said, "Don't worry Connie, I'm well versed in the wicked ways of Rusty Slump."

Over the past few years there'd been a tragic spate of public defections in Fremont. Several of the finer establishments in town had been defaced with feces – the Rutherford B. Hayes Memorial Fun Park, the Other One True Way Church, and Police Chief Pendleton's own front porch. Many witnesses had come forward and fingered Rusty Slump as the perpetrator (or "poopetrator," as *the Rutherford B. Hayes Memorial Picayune-Times* had dubbed the defecator) but nothing could done, as Rusty's father was a judge and knew exactly what the job of judging's all about.

But with Connie's sworn testimony about Slump's involvement with the production and distribution of Purple Hayes, all of that could change. The Police Chief imagined forcing Judge Slump to issue him a warrant to search Rusty's luxury treehouse and if he happened to find a stash of Purple Hayes, or, even better, the decomposed body of Rutherford B. Hayes himself... dear Sweet Baby G.

"Connie, did you see anyone else partaking of that purple crud?"

The girl licked her lips, narrowed her eyes. Her tears had dried. "Yes, sir. Rusty was sharing it with CoCo McArdle. She's his new girlfriend but she totally doesn't deserve him. I call her the Whore of Fremont and--."

"That's great, Connie, just great."

Her father hugged her. He gave the greatest hugs, especially after a savage beating.

He who neglects what is done for what ought to be done, sooner effects his ruin than his preservation, read Rusty Slump, slamming the tome shut, dust fluttering.

"Truer words have never been spoken, Machi," said the young drug dealer, who was alone in his luxury treehouse.

Slump was tripping balls on his dwindling supply of Purple Hayes, thumbing through the copy of Niccolo Machiavelli's The Prince that CoCo had forced him to read. The book, when he first attempted it, didn't make much sense to the young man. All big words and gobbledygook. But now that Rusty was climbing the ladder in the vast and dangerous criminal underworld of Fremont, Ohio, this Machiavelli dude was starting to make sense.

Not long ago a considerable number of Rusty's illegal endeavors revolved around taking dumps in public - daring but not exactly a friend-winner amongst the criminal element - but since stumbling upon the secret of Rutherford B. Hayes' magical penis meat, he was on the verge of becoming Fremont's next drug kingpin. Only one man, CoCo liked to remind him constantly, stood in his way.

Loco Lenny Labovitz. The boss of all bosses in the vast and dangerous underworld of Fremont, Ohio.

But CoCo had convinced Rusty this position was his for the taking.

During their first date - a visit to the Rutherford B. Hayes Memorial Hairstyles Museum - CoCo had cajoled him into a bit of petty thievery. A package of gum here, a box of condoms there. But CoCo wanted more. She wanted the corpse of Rutherford B. Hayes.

When he first absconded with the body of the nineteenth president, he'd planned - well, CoCo had planned - to wait until the furor over the theft reached fever pitch, when there were riots in the streets, and then they'd send a ransom note to the *Rutherford B. Hayes Memorial Picayune-Times*. CoCo dreamed of getting ten, maybe twelve thousand bucks for the safe return of the cadaver.

But there had been no furor, no public outcry, no riots. The story never even appeared in the pages of the *Picayune-Times.* The couple was now stuck with a moldering corpse hidden behind the *fin-de-siecle* chifforobe in Rusty's treehouse. To make matters worse, his father, who had a very sensitive nose, was beginning to complain about the stench emanating from the backyard.

For the first time in their relationship, Rusty made a suggestion to CoCo. They could simply get rid of the body, dump it on the town square in the middle of the night. Maybe shit on it. That would be a fine prank.

CoCo lashed out at him, as she often did. She would not be denied. Reminding her boyfriend, during a bout of slapping, she'd worked hard to make him the motherflocking Prince of Fremont. She vowed they'd find a way to turn this dead president into some dead presidents.

One rainy day not long after, CoCo and Rusty were hanging out in the treehouse. After she'd administered one of her trademark boisterous but toothy blowjobs, she paced the Safavid silk, wool, and metal-thread prayer rug. Antsy, she pulled out a small bindle of ecstasy in powder form and studied Hayes, who was stretched out on the four-poster bed once owned by Thomas Jefferson.

"I'm gonna do some molly off this dead dude's dick," she announced and laughed in a way that made Rusty even more nervous than he usually was around his girlfriend.

When the presidential trousers were removed, the junior criminals received quite a shock.

Having been raised in Fremont, Rusty thought he knew everything there was to know about native son Rutherford B. Hayes. He'd read every book, seen every movie, played every board game.

But none of those mentioned his prodigious penis.

The presidential meat, unravaged by time unlike the rest of his body, was truly a top shelf schlong. Thick and veiny, the purple-headed monster hung off Hayes' dead body like a mighty tuber.

"I don't mean to be mean, Rusty," said CoCo, a smile in her voice, "but you could take a page or two out of this dead dude's dick book. Sure, your huge nutsack is pretty great but you've got something of a gnat cock."

Before Rusty could defend his maligned trouser trumpet, his gal pal dumped out a line of molly on the dead president's donkey dick and obliterated it. CoCo went as cuckoo as a clock. She began talking a mile a minute to a gathering of unseen partiers. Giggling, curtseying, waltzing. When CoCo finally came down, many hours later, she tried to describe an indescribable high. Pouring out a line on the presidential pecker, she pushed Rusty's head peniswward. Ordering him to snort it. Per usual, he did as he was bade.

Usually, with molly, there's an overall feeling of elation, an increased energy level. Things were different with a little of Hayes' one-eyed trouser snake thrown into the mix. The world slowed, blurred. Everything around Rusty became washed-out, sepia-toned. All about him, the boy saw men in long coats and long beards, women in hoop skirts, hoisting parasols. In the distance, he heard the smithy hammering, smelled horses.

It was flocking crazy and it was flocking glorious.

That night CoCo came up with the formula for Purple Hayes: part molly, part cock, with some grape Jell-O powder for flavor and coloring.

Once word got around, that shit sold like a storm. At three hundred bucks a bindle.

It was a great ride but Rusty knew that it couldn't last forever. Hayes' cock, though massive, had been whittled down to dregs. Desperate, Rusty tried harvesting what little flesh there was left on other parts of the dead president's body but none of it had the same kick as that magic penis meat.

After the criminal couple concocted their last batch of Purple Hayes, they dragged the penis-less president to the dump and buried him under a pile of soiled diapers. Rusty cried. Not about the flocked up funeral; he was fretting over his clientele, as they were a violent stripe of ne'er-do-well and he'd created a demand that he could no longer supply. He feared when people found out the Purple Hayes was all gone, he might be tarred and feathered and run out of Fremont before even getting the chance to climb to the top of its vast and dangerous criminal underworld.

Sitting in his *Fauteuil aux Dragons* chair, Rusty thought over his woes. To relieve his anxieties, he pulled out his last baggie of Purple Hayes and was surprised to discover he was down to just a few measly ounces of the drug.

"Flock it," he said, snorting a bump and diving back into Machiavelli.

But Rusty's reading was soon interrupted when the door to the treehouse burst open and in rushed every single cop employed by the Fremont Police Society. All three of them. Salivating and grunting, they towered over the prone teen.

In Rusty's boggled brain, they were all Union soldiers, complete with blue wool coats, swords, and antiquated handguns. At the head of this pack of jackals was Police Chief Pendleton. Hands on his hips, he surveyed the blissed-out teen and his environs. The cop's face was ninety percent smug smile.

Bellowing about dead presidents and mountains of drugs, Pendleton and the other soldier cops tossed the place. Tearing it apart. They found nothing but the meager amount of Purple Hayes in Rusty's baggie – enough for possession but not enough for intent to sell.

The Police Chief's sweaty face turned the color of uncooked hamburger and he started in on his old-timey swearing. This got Rusty laughing. He continued cackling as they slapped the cuffs on him, read him his rights, and dragged him out of the treehouse.

His father stood on the lawn. Dressed in his robes, as always, the judge, who'd gotten his boy out of all his pooping related troubles, was shaking his head.

There was something in Judge Slump's eyes that made Rusty stop laughing and realize he was flocked.

No one likes a rat.

This venerable adage was brought home to Connie Pendleton on the days following Rusty Slump's arrest and incarceration. Usually at school she was ignored, most of the other students didn't deign to look her way, even as they jostled her in the hallway, forcing her to drop her sackcloth book satchel.

Now, she was a celebrity, but the wrong kind. Connie was continually glared at, gestured towards, mocked by sneers.

She had no idea how everyone knew. Her father, the Police Chief, had done everything in his power to keep her name out of the account published by The *Rutherford B. Hayes Memorial Picayune-Times.* But somehow, her fingering Rusty Slump was the worst kept secret in all of Sandusky County.

Connie strongly suspected it was CoCo McArdle who'd put it all together. She was the glariest, gesturingest, sneeriest of the kids at Rutherford B. Hayes Memorial High School.

And glaring wasn't the worst part. Connie was tripped, shoved into the lockers, and had to face the slanderous slogans, concerning her and her nether regions, scrawled on every bathroom wall in the school.

But what froze Connie's blood was the notes taped to her locker. Several hastily scrawled missives threatening her life, all written in a different hand.

Connie begged her father for release. She pleaded, spewing tears, to be allowed to stay home and school herself, a petition she'd made before but never so heartily. The Police Chief just shook his head, offering up some tired Bible verse about the Sweet Baby G and his gang of angles protecting her from evil.

Then came the terrible news, whispered with great excitement in the halls of Rutherford B. Hayes Memorial High School, that Judge Slump had, thanks to a popular Kickstarter campaign, secured the hundred thousand dollars Rusty needed to post bail. The doors were swinging wide at the Rutherford B. Hayes Memorial Prison for the young man.

The idea of Rusty Slump roaming around Fremont as a free man until his trial started in six months did not sit well with Connie. In fact, it gave her weird, vivid nightmares in which she ran through the Rutherford B. Hayes Memorial Cemetery, pursued by a shirtless and muscular Rusty. When he caught her, he tore away her sackcloth dress and had his way with her before gunning her down.

One, two, three quick shots.

Then came the heartrending day when Rusty actually showed up at school. To make matters worse, it was Halloween, yet another holiday that, thanks to her father's draconian religious convictions, she was not allowed to celebrate.

Never before had Rusty been terribly popular - no one likes a public defecator - but his short stint as a drug dealer and his brief stay in the clink had raised his cachet. He was now the newly crowned king of the ne'er-do-wells.

As he walked the halls of Rutherford B. Hayes Memorial High School, several people, many of whom were dressed in gory Halloween costumes, flocked around him, offering high-fives, chattering like monkeys. But the prodigal teen wasn't paying them much attention. Rusty searched the crowd and found who he was looking for. Connie, standing at the periphery. He wasn't glaring, he wasn't sneering. In fact, he was smiling with his straight, white teeth.

Ever so slowly, he brought up his hand, which he shaped into a gun, and pointed it in her general direction.

Silently, he fired one, two, three shots.

She was so flocking horny.

Hot lesbian sex. That's what she wanted, what she needed. Her last relationship had ended, badly – a very public argument in the atrium of the Rutherford B. Hayes Memorial Planetarium – over a month ago and, since then, dry rot had settled into her nether regions.

After a long, lusty sigh, Daniella Locke dropped her head into her hands. Lately, she'd done a lot more sighing and head-dropping than finger-blasting and scissoring. It was downright depressing.

Her bout of self-pity was interrupted by a soft knock on her office door. She looked up to see Connie Pendleton standing there. Though technically female, Connie was about as far away from hot lesbian sex as a girl could get. She was shy, skittish, and always wore long scratchy dresses.

"What do you want?" snapped the gym teacher.

"Well, uh, I came to you, Ms. Locke, because I, well, you're the only female teacher I have and I thought it might be easier to talk to you."

Daniella felt her anger slacken. Like everyone in Fremont, she was well aware Connie didn't have a mother and her father was a religious dingleberry. This girl was obviously experiencing period problems and needed a little guidance.

"Okay, first things first, a lot of people, especially boys, will say you shouldn't have sex during your period, but that's simply not true. Personally, I enjoy going with the flow-."

"No, Ms. Locke, this isn't about menstruation, my goodness. It's about a boy."

Daniella smiled. At least once a week, a love-sick young thing wandered into her office and spilled her guts about some stupid boy who didn't know she existed. From there it was an easy segue into a discussion about the joys of carpet munching.

For the first time ever, Daniella really studied Connie Pendleton. Looked past the scratchy dress. Saw that the girl had sweet eyes, soft skin, a constellation of freckles. The gym teacher pulled out a chair, motioning for Connie to join her at the desk.

The girl took the seat tentatively, as if she were sitting on a hotplate.

"So," began Daniella, "let me guess. You like a boy but he doesn't know you exist. Well, I'll let you in on a little secret, males are terribly people-."

"No, sorry, Ms. Locke, it's nothing like that. This isn't about love, it's about hate. I think Rusty Slump wants to do me harm."

With these words, all the blood fled from the girl's face.

Finally something interesting was happening in this dull berg. Daniella's breath caught as she leaned forward. "What makes you think that, Connie?"

"Cause his girlfriend, CoCo McArdle, is walking around telling everyone he's going to kill me."

"That certainly sounds serious." The gym teacher, her heart

trembling, leaned so far forward that she was nearly touching the teen. She could feel the heat of fear roiling off young Connie and she wanted to be enveloped by it.

Reaching out, Daniella gripped the girl's thigh as if it were the last loaf of bread in the supermarket.

Felt the girl squirm, felt their blood flowing together.

"Rusty Slump, dear girl, is an evil bastard, just like all men. All they desire of us is our nether regions, nothing more. They don't really want us, our souls. They don't want us to pull them up to heaven with our strong wings."

With a small gasp, Connie tried to stand. "Ms. Locke, I don't think we're talking about the same thing."

The gym teacher held her pupil tight, held her down. Daniella loved this part, the battle, the fight, the inevitable conquest. "There's really only one subject in this world, Connie, and that subject is sex, in particular hot lesbian sex."

Her breathing ragged, the girl tired to pull away, screamed a little. The gym teacher knew no one could hear. Her office was lodged in the bowels of Rutherford B. Hayes Memorial High School.

Thinking she had this girl, that heaven was just a touch away, she reached up and undid the top button of the ridiculous dress Connie wore.

This gave the girl room, time. Moving much faster than she ever had when playing dodge ball, she slapped away the gym teacher's hand. With more strength than she ever displayed during crab ball, the girl jumped to her feet.

Connie fled the gym teacher's office with a squeal, with tears.

It certainly looked pretty, the purple powder. Inviting, enticing.

Police Chief Pendleton removed the baggie filled with Purple Hayes from the evidence locker, sat it on his desk, and simply stared at it. Hypnotized. He'd done this every day since confiscating it from Rusty Slump. Ogling the drug, licking his lips, allowing his mind to wander.

Wondering if the crazy rumors about Purple Hayes were true. Cactus-fucker Rob Allen had claimed when you ingested the drug, it was like going back in time. The world turned black and white and more pleasant. You saw people – not quite ghosts, not quite real – dressed in clothing from yesteryear. Smelled sweat, dust, and animal droppings.

To Pendleton it sounded too good to be true.

The cop wanted to try the drug so bad his uvula hurt.

That's crazy talk, he thought, pushing the baggie away.

Never had Police Chief Pendleton snorted or shot or smoked an illegal substance. In fact, he steered clear of most of the legal ones. Not once had he touched tobacco or had a drink of alcohol or even owned a TV. He was tight with the Lord and he wanted to keep it that way.

But sitting at his desk, studying the Purple Hayes, a thought crept, the way they do, out of the primordial sludge at the bottom of the cop's mind.

His snorting of the Purple Hayes wouldn't be for entertainment but for research. A way to enhance his favorite pastime.

Police Chief Pendleton was a Civil War reenactor, a very earnest one. Believing that he was born a century too late, Pendleton took his beloved War Between the States quite seriously. The Civil War, despite being a war, was a much better time, a much simpler time. When all mankind bowed down to the Creator and knew their place in the universe. Not like today with atheists and feminists and lefties running wild in the streets, preaching their free love and having sexual congress in the anus.

Reaching for the baggie, the cop stroked it. Just as he was on the verge of dipping his trembling fingers into the lavender powder, a sour image materialized in his brain. Sergeant Snoopers, long dead, standing right before him. Forlornly shaking his head at the Police Chief, disgusted by his weakness, his dereliction of duty.

Dropping the drug, Pendleton made a mental note to place a new wreath on the grave of the best officer he'd ever known.

Before he could head for the Rutherford B. Hayes Memorial Cemetery, his office door flew open and Officer Rumpza rushed in.

To Pendleton, Chrissy Rumpza was a vexing woman. Though thoroughly modern - she wore her hair short, eschewed make-up, and didn't own a single sackcloth garment - the Police Chief found himself strangely attracted to her. Had since the day he hired her. He'd have asked her out on a date, perhaps to attend services with him and Connie at the Other One True Way Church, but he never found the nerve to do so. For she was a brazen woman, Chrissy Rumpza, brazen and forceful. She swore like a sailor, drank like a soldier, and cracked jokes that would've made a Marine blush. Those traits reminded Pendleton of his wife the whore, which seared his soul.

The Police Chief would have fired her, as he'd received several complaints about her brusqueness, but she was a good cop. Nearly as good as dearly departed Sergeant Snoopers.

"Hey Chief, we just got some bad... hey, why do you have the Purple Hayes?"

"Just... just... just looking at it so I can understand its evilness. What's up, Officer Rumpza?"

"Oh, we just got some bad news, that dickstain Rusty Slump is out on bail."

Pendleton winced at Rumpza's corrupt tongue but decided it was a waste of time and breath to chastise her yet again. "Well, I'll be cussed."

"Yeah, it sucks mega-balls. So, should we offer Connie police protection?"

"Why would my daughter need such a thing?"

"Well, she's so young and defenseless and that cumsplatter Slump has made threats on her life."

"Oh, that's ridiculous."

"But aren't you going to be out of town for the next couple of days?"

"Yes, I'm going to a reenactment of the Second Battle of Bull Run, but I'm not worried about Connie. She's got the Good Lord watching over her."

"Okay, yeah, alright. But still, I might check in on her tonight, it being Halloween and all, you know how the kids of Fremont can get all goofy."

The Police Chief shrugged. "As you wish, Officer Rumpza."

Pendleton stared at her. For the briefest moment, he pictured holding her hand and discussing their favorite Bible passages, but that thought, ludicrous, fled.

"I better get back to the front, that cuntturd Killion was pulling the Jarts out of the games closet and I think you remember what happened last time ."

She ducked out and, immediately, he missed her. He felt a Rumpza shaped hole in his life.

Depressed, he looked back at the Purple Hayes.

Rushing like a bat out of Hades, he grabbed the baggie, that plastic temptress, and scurried back to the evidence locker.

Douglas Kennedy hated kids with the heat of a thousand burning anal warts.

To a degree, this made his job as principal of Rutherford B. Hayes Memorial High School somewhat difficult.

Not that anyone knew of the dark thoughts lurking, like Great Whites, in the ocean of Kennedy's mind. Every morning, he stood at the front doors of the school, greeting students with warm salutations and smiles, while inside he was screaming.

I want to squash your stupid teenage face with a school bus! I want to cram the cafeteria's ass-searing chili down your throat until you choke! I want to throw you from the theater's catwalk!

The character of the young person didn't matter, Kennedy hated them all. The jocks, the geeks, the squares, the cripples, the dopers, the fuzz-bottoms, the student council. They were all awful, for they all wanted something from him, taking up all his time with their pitiful lives. Coming into his office for pep talks about faltering grades or requests for money for sombreros for the stupid Spanish Club. He didn't want to fund the Spanish Club's ridiculous hatwear habit, he wanted to lock them all in the boiler room and burn the school to the ground while they screamed their bilingual lungs dry: *Ay, caramba! Ay, caramba!*

Someday, he knew, he'd fail to keep all of this umbrage under wraps. He'd simply erupt. His anger would bubble to the surface like lava, smothering all around him, extinguishing their worthless lives under mountains of volcanic vitriol and, at last, he'd be released. Released from his job, released from his burdens, released from his shitty, kid-filled life.

Kennedy both feared this day and longed for it. It would be so much like death, so much like birth. Whenever he thought about this oncoming onslaught, each time he pictured choking a cheerleader while explaining to her how empty she was, it made him hard, his cock pressing polyester.

He'd felt this hatred of the young, even when he was young himself, so it was odd that he ended up as a high school principal. As a boy, he'd wanted to be a stevedore, working shirtless and sweaty with all the other burly, hair-encrusted men down on the docks. But growing up in Kansas, without a substantial body of water within a thousand miles, he knew that was just a silly dream. His father was a high school principal, which allowed the elder Kennedy to pursue, with gusto, his two favorite pastimes:

infidelity and inebriation. All day he'd hang out in his office and bang a succession of teenage girls while shitfaced. It seemed, to the junior Kennedy, this was not an unpleasant way to spend one's life, so Douglas followed in his father's rum-soaked and cum-stained footsteps.

Of course, thanks to that goblin "political correctness", it was now frowned upon to run a place of education while wasted, and banging students was right out.

So, he was stuck, sober and pussy-free, with all these awful and needy kids.

Like this girl sitting across from him. Tears glittering her eyes, her hands wrung into knots of worry. Though he played the part of the concerned surrogate father, he had no patience for this little turd. He didn't even know her name. It was something old fashioned and woeful. She was one of the quiet girls, the mousey ones who clung to the shadows and didn't make waves. God, he hated that type, wasting their lives on silence and security. He wanted to throttle them, force them to confess they lusted after the dirty boys with their dirty dicks.

Studying her stupid face, Kennedy had a feeling that this girl's name began with a C, not that he honestly gave a flock.

"And what can I help you with today, sweetie?" Nicknames were how Kennedy got around his poor memory and the little turds were too vapid to notice.

"It's Rusty, Rusty Slump, sir. I'm afraid… I'm afraid he's going to hurt me."

Though he didn't know a majority of the school's population, Kennedy was well acquainted with Russell Slump, a senior who was suspected of breaking into Rutherford B. Hayes Memorial High and taking a dump right on Kennedy's desk. The disgust he felt watching his secretary pick up the ochre log with her bare hands was etched upon his mind.

If Kennedy ran the world, the walking shit-pile known as Russell Slump would have been executed in the town square but it just so happened the boy was sired by a local judge and was, therefore, untouchable.

Recently, Slump had been busted for drugs and sent to the big house where, Kennedy hoped, he'd be raped repeatedly before being shived into the Sweet Hereafter. But that didn't happen. Daddy pulled a few strings and the walking shit-pile was now back on the streets, infecting Kennedy's school.

"And why do you fear that, my little cupcake?" asked the principal. Not that he cared.

Now the tears came in earnest. There was nothing worse than one of these little turds getting all emotional.

"I… I was the one who went to the police… I ratted out Rusty because I overhead him talking about manufacturing and distributing Purple Hayes."

"That was brave of you, my little pumpkin."

"But now I wish I hadn't done it. Like I said, I think Rusty knows and, I fear he's going to hurt me."

So many tears now, a river of them. And strings of snot. What she wanted, Kennedy knew, was for him to put his arm around her and assure her everything in her shitty little existence was going to work out just peachy. That Rusty Slump would be sent away to prison for the rest of his life and she would grow up unmolested and go to Rutherford B. Hayes Memorial Community College right here in town and meet some boring boy and they'd get married and have lackluster sex with the lights out and she'd shit out some unimaginative kids and the whole cycle of awfulness would simply start all over again.

He'd given a version of this speech a thousand times before, and he was just about to grit his teeth and deliver it again when something snapped in his brain. A *FWAP* noise filled his head. It sounded as if a rope that was holding a piano aloft broke and said piano nearly crushed a shirtless and sweating brawny stevedore.

Kennedy smiled his first genuine smile in years. He could feel a change coming, though this was just the beginning, the tip of the iceberg of hate.

Cleaning his fingernails, he rested his elbows on his desk and calmly informed the girl that he honestly didn't care if Russell Slump tore her lungs out and wore them as an ascot.

Jolted from her crying, the little turd looked at him with red eyes, her brow knitted into an ugly sweater. "Excuse me?"

"You heard me, those ears are certainly big enough. I said I don't care, by which I mean, I truly don't give a flapping flock if Slump kills you. All that really means to me is two less diplomas I have to pass out in the spring."

She shook her stupid head. "I... I can't believe you're saying these things."

"I can. And it's about flocking time I informed one of you worthless turds how I honestly felt. Sweet Baby G, I really feel good about all this honesty, don't you?"

"I'm... I'm going to tell my father about what you said, he's Police Chief Pendleton, you know."

"That's right, that's right, God that's been bothering me, now I know who you are. And I know your father, that religious bag of poopswill. Go ahead, tell him, he'll never believe you. Everyone loves smiling, glad-handing Principal Kennedy but, I'd hazard, no one really loves little quiet mousy Clara Pendleton."

"It's Connie."

"My point exactly. You're nothing, a nobody who cowers while life swirls around them. I bet your father doesn't even listen to you, does he, Clara? Doesn't have the time for his little quiet girl who stands in the corner."

Crying again in earnest, the little turd sprang to her feet and rushed from his office, leaving him in the first peace he'd felt in years.

There were times when Rusty Slump feared he feared his girlfriend. Her angry outbursts, her steely stares, her boisterous but toothy blowjobs. But what really turned his blood to toothpaste was the way she pushed him to become the king of the vast and dangerous criminal underworld of Fremont, Ohio. His first acts of non-feces malfeasance - stealing a dead president and manufacturing a powerful drug from dead president dick, both of which had been CoCo's idea - had landed him in the Rutherford B. Hayes Memorial Prison.

Oh, how he longed for a simpler time. A time when he was free to walk the streets of his hometown and drop the occasional deuce on an unsuspecting public. No cells, no record, no CoCo.

But now, that was just a dream.

For although he was, at the moment, a free man, the specter of a real prison stretch hung over him as he lay on the fainting couch in his luxury treehouse, CoCo kneeling before him, naked, her bleached blonde head buried in his lap, scaring and scarring his manhood, which was being uncooperative. Flaccid, limp, unwilling.

With disgust, CoCo threw in the blowjob towel. Sat up, glared at him. "Your worm won't waggle. You know what you gotta do to solve your dick issues."

A fine patina of dread settled over Rusty, for he knew exactly what she was talking about: CoCo had been threatening him to keep threatening Connie Pendleton. She wanted to get the poor girl so scared she wouldn't testify against him in a court of law.

Rusty had to go on the offensive. "You know, CoCo, my time behind bars really got me thinking about Machiavelli and what he meant--."

"You've got to kill her, you know, for realsies."

These words, like fragments of angry candy, cut Rusty's brain. Sitting up, he asked CoCo what the hell she was talking about.

"That little bitch Connie Pendleton's not going to back down with just idle threats. She's made of tougher stuff than that. Her testimony could put you away for a long time. She saw us sniffing Purple Hayes at the quarry, overheard you talking about manufacturing it. But, on the bright side, without her testimony in court, you could be a free man. The pigs only found a trace amount of Purple Hayes in your possession and, since it's your first offense and your father is a judge, you'll get just a slap on the wrist. But if Connie Pendleton is allowed to open her trap on the witness stand, then you can kiss the outside world, and your ass cherry, goodbye."

The queasy hand of fate reached up through Rusty's puckered butthole and gripped his heart. "Well, yeah, sure, but, but, but, I can't kill Connie. That's ridiculous, it's not how I roll, Sugar Uvula."

"You have to," she said.

Shaking his head, he said, "I'm a crapper, not a fighter."

CoCo smiled a smile that wasn't really a smile at all. Stretching out beside him on the fainting couch, she said, "'He who neglects what is done for what ought to be done, sooner effects his own ruin than his preservation.'"

Rusty gasped. Having Machiavelli's words thrown in his face made him stop, made him think. He lay back on the fainting couch, clasped his hands behind his head, and studied the Pierre-Philipe Thomire chandelier which hung from the treehouse ceiling. It pained him, but he knew, of course, CoCo was right. The road back to the big house was paved with Connie Pendleton.

But there was no way he could harm a hair on her pretty little head.

Not that he'd ever admit it to anyone, especially CoCo, but

he sort of liked Connie. Not in a sexual congress kind of way, of course, just that he was always pleased when he saw her at school. She wasn't like all the other girls in Fremont. She didn't swear, in fact, she rarely spoke, but when she did, it was something smart. She didn't show off her body, she wore long dresses made out of some kind of burlap material. She didn't flirt; she just pressed her books against her flat chest, cast her eyes down, and scurried through the halls of Rutherford B. Hayes Memorial High.

But it was these same traits – her seriousness, her studiousness – that Rusty knew would sink him if she stood witness against him. A jury would believe everything she said and, if it came down to her word against his, he was a goner. When it came out that he'd stolen the body of Rutherford B. Hayes, the fine folks of Fremont would probably lynch him, then tear him apart, then relynch each and every individual piece of his corpse.

Of course, if she couldn't get up in front of a jury because she was in the ground...

"You're right," he said, his voice soft, pliable, pained.

CoCo leaned forward, her large breasts swaying like untethered zeppelins. She kissed her man, kissed him hard. "I knew you'd come around."

Though the thought sickened him, a plan formed in his head. His voice grew stronger as he said, "I have money, thanks to Purple Hayes, to get someone to do the job. Perhaps I'll hire one of the many young toughs who call Toledo their home."

Connie shook her head. "No, Rusty, you can't hire someone to do this. That would mean just another person in the loop, another person who, if the shit hit the fan, could go squawking to the police. You have to do this yourself."

"I don't... I don't... there's no way."

Reaching over the side of the fainting couch, CoCo retrieved a .38 that she had hidden in her clothes, which were sprawled on the bamboo floor. She held up the weapon, turning it this way and that, its blackness catching the light, absorbing it.

Rusty felt his eyes bug. Despite being part of the vast and dangerous criminal underworld of Fremont, Ohio, he'd never actually seen a real, live gun. It both thrilled and repulsed him. He wanted to both hold it tight and get the hell away from it.

"Where'd you get that thing?" Rusty asked.

"It belonged to my dear, departed dad," she said, her voice choked with emotion. "Now there was a real man. When things needed to get done, he did them."

Jinx McArdle had run the Rutherford B. Hayes Memorial Slightly Dangerous Petting Zoo until he was humped to death by a rabid ocelot. Often, CoCo spoke of him and his adventures, his manliness. Traveling to distant, dangerous lands to retrieve exotic animals. Wrestling wild animals as big as an ibex to the ground with his bare hands. The implication was always that Jinx was a real man and Rusty was a pale imitation.

CoCo handed the .38 to Rusty. He took it reluctantly. It felt like the weight of the world was in his hand, as if it could drag him straight through the Safavid silk, wool, and metal-thread prayer rug and down into the bowels of hell.

Unburdened of the gun, CoCo once again rifled through her discarded clothes. This time she returned with a baggie of purple powder.

Once more, Rusty's eyes leapt out of their respective sockets.

"Is that what I think it is?"

"Sure is. The last of Purple Hayes not in police custody. I wisely stole it from you a few days before the pigs nabbed you. I was gonna save it for our honeymoon but it feels like you might need a little bump tonight to help you with the killing."

"Tonight?"

"Sure. It's Halloween and Jugsy Jaspburger's having his famous party. Conveniently, he lives only a few blocks from that bitch Connie Pendleton. You and me are gonna go to that party and talk to a bunch of people, make sure everyone sees you. Then we're gonna head upstairs, tell some people we're gonna go bounce refrigerators. But we ain't gonna bounce anything. You're gonna slip out a window and sneak over to the Pendleton house. I heard Police Chief Pendleton's out of town for some Civil War bullshit, so Connie will be home alone. Ring her doorbell and, when she answers, say trick-or-treat with that .38, then hustle back to the party."

Rusty felt lightning striking his nuts region. It was a great plan but it was also the worst thing he'd ever heard. Mentally, he poked around for flaws, but there were none. Obviously, CoCo had thought this through.

CoCo took the gun away from him, he gave it willingly. She cracked open the cylinder and dumped the bullets, there were only three, onto the blanket.

He asked her what she was doing but she didn't answer, just smiled. Opening the baggie, she took a pinch of the purple powder and sprinkled it over the trio of bullets.

"Sugar Cheeks, don't waste it," he said, too late.

"It's only a smidge, silly. I thought it might be a good way to bless the little buggers." CoCo reloaded the weapon and turned to her boyfriend. "Now, let's get higher than flock and get ready for Jugsy Jaspburger's party."

Fags, Jews, Muslims, fornicators, atheists, menstruators, liberals, strippers, abortionists, black heathens in jungles all over the globe, drug addicts, drunks, prostitutes, pornographers, Catholics, the members of Satan's Butt Buddies, adulterers, Reverend Stevie G. Jones and his entire congregation over at the Other Other One True Way Church.

His joints barking in pain, Reverend LaRue Rump was down

on his knees, petitioning the Lord to smite these evil folks and toss them into the Fiery Pit for all eternity. Amen.

Mentally running through his prayer checklist of mortal enemies, the old minister was fairly certain he'd covered all his bases. But, being ninety-nine years old, he feared his memory might be slipping, so he said one more prayer for Reverend Stevie G. Jones' smiting just for good measure.

Groaning, he got to his feet. It took a minute and he arrived out of breath. Though he loved his job as Shepherd of the flock at the Other One True Way Church - not to be confused with the Other Other One True Way Church - there were times when he found it terribly taxing. Doing the Lord's work by keeping up a grueling retinue of praying for smiting took up much of his time and energy. Not that he would ever stop. There were dark moments when he overheard members of his congregation mentioning the specter of retirement, but Reverend Rump knew as long as fags were fornicating with children and impregnating them with future abortionists, he had a job to do.

Just as soon as he'd settled his wracked body into his favorite armchair and reached for his cooling cup of tea, there came a knock on his front door.

He cursed under his breath, then cursed himself for cursing. For a brief moment, he considered doing nothing. Let the knocker knock until they grew weary and went away. Then he could enjoy his tea in peace.

But he knew in his ischemic heart that that was not what the Lord wanted him to do. Whoever had darkened his door was in trouble. That's the only reason people ever came to see him on a Wednesday. Tearful men cheating on their wives, conflicted women considering an abortion, awful people, terrible people. It was his job to force them to their knees and put them right with prayer and the promise of perpetual suffering, just as Jesus would've done.

Despite the cracking in his aching spine, which was really just a collection of slipped discs, the minister rose and hobbled to the door. It was a painful journey and the only thing that kept him going was the promise of berating and shaming some poor sinner.

When he opened his front door, Reverend Rump's heart sank. It was only Connie Pendleton standing there.

Damn.

The Pendleton family were pure and good, the father and daughter were regular church goers, and truly some of the leading lights of the Other One True Way Church community. Never once did they falter in this sickeningly secular world. The Police Chief chaired the Let's Kill All the Abortion Doctors For Christ Committee and was the treasurer of the Fires of Hell Aren't Good Enough for Fornicators Club.

This visit was going to be disappointing; Connie had probably stopped by to pick up some more religious tracks to hand out to the little heathens this Halloween night or perhaps to drop off yet another basket teeming with her father's world famous hard tack.

But the old man's spirit soared when he spied tears cascading from Connie's red eyes. Her face was flushed, snot glistened. Reverend Rump could barely contain his enthusiasm. Perchance this good Christian girl had fallen, engaged in sexual congress with some lusty boy or – could he have hit the jackpot? – maybe she'd gotten herself with child. That would certainly brighten up a rather dreary day, as shaming a pregnant teen was right up there, in the reverend's book, with forcing fags to renounce their wanton ways.

Barely able to keep the excitement out of his voice, Reverend Rump asked, "My dear child, whatever could be the matter?"

Between cloudbursts of tears, the girl managed, "It's… it's Rusty Slump."

Of course it was.

Though the Slumps weren't members of the Other One True Way Church, the minister was well acquainted with the boy and his nefarious activities. A few Christmases ago, the reverend went out for a walk and was sickened to discover some fecal matter snuggling with the Sweet Baby G in his life-sized crèche on the church lawn. He called 911 but Police Chief Pendleton was at one of his reenactments and that idiot Junior Officer Killion showed up. He was no help, stifling his laughter, shrugging his stupid shoulders. Even refusing to retrieve the turd, forcing the minister to do so himself. The only help that cretin offered was to say that the crime certainly looked to be the work of one Rusty Slump, who the Fremont Police Society suspected in a string of defecation related offenses, though apparently, thanks to his father the judge, he and his felonious colon lived and shat above the law.

After that incident, there were several nights when Rump got down on his feeble knees to pray for God to send an asteroid down from heaven and obliterate the Slump home, just as He had done to the godless dinosaurs.

Laying his liver-spotted hand upon Connie's slender shoulders, the minister asked, "Has he… has he been at you?"

The old man trembled with anticipation and he had to suck in a stalactite of saliva that had formed in the corner of his mouth.

Her face scrunching into a mask of disgust, Connie groaned. "Ewwwww, gosh, no, that's… that's… I don't even want to think about such a thing. No, Rusty Slump is threatening to kill me."

"Oh. Is that all?"

"Is that all?!? Reverend Rump, my life is in danger and my father refuses to help me!"

"Of course, you poor girl. I simply meant that through the Lord's strength and might, it will be easy to defeat such an unworthy foe. God has vanquished the devil on several occasions, surely he can dispense the wanton defecator Rusty Slump like that." Reverend Rump attempted to snap his fingers but, thanks to his arthritis, the act was as impossible as a camel passing through the eye of a needle.

Plastering a sham of a smile on his gob - which was the same expression he wore during wedding ceremonies of marriages he knew would be torn asunder by adultery and divorce - he led Connie deeper into his living room.

"The first thing that God wants out of us," he informed the girl, "is supplication. So, let's get down on our knees to show the Great Master that we are not worthy of his grace."

Gripping her by the arms, Reverend Rump rode Connie to the ground. They landed with a minor thud and pain coursed through the old man's body. Recovering, he looked up toward the cobweby ceiling and intoned loudly, "Lord, I bring before you this day one of your flock, Connie Pendleton. Unfortunately, she has performed some rather nasty impure deeds with one Rusty Slump and--."

"Wait, sir, no I haven't!"

"That's right, that's right, of course." Again, the ceiling, the cobwebs, the intoning. "This poor girl, dear Lord, has had impure thoughts about one Rusty Slump and his bit of beef-."

"No, Reverend, that's not it either. I haven't had impure thoughts about him, he's had impure thoughts about me. He wants to kill me, remember?"

Looking at her with lightning in his eyes, the old man barked, "Of course I remember, I'm not senile or anything!" With a labored sigh, he spoke to the ceiling again. "Dear Sweet Baby G, this girl, who sometimes suffers from impertinence, has been threatened with bodily harm by one Rusty Slump, a servant of the devil if I ever met one and a major league crapper. Now, how shall thee protect her?"

Cocking his head to listen, the minister heard a storm brewing outside and saw, out of the corner of his eye, his cup of tea, no longer steaming.

"That's good news, Lord, certainly good news." With a smile, he turned back to the girl and said, "The Lord has promised to protect you. He wants you to have this."

The reverend held out his empty hands, bowed a little.

"What… what is it?"

"Can't you see? It's the sword of righteousness. Take it!"

With some hesitation, Connie grabbed at the vacant space between Rump's outstretched hands and pulled back.

"Be careful not to cut yourself," the old man warned.

Then, once again, he extended an empty hand.

"Oh. Thank you, Reverend Rump. Is this another sword?"

"Obviously it's not another sword, you silly girl! Who needs two swords of righteousness? This is a shield, the shield of rectitude."

She took it. "These… weapons… they're… they're great, but what I really was hoping for was for you to talk to my father. You see, he doesn't believe I'm really in danger and he's leaving town, leaving me alone. He has such respect for you and if you could just have a word with him about-."

"Do you honestly believe your father can protect you better than the Lord can? Sure, your father carries a badge and an antique handgun, but I've just given you the sword of righteousness and the shield of rectitude."

"Well, yeah, sure, but… but you know, really, there's nothing in my hands but air."

His eyes burning, the old man leapt to his feet, all pain vanquished. "Nothing but air?!? You dare to call the blessings of the Lord nothing but air?!? Do you not believe in the power and the glory of the Sweet Baby G?!?"

"Certainly I do, but still, you know, I just want something a little more tangible, something I can actually see."

Leaning over, he grabbed the space before her. "Give these back to me. You don't deserve the sword of righteousness or the shield of rectitude. What you deserve is the fires of hell! Just like your harlot mother, you are no better than the Jews and the strippers! Get out of my sight, get out of my house, and never come back to the Other One True Way Church again!"

Her tears returning with a vengeance, the little whore clamored to her feet and ran out the front door into the rain that had just begun to fall.

His heart pumping, his blood flowing, feeling better than he had in years, Reverend Rump finally took a drink of his tea.

It was cold.

A thorough man, Police Chief Pendleton once again unpacked his rucksack and laid its contents on his bed to triple-check that he hadn't forgotten anything for the Second Battle of Bull Run: Union Army uniform, Hardee hat, musket, knapsack, bayonet, bayonet scabbard, baggie of Purple Hayes stolen from the evidence locker, cartridge box, forty cartridges (faux), percussion caps, percussion cap box, gum blanket, a pair of scratchy wool socks, and enough of his world famous hard tack to choke a horse.

Pendleton could feel electricity coursing through his veins. Not only was the Second Battle of Bull Run his favorite Civil War engagement (so much better, so much bloodier than the First Battle of Bull Run), he'd definitively decided it was more or less his duty to give Purple Hayes a shot. As long as he only did it once, wasn't on the clock, and was far away from his friends and family. Since the Second Battle of Bull Run was going to be played out on the fields of Old Virginia, it was the perfect place to try the illicit drug. For research purposes, of course.

Repacking his rucksack, he slung it over his shoulder and headed for the front door, for freedom.

As he stepped over the threshold, he stopped, turned his head and called, "Hey Connie, don't forget tonight's Halloween. I've put a bowl of religious tracks by the front door. Oh, and be careful, Rusty Slump just might try and kill you."

Not certain whether Connie was even home, he stepped outside and slammed the door behind him, which reminded him of the boom of the cannon. By the time he reached his El Camino, he'd forgotten that he, Private Pendleton of the First Regiment, even had a daughter.

Connie felt delicious.

This sensation brought forth pangs of guilt, which, in turn, made her feel even more delicious. It was a vicious cycle and she was really enjoying the ride.

She'd had a shit day. Her gym teacher grabbing at her nether regions, her principal mocking her, and her minister arming her with invisible weapons. Not to mention her father heading off to fight a mock battle though the real battle was right here in Fremont.

Everyone had failed her.

After fleeing the Other One True Way Church, running through the rain, which hid her tears, she sought shelter in the Red Cross Drug Store.

And there, standing before her like an altar to sugar, was a display of Halloween candy. Plastic bags filled with tiny chocolate bars glittering. The girl could hear her mouth watering.

Never in her life had Connie been Trick-or-Treating, as her father saw Halloween as just another pagan celebration. They'd spent every October 31st at home, passing out religious tracks to any kids unfortunate enough to darken their door with their cuteness. Though she prayed against such feelings, she always felt a twinge of anger about handing a pamphlet about the Lord and his bounteous rules to some little cowboy or cheerleader. Even as the tot looked up at her perplexed, she had to keep her smile plastered, for she knew that her father was right behind her, watching.

He was always watching.

But he couldn't see her from Old Virginia.

Standing in Red Cross Drug dripping and downtrodden, Connie decided this Halloween was going to be different, this Halloween was going to be fun. Disobeying a direct order from her father, she grabbed two bags of what appeared to be the most decadent-looking candy and rushed to the registers, afraid she might lose her nerve.

Back home, she dumped the bowl of religious tracks into the fireplace, struck a match, and laughed as they went up in flames. Hundreds of images of the Sweet Baby G turning black, disappearing, becoming ash. She filled the bowl with the tiny candy bars. Running her hands through the shiny orange packages, she felt quivers in crevices she never realized she had. Before she could stop herself, Connie ripped open one of the candy bars and devoured it in one quick bite. Her first ever experience with candy.

Sin coated with chocolate was delicious and it made her feel delicious. A sensation she'd never had before. Though she told herself not to, she ate another and another and another. Cramming the bars into her mouth, chewing and laughing, chocolatey spittle sluicing down her chin. All her cares about her father and Principal Kennedy and Reverend Rump and Ms. Locke and, even, the cute but deadly Rusty Slump, fled.

Connie only stopped stuffing the treats into her wet hole when she saw half the bowl was gone. She feared she might eat them all, then there'd be nothing to hand out to the little kiddies except a pile of ash. She couldn't deny the youth of America this amazing feeling.

Clasping the now half-empty bowl to her stomach, she stood near the front door, a chocolatey smile smeared. As she waited for the sun to make its slow descent, her mind drifted. Closing her eyes, Connie pretended this was her house, her bowl. And she had her own family: a ruggedly handsome husband and a mischievous but beautiful boy, Rusty Slump Jr.

Shocked at this thought, her eyes ripped open and she shook her head vehemently.

Laughing at herself and her crazy imagination, she had another candy bar to smooth her nerves, readjusted the bowl, and went back to waiting.

Hours passed, the sun set but her doorbell remained unrung. Of course. Word had gotten around the kid world to avoid the Pendleton house like the plague. All you'd get there would be a small picture of a bearded dude embossed with a quote about fishes or lepers. Kids weren't stupid, they didn't want that crud.

Okay, thought Connie, *if Muhammad isn't coming to the mountain of candy, then she would bring the mountain of candy to Muhammad.*

The girl threw open the front door and headed out into the night to distribute her bounty but stopped, shocked, when she spied who was waiting on the doorstep.

Officer Rumpza was standing there, preparing to knock.

They studied one another, not a word passed between them. Connie had always liked the woman who became her father's second-in-command when Sergeant Snoopers was run over. As she was not allowed to befriend any of the girls at Rutherford B. Hayes Memorial High School, Officer Rumpza was as close to a friend as Connie had. Sometimes, during the fleeting moments when they were alone, the older woman had schooled the girl on fashion and make-up.

"That's a great costume," Connie joked, motioning toward the uniform that clung to the policewoman's body.

Although she smiled, Rumpza said, "This is no laughing matter, Connie. Your father seems unconcerned that that turdwipe Rusty Slump is free and dangerous, like all men, but I feel you might need a little protection. With the Police Chief out of town, I guess it's up to me to stay close to you."

Connie didn't know what to say, she was too dazzled by the way the streetlights on Rutherford B. Hayes Memorial Avenue sparkled in Officer Rumpza's golden hair, like tiny, shiny candy bars.

The girl stood aside and let the cop into her home.

For a long time, they didn't speak. The pair just sat in the living room – Connie on the couch, Rumpza sprawled on the matching love seat – staring at one another. When the girl realized that she was still gripping the bowl of candy, she offered one to the other woman.

"I'm watching my figure." Rumpza patted her stomach.

"You don't need to. You're quite beautiful." The words were out of Connie's mouth before she could think.

A heavy, mossy silence settled over everything.

Outside, a sudden shower, coming down in black sheets. Both women jumped as lightning cracked the sky and illuminated the night.

Rumpza was just like the lightning. The way she moved, crooked but with intent, fast and indelible, how she was one place then another, bringing light. She was out of the love seat and on the couch before Connie could move or even grasp what was happening. Rumpza was all over the girl, her mouth, her hands, her spit, her scent. The bowl fell from Connie's grasp, shattered on the floor, scattering candy.

Then came the thunder crash, shaking the house but Connie didn't even notice, didn't even feel it.

Many things about Civil War reenactments brought Police Chief

Pendleton great joy – the smell of gunpowder, the pounding of the canons, the cries of the dying as they fell – but there was one thing about the experience that drove him absolutely mad: the camaraderie. His fellow reenactors, dullards all, treated these great battles like some kind of vacation. Spending their nights in RVs, these lowlifes lounged around in modern clothing and watched sporting events on their portable televisions or cranked up some heinous Satan's Butt Buddies' CD on their stereos. Some of them even had the gaul to bring their cell phones onto the field of battle, place calls to their loved ones back home or, even worse, take selfies. None of them took it seriously enough for Pendleton's liking.

As much as possible, he avoided his fellow combatants. Not joining in on their parties, he chose to sleep on the cold, hard ground under his thin gum blanket. Just like the real men who bravely fought in the War Between the States.

He didn't care that he was alone. It's where he wanted to be. Out in the elements, beneath the stars, chewing diligently on some of his world famous hard tack, which the other reenactors not only refused to touch, but openly mocked.

As he lay amongst the cedars of Prince William County, Virginia, Pendleton found himself more distracted than usual by the sounds of partying bleating through the trees. Those dratted fools were ruining a perfect evening with their fraternizing. Pendleton couldn't sleep, which meant he couldn't dream about the glorious battle that awaited them at first light. He could only fume.

To take the edge off, Pendleton reached into his rucksack and pulled out the baggie of Purple Hayes. In the light of his dying campfire, he considered the lavender powder. On the long drive down from Ohio, he'd formulated a plan. He'd snort a little with his breakfast of bacon fat and cold coffee and experience its effects, if there were any, as he headed into the Second Battle of Bull Run.

But as he lay there not sleeping, he quickly changed his plan and ripped open the baggie right then and there. Amongst the cedars, an owl barked a warning but the Police Chief paid no heed. He wanted to go back in time and he wanted to go now.

Pendleton froze when he realized he had no idea how much he was supposed to ingest for the perfect trip. There was only a few ounces left at the bottom of the baggie. Although no one knew the exact amount the Fremont Police Society had, the cop was aware that if too much went missing from the evidence locker, there might be questions.

A terrible roar of camaraderie rose from the bivouacked RVs and Pendleton jumped, nearly dropping the baggie. He groaned.

Before he could stop himself, the Police Chief snorted the entire contents of the baggie. As the great Rutherford B. Hayes once said, "The bold enterprises are the successful ones."

The effect was almost immediate.

Suddenly, all around him were men, thousands of them, wearing blue wool uniforms, toting muskets.

They were the real Union soldiers of Major General John Pope's army.

Every organ in Pendleton's body smiled.

He was smack dab in the middle of their encampment. In a haze of complete wonderment, he walked amongst the army preparing for battle the following day as if he were the one who was a ghost.

These brave young men weren't lollygagging about in RVs, they were huddled around dying fires, playing mournful harmonicas or speaking to one another in hushed tones. Some were off on their own, curled beneath their gum blankets, looking for sleep. Though Pendleton knew they wouldn't be traveling to the Land O' Nod that night, as they were anxious for the morning. The battle. The fire and flames.

"Hey there, Private Pendleton, look sharp!" A voice carried across the breeze and cut through the cop's solitude.

A bewildered Pendleton spun in circles attempting to find who could possibly be addressing him. Near the tree line he spied a figure that he recognized instantly though he had to blink a few times to believe his eyes or his luck.

It was Rutherford B. Hayes who, at that time, was a lieutenant colonel in the Union Army. The future president stood proud, his head back, his back straight and, Pendleton noted with astonishment, quite a prodigious bulge in his woolen trousers.

The lieutenant colonel motioned for the cop to follow him and dipped into the trees, out of sight.

As fast as his legs could carry him, the Police Chief followed suit.

When he entered the copse of cedars, the sounds of the soldiers and the horses disappeared. The woods were dark and claustrophobic; it felt as if every tree branch were reaching out for him. Hayes was nowhere to be seen. Dashing this way and that, Pendleton looked for him, for anyone. Fear crept out of the darkness and gripped Pendleton. He felt all alone, abandoned.

His dream had become a nightmare.

"Private, you are a dad-blamed scalawag," said Hayes, appearing from behind a tree.

The Police Chief didn't hear the future president's words. He was too busy considering whether to genuflect or not. "Lieutenant Colonel Hayes, I am at your service."

"Then I am truly in a hell-fired mess. Though you wear the uniform of a Union soldier, I need your service, sir, about as much as I need more penis."

This harsh besmirching of Pendleton's character stung the Police Chief.

His lips trembling, the cop asked the future president what he was talking about.

Motioning toward his gabardines and the prodigious trouser knoll contained within, Hayes explained, "Can't you see for yourself, man, my cock is much like the cock of the mighty ibex."

"No, no, I understand that part, believe me. But I will not accept your indictment of my character. I'm a good solider and I would lay down my life for you."

Hayes snorted. "Unfortunately, your life is worth nothing, nancy-boy. For you, sir, are the consummate boot-licker. Stealing illegal drugs from your own constabulary and then consuming them.... that, young man, is the behavior of a true rapscallion."

"But, but, I only stole those drugs and consumed them so that I could travel back in time and meet great men such as yourself."

"That, Private, is a tarnal lie. You stole the drug – which, I might add, is made from flesh shaved from my massive kidney-buster – because you have a weak spirit and a wanting soul."

Nodding, the Police Chief said, "Oh, I get it now, you're just a figment of my imagination standing in for my conscience."

"If that is what you choose to believe, you lowly cockchafer, believe it."

The fashion in which the great Hayes swore both surprised and excited Pendleton, for it made him think of his very own Officer Rumpza.

The lieutenant colonel continued, "Whether I'm a ghost or an effect of the drug or your own crippled conscience, I find you reprehensible and silly. Why would any sane man choose to leave the comforts of his home to play pretend soldier and sleep on the ground?"

"I... I want you honor your men, your sacrifice."

While shaking his head, Hayes tittered. "You cussed lickfinger, we fought to obtain peace, stability throughout the country. Now that you have that, why do you wish to relive the horrors of war as if they were some sort of game? My men slept on the cold hard ground and partook of that awful hardtack crap because we had to. If any of us had a choice, we would have stayed home with our loved ones. Eating pussy and pot roast. Just as you should have."

"Well, I, ah, I--."

"Shut up, you blamed idiot. I abhor you, sir, and your actions. Abandoning your daughter though you know full well there's trouble brewing in my beloved burg of Fremont."

"I, but, yeah, but Connie has the Good Lord looking out for her!"

"Oh, be still, you poxed snatch, the Lord is as much of your imagination as I am. The truth is that your daughter's alone and scared. You left her to play soldier and do drugs. That is beyond reprehensible in my book, you fool. Now be gone, scalawag, get out of my sight!"

His soul ablaze, Pendleton turned and skulked away. He knew that, besides the surprising amount of swearing and the harsh words concerning the Almighty, Hayes' words rang true. He'd abandoned his daughter when she needed him most.

No amount of Purple Hayes would have made him feel better at that point.

By the time he stumbled back into the clearing, gone were the soldiers and the horses and the harmonicas. He was back in his own awful time, his own awful world.

Satan's Butt Buddies' latest abomination - a song called *Give Me Every Inch of Your Horn, Beelzebub* - was roaring from the RVs.

Taking a deep breath, he raced back to his tiny campsite, gathered his meager possessions, and tossed them into the rucksack.

He had to get back to Connie, back to Fremont, back to where he belonged.

Little did he know, he was already too late.

Another coupling of thunder and lightning woke Connie Pendleton from her slumber. She refused to open her eyes though, because she knew if she did, her dream would dissipate and what a splendid dream it was. Chrissy Rumpza's tongue and hands roaming her body. Tugging off her sackcloth dress, her wilted bra, her granny panties, tossing them. Their bodies locked together, grinding. Moans of pleasure filling the living room while outside, the rain with its small hands knocked. Then finally, they both came, crying out, clinging to one another. In that moment of ecstasy, Connie wondered if she should feel ashamed for acting like a common beast of the field, but decided she didn't care that she didn't care. After the shuddering finally wound down, she looked the cop right her green-with-brown-flecks eyes and told her that she loved her. Chrissy Rumpza responded in kind and they kissed and they kissed and they kissed.

As these wanton and joyous images filled her head and heart, Connie felt blessed that she'd had such an amazing, graphic, sweet, demented dream. Too bad it was over.

But then she felt a heartbeat *outside* her body.

Opening her eyes, she nearly cried out in joyance. For she was laying on the couch naked and pressed against an equally naked Chrissy Rumpza. The girl's smile widened to the point of pain. Though she wished to grab the other woman, tweak her nipples, message her breasts, run her hand over her pulsating mound of love, Connie controlled herself and her brand new libido. She let her love sleep while she ran only her eyes over Chrissy's body sprawled.

The girl had never seen another human naked before. Her father had signed a permission slip that excused her from PE. She had to sit in the library while the other girls ran around the gym, getting good and sweaty, and showering together, laughing. Many times, as she sat under the harsh fluorescent lights of the library, pretending to read her well-thumbed copy of *Heaven is For Realsies*, Connie wondered what being naked in front of other females would be like.

Now she didn't have to wonder, it was wonderful.

Bereft of clothing, Chrissy was a masterpiece. Connie would have hung her in the Rutherford B. Hayes Memorial Art Gallery, though she didn't want to share her.

Round where Connie was flat, defined muscles ran up and down Chrissy's arms and legs. Her golden hair, her pouty lips, always ready for a kiss.

It was all too much and, yet, not enough. Never enough. The girl knew that if she and Chrissy made sweet, passionate love until they both curled up and died, Connie would never be sated. That was a glorious feeling, a feeling of peace, of bliss that she'd never obtained from the sermons of Reverend Rump in the confines of the Other One True Way Church.

Never again did she want to see Chrissy ruined by clothing. Never again did she want to be more than two feet away from this beauty. Never again would she dream of Rusty Stump, as she recalled with disgust his scrotum, huge and pulsing, sullied by disease. Not soft and inviting and moist like the undercarriage of her lover, Chrissy Rumpza.

Unable to stay her hand, she reached out and gently took the cop's nipple between her thumb and forefinger and rolled it around, hardening it. The woman stirred, groaned.

Scolding herself for breaking her promise to let this lovely creature rest, as their sexual congress had been exhausting, Connie let go of the nipple and untangled herself from her lover carefully, enjoying every accidental caress.

The girl stood and stared down upon the glory that was Chrissy Rumpza's nakedness. She could have stayed and stared all night but her bladder was full and screaming for release.

On the toilet, Connie relived every touch, every tingle. When she finished urinating, she carried herself to orgasm with two fingers and memories.

Returning to the living room on shaky legs, she found her lover still asleep. Connie imagined waking up every morning next to this for the rest of her life and the thought made her nearly burst with joy.

Spinning a circle of unbridled bliss, Connie nearly tripped on Rumpza's uniform, which was scattered across the living room floor like a chain of islands. She grabbed the dark blue shirt, pressed it to her face, and inhaled the scent of her lover. A little sweat, a little sweet, like a strawberry left out in the sun.

Though it was far too large for her, Connie slipped the shirt on, buttoned it. Hugging herself, she felt as if she were drowning in an ocean of Chrissy Rumpza. Pulling on the cop pants, she cinched them as tight as she could with the leather belt. She felt the weight of the cop's Savage 1861 Navy revolver against her thigh. As if she were crowning herself, she placed Officer Rumpza's stiff peaked cap atop her head, it was so big it slipped down to her eyes.

As best she could in the ridiculous get-up, she ran to the bathroom to check herself in the mirror. It surprised her how much she looked like her father. This made her gasp. Inside her head, she could hear his wrathful laments about her mother being a whore, an adulterer, a garden-variety harlot. Connie knew that if he could see her now with her hickies and lust-filled heart, he would spit the same irate words in her face. For a moment, she was mortified. She cowered in shame, which is exactly how God liked his humans.

Then she thought: flock it. Flock her father, flock her shame, flock, even, God.

This thought made her burst out laughing so hard she fell to the floor.

When the laughter subsided, she had a vision of herself, out in the streets, in Chrissy's uniform. It made perfect sense as this was Halloween, the night where you got to be what you weren't. She knew it was wrong, was well aware it was actually against the law, but she couldn't help herself, she wanted to be out in the rain, disguised as her lover. Maybe, if it weren't too late, she'd knock on a few doors, get some more of that delicious, delicious candy. Bring a handful back to her lover and they'd eat it and laugh and grind together like glorious beasts of the field.

After donning her lover's shoes, which were three sizes too large, Connie slipped out the front door, out into the world.

Feeling ridiculous in a ski mask and hoody, Rusty Slump hid in the evergreen bushes outside the Pendleton's front door. Finding it hard to breath though there was air all around him, the young man stood perfectly still.

When he arrived on the scene, he discovered there was a cop car parked in the driveway. This froze him in his tracks, made him scratch his head. CoCo had promised the Police Chief was out of town, but he swore he heard voices coming from inside the house and what certainly sounded like really hot sexual congress. Perhaps Connie had a boyfriend over while her father was off fake fighting in the fake Civil War. Maybe that cop no one liked, Killion.

For some reason, this thought made the back of Rusty's neck burn, itch.

He decided to wait in the bushes until Connie's lover left. Then he could gun Connie down in cold blood. A thought which made him want to vomit up all his internal organs.

After the sounds of sexual congress died out, no lover left. Rusty had no idea what to do. He couldn't kill Connie Pendleton, but at the same time, he couldn't return to Jugsy Jaspburger's party and face CoCo without having killed Connie Pendleton. As he was at something of impasse, he stayed in the bushes and waited for the world to end.

Then a thought struck him. He realized that his alibi would no longer hold water. According to his iPhone, he'd been gone from the party for over an hour. This was supposed to be a quick operation, in and out, *bang, bang, bang.* With this much time having elapsed

– no teenagers engaged in sexual congress for more than twenty minutes – all the other partygoers would surely have noticed his absence and would be able to testify as much. As he would already be the prime suspect if Connie ended up dead, carrying out this mission seemed like a bad career move. He should probably just go forward with his trial, perhaps the judge would be lenient on him, seeing as this was the first time he'd ever stolen a dead president and manufactured drugs from dead president's penis.

An unexpected sense of relief washed over Rusty as he climbed from the bushes to head back to the party, the .38 hanging at his side. He'd confess to CoCo that he couldn't go through with her plan, as Connie had someone over, probably a cop, and he'd simply run out of time. Surely CoCo would understand. Hopefully she would. And, if she didn't, hopefully she wouldn't hurt him too much.

When Rusty reached the street, the front door of the Pendleton residence was thrown open and out into the shadows danced a cop. Obviously, this was the dude who'd been engaged in sexual congress with Connie. His blood simmering, Rusty ducked behind a streetlight.

Skipping in a very uncoplike fashion, the dude made his way down the driveway and into the eerie glow of the sodium-vapor streetlights. To Rusty's great surprise, he saw that it wasn't Junior Officer Killon. It was Connie herself. Wearing her father's ill-fitting uniform, like a child.

And she was beaming. Rusty had never even seen her crack a smile before. She always looked so serious, as if she were perpetually solving an algebra problem in her head.

But skipping down Rutherford B. Hayes Memorial Avenue, she looked resplendent.

Her smile made him smile.

When Connie reached the middle of the deserted street, she

held out her arms, threw back her head, and spun in circles. A slow, crazy dance. Humming to herself. Not caring if anyone saw, safe in her own little world. She made her way down the street in this fashion, the happiest soul in Sandusky County.

Rusty was well aware he should flee, return to the party, but instead, he trailed the dancing girl. Unable to take his eyes away from her performance of pure joy. He stuck to the shadows, not making a sound, the gun, forgotten, dangling at his side.

Rusty could feel a smile burning his face, could feel tears of joy welling. He'd never experienced this level of happiness with CoCo, even when they were high on Purple Hayes and she was administering one of her boisterous but toothy blowjobs.

Needing to get closer to this elation, Rusty stepped from the shadows.

"Hey, Connie," he called.

She stopped. She stopped spinning, she stopped humming, she stopped everything and the world stopped with her. Connie's smile vanished as her mouth dropped. Where he had eyes only for her perfect beauty, she had eyes only for the .38 clasped in his hand.

All the blood drained from her face so fast Rusty could hear it. She let forth a bloodcurdling scream.

Recalling that he was wearing a ski mask and hoodie, Rusty tried to explain who he was, a friend, a lab partner. "No, no, I'm…"

But Connie was already running away, disappearing into the smothering darkness that was the Rutherford B. Hayes Memorial Cemetery, which lay at the end of Rutherford B. Hayes Memorial Avenue.

Thanks to her ridiculous costume, she couldn't run properly. Afraid she might trip and bash her pretty head on something, Rusty took off after her.

The graveyard was empty, quieter than quiet, darker than dark.

With a half-loaded gun in his hand and hundreds of headstones haphazardly placed, Rusty had to be careful with his step. Therefore he couldn't catch up to the fleeing Connie, who was running full-tilt boogie, but he kept her in sight. Calling out her name again and again in his softest, least threatening voice didn't help. She didn't slow. Holding up her pants with one hand, she kept scrambling, looking over her shoulder at her perceived pursuer, her face so white. Still screaming loud enough to wake the dead.

After several minutes of this slow chase, Connie caught her foot on a tree root and fell, face-first, onto a pile of dirt beneath a monument of a dog wearing a badge. Her legs still kicking, trying to run, trying to get away. With a squeal of pain – she'd obviously hurt her ankle in the tumble – she spun to face Rusty as he approached. Her eyes wide, shaking her head.

She looked so ridiculous, sprawled out in that silly costume, that Rusty couldn't help but chuckle. Years from now, sharing their lives together, they'd tell their children about this absurd misunderstanding and laugh.

His chuckling came to an abrupt halt when Connie drew the Savage 1861 Navy revolver holstered at her side. With shaking hands, she raised the weapon, aimed it at Rusty.

Later, he'd wonder if he'd had a choice, if there had been any other way. But in the moment, there was only one course of action. He brought up the .38.

Fired all three of the Purple Hayes laced bullets into her chest.

Part Two:
Dope Tits

Spring.

The time of year when the earth girds its loins, gathers its resources, and raises its voice to tell Old Man Winter to flock off. When the smallest sprout becomes potent and fists up through the thawing ground. When leaves unfurl to soak up the sun. When coats and boots are relegated to the back of the closet as shorts and skirts take center stage.

Spring, when a young man's fancy lightly turns to thoughts of love.

Unless, of course, that young man happens to be Rusty Slump, whose fancy was lightly turning to thoughts of how much he hated the blowjob he was currently receiving.

First off, as always, it was boisterous but toothy, but that wasn't the real problem. He loathed watching CoCo's head bob, listening to her slurp, the smug smile she shined when she swallowed.

Not that he would ever voice his displeasure.

The young man knew he had no right to be in such a dour mood. All in all, the last six months had gone his way. His trial had been a complete bust for the Fremont Police Society. Somehow, the small amount of Purple Hayes that the cops had found on his person went missing and the prosecution's star witness, Connie Pendleton, was unable to testify.

Probably because she was dead and buried under three feet of ground.

Not that anyone knew that.

That was yet another thing that had gone Rusty's way, no one ever found Connie's body because he'd buried it in the grave of Sergeant Snoopers where she'd fallen. A search was conducted for the missing girl, led by Police Chief Pendleton, while Rusty fretted and CoCo made him tell and retell the story of her death, begging for gory details. The searchers found nothing, no trace of Connie. Reverend LaRue Rump, the last person to see Connie alive, came forward to testify that she'd visited his house and was very distraught about something. What, he couldn't exactly remember. Though the minister offered her the guidance and protection of the Lord, she left petulant and upset. Rumors started flying around town that she'd run away to the bright lights of Toledo or, less horribly, had thrown herself into the Sandusky River.

Seemingly, Rusty Slump had gotten away with murder.

But still, he felt very unMachiavelli.

Connie's death brought him no joy. In fact, whenever he thought about it, which was often, he felt as if someone had shoved his guts into a blender.

In the last moments of Connie's life, Rusty had fallen in love with her. Whenever he was alone and had a minute, he sobbed over his loss.

As if murdering his unrequited love weren't bad enough, Rusty had other travails. He was disgruntled that his life of crime was ostensibly over. For a few short, shiny weeks, he'd become, thanks to Purple Hayes and CoCo's constant hectoring, a mover and shaker in the vast and dangerous criminal underworld of Fremont, Ohio. Now that the drug was gone and there was no hope of ever acquiring more, his thoughts returned to taking unlawful dumps. CoCo forbade him from doing so. She kept reminding him she had plans for him, big plans, not that she'd ever divulged what those big plans were.

Another thing bothering Rusty was Loco Lenny Labovitz, the local drug kingpin.

Often CoCo would dispatch Rusty to Loco's mobile drug emporium to score some weed. Whenever Rusty came face-to-face with Fremont's current crime lord, he was terrified. During his brief stint as a drug dealer, Rusty had worked hard at keeping his identity a secret. If Loco had ever found out it was him who'd invented Purple Hayes and poached his clientele, the kingpin would have not reacted kindly. In fact, he most definitely had Rusty killed in some unpleasant way.

Whenever he was in the tubular confines of Loco's mobile drug emporium, Rusty felt that Loco was looking at him with anvils for eyes.

Another persistent thorn in Rusty's side was CoCo herself. He'd grown tired of his girlfriend. He'd never particularly cared for her, but now he was stuck with her. For they shared the deepest, darkest secret a person can possess. She knew Rusty was a murderer. This bound them together, though he loved another. A girl smarter than CoCo, more beautiful, but, unfortunately, more dead.

As their graduation approached, CoCo had begun to drop hints that, after they'd doffed their caps and robes, perhaps they should get hitched.

This dark cloud of inescapable fate hung heavy over every one of Rusty's moments, each movement.

Unless, of course, I killed CoCo too, he thought, glancing down at the blowjob in progress.

Though he'd been having trouble getting into this particular blowjob - even though he closed his eyes, as he often did, and thought of Connie - the image of CoCo in a casket flung him into the pit of ecstasy. His thighs jostled as he shot a fist of steaming cum into CoCo's mouth. She whooped with either joy or surprise, he didn't care which. Laughing or gagging, his girlfriend fell back onto the Safavid silk, wool, and metal-thread prayer rug.

Looking away, Rusty stuffed his penis back into his trousers, stretched out on Thomas Jefferson's four-poster bed, and turned his back.

Climbing to her feet and wiping the last dollop of dick dew from her chin, CoCo said calmly, "You know you're going to have to kill him."

Rusty jumped, faced her. "Kill who?"

"Loco Lenny Labovitz."

Rusty laughed, or tried to anyway. "What are you talking about?"

Laying down beside Rusty, she curled into him. "That's the big plan I've been talking about, the thing to get you back on top. Think about it. When you were selling drugs, you were the Prince of Fremont, everyone looked up to you. Now you're a nobody who dreams of shitting in the Rutherford B. Hayes Memorial Swimming Hole."

"Last time I did that, they had to close for the day," he pointed out with pride in his voice.

"I hate to be the one who has to break this to you, but you can't monetize crapping. You need a real job in the vast and dangerous criminal underground that is Fremont and I'm thinking drug kingpin. You've got the cred and I've got the brains, the brawn, and the guts. There's only one person standing in our way and that's Loco Lenny Labovitz. Hell, you've already killed, putting that little bitch in the ground. Now you just have to do is the same thing to our local insane drug dealer to become king. Pop Loco, don the crown."

CoCo's glittery words sounded good, sounded right. But, Rusty reasoned, there were a few flaws in her plan. One, he wasn't really a killer, although he had technically killed. And two, Loco had a pair of burly henchman, named Right and Left, who followed him wherever he went, flashing their fake smiles and real guns.

"Me murdering Loco ain't gonna happen, Sugar Labia, so you can just put that dream back in the freezer."

"'There is no avoiding war; it can only be postponed to the advantage of others,'" she purred.

Pushing her away, he said, "Stop throwing the great Machiavelli's words in my face. That's not going to work a second time."

CoCo rose, her back straight, her head held high, her eyes as inscrutable as soccer.

"Huh," she said, somehow turning it into a threat.

Now it was her turn to turn her back on him. She stood there, thinking dark thoughts.

Silence cluttered the luxury treehouse.

At last, she said in a voice as soft as summer skin, "It would certainly be a shame if the Fremont Police Society got an anonymous tip about where that little bitch was buried and who put her there."

Feeling vomit moving throughout his system, Rusty asked his girlfriend if she could possibly be serious.

"Kill Loco Lenny Labovitz or I'll show you how serious I am. Rusty, you and me, we need a lot of money to make our lives turn out the way I want. I want a really nice, top-of-the-line trailer, a couple of rugrats, and all the weed I can smoke. You can make all of these dreams come true. Just kill Loco Lenny Labovitz. Or go to jail."

Rutherford B. Hayes caught him masturbating again.

Police Chief Pendleton was really going to town self-pollution-wise, gripping Officer Rumpza's official police portrait in one hand, his solidified schlong in the other, when he looked into the bathroom mirror and spied the ghost or drug hallucination or whatever of the nineteenth president. Hayes' beard was frowning, he was shaking his head, arms folded across his bow.

Talk about erection killers.

Pendleton dropped both his penis and the official portrait of Rumpza. The glass in the frame shattered but neither man flinched.

"I wish you wouldn't do that," said the Police Chief, stuffing his defeated penis back in his trousers.

"And I, sir, wish you'd stop defiling yourself, as least as long as I'm haunting you or whatever it is that I'm doing."

It had been six months since that fateful Halloween night, six months since Pendleton, in a moment of weakness, had snorted what was left of the Purple Hayes, six months since Connie had left the front door open and disappeared into the night. It had been the worst night of Pendleton's life, as a father and as the Police Chief of the Fremont Police Society.

Looking down upon the shards of glass tiled across the bathroom floor, the cop said, "I'm sorry, Lieutenant Colonel Hayes."

"That makes two of us, you worthless scalawag. You are about as worthless as a fart in a whirlwind. Need I remind you that your daughter is still missing, and what are you doing about it? Except the defiling yourself, of course."

To make matters worse, over the last six months the ghost or drug hallucination or whatever Rutherford B. Hayes was, would appear to Pendleton at the most inopportune times, primarily while engaged in the act of self-defilement, and chastise him. There was no one Pendleton could turn to for help with his predicament, for he feared being tossed into the Rutherford B. Hayes Memorial Nuthouse.

There were a handful occasions when he almost shared his secret with Officer Rumpza. But he couldn't. For it was always her that he thought of during his numerous bouts of self-abuse.

Besides, over the last few months, Rumpza had changed. She

appeared to bathe with less frequency, her uniform was often mis-buttoned and befouled with stains, and her repellent temperament had grown worse and was now bordering on insubordination. When she wasn't taking the name of the Lord in vain or throwing Jarts at Junior Officer Killion, she spent a fair amount of time staring out the window. She seemed, in a word, distracted. A few days previous, the Police Chief caught her gazing at a photo of his daughter on his desk and everything suddenly made sense. Apparently, Connie and Chrissy were better friends than he realized, and Connie's disappearance had hit her hard.

This fact made the Police Chief overlook Rumpza's many damnable personal flaws and made him desire the young officer even more, which was not a good thing for his soul or his career, the two things that mattered most to him. But he couldn't help himself. He'd stolen her official police portrait, hung around outside her house at all hours of the night, and often got caught in the act of self-pollution by Rutherford B. Hayes.

Deciding it best to change the subject from his self-abuse, Pendleton looked Hayes straight in his brilliant blues and asked, "Listen, if you're all knowing, why don't you just tell me where my daughter is? Did she run away to the bright lights of Toledo and become a prostitute?"

This was the Police Chief's greatest fear, that Connie had lost God and found men.

After a chuckle, Hayes said, "You've asked me that time and again and I've always given you the same answer. This spiritual quest is *your* spiritual quest, not mine. I've already found everlasting peace and salvation. I can lend you a hand but I cannot lead you along, you dad-shamed cockteaser."

The cop sighed.

"Well then," he said with mock enthusiasm, "I better get to work."

Stepping over the shards of glass, he brushed roughly past the broad chest of the dead president, and stomped down the hall to get dressed.

Spring.

The time of year when the earth girds its loins, gathers its resources, raises its voice, and tells Old Man Winter to flock off. When the smallest sprout becomes potent and fists up through the thawing ground.

Spring was certainly busting out all over the Rutherford B. Hayes Memorial Cemetery. The leaves of the mighty oaks unfurled to soak up the sun. All along the wrought iron fence the daffodils burst into bloom. Buds appeared on the peony bushes guarding Rutherford B. Hayes' empty mausoleum.

Even at night, things came to life.

Shoots of grass were finally coming up through the dirt of Sergeant Snooper's grave.

Along with a hand.

Then another.

Shocking white, the pair of hands clawed their way out of the earth. Long fingernails, sharp and painted the color of spilt blood. As they so often are, these hands were followed by slender wrists, lithe limbs. Twisting, turning.

In nearby trees, birds awoke. Disturbed by the thing coming out of the ground, they flew away from their nests, their eggs, that town. Never to return.

Back at the grave, a head, gasping for that first kiss of fresh air in such a long time, poked up through the soil, a sneer for a smile.

This thing was Connie Pendleton but most definitely not Connie Pendleton. Not at all. She'd completely changed during her time beneath the earth. Her limp strawberry hair was now a fiery red. Once a muddled brown, her eyes had turned the green of an ocean that lived only to swallow ships. Her once pug nose was now pert and turned up subtly and pierced with a diamond stud. No longer was her face skinny and dotted with freckles, but full and round. Just like her crimson lips.

Using her skinny arms for leverage, this thing that was definitely not Connie Pendleton but a demon wearing Connie like a dress, pulled her body out of the grave. And what a body it was. No longer obscured by an oversized cop uniform, everything was on display. She wore a faded Lynyrd Skynyrd T-shirt, black and cropped, that showed off her flat, pale stomach. Her jeans skirt, which didn't have enough fabric to make a burka for a Muslim mouse, showed off her tenacious tuckus and shapely legs.

And those tits.

They were the type of perfection that would have brought tears to the eyes of Michelangelo and hard-ons to every other male. Spherical and firm, perched, unhindered by gravity or reality. They were like balloons filled with wet dreams.

Taking in her environs with a bemused eye, the demon smiled. She felt great, freed from her dirt jail and back on the right side of the grass.

Tripping on her new legs – and unused to six-inch platform heels – the creature stumbled away from the grave and turned, studying the unusual gravestone towering over her. It was shaped like a dog and carved into the base were the words SERGEANT SNOOPERS, DEARLY DEPARTED FRIEND AND INVESTIGATOR.

This demon already had a name, had had one for millennia. She was Maude the Layer of Waste. The one who will give birth to the ultimate demon who will lay waste to all mankind. But that was too long of a name. She needed a new one. Something snappy. Something modern.

Studying the tombstone, she found a good name for her new

life. Not Sergeant Snoopers, that was a silly name, but Dearly Departed. Nodding, she decided that's what she would call herself.

Hunger burned in her stomach. That's what a decade trapped beneath the ground got you. She needed flesh. Red, raw flesh. After which, she needed to mate with a puny human, as scrawled in the ancient scrolls, to create the monster that would eventually destroy the world of men.

But first things first.

Despite her rocking body, she looked like crap. Her wan skin was flecked with splotches of dried blood, and dirt was tucked everywhere: in her hair, beneath her fabulous nails, pressed into the corners of her mouth. Even wedged between her marvelous mammaries.

Lurching across the dewy ground, Dearly Departed made her way toward the gurgling fountain at the front of the Rutherford B. Hayes Memorial Cemetery. During her journey, she came across a wandering raccoon. When the critter spied her, it stopped moving, its tail fluffed, its eyes full of fear. She smiled at the creature and it took off, running as fast as its little raccoon legs could carry it.

Dearly frowned. If she could have befriended the small animal, calmed it, coaxed it, she could've had a nice meal.

With a shrug, she continued toward the fountain.

At the water's edge, she tugged off her top, stepped out of her her skirt and frilly red panties that were more of a conceit than an actual article of clothing.

In the measure of moonlight, she checked herself out.

Despite the dirt and blood, Dearly Departed was resplendent.

Pleased with herself, she leapt into the fountain, which featured a statue of Rutherford B. Hayes crossing the Delaware, liquid spraying out of every orifice.

The water was bracing, cold but effective. Washing away the

blood, the dirt, the past. She felt renewed, reborn, wet from the womb.

Smiling, she couldn't stop massaging her breasts. In addition to being aesthetically pleasing, there was something about them that was, in a word, magical. She could feel it, pouring out of every pore. Something purple, something powerful.

Interrupting her inspection, a truck happened past, rusty and mufflerless, a hefty puny human behind the wheel, staring at her as if he'd never seen a naked female frolicking in a fountain before.

Though she smiled and waved, took an inviting step forward, the puny human's eyes went wide and worried and, just like the raccoon, he scurried away into the night. The scratch of rubber meeting pavement.

Too bad. He would have made a great meal, lots of juicy flesh. Though she never would have mated with him. Too fat, too stupid, too drunk. The demon needed perfection - or as close as puny humans could get - for her child of fire.

Though she'd fled from Police Chief Pendleton's house completely naked on the night Connie disappeared, Rumpza hadn't left empty handed. On the way out, dazed and panicked, the cop had grabbed Connie's panties, which were splayed on the floor amongst the spilt Halloween candy.

There was nothing special about this particular pair of panties. They weren't crotch-less or hot pink or decorated with tiny Rutherford B. Hayes faces. In fact they were rather pedestrian, bordering on matronly. Lots of material, covering as much skin as possible. Once blue, they had faded to a near white after numerous washings.

But still they sent battering rams of electricity surging through Rumpza's nervous system whenever she touched them. They had been on Connie's body, rubbing shoulders with her nether regions. Rumpza had removed them herself, tossing them with a laugh.

Now the cop, as she did every night, pressed the panties into her face.

They smelled of Connie, her sweet lollipop pussy, but Rumpza noticed, with distress, her lover's scent was waning. With each passing day, the odor of Connie's glorious cod trench was growing fainter, harder to detect.

Soon, the snatchy smell would be gone forever. Just like Connie herself.

Most Fremontonians labored under the delusion that Connie, driven mad by her religiously oppressive father, had simply fled to the bright lights and dark streets of Toledo to become a prostitute, following in the soiled footsteps of her garden-variety harlot mother, but Rumpza knew this wasn't the case. Something had happened to her lover, something bad. The cop knew that she and Connie, although their relationship had lasted only an hour, had had something special. They'd entered each other's souls, using their vaginas as portals. Connie would never have taken off, leaving Chrissy alone in the cold world of Fremont.

She'd been taken.

If Rumpza just would have gone by the book, if she'd been any kind of cop at all, she'd have called in Connie's disappearance immediately, exposed herself, and let the chips fall where they may. That way, the search for Connie would have begun at once.

But she didn't.

Scared of discovery, scared of losing her job, losing everything, she snuck out of the Pendleton house and into the night, the rain, clutching Connie's panties, as naked as the day she was born.

This bevy of secrets, of lies – that she loved Connie Pendleton, that they'd had hot lesbian sex, that she was there when the girl disappeared – which Rumpza kept concealed in her soul burned her from the inside out and left nothing but a husk. Now Rumpza was just a ghost haunting her own life.

This unsettling thought brought tears to the cop's eyes. The wet interlopers slid down her face, spotting Connie's panties.

To cheer herself up, Rumpza decided to masturbate. Which was what she decided to do quite often these days.

With a practiced hand, she pulled the elastic of her own panties down and found her love cranny, waiting, moist.

She was only a few strokes into her bout of self-love, picturing sweet Connie writhing beneath her, when she heard a sound outside. It wasn't much of a sound, just a muffled footfall on Rutherford B. Hayes Memorial Drive, but it made Rumpza sit up straight in bed and unhand herself.

"Connie," she whispered.

In an instant, the cop knew her lover was alive, that she'd returned to her. She knew this in her heart, her soul, her vag.

Dropping her lover's unmentionables, she sprang from the bed and checked the window. The street was deserted. Still, she sprinted downstairs. Wearing next to nothing, she burst through her front door and out into the chilly April air. She didn't mind the cold for her mind was burning bright.

On goosepimpled legs, the cop raced across her lawn, the dew. Stopping only when she reached the middle of Rutherford B. Hayes Memorial Drive.

Gasping for breath, she looked right, she looked left. There was no one there, not a soul. Well, there was one thing. A smell hanging on the air. The faint scent of decay, of earth.

Standing in the middle of the street, Rumpza cursed herself for believing, hoping, but then, out of the corner of her eye, she spied a shadow moving amongst the shadows congregated at the corner of Rutherford B. Hayes Memorial Drive and Rutherford B. Hayes Memorial Court. A person walking.

Her heart raced and once again she nearly called out Connie's name.

But then, even at this distance, she could tell that the shadow in question, though a female, was not her missing lover. This young woman moved differently, with a rangy lope in her step, just another drunk stumbling home from the Rutherford B. Hayes Memorial Tavern.

Her shoulders hunched, a fresh team of tears forming, Rumpza returned to her bed, chilled and feeling like an idiot. She berated herself. Her lover was gone. Probably dead and gone if Rumpza's gut was right.

And Rumpza's gut was always right.

To alleviate her pain, she returned to her panty-sniffing and masturbating.

Stalking through the deserted streets of Fremont, a curious disquiet settled over Dearly Departed. For everything in this town of puny humans was, at once, both familiar and strange. She recognized some of the insignificant abodes, a handful of the sad businesses, a few trees. The noxious tire stench floating up from Akron.

But that was impossible, Maude the Layer of Waste had never passed this way before in her many incarnations.

That could only mean one thing. One terrible thing. The girl whose body she was using wasn't entirely dead, wasn't completely gone. She was there, lurking, hiding in the shadows of the underbelly of Dearly's brain.

That had certainly never happened before.

Brought into existence at the ass end of the Akkadian Empire by a warlock jonesing for a sex partner to help him produce an offspring so deadly, so dangerous that his seed could rule the world, Maude the Layer of Waste was semi-banished by a half-assed oracle with a club foot. As this oracle was wasted on sand wine at the time, the banishment didn't quite take and the demon had, ever since, returned to the world of the puny humans every decade and taken the body of a recently dead, fertile young female. Using this sexy corpse, Maude the Layer of Waste forced unsuspecting men to mate with her in hopes of producing a child that would lay waste to the world.

Not that that plan had ever panned out. Somehow the demon had always been discovered and sent back to the underworld before she gave birth.

But not this time. This time she was going to be careful, cautious. Find the perfect mate, make all the right moves, raise as little suspicion as possible.

No, you won't! I won't let you! screamed the girl who lived beneath her brain. This interruption frightened Maude the Layer of Waste, she stumbled.

But, as always, she regained her footing.

Be still, Other Girl, you are no match for Maude the Layer of Waste!

The Chief of the Fremont Police Society will stop you! He's brave and strong and true.

With pride, the Other Girl pictured a quaint house and the route there.

Dearly thanked the Other Girl for providing her with a perspective mate.

The Other Girl screamed and screamed.

Soon, Dearly found herself standing before 667 Rutherford B. Hayes Memorial Avenue. She studied the small house. Though it was dark, there was something about this house that was welcoming, inviting her inside.

Dearly slinked to the front door and rang the doorbell. Licked her lips, waited.

Lights, lots of lights, sprang to life in the small house and the front door was flung open. The man standing there, barrel-chested, breathing heavy, had a gun in his hand. His face, which was perched near excitement, fell when he saw who was standing there.

"Oh," he said, "I thought..."

"Good evening," said Dearly, though she was disappointed. The Other Girl had lied to her. This was not the perfect mate. He was old and sour and reeked of religion. But he still might make a nice meal.

Rubbing the sleep from his eyes, the puny human looked her over. A crooked smile lifted the corner of his mouth. "Okay, I get it. Someone sent you here as a practical joke. Who was it, Killion? I know it wasn't Rumpza, she may have a foul mouth and tarnished soul, but she'd never stoop so low."

That name, Rumpza, Dearly recognized. It would have made her heart skip a beat if it had been beating.

She said, "I don't know what you're talking about."

"Well, obviously, you're a garden-variety harlot and someone paid for you to show up on my doorstep in the middle of the night. Now I'm just trying to figure out if they did it as a joke or a misguided favor."

Narrowing her eyes at him, she said, "I'm no prostitute, I'm just a lost little girl looking for a place to rest my weary head. And it's just for the night, in the morning I'll be gone."

"But I... but I don't even know who you are." He looked closer, squinted. "Do I?"

"Seems highly unlikely, I'm not from around here."

"Just as I suspected, you're from Toledo."

"Regardless of from whence I hail, I'm only seventeen, I'm scared, and I seek shelter."

He laughed but there was no mirth in it. "This is ridiculous. Go away, you hussy, you're disturbing my sleep."

That's a good idea, thought Dearly. *I'll go away once I've made a meal of your guts and your bones.*

The Other Girl screamed so loudly that the inside of Dearly's head vibrated. The demon decided to play along. For now.

Letting her eyes go wide, her mouth coil into a pout, Dearly produced a tear, a real whopper.

The man froze, studied her. Unlike the lusty driver of the rusty truck, this puny human had no lust in his heart. "You… you remind me of someone I know, I knew. Sort of. She too lost her way."

Dearly forced another tear.

After he thought for a moment, he said, "Come in, come in."

The man put his arm around her, guided her into his home.

"Tarnation, I can feel your bones poking through. Do you need something to eat?"

Though her mouth was pressed against his flesh, she didn't bite, didn't even nibble. Every time she thought of such a thing, a fist of paint punched her brain.

Dearly cursed the Other Girl.

As was his custom, Police Chief Pendleton woke at dawn, fell to the floor and did a hundred push-ups and twice as many crunches. He did this routine naked while reciting the Lord's Prayer. He had to get prepared, get into top physical and mental condition, as Hayes Dayes, Fremont's annual three-day bacchanalia celebrating their native son, was nigh and there would be plenty of arresting to do and police brutality to engage in.

Only after completing his exercise regimen, while he was wiping the sweat from his broad, hairless chest, did he think about the girl who showed up the previous night.

When he first opened the door, he assumed it was Connie returning from Toledo after months of whoring. Probably pregnant and riddled with several cases of chlamydia, she'd come home, the prodigal harlot, begging for forgiveness which would be in short supply. But then he saw the roundness of her face and breasts, smelled her sweet scent of decay, and realized it wasn't Connie.

In fact, it wasn't anyone.

It had all been a dream. His mind, overwrought due to his daughter's disappearance, was simply playing tricks on him. It was impossible that a strange young woman had shown up on his doorstep and he'd offered her shelter. That was unthinkable.

The absurdity of the whole scenario made him chuckle, an act he didn't particularly care for.

But then he heard a sound. A footfall. Someone was in his house.

Moving like liquid lighting, he donned a robe, grabbed his Savage 1861 Navy revolver, and dashed from the room.

Racing into his living room, he discovered the girl hadn't been a dream. There were blankets and pillows scattered on the couch.

He found her in his kitchen, dressed in her poor excuse for an outfit, cracking eggs on the edge of the sink and, hoisting them high, allowing their gelatinous contents to slide down her throat.

She didn't stop eating when he entered the room but she did wave.

"You shouldn't do that."

"Do what, puny human?"

"Eat raw eggs."

"Why not?"

"Salmonella."

That just made her laugh. She held another egg aloft and the yoke and the albumen slowly slid down her tender and pulsing throat. Some got on her chin, which she licked off with a surprisingly long tongue.

This both excited and repulsed Police Chief Pendleton. He had to adjust his robe, cough.

"Listen, last night, you, uh, you said that you'd be gone in the morning."

"And I will, once I finish my breakfast."

"This is… this is, well, this is highly unusual. I want to assure you that never before have I let a strange female into my house in the dead of night."

Finally, the girl looked at Pendleton. Narrowed her eyes. "Sweet Baby G, it's not as if we mated or anything."

He felt his face burn with embarrassment and had a hard time finding words. "Please, Miss, do not blaspheme in my house and do not speak of carnal activities, especially carnal activities that never happened."

She shrugged.

Shaking his head, he said, "Listen… you… tarnation, I don't even know your name."

"It's Dearly, Dearly Departed."

Of course it was. A stage name if he'd ever heard one. Regardless of what this young woman had claimed, she was either a lady of the night or working the pole at one of the many Rutherford B. Hayes Memorial Strip Clubs in town.

"Well, Miss Departed, I believe it is time you did, in fact, depart."

"That's my plan."

Brushing up against him with a twinkle in her eye, she walked out of his kitchen, out of his life.

Howling into the the Fremont Police Society Headquarter's toilet bowl, Officer Chrissy Rumpza threw up her breakfast and an unhealthy dollop of bile. This development would have been more disturbing if it hadn't been a daily occurrence since she'd woken in her boss' home, her uniform and lover gone.

Wiping sausagey swill from her chin, Rumpza left the bathroom without flushing and returned to her desk.

There she sat, staring out her office window, thinking about Connie and waiting for the time she could go home and sit and stare out her bedroom window.

Her rectitude was ruined when the intercom on her desk

buzzed, a mechanical insect. It was Junior Officer Killion and his room temperature IQ.

"Hey Officer Rumpza, you've got a call on line two."

"Who is it, cum-slurper?" inquired Officer Rumpza.

The name calling no longer fazed Killion. "It's a man saying he saw something fantastic in the graveyard last night."

Just another dick-minded lunatic, thought Rumpza who wasn't surprised. Fremont was bursting with lunatics and freaks and weirdos and cactus-fuckers and oddballs and morons and fiends and porno burn-outs and dopers and perverts and clove cigarette smoking cretins and occultists and Christians and other zealots. Certainly the cop had been aware of this unsettling fact before her lover disappeared, but now the world around her felt darker, even more filled with cactus-fuckers.

Groaning, Rumpza picked up her phone and tried to sound chipper as she announced herself.

Without salutation, the man on the other end of the line, who certainly sounded like a dick-minded lunatic, shouted, "I saw something weird in the graveyard last night!"

"Oh really? Let me guess, you were drunk at the time of this sighting."

"Okay, you've outfoxed me, I confess, I was more skunked than a raccoon, but that don't change what I saw."

Picking up a pencil though she had no intention of writing down anything this fool said, Rumpza asked, "And what did your pickled eyes behold in the graveyard?"

"A young woman, but I don't think she was was human, as she wasn't like nobody I've ever laid eyes on before."

Rumpza had to admit that this call was more interesting than the usual I-didn't-mean-to-kill-my-brother-in-law-and-defile-his-corpse case that usually came rolling in in the morning.

"In what way?"

"Well, for one thing, she was moving real weird, kind of stumbling, real herky jerky, like she'd never used them long legs before. She was in the fountain by the gates of the cemetery, washing what appeared to be blood and dirt off her rocking body."

There was something about this call, the way the drunk's voice trembled, that wrapped around Rumpza's mind. She thought about the previous night, how she'd been interrupted during a nice bout of masturbation by a young woman walking past her house.

The cop actually employed her pencil. She wrote down "rocking body."

Leaning forward, gripping the phone a little tighter. "Can you describe this young woman?"

"Well, I only saw her for a moment, as I got the hell out of there and fast, but I do remember one thing: she had hellacious boobs."

"Hellacious boobs" Rumpza scrawled, suddenly interested.

Like most teenagers, Rusty Slump hated his life. Unlike most teenagers, he had good reason. A whole buttload of good reasons actually. His girlfriend wanted him to kill the most dangerous man in Fremont, Loco Lenny Labovitz. His father, the judge, was always on his ass about one thing or another. And the only woman he'd ever loved was now moldering in the grave.

When he was at school or around CoCo, he kept his shit together. But when he was alone, in his bedroom or his luxury treehouse, he cried. Thinking of Connie laying in the cold ground, three Purple Hayes laced bullets in her chest.

Sometimes he thought of her alive. Like in Chemistry, where they were lab partners. Though they rarely spoke, but she sometimes looked at him with the most unnoticeable smile. When Rusty thought of Connie that way, he couldn't help but masturbate with one hand and use his other hand to wipe away the tears. Afterward, he held his pillow tight, pretending it was

Connie, making promises about their future he knew he couldn't keep now that she was dead.

Now that he had killed her.

He was in the middle of one of these phony lovemaking sessions when a thunderous knock landed upon his bedroom door. It was his father, who always knocked like that, as if an astroid were headed straight for Fremont.

Rusty stuffed his chubby back into his sweatpants and allowed his father to enter.

Throwing open the door, Judge Slump stood there dressed in his robes, like always, looking pissed, like always. "You're late for school."

"I don't think I can go, my stomach."

"That's the same excuse you used yesterday."

"My stomach was bad yesterday too."

Rusty wasn't lying. His stomach, his bowels, his heart hadn't been right since Halloween night. He always felt as if he were going to throw up or shit or lay down and die.

The judge judged, "I think you're faking. Get up and go to school or I'll demand the cops reopen your drug possession case and maybe this time, things won't go your way."

Sitting up, Rusty said, "You wouldn't dare."

"Oh, yes I would. Even though those dunderheads down at the Fremont Police Society botched the case, there still could have been trouble for you. My influence kept you out of jail. Now I expect a little consideration in return. Put an end to this juvenile delinquent crap. No more public crapping, no more running around with that CoCo McArdle, no more staying in bed all day. You're not going to make me look bad. Especially with Hayes Dayes right around the corner. I vouched for your character, don't make me regret it. You won't like me when I'm full of regret."

Not even waiting to see if his son obeyed his command, Judge

Slump stomped away, slamming the door behind him.

With a sigh, Rusty rose, dressed in the same clothes that he'd worn the day before, and headed for school, forgetting his backpack.

Pissed at his father for threatening him, pissed at CoCo for threatening him, pissed that he killed the only woman he'd ever loved, Rusty climbed behind the wheel of his safety-conscious Volvo, which had been his mother's car before she passed, and roared out of the Slump Mansion driveway and down Rutherford B. Hayes Memorial Boulevard.

As he drove toward Rutherford B. Hayes Memorial High, Rusty considered ditching school. Heading out to the Rutherford B. Hayes Memorial Rock Quarry, spending some quality time alone, crying and masturbating until the sun threw in the towel.

But, as cool as that sounded, he knew it was just a dream. Ditching school would be a total mistake. Principal Moorhead, Principal Kennedy's replacement, would call his dad who would proceed to come down on him like a ton of robed bricks.

Though it pained him, he had to go to school, where he couldn't cry or masturbate.

Thinking of how much his life sucked, his stomach lurched.

It lurched again when he spied the most beautiful girl ever walking down the sidewalk.

Even from behind, it was obvious that she was a total babe. Those curves, that flowing red mane, and that slow, stumbling way she walked.

Surveying her ass, Rusty could tell that she was about his age, but he'd never seen this beauty before, unusual in a city of 16,000 souls. She must have been new in town.

Rusty braked as he passed her, trying to slow down time.

As he suspected, her babeness continued in the front. Tight, cropped Lynyrd Skynyrd T-shirt, flat stomach, and a face that was wan and unforgettable.

And her tits, they were dope.

She was an earthbound angel and Rusty instantly had a stiffy moldering in his pants.

He hadn't felt this way since the last few moments of Connie Pendleton's life, which made him feel a little guilty, like he was cheating. But guilt is a fleeting emotion in the young especially when there's a blue-veiner involved.

Pushing Connie out of his mind, Rusty replaced her with this girl, who did, if you squinted just right, bear a resemblance to Connie. If Connie had been super hot.

As he drove past her, the young man tried to force his dizzy mind to formulate a plan of how to get this young woman into his life. First, he had to get her into his car.

He planned to loop around the block, pull up next to her, casually roll down his window, and ask if she were heading to the high school.

With his winning smile, bedroom eyes, and safety-conscious Volvo, she couldn't help but climb in beside him. It would be love at first touch. They'd be necking by the Rutherford B. Hayes Memorial Lawn Jockey Factory and, by the time they arrived at school, they be engaged in wild, unprotected sex. After graduating, they'd get married, have a ton of unprotected sex, and live happily ever after. Somewhere far away from Fremont, far away from CoCo, the judge, and the ghost of Connie Pendleton.

Perhaps Toledo.

Rusty circumnavigated the block and easily found the angel; she hadn't traveled far during his absence with that stumbling gait of hers.

Pulling even with her, he slowed. Just as he was about to roll down his window and introduce himself to his future wife, she looked his way.

There was a hunger in her eyes, palpable even at a distance.

She looked as if she wanted him, his heart, his penis. But not in a carnal pleasure way. In a meal way.

His nerve went south.

Shivering, Rusty sped away. Cursing himself for not speaking with the angel, terrified that he might have. This was the conundrum of teenage boys all over the globe.

Not that it mattered now, he'd blown his chance. Slowly, he realized this meant he was going to die alone or, worse, spend the rest of his life with CoCo McArdle by his side, berating him and doling out boisterous but toothy blowjobs.

When he reached the high school, he found a spot at the back of the parking lot and waited. Watching a steady stream of uninterested students pour into the building. Rusty couldn't move, couldn't stop crying. He couldn't even breath right, it felt as if his nose were packed with sand. Actually, it felt as if his whole body were packed with sand.

In the distance, he heard the late bell ring, sealing his fate. Taking a deep breath, he restarted his car and roared out of the parking lot.

He didn't know where he was headed but found exactly what he was looking for. The dangerous beauty, her dope tits and crazy walk, still stumbling down Rutherford B. Hayes Memorial Street.

Somehow she'd grown even more beautiful since the last time he'd seen her. Not wishing to draw her attention, he hung back, trailed her. Watching that fine ass swamp and sway, take his breath away.

After several minutes and many turns, Rusty began to suspect that this lovely creature was just wandering Fremont with no particular place to go. Just like him, no direction in life, lost.

But she proved him wrong by stopping before the Other One True Way Church and staring at it. This rather pedestrian house of God wasn't worth such study. It was hideous, squat and boxy. The only thing of consequence that ever happened there was that one glorious Christmas Eve Rusty crapped in their creche. An impossibly long turd, a Christmas miracle if you will.

The girl stood there, unmoving, for so long that Rusty actually grew bored pondering her perfect ass. Just as he began to wonder what the kids were doing in his Horses of Rutherford B. Hayes class, the young woman moved, swayed away.

She headed for the small house next to the small church. From his pre-crap reconnaissance, Rusty knew that this house belonged to the minister of the Other One True Way Church, that old fart LaRue Rump.

Surprised that this angel would have anything to do with religion, Rusty watched her knock upon Rump's front door. When the minister appeared, the young woman flew into the old man's arms, wrapped herself around him, smothering him. This wasn't the hug of a friend or parishioner. It was the hug of a lover. Ensnared in each other, the couple disappeared into the depths of the small house, and the door slammed behind them.

Surely to have sexual congress.

"Huh," Rusty said to himself.

Disgusted that he'd ever lusted after this female who would bone a 99 year old jerk, the young man threw the car into gear and raced away. Heading for Rutherford B. Hayes Memorial High and concocting an excuse for his tardiness.

During the drive, Rusty chided himself for being unfaithful to his one true love: the ghost of Connie Pendleton who haunted his mind, his days, his libido.

It was like a dream, how she got there.

When she'd stormed from the cop's house, the only thing on her mind was snacking. The raw eggs hadn't curbed her hunger; she craved the flesh and blood of puny humans. A simple solution would have been to nosh on the cop but the Other Girl kept kicking, kept screaming, when that thought crossed her mind.

To shut her up, Dearly walked away. Quickly.

Then an image of a human flashed through her mind. An old man, dressed in black, forcing her to her knees to pray. A puny human the Other Girl hated.

It was funny to be so picky about snacking. Blood was blood, creamy and delicious, but she felt compelled to find this old man.

No, screamed the Other Girl, *not Reverend Rump.*

Yes, thought Dearly, *Reverend Rump. You despise that man of God.*

Sure, he's a little pushy sometimes, but he doesn't deserve to die.

Everyone deserves to die, Dearly promised, *and everyone will.*

The Other Girl spidered off and hid in her little corner of Dearly's brain.

As she sauntered through the streets of Fremont, having a vague idea of where to go thanks to the Other Girl, a car pulled up beside her. The boy driving it was so cute that she stopped in her tracks, he made her magical nipples harden.

This one, this cute breather, she knew instantly was the perfect mate. Even at a distance, she could smell the semen that filled his substantial scrotum to capacity.

Dearly smiled at him but it must have come out all wrong as the cute human drove away quickly.

She would find him again. Find him and mate the living daylights out of him.

After she filled her stomach with a little Rump.

As one approached the century mark, there was a lot of reflecting. Reflecting and waiting for a decent bowel movement.

Sitting in his battered armchair, enjoying a cup of tea, Reverend LaRue Rump recalled the turbulent history of the Other One True Way Church.

It started back in the 1980's when he was teaching at the One

True Way Bible College in Columbus. Although he'd served God for over fifty years and was on the verge of retirement, he still loved his job, as meeting young people who were blindly obsessed with the Lord brought him great joy.

During his last year of teaching he met Stevie G. Jones, a pious young man with bright eyes, a quick smile, and a heart set ablaze with the love of Christ.

At least, that's what Rump thought.

During many meetings in Rump's office, Jones convinced the older man his time of serving the Lord was far from over, that he needed Rump to help him to make his grand schemes for God play out. When he graduated, Jones explained, he planned on founding his own congregation, the One True Way Church, and he wanted Rump for a partner.

At first, the old man balked. He dreamed of a rocking chair, of peace, of being left alone. But Jones was persuasive and persistent. He talked about how the called never truly stop being servants of the Lord. In confidence, he confessed the Sweet Baby G himself had appeared to him in a dream, astride a large breasted unicorn, and instructed the young man he'd been chosen to lead mankind out of the darkness. But Jones, tears welling, admitted to Rump that he needed his help to make the Sweet Baby G's dreams come true.

Once he was made privy to the vision of the Sweet Baby G and the large breasted unicorn, there was no option for Rump but to join Jones on his mission. They used Rump's money to buy an abandoned church in Fremont, Ohio. A berg that, Jones assured Rump, was in desperate need of intervention from a higher power.

With Rump's bank account and Jones' charm, especially with the fairer sex, their flock quickly multiplied. Rump was so pleased with this development that he turned a blind eye to what was happening right beneath his nose. Any fool could see that Jones was a charlatan but Rump kept mum and continued working for the Lord. It took a teary Relinda Horst, a young woman who had spurned Jones' advances, to help Rump see what kind of vile human his partner was.

Together, he and Relinda shadowed the young minister and found that he was too busy serving his self-interests to serve God. Regularly Jones pilfered from the church's Let's Save the Darkies Poor Box, his Let's Talk About Our Infidelities Workshop was really just a garden where Jones cultivated his sexual conquests, and the young man spent a surprising amount of his free time drawing dirty pictures of Rump with a small penis - accurate but still alarming - on the walls of several public bathrooms around town.

When Rump confronted Jones with these accusations, the young man, sporting a squalid smile, explained that the whole thing had been a ruse. He'd never had a vision of the Sweet Baby G riding a large breasted unicorn. The entire let's-start-a-church thing was just a scam, his hopes to "… get himself a nice, juicy slice of the lucrative God pie."

Such anger flowed through Rump's system that he considered, briefly, killing the young man. Luckily, the elderly minister reined in his murderous rage and simply walked away.

Shaken, Rump decided to return to his original dream. To retire and be left alone somewhere far, far away from Fremont, Ohio. But while waiting for his bus in the Rutherford B. Hayes Memorial Transit Station he spied a poster that changed his life and his direction once more.

On the poster was the picture of a scantily clad woman on her knees before the devil. Looking over her shoulder at the viewer, her chin glittering, her tongue lolling, she bore a wicked smile. One was obviously supposed to gather that the woman had just provided the Dark One with oral sex. The text of the poster read: SATAN'S BUTT BUDDIES/ RUTHERFORD B.

HAYES MEMORIAL ARENA/MAY 6th/LOCK UP YOUR DAUGHTERS, WIVES, AND DOMESTICATED ANIMALS!

A heavy metal rock band, the lowest of the low in Rump's opinion. Even worse than fags. He'd heard rumors of this band, Satan's Butt Buddies, before. How they spewed filthy lyrics about fornicating while worshipping Beelzebub or, to change it up, about worshipping Beelzebub while fornicating.

The old man could barely conceive of a world where this kind of filth, and filth like Stevie G. Jones, could exist. Although Jones was a filthy heathen, his words came back to Rump. The Lord was not done with him, not done with his service.

After ripping down the poster, Rump declared, internally, his intention of ridding the world of such rot. People like Jones and the four hoodlums who made up Satan's Butt Buddies. Also Atheists, Jews, feminists, and all other depraved lumps of godlessness.

He would remain in Fremont, which was rife with godless behavior, and build his own house of God, the Other One True Way Church, and defeat "Reverend" Stevie G. Jones, send him spiraling into the flames of hell.

Unfortunately, the intervening thirty years hadn't work out the way Rump and the Lord had planned. Jones wasn't defeated or sent spiraling into anything. Instead, he also started a new church, the Other Other One True Way Church, and his congregation flourished. It included several prominent leaders of the Fremont business world, a whole peck of ombudsmen, and, of course, hordes and hordes of garden-variety harlots. Jones built a mega-church right in the middle of town, which was filled with giant TV screens and several stained glass windows featuring Jones interacting with the Sweet Baby G himself. Rump's congregation, on the other hand, was small, and sometimes off their collective rockers. He made just enough money to get by, never took a vacation, never even had a day off even though he was suffering from many maladies during his misnamed golden years.

Just like the resilient Jones, Satan's Butt Buddies continued to tour, spreading their depravity to the youth of the world.

But Rump carried on, continued to fight. When his arthritis wasn't enflamed or his cataracts wasn't too bad or his lumbago wasn't acting up.

As he sat in his tattered chair, reflecting on his shared history with Stevie G. Jones and waiting for a decent bowel movement, he thought a thought he'd never thought before.

Perhaps the Lord was a jerk.

For LaRue Rump had served the Almighty from his first breath and now, as his last breath approached, he didn't have much to show for it. But that ass Jones, he had everything. Everything and more.

Without realizing what he was doing, the reverend crushed his tea cup in his hand.

As he stared down, shocked, upon the shards and blood, a knock fell upon his front door.

Somebody wanted something from him. Again. Well, the reverend decided, he'd share with them the important life lesson he'd just learned: God was a complete prick and that praying to him was a waste of time and serving him was a waste of life.

Despite his sciatica, scoliosis, and spinal stenosis, Rump practically bounded from the chair and threw open the front door, ready to share the Bad News.

But he stopped when he saw what was waiting for him. Despite being ninety-nine years old and not having had achieved an erection in decades, Rump was still a man and the female on his front step, blocking out the sun, was quite a looker.

Obviously, with the way she was dressed, this trollop made a living selling her body, much of which was on display, to grubby men with greedy hands. But she was no garden-variety harlot. She was beautiful and as big breasted as any unicorn imaginable.

"Hello, Reverend Rump," the young woman said, her voice dripping with honey.

He stared at her closer. "Do I know you?"

"Yes and no."

This response came as no surprise to the reverend. There was something about this girl, something that was familiar and distant at the same time.

What did come as a surprise was her smile, which accompanied her comment.

There were a staggering number of teeth in her mouth and they were all as sharp as the sword of Damocles.

This is no girl, Rump perceived, this is Satan himself.

Even though Rump had come to the realization that praying to God was a waste of time, he was just about to do so, hoping to drive the devil back into the wild, but he was not allowed the time.

In a blur, the demon was upon him, wrapping her arms around Rump and dragging him deeper, darker into his home. Magically, the door closed behind her.

The final thought Rump had on this earth, as the devil opened that impossible mouth impossibly wide and latched onto his throat, was: *yes, I was right, God is certainly a prick.*

Academics had never been his strong suit, but since taking Connie's life, school had become unbearable for Rusty Slump. He simply floated through every class, every paper, every test. The halls of Rutherford B. Hayes Memorial High were just a dream, billowing. He high-fived his peeps, made out with CoCo in the back of his safety-conscious Volvo, and tried to stay awake while his teachers blathered on about nothing. Just waiting for the final bell so he could retreat to his treehouse, his tears.

The only way this day was different from the previous day and the day that would follow was that girl. The vision of beauty he'd seen on Rutherford B Hayes Memorial Drive. She kept walking through his mind, smiling at him, waving. He tried to keep her at bay, picturing the way she hugged that creepy old preacher who hated Satan's Butt Buddies, Rusty's favorite band, but she hung around.

All day she stayed with him, in his head, in his heart, in his penis, until his final class of the afternoon, Favored Desserts of Rutherford B. Hayes, taught by Mrs. Armknecht. That day they were supposed to take an exam covering Hayes' befuddlingly intricate list of top ten pies, but the class got off to a rocky start when a new student swam into class.

The vision of beauty.

No longer was she in Rusty's mind, she was perched on a desk at the back of the classroom.

Apparently, Mrs. Armknecht was just as flummoxed by this girl as Rusty was. "And what is your name, young lady?"

"Dearly, ma'am, Dearly Departed."

As snickers rippled through the classroom, the elderly teacher frowned. "That cannot be your real name."

The girl smiled. It was thin. "Why not?"

Crossing her stick arms across her flat chest, Mrs. Armknecht asked the new girl if she had any paperwork.

"Paperwork?"

"Yes, your parents had to fill out paperwork for you to start here at Rutherford B. Hayes Memorial High, yet I haven't heard anything about a new student."

"That's probably because I don't have any parents."

Having taught for fifty years, Mrs. Armknecht wasn't about to be thrown. "Then who is your guardian?"

With a shrug, the girl said, "I guess I'm my own guardian."

Shaking her head, the teacher retreated to her desk. "Well, we've wasted enough time on horseplay, we'll sort it all out later.

For now, Miss Departed, you can read a book or stare out the window, I don't care which, as the rest of the class is going to take an exam covering President Hayes' love of pie for which, hopefully, they are prepared."

"Oh," said Dearly, a twinkle in her eye, "you're talking about Hayes' unusual love of rhubarb and carrot pie. Well, that is, until he entered the White House, after which he inexplicably changed his allegiance to mangrove pie."

This stopped the class as if the brakes had been applied to the universe. Everyone stared at the new girl, including Mrs. Armknecht.

"Well," said the seasoned teacher after some time, "it appears, since Miss Departed knows everything about everything, our scheduled exam won't be necessary. So instead, you will all, and I'm including you in this Miss Departed, write a 2,000 word essay about Hayes' disdain for divinity. fudge It's due at the end of the period."

Like a snake unfurling in the sun, Dearly's arm stretched toward the false ceiling. "Mrs. Armknecht, can we also write about how Hayes hated peanut brittle, as it stuck to his false teeth?"

"Of course you can," said Mrs. Armknecht crisply. "Now get to work, and keep in mind that this essay is going to count as a quarter of your grade."

Groaning, the entire class drew out their notebooks and began, with some difficulty, to write.

Though he throttled his pencil, Rusty couldn't compose a single word. Instead of writing, he sneaked peeks at Dearly. Her pen was flying across her borrowed notebook, filling page after page, she never stopped to rest her hand or take a breath.

Everything about her was amazing. The beautiful face, the big old bucket of brains, the brazen mouth, and, of course, those dope tits.

When the final bell sounded, Dearly was the first person

to hand in her paper. She traveled quickly to the front of the classroom, a smear of colors, seemingly without moving her long legs. With a flourish, she slapped her thick sheaf of papers on Mrs. Armknect's desk. Dearly smiled but she wasn't smiling at the teacher, she was smiling at Rusty.

His blood flowed upstream.

Then Dearly disappeared. Gone before anyone could say a word, which was good, as no one knew what to say.

For some reason, Rusty felt compelled to turn in his blank sheet of paper, which didn't even have his name on it. He was dazed, dazzled, not thinking straight.

Rushing out into the hall, which was packed with students fleeing school, he spied Dearly, already impossibly far away. She was at the end of the hallway, looking over her shoulder at him.

With the smallest of gestures, an imperceptible wave of her hand, she beckoned him to follow. Then walked away.

With legs of rubber and feet of clay, Rusty ran after the sauntering Dearly. But he couldn't close the gap between them. It was like swimming in a sea of quagmire.

Of course it didn't help matters that, thanks to his case of orchitis, his balls were the size of pomegranates. This made running out of the question, even trotting brought testicular pain down like thunder.

Not once did Dearly turn around to make sure that he was following. She sashayed down the hall and through the doors to the outside, along with seemingly every other student at Rutherford B. Hayes Memorial High. All trying to reach the fresh air, the real world, freedom. Everyone was chattering about the upcoming Hayes Dayes celebration. Shouldering his way through the crowd, Rusty received plenty of dirty looks but no one dared rebuke him, for, though it was brief, he'd been behind bars.

When he burst through the doors, through the people, the

cool April air wrapped its tendrils around him. He spotted Dearly walking across the lawn of the school, toward the parking lot. Knocking the kids who were waiting for buses out of the way, he followed her.

For a moment, he lost sight of her in the parking lot. Making whimpering sounds, Rusty spun in circles.

Then he spotted her.

Waiting for him.

Leaning against his safety-conscious Volvo as if she owned it. Approaching her, he tried to gather his thoughts, his breath, both of which were elusive.

"I saw you this morning, did I not, puny human?" she asked.

Rusty tried to smile but didn't have the strength. "Yeah. And I saw you, hugging Reverend Rump."

Something flashed across her face, something unkind. But it quickly fled. "That particular puny human is my uncle. Do you like my breasts?"

Uncertain he'd heard right, he asked, "Excuse me?"

"I find them not only aesthetically pleasing but also magical."

"Yeah, sure, 'magical' is probably the word I'd use."

"And I admire your rather bulbous testes."

"Oh. Those. They're not always like that. It's a inflammation called orchitis. I got it from a case of chlamydia I caught from… from a toilet seat."

Rusty really wished he hadn't brought up sexually transmitted diseases as it was usually something of a mood killer.

But Dearly appeared undaunted.

"Alright. But I'm certain they are still bursting with semen."

"Well, yeah, probably."

"Good. We're on the same page then, dear breather. Let us engage in sexual congress in your car. I'll assume that is what you desire."

Of course he did. Desired it more than anything, including

becoming the leader of the vast and dangerous criminal underworld of Fremont, Ohio. But he couldn't put this concept into words, so he simply smiled and he and his inflamed nutsack leaned toward her.

Without a thought of CoCo McArdle or the ghost of Connie Pendleton, Rusty dove into Dearly's face and, despite the fact she smelled like a pile of leaves when he got close, kissed her hard.

Inside his head, Niccolo Machiavelli was cheering his Italian head off.

After swapping spit for several rapturous minutes – with much grinding of pelvises, tweaking of nipples, and groans of ecstasy from both participants – they decided it best to take refuge in the backseat of his car to evade the prying eyes of the passing classmates.

When settled, Dearly wasted no time. She pulled the Lynyrd Skynyrd T-shirt over her head and there they were, front and center, those tits. More perfect than he'd imagined and he'd imagined perfection. Firm and round, high, big but not floppy, with pert nipples the color, but not the texture, of pink granite.

There was only one small problem, tit-wise. A constellation of dried blood drops decorated her mammeries. Despite the hungry hard-on and the salivating and the fluttering in his stomach, Rusty hesitated.

Narrowing her eyes at him, Dearly asked, "Is there a problem, dear puny human?"

"You... you have blood all over your tits."

"Oh, that. Don't worry, it's not mine."

With a flick of her tongue, which was preternaturally long, she licked the blood from her funbags. "Oh, my breasts are certainly delicious today. Would you like a taste?"

Of course he did, so he stopped thinking about her bloody boobs and her tongue as it spooled back into its lair, and he nuzzled her nipples.

After just one lick, Rusty felt the world slide, reality fade. His entire existence roiled.

Everything turned sepia and he could hear horses clomping through the parking lot.

Looking out the window, he spied men in long wool coats and women in long wool dresses. There were parasols and waxed mustaches.

It's just like Purple Hayes.

That was his last thought before he passed out.

"Sweet Baby G, we got a lion on the loose here!"

Officer Rumpza pulled the phone away from her ear as Junior Officer Killion was shouting. Rolling her eyes, she ordered him to slow down, enunciate, and try to make sense.

He refused. "Or maybe it was a tiger! Whatever it was, it must have escaped from the Rutherford B. Hayes Slightly Dangerous Petting Zoo and now it's terrorizing the town!"

"Killion, get a hold of yourself. That cunt-blogging zoo's been closed since that jizz-faker Jinx McArdle got humped to death by that rabid ocelot."

"That's what it must be, a rabid ocelot. This ain't good with Hayes Dayes coming up this weekend. No one wants to party when they know a rabid animal's on the loose. Oh, how I wish Sergeant Snoopers wasn't so dead, he'd be able to tell us what kind of animal this was. Being an animal himself and all."

Though emphatic, Junior Officer Killion's words evaporated in Rumpza's ears as fast as he said them. She didn't have time for this tomfoolery, she had to get back to staring out the window and ruminating about Connie. "Jeff, I can't understand a cock-chugging word you're saying. Why don't you try to start from the beginning, you taint-taster?"

She heard him take a deep breath. Rumpza could tell that something had really spooked Killion. She tried to focus, tried to listen.

"When all two members of the Anti-Satan's Butt Buddies Committee arrived at Reverend Rump's house for a meeting, they found the old man had been murdered. But he ain't been shot nor stabbed nor strangled nor anything humane. He's been ripped apart. There's chunks of him all over the place. Hell, I tripped over half of his pancreas in an upstairs bedroom, I assume the other half got ate. He's like a jigsaw puzzle and I'm sure glad it ain't my job to put him back together again."

As Killion described the carnage, Officer Rumpza sat up, took notice. She may have been lovesick but she was still a cop and a brutal death had gone down on her beat.

"You mean like he was torn up by a dick-pinching wild animal?" she said, a little breathless.

"That's what I've been trying to tell you. We got a rabid wolf or lion or ocelot on our hands or, now that I think about it, I suppose it could have been a jaguar. Man, I wish we still had Sergeant Snoopers."

"Well, we don't. That four-legged fuck-fart Sergeant Snoopers is dead and gone, Jeff, so it's up to us to solve this jizz-fonduing crime."

Even though she tried to sound strong, Rumpza felt no real conviction in her words.

"What about Police Chief Pendleton? Where's he at?" asked Junior Officer Killion.

Officer Rumpza admitted that she had no idea where the Police Chief was. She didn't tell Killion she'd tried calling him several times that morning. She'd left many messages, all unanswered.

"I'll be there in a minute, Killion, just hang onto your tangy squat-balls."

He was on the precipice of orgasm. That special tingling feeling had started in the basement of his balls and was pushing the express button.

Police Chief Pendleton was pleased for two reasons. One, he was about to shoot some steam. Secondly, he'd finally outwitted that nosy and verbally abusive Rutherford B. Hayes ghost or drug hallucination or whatever by hiding in the garage for his bout of self-abuse.

The orgasmic scenario playing out in his mind was an image of himself, a Union soldier separated from his company, stumbling out of a copse of magnolia trees and coming upon a plantation engulfed in flame, set afire by retreating Confederate soldiers.

There was only one survivor: Officer Rumpza. Only she wasn't a cop, she was wearing a sackcloth gown that, as she lurched away from the inferno, ripped in all the right places. Collapsing to the ground at his feet, she soiled the soil with her tears.

As Private Pendleton pulled Rumpza to her feet, her breasts escaped the confines her dress. Either she didn't notice or didn't care, as she did nothing to right this wardrobe malfunction.

She gripped him, tight. "Thank you, kind soldier, for you've saved my life. As a way to repay you, please have your wanton way with me."

Gentle as a bear, he laid her down upon the soft grass, pulled her sackcloth gown up to reveal her crotchless bloomers and--.

"Well, quite an exciting story of love and conquest, but I do have one blamed important question, who set fire to this poor naked woman's house?" asked Rutherford B. Hayes as he stepped from the shadows.

The burning manse, the beautiful woman, and her exposed *mons pubis* all evaporated, along with his erection and any hope of orgasm.

Pendleton, who was dressed in his Union uniform for the occasion, spun on the ghost or drug hallucination or whatever. Stuffing his stifled erection back in his pants, scratching his poor penis on the wool, he asked, "What are you talking about?"

"Well, you cussed moron, you put the blame of the arson on Johnny Reb, but it's much more likely, since you're picturing a plantation, that that cockchafer Sherman and his army were the ones who struck the match and rent her clothing *in all the right places*, as you so delicately put it."

If this hadn't been the twentieth time in as many days that Hayes had caught him polluting himself, Pendleton might have blushed or turned away. "Do you have a reason for being here? I mean, besides snuffing out the only spark of joy I have left in this dark and dismal world?"

"I come bearing news of the unpleasant variety. Reverend Rump is dead, dispatched from this world in a most horrendous way and I believe, you reprobate, it's your responsibility to find out who would do such a thing."

Without changing out of his uniform, Police Chief Pendleton rushed out to his squad car and roared away.

When he arrived at his luxury treehouse, Rusty was in desperate need of a nap. He was wiped. Twenty minutes before, he'd awoken, alone, in the back of his Volvo. There were no students, of any era, milling about in the parking lot, and there was nothing left of Dearly Departed but the lingering scent of earth.

Rubbing the sleep from his eyes, Rusty realized he'd ruined his relationship with Dearly Departed before it had even begun by passing out during foreplay. An act for which he had no excuse, only shame.

Rusty needed to seek refuge in the Land O' Nod.

But there was no nap in Rusty's future.

For he found CoCo sitting on the Safavid silk, wool, and metal-thread prayer rug, her legs splayed, a majority of her thighs available for inspection. She was grinning like the cat who'd flocked the canary.

"What're you doing here?" he asked. Thinking about licking Dearly's dope tits, Rusty felt his face shift toward crimson.

"I brought you a present."

Rusty assumed his girlfriend was talking about yet another boisterous but toothy blowjob. Thoughts of attempting his second erection of the afternoon tore at him.

But CoCo wasn't talking about blowjobs, boisterous but toothy or no.

From behind her back, she pulled three bullets. In the light of the Tiffany leaf turning table lamp, they gleamed like a triumvirate of tiny suns. Rusty felt as if he should shield his eyes.

"I assume you still have my dad's .38."

The young man nodded. He knew he should have ditched the murder weapon long ago but he couldn't bring himself to do so. It reminded him of Connie.

"I found these bullets hidden in my father's machete drawer. Now you can kill Loco Lenny Labovitz, just like we talked about, and become the leader of the vast and dangerous criminal underworld of Fremont, Ohio."

"I don't know, Sugar Canthus. I'm kind of tired and my feet hurt and--."

Her scowl stifled him.

"Don't talk crazy, Rusty. Tonight's the perfect night to off Loco. He's going to be in his mobile drug emporium, selling weed down by Rutherford B. Hayes Memorial Water Park. But it's going to be a slow night. Everyone is saving their money for that sweet Hayes Dayes Methmatch. So, it's simple, you just walk in and pop him and his henchmen."

One, two, three.

It was worse than she feared.

Thanks to the vast and dangerous criminal underworld of Fremont, Ohio, Officer Rumpza had seen her fair share of death in her decade as a cop, but she'd never witnessed anything this gruesome.

Blood painted every wall of Reverend Rump's home, chunks of flesh rested on several surfaces like grisly tchotchkes, everywhere internal organs were now external. Whatever had ripped Rump apart had done a disturbingly thorough job.

Every cop knows to be careful of contaminating a crime scene. Don't touching anything, be heedful of every footstep. But in this case, that was impossible, as the entirety of Rump's living room floor was splatter, every inch gore.

Tiptoeing through the minefield that was the minister's remains, Rumpza made her way to the kitchen where she found Killion. And some more chunks of Rump.

The Junior Officer, his thick head in his thin hands, was seated at a blood speckled Formica table, openly weeping.

Rumpza wanted to both strike and soothe him.

She settled for landing a firm hand on his shoulder.

Not bothering to look up, he said, "See? Just like I told you, ain't it a mess? And to think, tonight I was going to attend Reverend Rump's Hell Is Most Likely Your Next Stop Symposium at the Rutherford B. Hayes Memorial Community Center. I guess that talk's gonna have to be postponed."

Rumpza was only half-listening to the sobbing man. She was busy studying the lump of lung that clung to the refrigerator door. Almost imperceptibly, it was sliding toward the linoleum.

"What kind of animal could do this?" she wondered aloud.

Killion said, "I'm beginning to suspect rabid giraffe. I mean, it had to be something tall. How else could the good reverend's lower intestine be draped all through the dining room chandelier?"

Though she wanted to, Rumpza couldn't argue with the insanity of this assertion, as every aspect of this business was insane. Any answer for this carnage had to be just as ridiculous as any other.

Leaving Killion behind, she returned to the living room for a closer look. If her eyes had not already been burned by the butchery, the scene would have been too terrible to gaze upon. Near a ratty recliner sat Reverend Rump's head, oddly intact, staring out at the eternal nothingness that is death.

So absorbed was Rumpza she didn't notice Police Chief Pendleton until he cleared his throat. She looked up to find him standing in a lagoon of blood near the front door, dressed in his Civil War garb, not giving a damn about contaminating the scene.

Like her, his mouth was agape, his eye wide, wild.

"What in tarnation..." he whispered.

Rumpza said, "A taint-texting animal of some kind, apparently. A big one."

A tear appeared on Pendleton's face, slouching toward his quivering chin. "I can't believe I would do that to the poor girl."

Apparently, this tear was not shed for Rump.

"What girl?" Hairs on the back of Rumpza's everything stood on end.

Pendleton looked into her eyes but didn't see her. "A girl who I turned my back on, a girl I shoved out into this dark and dismal world as if I had no heart. I have to find her."

Studying the charcoal sketch she'd done of a moist *mons pubis*, Dearly reflected upon how much she'd enjoyed art class. The rest of the day spent at Rutherford B. Hayes Memorial High was tedious. Rutherford B. Hayes this, and Rutherford B. Hayes that, and all the puny human talk of the upcoming Hayes Dayes.

Unimaginative and dull.

The only reason she'd gone to school, after ripping that reverend to shreds and eating the nice bits, was to see that cute breather again. Have sexual congress with him, let him spill his substantial semen supply into her. Then go all praying mantis on his sweet ass.

But he'd foiled her plans by fainting before she was properly introduced to his penis. This infuriated her. She considered simply snacking on him but found she couldn't. Inexplicably, she felt herself drawn to the puny human but not in a bloodlust way. She understood this was just more interference by the Other Girl. During her short human existence, she'd obviously had feelings for this boy.

That's the reason Dearly found herself on his front porch a few hours after ditching him, waiting for him to return from school.

With a sly smile, she went back to examining her drawing.

Though the old woman who taught art pretended to be shocked – fluttering eyelashes, hand clutched to her chest – Dearly could tell that she was impressed with the drawing. Of course she was. The rendering of the female genitalia was spot on.

When she squinted, Dearly could nearly recognize the *mons pubis* in question. Swollen, glistening, with fine blonde hairs.

She'd been there, had her face burrowed in this particular oyster ditch. Well, the Other Girl had. That impressed Dearly, apparently the body she was inhabiting, who felt so milquetoasty the demon assumed she was a virgin, had not only played, but played for both teams.

The door behind her swung open and Judge Slump stepped out onto the porch. He was wearing a dark robe and a dark scowl. "May I ask, young lady, what you're doing lollygagging on my front porch, looking at an indecent picture."

Turning on him with her smile and sparkling eyes, Dearly saw the scowl falter. "I'm waiting for your son to come home."

"Oh... are you a friend of Rusty's?"

"More than that. I'm his girlfriend."

"But I thought… I thought that he went with that awful McArdle girl, the one with all the tattoos and the dead charlatan father."

"Not anymore. He's with me now. And when he comes home, I'm going to have sexual congress with him right here on these steps."

The old man's flabby jowls flapped as if they were trying to take flight. "I… I…"

"You could prime the pump, old man." She turned toward him, spread her legs. The short jeans skirt rode up her thighs, exposing her frilly panties which left little to the imagination.

Judge Slump made a gargling noise low in his throat, where men keep their lust anchored. But he didn't take the glistening bait. Bewildered, he bumbled back into the house, mumbling to himself, sweating. Dearly didn't bother to watch his departure, for she had other things on her mind. Like who was the owner of this stunning *mons pubis* and what was she doing right then.

So enraptured was Dearly that she didn't even notice Rusty sneaking down the side of the house, hand in hand with CoCo McArdle, on his way to kill Loco Lenny Labovitz.

Though she could feel bile gathering in her throat, she was a cop and she had a job to do. Forcing herself, Officer Rumpza searched every bloodstained inch of Reverend Rump's house. Somewhere there had to be a clue as to what kind of animal had slaughtered the reverend: a hair, a bit of tooth, a paw print.

She found what she was looking for behind the ratty recliner.

A bloody footprint.

A bloody, human footprint.

Wiping tears from his eyes, Police Chief Pendleton drove the streets of Fremont, ignoring the speed limit and the many calls that came over his police radio – Officer Rumpza hysterical about some footprint she'd found at Rump's – looking for Dearly Departed in every alley, every shadow, every memory.

The sun went down, the stars came up.

Like all Americans, Carl Cagney hated his job. Daily, he considered setting his boss, who was also his father-in-law, on fire. Of course, Carl never acted on this impulse because, like all Americans, he was basically a quivering bundle of fear.

As a boy, he'd dreamed of being a hobo. Riding the rails, living in a corrugated tin hut down by the river, and eating cold beans out of a can.

But life held different plans for Carl.

During his senior year at Rutherford B. Hayes Memorial High, Carl fell in love with Blenda Troost, who, as his lab partner in biology class, had dissected their shared frog while Carl stood by wringing his hands.

This selfless act endeared Blenda to Carl for eternity.

It just happened that Blenda was the daughter of Spleen Troost, warden of the Rutherford B. Hayes Memorial Prison. When Blenda found herself pregnant, the elder Troost informed the young Cagney of two facts: he was to marry Blenda as soon as possible, which Carl didn't mind, and he was to take a job at the prison, which he minded very much.

Every night for the last twelve years, Carl had sat in a small chair at a small desk in the small room that served as the surveillance center for the prison, watching a bank of small monitors until his eyes burned.

This was about as far away from riding the rails as one could get.

When he first started, Carl took some enjoyment from watching the prisoners furtively masturbate in the dead of night on the monitors but even that, over time, had lost its appeal. Now it was a nightly battle to stay awake until dawn and not daydream about getting beaten senseless by railroad bulls.

Which is what he was doing when he heard the knock on the front door of the prison.

Knock, knock, knock.

Unlike most prisons in the prisonful United States of America, the Rutherford B. Hayes Memorial Prison was not originally constructed to house criminals. In fact it was actually a three-bedroom house built in 1858. It had been Rutherford B. Hayes' first home in Fremont. There were no bars on the windows, no gates, and the plumbing was, at best, questionable.

The Hayes House was converted to a prison for reasons of thrift. Money was always tight down at Fremont City Hall. Mostly due to graft and simple misplacement.

The small room where Carl had his small chair and small desk was once the Hayes' front parlor, and the front door of the house, which was now the front door of the prison, was in the same room. Carl was in charge of opening and closing said door when it deserved to be opened or closed.

Knock, knock, knock.

The loud knocking, which continued unabated, surprised Carl as none of the prisoners had ordered a pizza or called up to Toledo for a whore. Well, the *prisoner* hadn't done either of these things, for there was only one ne'er-do-well lodged in the Rutherford B. Hayes Memorial Prison that night. Former Principal Douglas Kennedy, who had been arrested for urinating on a student.

Reaching into his desk, Carl consulted his handy (and well-thumbed) copy of *Prison Guarding For Dummies*. Although he knew the publication, which had been written by the Spleen Troost himself, backwards and forwards, he re-read the section entitled KNOCKING ON THE FRONT DOOR WHEN NONE

OF THE PRISONERS HAVE ORDERED A PIZZA OR A TOLEDO DICK-SUCKER. It stated, in no uncertain terms, that he was to A) check the video monitors to identify the knocker and B) pretend no one was at home so they would simply go away.

Knock, knock, knock.

Although, like all Americans, Carl Cagney hated his job, he had to hold onto it as not only did he have a wife to support, he had four kids and there was another little Cagney on the way. So, Carl followed the directives of *Prison Guarding For Dummies* to the hilt.

But he received quite a shock when he checked the video monitor for the security camera mounted above the front door. Despite the fact that he could clearly hear someone knocking, he plainly saw that there was no one there.

If he didn't suffer from a formidable case of psoriasis, Carl would have scratched his tiny head. As it was, he stood and performed a series of stretches, hoping the invisible knocker would simply give up of their own volition.

That didn't happen.

Knock, knock, knock.

Prison Guarding for Dummies didn't cover this peculiar situation.

It was times like these that Carl wished the Rutherford B. Hayes Memorial Prison was a proper prison with barbed wire, towering towers, and guards who were A) armed and B) hadn't married into their jobs.

Knock, knock, knock.

Curiosity finally got the better of Carl. He raced across the room, slid the dead bolt, and threw open the front door.

There, regardless of what the security camera said, stood the most beautiful woman Carl had ever laid eyes on. She made Blenda look like a fleshy turd.

The young woman was tall and lithe but had breasts the size of Packards parked on her chest. Her shock of red hair flowed on the breeze. Sparkling eyes that could have passed for precious stones were embedded in her wan head. A smile that was as salacious as it was wide seeped across her face. The scant amount of clothing she wore – a cropped Lynyrd Skynyrd T-shirt and short jeans skirt – showed off more than obscured her amazing figure.

Clearly, this was no pizza delivery girl or Toledo dick-sucker. This beauty, this dream wasn't there for the pisser Douglas Kennedy, the prison guard was certain of that.

She was there for him.

Carl, who suffered from an imagination, knew this lovely lady was the ticket out of his shitty life. Together they would ride the rails, steal pies cooling on windowsills, and sleep under trestles to avoid the rain.

Carl's dream had finally come true.

Well, that is until the young woman reached out her lovely hand, punched through the skin of his gut, and started pulling out his intestines.

It wasn't a walk in the park being the king of the vast and dangerous criminal underground of Fremont, Ohio.

For one thing, the cops were always breathing down his neck, begging bribes or trying to bust him. Then there was his henchmen – a pair of muscleheaded twins he couldn't tell apart so he called them Right and Left. They were intimidating but they were also as dumb as a continent of rocks. Lastly, Loco had to continuously be looking over his shoulder, keeping an eye on all the Young Turks of Fremont who were looking at his underworld throne and salivating.

One of those Young Turks, Rusty Slump, was currently standing before Loco in his mobile drug emporium. Loco didn't care for

Slump. His stupid toothpick arms, his massive nadbag, and the fact that his wardrobe consisted solely of Satan's Butt Buddies T-shirts. The boy was on the bottom rung of the Fremont crime ladder, his only claim to fame was taking massive dumps in public places. Despite this meager crime resumé, Slump had a super hot lady friend. Like every male in Fremont with a dick and a pulse, Loco lusted after CoCo McArdle and couldn't see what she saw in Rusty.

Maybe the rumors were true. Perhaps Rusty Slump was the genius behind Purple Hayes. As it seemed highly unlikely that this floor-shitter had invented the wonder drug that had captured the hearts and wallets of Fremont, Loco ignored the rumors. Then Purple Hayes dried up and blew away and the issue, at least in Loco's mind, was settled. He remained the king of the vast and dangerous criminal underworld of Fremont, Ohio, and that's all that mattered to him.

When Slump had shown up at his mobile drug emporium, Loco had been brewing a batch of his famous Hayes Dayes Methmatch, which was a semi-lethal bouillabaisse of many drugs: weed, blow, H, crack, crank, crabs, barbs, bennies, tweezies, red hibnobs, blue hibnobs, brussel sprouts (the cultivar not the drug), electric hobos, ploppers, screaming teens, cilantro, the Rez, Flonase, black licorice, brussel sprouts (the drug not the cultivar), and a little meth thrown in for the ladies.

Although a great drug, Hayes Dayes Methmatch was also something of a curse. For the weeks leading up to Hayes Dayes, Fremont's boisterous and often deadly weekend-long celebration of its favorite son, business was dead around the old mobile drug emporium, as everyone was saving up to buy a bunch of Hayes Dayes Methmatch and didn't want any weed or blow or stink sink.

Hence, Rusty Slump was his the only customer that night and something about the little creep was making Loco loco.

The kid kept looking over the bags on the merch table but couldn't make up his mind. Most dopers were quick in their purchase of crank or heroin or Shepherd's Pi. Also Loco caught Slump staring at him, as if he were measuring him for something. Sweat coated the kid's brow and his hands were shaking.

It was as if he were itching for a fight. If so, Loco could easily scratch that itch. Or, more accurately, have Right and Left, who were in the back of the mobile drug emporium playing Pong, scratch that itch.

"You gonna buy something, boy, or are you going to sniff around all night? I got brewing to do."

Slump stared at Loco, opened his mouth as if he had something to say, but remained quiet and, after a few moments, simply split. Ran out into the night, disappeared as if something spooked him.

Turning toward Right and Left, Loco was about to say something about how odd the kid was acting but he realized he'd be wasting his breath on his two imbecilic goons.

Douglas Kennedy trembled when he heard the screams coming from the jail's first floor.

Though he'd been a high school principal all his life, he'd surprisingly never witnessed a murder. But he was, without a doubt, hearing one now.

Another thing he knew for sure was he was going to die that night and it wasn't going to be pretty, for whatever was killing that guard downstairs, it was here for him.

The previous night Kennedy had had a horrendous nightmare. He was back in his office at Rutherford B. Hayes Memorial High when he heard a noise out in the hall. Clicking. Ever vigilant, Kennedy, rushed to investigate. Though the logical part of his brain knew that it was no longer his high school, no longer his turf, he still didn't want anyone, anything screwing with it.

When he exited his office, he was no longer in the high school but in a graveyard. Before him stood a prodigious tombstone with the name CONNIE PENDLETON carved into it.

He also discovered the source of the clicking sound. It was a pair of claws opening and closing as they dug their way out of Connie's grave.

Kennedy knew the best course of action was to flee. As fast, as far. The only problem was his legs weren't cooperating. They couldn't move, they could only quiver.

Something that was part Connie Pendleton and part creature shat from the bowels of hell crawled from the soil. This towering demon had Connie's face but the rest of it was covered with hair, bristling. Red skin torn, puss-oozing sores, those claws, opening and closing. It reeked of earth and death and blood.

Shaking dirt from its mane, the creature stalked toward him. Taking its sweet time while he pissed his pants several shades of yellow. Snapping its claws.

Click, click, click.

"Hello, Principal Kennedy. I came back to ask you why you didn't tell the police what I told you about Rusty Slump."

It was a fair question, but he had no words. Only urine.

"I see you have no excuses for your life," it said. Then smiled. He couldn't avert his eyes from the thing's maw. For it was a cave with hundreds of teeth sharp as spades.

As it drew closer, he noticed the beast had a second mouth. Between its legs. It too was filled sharp teeth.

When the beast finally reached him, the only thing Kennedy could do to defend himself was continue to piss as those two mouths, opening and closing, drew closer and closer and everything grew blacker than black.

That's when he woke up. Screaming.

After the murdery sounds came to a conclusion on the first

floor of the jail, there was a deafening silence.

"Flock this bullarkey," Kennedy cursed his luck.

He knew he should have told the police the truth after the Pendleton girl went missing, made them aware of her suspicions about the Slump boy. But what he'd told them was that she'd come to him and mentioned some vague "boy troubles." He'd lied because he just didn't give a shit and that was Connie Pendleton's fault.

When he told her to flock off, he felt alive for the first time in several years. Over the next few days, he'd told several students to flock themselves. This power trip ended when he went too far and held down the president of the student council, the hideous Julia Sheehan, and pissed on her as he bellowed the National Anthem. Not only had this lost him his job, he was arrested.

And now he was trapped in the Rutherford B. Hayes Memorial Prison waiting for something to kill him.

Though he'd learned through years of being around high school kids there was no God, Kennedy prayed. Prayed like there was no tomorrow.

Which there wasn't.

"Dear Sweet Baby G, it's me, Douglas Kennedy, the guy who held down Julia Sheehan while urinating on her. Though that act was totally justified, I mean, how many balloons can one turd request for a simple awards banquet, pissing on her in front of an assembly was probably not the best course of action. I'm kind of sorry for the whole thing. Also, I feel a little bad about the Connie Pendleton situation. I fear, with that snapping snatch nightmare, that something bad might have happened to her. I always just assumed she'd fled to Toledo to be a dick-sucker, which is what she totally deserved, but now I think she might be dead, which would be kind of bad. Also," he said in conclusion, "could I please have a bigger penis. Amen."

When he finished talking to the Lord, who wasn't listening, he heard something coming up the stairs. Slowly, slowly. Whatever it was, it was taking its sweet time.

Kennedy stood at the door of his cell, which was really just a bedroom doorway with bars. He didn't run, he didn't hide, as there was nowhere to run, nowhere to hide. Besides, he was compelled to see what was coming to kill him.

When the beast finally appeared at the top of the stairs, it was just like his dream. This thing was Connie Pendleton and it wasn't Connie Pendleton. Only the part that wasn't a real girl wasn't covered in fur and rent skin, it was covered in marvelous breasts.

The only thing that marred this lovely girl's appearance was the blood. She was caked with it though she sported no wounds of her own.

They studied one another for a moment. Prey and predator.

With a quick smile and slow steps, the girl made her way down the hall. Her platform heels clomp, clomp, clomping on the hardwood floors.

Also just like in the dream, he pissed his pants.

Arriving at his cell, the girl he knew wasn't a girl, but something even worse, leered at him like she wished to have sexual congress. But even the most optimistic part of his brain knew that wasn't what this thing really wanted. It wanted his blood, every drop of it.

They stood like that, two fighters in the ring, sizing one another up, for several minutes. Kennedy so wanted her to talk, defend her actions, explain herself.

But she said nothing.

Finally, the girl creature reached through the bars and grabbed him by the collar of his old fashioned nightshirt. He thought she was going to throttle him or pull him close to the bars to whisper in his ear.

But she did neither of those things.

Instead, with a jerk and a laugh, she pulled Prisoner #1 of the

Rutherford B. Hayes Memorial Prison, Douglas Turner Kennedy, through the bars, basically julienning him.

Suicide. That was the only answer.

He'd failed miserably at killing Loco Lenny Labovitz, unable to even draw Jinx McArdle's .38, scampering away into the night.

If he returned to the treehouse as planned, CoCo would light into him something fierce. His spirits were too low to survive such an emasculating onslaught. He had nowhere to go, no one to turn to.

The only person still drawing breath who he liked, Dearly Departed, was not an option. For passing out during sex, she probably hated him nearly as much as he hated himself.

Out of options, Rusty chose the only option that was still available to him: he was going to end his life.

Not with the gun, though. He didn't deserve to be killed by the same weapon that had ended the life of sweet Connie Pendleton.

With determined steps, the young man marched through a mostly deserted Fremont, his ultimate goal the unimaginatively named 20th Street Bridge and the muddy waters of the Sandusky River below.

As he walked, Rusty looked up. He'd always enjoyed a bit of night sky now and again. But that night, his last night on earth, the sky taunted him. The moon wouldn't look him in the face and the stars were cold and distant, like a thousand little CoCo McArdles.

When he finally arrived at the 20th Street Bridge, he checked to be sure there was absolutely no traffic – Rusty saw no reason to spoil anyone's evening with a suicide, especially so close to Hayes Dayes – to climb onto the railing of the bridge.

Standing there, the wind mussing his hair, finally the master of his own destiny, Rusty thought about what he should think about before jumping. This was a big decision, the last thoughts of one's life. He didn't want to think about his mother being smashed to death by a pancake or his overbearing father or CoCo and her berating. He wanted something positive. There were a handful of epic shits he'd taken in public, like that one in the fountain at the Rutherford B. Hayes Memorial Shopping Center during Black Friday, but even those monumental bowel movements brought him no solace during this trying time.

The only thought which didn't blemish his soul was of Dearly Departed. Her face appeared before him, twenty feet high and luminous, floating over the sluggish Sandusky.

Unexpectedly, the young man felt a chubby gathering force in his gabardines. Outside of a sexual situation, chubbies are always embarrassing, but this one was particularly so, as Rusty was in the midst of his suicide.

Though alone, he could feel his face go crimson.

Desperate, the young man tried to think away the crotch zombie. But even his old standbys – his mother's flat coffin, CoCo berating, his father yelling – did nothing to quell the throbbing gristle in his pants.

Rusty examined his options, boner-wise. It certainly felt as if an erection, especially one as dynamic as this one, was unfinished business, no way to go to the grave. Studying the tent pitched in his pants, the young man wondered what Machiavelli would do with such a poorly timed screaming flock weasel.

The great statesman had said, "Whosoever desires constant success must change his conduct with the times."

Though the connection was tenuous, Rusty interpreted this quote as Machiavelli coming down squarely on the side of a little pre-death masturbation.

Convincing himself that a quick polish of the old dolphin was a solid plan, Rusty put a pin in the whole suicide thing. He jumped down from the railing and rushed to a clump of bushes at the end of the 20th Street Bridge to rub one out.

Which took a surprisingly short amount of time considering his dour mood. Thinking of Dearly and her dope tits, it took only a handful of tugs before Old Faithful issued forth and the young man, as young men are prone to do, coated the surrounding foliage with cobwebs of cum.

Feeling better, as one always does after an act of self-love, but still suicidal, Rusty stepped out of the bushes ready to face his demise.

But it wasn't death who was waiting for him on the 20th Street Bridge, it was Dearly Departed herself. Her arms crossed over that magnificent chest, blocking his path.

He felt himself blanche as he wondered if she'd heard him bashing the bishop.

"Good evening, cute breather. What were you doing in the bushes?" she asked, her voice as cool as the evening air. There was something which appeared to be a smile on her face but it was hard to tell.

Rusty stammered, "Looking for something."

"Did you find it?"

"I think so, yeah. So, I see you're covered with blood again."

With those eyes that glittered even in the darkness, Dearly looked down. Her clothing was drenched in blood.

"Oh," she explained, "I'm menstruating. Perhaps we should go for a swim in the river."

"So… you're not mad at me?"

She definitely smiled. There was blood in her teeth. "Oh, puny human, why would I be angry with you?"

"For this afternoon… in the back of my car… I, I passed out while we were, well, you know."

Unfolding her arms, she stepped forward. Ran a hand sticky with blood through his hair. He didn't mind, not at all. "I've had a very strenuous day, dear breather. I need to bathe. Let us go skinny dipping, that will make both of us feel better."

As most of his blood was employed in his penis, Rusty was astounded that he could still use his brain to think about the muddy waters of the Sandusky River and how they'd nearly been his grave. He said, "Let's go the Rutherford B. Hayes Memorial Public Swimming Hole, the water is much cleaner there."

"Isn't that closed at this time of night?"

"Sure. But I've hopped the fence tons of times before."

He had, with CoCo standing behind him, berating him.

Taking his hand, Dearly said in a soft voice, "Then let us go, cute breather, together into the night."

Without fail, Blenda Troost Cagney brought her husband a midnight snack at the prison. Without fail, it was a peanut butter and cheese sandwich, his favorite. Without fail, she sprinkled just a little bit of arsenic on it.

Like all Americans, Blenda hated her spouse and longed for his demise. She couldn't take how he depended on her father for a job, the fact that he ate a peanut butter and cheese sandwich every night, and his incessant pining for the hobo life.

But she didn't wish to get rid of him in any obvious way. Blenda was smarter than that; Spleen Troost didn't raise no dummies. She wasn't going to the chair for that peanut butter and cheese loving fool. Her plan was to poison Carl so slowly, and with such trace amounts, that no one, not even the medical examiner, would uncover her deceit.

As she approached the Rutherford B. Hayes Memorial Prison, Blenda began to suspect something was wrong. For one thing, the front door was wide open, which was an obvious breach of security covered several times in Prison Guarding For Dummies. The next thing she noticed, which made her certain something was amiss, was the blood. Gallons and gallons of it, splashed all over the porch.

Stepping over the sticky threshold on jittery legs, Blenda was about to call out for her husband, but what she found inside made her realize that calling out his name (or slowly poisoning him for that matter) was no longer necessary. For Carl had already met his demise, chunks of his person were spread all over the floor. It was as if a bomb had gone off and blown him all over the front parlor/surveillance room. A hand here, a foot there, hair everywhere. His intestines were strung from surface to surface like the world's ugliest bunting.

She should have been pleased, ecstatic even, but instead, she felt an emptiness inside her that was bigger than her insides.

Collapsing, Blenda cried out, astonished to find tears cascading from her eyes. Spying what was left of his face on a nearby radiator, she suddenly missed her husband and his stupid sandwiches.

Lounging in a steamy bath, Officer Chrissy Rumpza masturbated with wild abandon, thinking about Connie Pendleton and her lollipop pussy. Every fourth or fifth stroke, her lost love was forgotten and the cop thought about the bloody footprint she'd found in Reverend Rump's living room. It was amazing, and a little unnerving, how easily she could alternate between those two disparate thoughts while continuing to toggle the little man in the boat.

With an arch of her muscular back, Rumpza peaked and tendrils of pleasure burrowed through her body. She shuddered, mumbled Connie's name, splashed water outside the tub.

When her moaning slowed, Rumpza noticed that her cell phone was ringing. For how long it had been doing so, she had no idea.

Leaping out of the tub and slipping on the water spilt, the cop found her chirping phone in the garble of uniform strewn across the floor. Answering it, she sank to the tiles. Though still tingling from her orgasm, she sensed a darkness all around her. Something was coming, something bad. No one called in the middle of the night unless the shit and the fan had become acquainted.

"Rumpza here," she yelled into the phone. Hoping it was just the acoustics of the bathroom that made it sound as if she were shouting.

It was Junior Officer Killion. Rumpza could tell by the squeak in his voice that he'd yet to recover from finding bits and pieces of Reverend Rump scattered. After identifying himself, Killion said, "We gotta talk about this animal attack on Reverend Rump…"

Rumpza had kept quiet about the human footprint she'd found behind the ratty recliner. She was well acquainted with Killion's big mouth. He'd squawk and soon every Fremontonian would know there was a savage killer on the loose. Before she said anything to anybody, she wanted to have a conversation with Police Chief Pendleton, but she'd been unable to reach him all day.

No longer could she keep her secret from the rest of the Police Society. "It's not an animal, Jeff."

"What?" he shrieked.

"It was a dick-dancing human who killed Reverend Rump," said Rumpza. She filled her in fellow officer about the footprint.

Just as Rumpza feared, Killion freaked out. His breathing went all weird and she could hear him hopping around. "Sweet Baby G, we got a serial killer on the loose here in Fremont. That's so much worse than a rabid ocelot."

"Now calm down, Jeff, no one said anything about a quiff-slinging serial killer, we have to keep our heads--."

"But he's struck again! The Fremont Fiend has killed yet another!"

Trying to keep her voice and heart still, Rumpza asked Killion what the clit-chucking hell he was talking about.

"That's why I'm calling! Our serial killer has struck again! This time he slaughtered two folks down at Rutherford B. Hayes

Memorial Prison."

"Who was killed?"

"That guard who always went on and on about being a hobo and the only prisoner they had locked up, the pisser, ex-principal Douglas Kennedy."

A bolt of Connie flashed through Rumpza's brain. It took her a moment to reckon why. The last person the doomed girl had spoken to – besides Rumpza herself and they hadn't wasted their tongues on talk – was Reverend Rump, now deceased. The second to the last person that Connie had spoken to was Douglas Kennedy.

Dropping the phone, Rumpza let her head fall back, smack the wall. She felt as if she were drowning in a whirlpool of thought. Rump, then Kennedy. Rump, Kennedy.

She did not care for how this cookie was crumbling.

It wasn't often that she missed Sergeant Snoopers. She always found the cocksure canine to be full of himself, something of a show-off. Not to mention, Police Chief Pendleton thought the sun shined out of that dog's ass. Often, Pendleton took Snoopers out to Rutherford B. Hayes Memorial Park, where they'd play fetch and talk over open cases, Snoopers doing the retrieving, Pendleton doing the talking.

But now that she felt overwhelmed by facts, she wished Sergeant Snoopers hadn't been killed by that hit-and-run driver.

But he had.

The dog detective was dead and gone, and solving these murders was up to her. Rumpza grabbed her phone by the throat.

Apoplectic, Killion was screaming her name.

"Jeff, Jeff, get a hold of yourself, I'm here."

"Oh thank God! When the line went dead, I feared the Fremont Fiend had claimed yet another victim. I imagined you ripped apart in a giant pool of blood."

"Well, I'm not. I'm just sitting here on my bathroom floor

trying to sort this hymen-gargling mess out. Meet me at the Rutherford B. Hayes Memorial Prison in half an hour. I have to get dressed and try to find Police Chief Pendleton"

"Is that police officer taming his beef weasel?" asked Dearly, laughing a little.

"I don't think so," Rusty replied. "He's not exactly the beef-weasel-taming type."

Though it certainly appeared as if Police Chief Pendleton was masturbating, right there in his patrol car, which was parked in the middle of the Rutherford B. Hayes Memorial Swimming Hole parking lot. Bouncing up and down in his seat, his right arm flapping, his face etched in ecstasy.

Regardless of all the evidence of some gherkin-goosing going down, it seemed highly unlikely to Rusty that this morally superior ass would be spanking the monkey so brazenly. Especially in public.

Just last year, Pendleton had spoken passionately at an assembly at the high school. His theme was the dangers of sex, pre- and post-marital. He intoned that, thanks to the atheists running Washington D.C., he wasn't allowed to arrest two consenting adults for engaging in sexual congress, but the Lord could. And Lord's jail was called hell and your sentence was eternity.

"Hey," Dearly brightened. "I know that breather who I'm sure his taming his beef weasel."

"You know Police Chief Pendleton?"

"Sure. Last night when I arrived in town, he let me stay at his place."

"What?"

"Yeah, I just walked up to his door and he let me spend the night on his couch. He was actually pretty kind for a puny human, said I reminded him of someone, but then, in the morning, he turned all weird and threw me out."

Rusty knew exactly who Dearly reminded Pendleton of, his sweet daughter, Connie. The young man had thought the same thing. In the moonlight, Rusty studied this strange woman. Though this young woman had a completely different face, totally different body, and definitely a different demeanor, there was something undeniably Connie-esque about her.

Suddenly, the flapping stopped and the etched expression disappeared from Pendleton's face, but Rusty could tell, from vast experience, that the cop hadn't shot his wad. Something had stayed his hand.

Pendleton whipped his head around, looked into the backseat, and screamed at no one, "There's no such thing as oral gangrene!"

Rusty pulled Dearly deeper into shadows at the edge of the parking lot.

Pendleton continued yelling. "Okay, great, I've learned a little known medical fact. Now is that the only reason you interrupted my pleasure or do you have more unpleasant news to relate?"

Dearly turned on Rusty, whispered, "Is that breather yelling at us?"

Rusty shook his head. "I… I don't think so."

"Then whom?"

"I have no idea."

Pendleton shouted, "Well, what is it? I don't have all night!"

Rusty continued, his voice tight, "Maybe he's gone loony. See, his daughter, that's who you reminded him of, she ran away about six months ago."

Pain passed over Dearly's face, darkening it. "What happened to her?"

"No one knows," said Rusty after he swallowed the lump in his throat that was the size of his throat.

Wiping away a tear, Dearly said, "Your human world can

certainly be a dark and dismal place."

The young man wanted to kiss her tears away. But before he could move, the Police Chief continued with his monologue, "Yes, I do, because it's agitating. Can't you appear to me while I'm engaged in prayer, which I often am, or, perhaps, just having a sandwich?"

Dearly said, "Boy, this puny human is beyond crazy. He must have really loved his daughter."

"Oh, tarnation!" screamed the cop.

It seemed unlikely to Rusty that Pendleton loved his daughter much, as he was too busy loving the Sweet Baby G, so the boy simply shrugged.

Pendleton switched on the patrol car's sirens and lights. He took off across the parking lot, spitting gravel, and out into the street, nearly taking out a telephone pole in the process.

Soon the world was quiet again.

Standing, Dearly said, "Okay, now we can climb the fence. I can wash off and then we will have sexual congress."

"Yeah, about that..." Rusty started but stopped. In the silence that followed Dearly simply stared at him.

Though he couldn't put his dark thoughts into words, Rusty was worried that if they tried to have sex, he might, for some inexplicable reason, pass out and embarrass himself yet again. Perhaps drown.

During their shared silence, Dearly came closer, stole all the air surrounding him so that he couldn't breath, and leaned into him. "Are you afraid, cute breather, that what occurred this afternoon will occur again?"

Shrugging, he said, "Maybe."

"I want you so bad," she whispered into his ear, "that I am willing to take that risk."

When she walked away, there was nothing he could but follow.

As a man beholden to the multifarious decrees of a very pissy God, Police Chief Pendleton had rarely engaged in the act of self-pollution. Certainly, during his teenage years, he'd experienced a few moral slips but mostly he defeated those dark desires with a cold shower or a long run. In retrospect, he recognized his pent up sexual frustration had been a major factor in rushing him to the altar with Runeé Pettigrew just a few months after they graduated. He and his underutilized penis didn't listen to his mother, who warned him that Runeé would be trouble, or his minister who compared the young woman, unkindly, to the Whore of Babylon, or the walls of every bathroom stall in town, whose graffiti guaranteed that Runeé's naughty bits could be had for a few slices of Kraft singles.

Though they'd been classmates at Rutherford B. Hayes Memorial High, the pair had never actually spoken to one another until that fateful day in July when Pendleton, a shiny new Junior Officer on the Fremont Police Society, pulled Runeé over for a broken taillight. He soon discovered that she was driving with a suspended license. When he accused her of being reckless and endangering her life and the lives of others, she broke down. With tears in her eyes, Runeé explained that she was broke and, if he gave her a ticket, she wouldn't be able to pay it and she'd have to go to jail, then she'd be fired from her job at the Rutherford B. Hayes Memorial Sex Shoppe #8, and then she'd be even more broke and be in more trouble than she already was.

With a teary wink, she assured him she'd do anything to get out of the ticket. He thought about that for a moment and smiled. He told her that although it was against Police Society policy, he'd tear up the ticket in trade for a favor. Instantly, her tears dried and, in their place, a libidinous smile ruled her over rouge-caked face.

Pendleton pulled out a religious tract concerning the Lord

smiting a buttload of people for some minor offense and told her to read it. They'd discuss it the next day.

Shrugging, Runeé grabbed the tract and raced off.

The following morning, Pendleton pulled into the driveway of Runeé's trailer. Certain she'd failed her assignment, Pendleton found Runeé in her backyard standing at a trash barrel. As he approached, he was surprised to see that she had gone through a dramatic transformation. This was not the old Runeé Pettigrew with her trashy clothes and trashy talk. She was now a proper young lady, tossing cartons of cigarettes into the flames along with stacks of fashion magazines and smutty video tapes.

Not only had she read the tract, Runeé told a stunned Pendleton, she'd perused it for hours. Stayed up all night, rethinking her evil ways.

Grabbing Police Chief by his lapels with trembling hands, she pulled him close and talked breathlessly about the kind and merciful Lord ripping those who disobeyed him limb from limb. Confessing that she'd, many times, been on the wrong side of the Lord. That she'd taken drugs too many times to count, had a score of abortions, and had even once been half a blumpy act. Pendleton had no idea what she was talking about but it didn't matter, as he wasn't really listening. He couldn't stop gazing into her unmascared eyes, studying her blouse, which was buttoned all the way to her throat, sniffing her hair, which had been dyed back to its original color and pulled into a severe bun atop her head.

Feelings, raw feelings, began to flow through the sewers of his body.

Unable to curtail his emotions any longer, he grabbed his convert and pulled her close. Runeé jumped, feeling his hard-on blossoming in his polyester shorts.

"I thought you were a man beholden to the laws of God," she whispered.

"I am, I am," he assured her as he exposed his penis. "But the Redeemer wants you to touch my manhood in a wanton way. Oh please, it ain't never been handled by a real woman."

Looking back and forth between him and it, she sputtered, "But that's… you're asking me to commit a sin."

Holding up a solemn hand, he promised, "It's not a sin if we're wed within the week."

Within the week, they were wed.

Despite the objections of his family and pastor and every bathroom stall wall in town, Pendleton was madly in love with this girl and knew in his heart that she'd left her hussy ways in the dust when she found the Lord. Plus, she doled out oral pleasure like a hurricane with teeth.

Their first couple of years together were pure bliss. There was only one bee in the ointment, they couldn't – thanks to Runeé possessing a tangled web of endometriosis throughout her well-worn womb – conceive a child. Every night they spent an hour praying over this dilemma and then they spent the next hour actually doing something about it by going to town on one another.

Soon their prayers were answered and the Good Lord thrust His Holy Fingers into Runeé's love cabbage, cleared away the endometriosis, and made her fruitful with child.

After Connie was born, Pendleton noticed things began to change, and not for the better. Runeé would, from time to time, engaged in a bit of backsliding. The cop tried to chalk this up to the stress of having a newborn who was plagued with several respiratory problems.

Pendleton caught his wife, with alarmingly regularity, in possession cigarettes or a pint of gin or going to PG rated films at the local movie house. But the worst offense was when he found her with Johnny Greene, the kid who mowed their lawn, just sitting around in the living room, acting as if blasting Satan's Butt Buddies' records were normal.

That night Runeé cried and swore she'd never touched the boy, didn't have feelings for him, that this would never happen again, that she'd do better, be better. She convinced her husband that they were a family and the best place for them to be was together.

Reminding himself the Sweet Baby G had said a thing or two about forgiveness, he exonerated his wife and they had the best sex of their lives as the infant Connie slept in a cradle nearby, breathing roughly.

Then came that dark and dismal Tuesday. Pendleton returned home for a surprise lunch and found Runeé in their martial bed with Johnny Greene. In a crib nearby was Connie, rasping, fussing. To the cop's surprise, there were darker things occurring than your garden-variety adultery.

For one thing, Runeé had painted, with menstrual blood, a pentagram on the wall above their bed. Johnny, who looked quite dismayed, had make-up and ashes smeared all over his naked body. Also, his hands and feet were bound. In one hand Runeé held a measuring cup of burnt offerings, in the other a sharp knife glittered.

His knees buckling, Pendleton asked what was going on.

"I don't rightly know, Officer Pendleton," said Johnny Greene, tears running down his face, ruining his make-up.

"It's a sacrifice, sweetie, for Connie. I've made a deal with the devil, one soul for another. I've said all the incantations, now all I have to do is spill this virgin's blood and our little baby will be better. In fact, she'll live forever."

"I'm beginning to suspect that I'm not about to get my dick wet, as promised," said Johnny Greene, not the brightest trussed bulb on the tree.

The cop said, "Incantations? Burnt offerings? That's crazy, it don't make no sense. We're a Christian family."

"Yes, I know, but Satan has power too, the power to save our child."

All his life, though he was a man beholden to the laws of God, Pendleton had struggled with controlling his anger. Many times, in his youth, there'd been fights. Bruises, bloodied noses, broken bones.

Without much thought, as so often happens, Junior Officer Pendleton drew his piece and put an ugly hole in the middle of Johnny Greene's sweaty brow. Blood spurted as he slumped.

Runeé smiled at her husband, though she was covered in another man's brain matter. "You did it, dear, you've given Satan exactly what he desires!"

Wishing to block out her mumbo-jumbo, he screamed, "I am the Power and the Glory!"

He fired a bullet into her belly.

While he went to put a new diaper on the baby – who was, surprisingly, no longer fussy though the room was still reverberating from the shots fired – Pendleton let his wife lay there and bleed out. She kicked a few times, mumbled unintelligibly, rolled around a bit.

By the time he'd rocked Connie back to sleep, the satanic harlot was dead. In a reverse of their wedding day, Pendleton carried her out of their bedroom. Heading to their earthen basement, he buried her and her lover deep, placing an old, broken dresser on their grave as a headstone. After taking a shower, he found the beers he knew Runeé had hidden in the crisper. Pendleton poured them all down the drain save one, which he poured down his own drain. Then he put the bloody sheets in the washer, scrubbed the pentagram from the wall, called into police headquarters, and told them he wouldn't be back that day, or the next, as he'd arrived home for a surprise lunch and found a disturbing note waiting for him. Apparently, Runeé, that garden-variety harlot, had cleared out, run off with the kid who mowed lawns in the neighborhood, leaving Pendleton and their infant daughter in her wake.

Everyone in Fremont loves a juicy tale of debauchery, so the general populace believed this tale spun. After a few days, Pendleton felt he was in the clear but he still scoured every inch of his bedroom with bleach daily in an attempt to cleanse all the bloodstains out of his life.

And just like that, Pendleton went back to being a bachelor. Well, he did have one woman in his life, little Connie. With his job and the baby, the cop found that he didn't have time for relationships, not even with himself. There wasn't even a need for cold showers or long runs to stay his hand. He was too exhausted, mentally and physically, for self-pollution, which suited him just fine.

That was until Officer Rumpza came to town.

When he first saw her, something weird happened in his polyester. He often caught himself thinking of her in a most unprofessional manner. He managed to keep these urges under wraps, succeeded in shunning the sin of self-pollution. It helped that she was aloof, cold, had a mouth on her. Also, Rumpza and Sergeant Snoopers, his favorite officer, got into many arguments laced with foul language and harsh barking.

It was only when Connie disappeared that Pendleton succumbed to the devil's wishes concerning his penis. The pious cop told himself there was only way to relieve the stress he was living under, engaging in self-pollution ten to thirteen times a day.

The intervening six months had done nothing to curb this reprehensible behavior.

Even after driving around all day, not listening to the frantic calls on his police radio, looking for that poor girl, Dearly Departed, whom he'd cast out into the dark and dismal world of

Fremont, he found himself in the parking lot of the Rutherford B. Hayes Public Swimming Hole, sitting in his patrol car with his engorged penis in his hand, committing the sin of onanism, while thinking about Officer Rumpza.

In the sexual scenario unspooling in his mind, Rumpza was a Civil War nurse at the Second Battle of Bull Run. Like an angel, she floated from tent to tent, tending to the wounded, covered with the blood of the dead and dying. She had a roll of gauze, a concerned look on her face, and that sweet posterior.

She gasped when she stumbled upon Pendleton, who was strikingly handsome in his uniform, which was soiled by a grievous gut wound. Even though she was but a woman, the sexy nurse could tell the soldier had only a few moments left in this world. She kissed his wound with tender lips. But she didn't stop there. Her kisses turned to licks and was soon tonguing his gaping wound and working her way south. Undoing his woolen trousers, she wrapped her lips around his engorged penis. Though he was on death's door, he felt a delicious tingling in the basement of his scrotum and--.

"Well, that's one way to contract a cussed case of oral gangrene, you dirty devil," came a sonorous voice from the backseat.

Pendleton jumped, dropped his cock, and spun around to face his accuser.

His long legs stretched out, Rutherford B. Hayes was reclining in the back of the cruiser.

"There's no such thing as oral gangrene!"

"Oh, sir, I beg to differ. The licking of a festering wound was an extremely dangerous practice to engage in, very unsanitary. If a drafted nurse had behaved in such unprofessional behavior in my unit, that nut-scooper would have been tossed from the camp before her bell-fired tongue have even began to turn green."

"Okay, great, I've learned a little known medical fact. Now is that the only reason you interrupted my pleasure or do you have more unpleasant news to relate?"

Leaning forward, the dead president said, "As a matter of fact, I do. Thank you for reminding me of my mission, you self-polluting wastrel."

"Well, what is it? I don't have all night!"

"You become quite agitated when interrupted indulging yourself."

"Yes, I do, because it's agitating. Can't you appear to me while I'm engaged in prayer, which I often am, or, perhaps, just having a sandwich?"

"I'm certain both of us would enjoy that, you cockchaffer, but have you not figured out the rules to our engagements? I can only appear while you are immersed in the act of self-pollution."

"Oh, tarnation!"

"Fortunately for both of us, you seem to engage in such deviant behavior on a regular schedule. But right now you should pack away your penis and head over to the Rutherford B. Hayes Memorial Prison as there have been two more blasted attacks. Bloody, bloody affairs."

After dropping this bomb, the ghost or drug trip or whatever he was simply disappeared.

Replacing his penis in its rightful place, Pendleton tore out of the parking lot and into the night.

Thanks to the gallons of blood splashed on her when she ripped apart Kennedy and the guard, all the water around her was tinged a magnificent pink.

Sitting on the bottom of the Rutherford B. Hayes Memorial Swimming Hole, legs crossed, Dearly looked up at the full moon struggling through the water and realized she'd lost track of time.

How long had she been down there? Ten minutes? Twenty? Long enough to get clean, she decided, and rose up through the pink.

Breaking the surface, Dearly discovered the cute breather standing at the edge of the swimming hole. She'd forgotten about him during her watery sojourn. Clad only in his underwear, which clearly defined his cumbrous scrotum, he looked as nervous as a cat in a room full of demons.

"How… how long can you hold your breath?" he asked, his voice choked with worry and admiration. "I thought maybe… I was afraid…"

"If you were so concerned for my safety, why did you not jump in and attempt to save me?"

"I… I can't swim."

She scoffed. "But you claimed to have broken in here many times."

"That was only so my girlfriend could go swimming." As soon as these words were released into the wild, a look of panic griped the breather's face. He turned the wrong color.

Laughing, Dearly pulled her T-shirt over her head. Wading it into a soggy ball, she tossed it to the side of the swimming pool. "You have a girlfriend, do you? Is she as pretty as me?"

To aid him in his decision, the young woman cupped her large breasts. Jiggled them a little.

"No one is as pretty as you, Dearly."

"Do you really mean that?" Tweaking her nipples, she could hear the cute breather salivating.

"I don't love her," he said, the words tripping over themselves.

"That's a shame. Why not?"

"She's bossy."

"Oh, there's nothing worse than a person trying to control your life. Now jump in."

"But… but I just told you, I can't swim."

Dearly studied the boy, his thin arms across his thin chest. He looked frail and weak, two things she despised. But still, he possessed a nutsack for the ages and she need him to impregnate her with evil.

Not to mention, something about him piqued her interest. She was curious about the Other Girl's reaction to him. She felt light and fluffy in Dearly's brain. Also, when she thought of the cute human, her chest hurt. This strange feeling was nearly overwhelming when they'd been talking about the cop and the daughter he'd lost.

Dearly suspected the Other Girl was the cop's missing daughter. But she hadn't run away. She was dead. Dead and gone and no one even knew it.

The demon was curious about this human girl who was dead but also refused to die. She hoped perhaps that the cute breather could answer a few of her questions, shed some light. Then they could have sexual congress which would end with her being with child. Then she could eat him and his super-sized jizzbag.

No, you can't, screamed the Other Girl from her hiding place amongst the weeds in Dearly's mind.

The demon told her to go away, though she knew the Other Girl wouldn't.

To Rusty, Dearly said, "I will not allow any harm to come to you, cute breather, jump in."

Eyeing the depth of the water, the boy seemed unsure about so many things in his life.

She said, "Explain to me how we can have sexual congress if you're so far away from me?"

This helped him make up his mind.

Taking a deep breath, he jumped, hung in the air for a second, flailing, and hit the water with a splash.

She watched the water swallow him until he was but a fleshy flapping speck resting on the bottom of the swimming hole.

With a giggle, Dearly dove, brought him back up. When they broke the surface, he sputtered, gasped for breath. Coughing a few times, he spat, "Why'd you do that? You said no harm would come to me!"

"And none did."

"I nearly drown!"

Pulling him tight, she kissed away his concerns.

When Dearly opened her eyes, she saw the boy looked dazed, as if he might faint again or simply die. She didn't want this to happen. Not yet anyway. She had to bring him back around.

While holding him afloat with one hand, she used the other to message her breasts. The cute human's eyes focused, a little. She asked, "My breasts, what do you think of them?"

"I think they're dope."

"Then why don't you lick them?"

"Cause I'm afraid of them."

"That makes me happy and sad at the same time. Here, let me help you."

As if bringing a babe to feed, Dearly forced the cute breather's face to her breast.

His tongue lapped once, twice, thrice.

"Whilst we engage in sexual congress, puny human, perhaps you could tell me of your relationship with the daughter of the police officer."

The human stopped lapping. She feared she'd drawn his ire with her question.

She looked down just in time to see his eyes roll back in his head.

Stupid flocking cop, dressed in some stupid flocking soldier costume, sitting in his stupid flocking patrol car, jacking his flocking meat and talking to him-flocking-self.

At least, Loco Lenny Labovitz thought he saw a masturbating cop playing dress up and delivering a monologue in his patrol car. But he couldn't be sure. For one thing, he was parked over a hundred yards away. Secondly, he'd been brewing a Herculean batch of Hayes Dayes Methmatch all afternoon and sampling his wares liberally, which made reality somewhat elusive.

But even if the cop was a drug hallucination, Loco felt he deserved to be mocked. The idiot was sitting right across the street from the biggest bust of his career - Loco's mobile drug emporium, which was ripe with illegal pharmaceuticals of all stripes - and the stupid cop, if he existed, was just sitting there, possibly polishing the dolphin.

Loco's heart, already pounding thanks to the Methmatch, nearly leapt out of his chest when the cop turned on his lights and siren and swerved out of the parking lot of the Rutherford B. Hayes Memorial Swimming Hole. Thinking the cop was coming for him, Loco nearly doused his trousers. His breathing slowed when he saw the patrol car turn and race off into the night.

When the memory of the cop faded, which occurred quickly thanks to the mind-curdling effects of the Methmatch, Loco returned to worrying about what he'd been worrying about all night.

That kid, Rusty Slump.

Thinking about how nice it would be to open his gut and let gravity do the rest.

Usually someone so low on the criminal ladder would not have drawn the attention of the king of the vast and dangerous criminal underworld of Fremont, Ohio, but there was something about Rusty that didn't sit well with Loco.

Loco didn't care for the way the little floor-shitter looked at him earlier that evening, didn't like the way he was fidgeting, didn't like that he ran away. Loco would have bet his mobile drug emporium - which he loved more than anything in the world, as it was the first thing he ever stole - that Rusty was up to no good.

Even in his addled state, he realized the rumors must be true. As hard as it was to believe, Slump had to be the genius who invented Purple Hayes. Which meant the kid wanted to be the king of the vast and dangerous criminal underworld of Fremont, Ohio, which meant he was gunning for Loco, which meant he had to die.

Turning, he spied Left and Right, lounging in the back of the tubular vehicle, playing Pong on a tiny TV.

Be-doop, be-doop, be-doop.

With an exaggerated sigh, Loco entered into his least favorite endeavor, attempting to converse with his two moronic henchmen.

"Hey guys, I've been thinking."

"Okay," said Right. Or perhaps it was Left. Loco couldn't really tell them apart unless they were standing on either side of him.

"Remember that kid who was in here earlier? Rusty Slump?"

"Nope," said either Left or Right.

Be-doop, be-doop, be-doop.

"He just stood around, saying nothing, buying no merch. Then he ran off."

"Is that a fact?" asked Right or Left. Neither of them bothered to look away from the TV screen, the bouncing square ball.

Be-doop, be-doop, be-doop.

"Guys, guys, I'm serious here. I pay you good money, so you have to pay attention to me. Now, shut off that stupid game."

With a palpable reluctance, Left or Right shut off the video game. They turned and looked at Loco with their droopy eyes, dull expressions. The king of the vast and dangerous criminal underworld of Fremont, Ohio made a mental note to run an ad in *the Rutherford B. Hayes Memorial Picayune-Times* for a new pair of henchmen.

"That Slump kid, as I was saying, has got me spooked. I don't like being spooked. I think you two should take care of this problem."

"Should we make you some warm milk or something?"

inquired Left or Right, motioning to the kitchenette that Loco had fabricated in the mobile drug emporium.

Groaning, Loco said, "No, you morons, I mean you should kill Rusty Slump as soon as possible."

Amongst the throng of sepia-toned folks who ringed the swimming hole, Rusty spied a man-sized frog, who, like the other figments of his imagination, was wearing an old-fashioned bathing suit.

The frog smiled. "It's nice to finally meet you, Rusty."

"It's nice to meet you."

Cocking his large, flat head, the frog asked, "Do you even know who I am?"

"You're Mr. Frog," Rusty said with all the confidence of a simpleton.

The frog's smile evaporated. "Mr. Frog? Mr. Flocking Frog is who you think I am? That's about the dumbest flocking thing I've ever heard and I don't even have ears. For one thing, I'm a toad, not a frog."

"Alright, sorry."

Taking an exaggerated breath, the toad said, "To be specific, I'm a Colorado River Toad. Does that ring any bells in that drug addled brain of yours?"

"I've never been to Colorado, Mr. Frog. Heck, I've never been west of Gary, Indiana."

After another sigh, the toad said, "But they got books east of Gary, Indiana, don't they, boy? I'm the Colorado River Toad, which means I have something in common with that girl's titties."

"That's really interesting, Mr. Frog, but I'm afraid I don't have the time for this discussion right now."

"Oh? And why not?"

"Cause I have to faint," said Rusty.

And faint he did, sinking to the bottom of the swimming hole.

"Officer Rumpza, tell me honestly, what do you think about the Civil War?"

"Excuse me, sir?"

"Oh, I was just wondering if you held any opinions about the glorious War Between the States. I mean, it was the last war fought entirely on American soil, I thought you might have a word or two to say about it."

"Police Chief Pendleton, do you really think this is the time or the place to hold such a discussion?" With a stern sweep of her hand, Officer Rumpza motioned toward their bloody environs.

They were standing in the Rutherford B. Hayes Memorial Prison, up to their ankles in Doug Kennedy's cubed guts.

Although it seemed impossible, Rumpza believed that someone, someone with superhuman strength, certainly the same person who so savagely disassembled Reverend Rump, had pulled the former principal and well-known pisser through the bars of his cell.

"Sorry," said Pendleton. His face flushed as he looked down upon the chunks of former principal. "I was just, you know, attempting to lighten the mood a little during this trying time. So, what in tarnation could have happened here?"

"It appears Kennedy was pulled through the bars of the cell."

Pendleton shook his head. "What kind of heinous animal could do such a thing? We're a thousand miles from the nearest shark. Hopefully."

"Well, sir, I believe it was a human animal," said Rumpza. As the words left her mouth, they sounded ludicrous.

Though he was the one dressed in Civil War garb, the Police Chief stared at his subordinate as if she were crazy. She couldn't really blame him. If it were physically possible, she would have stared at herself in the same fashion.

Through clenched teeth, Pendleton said, "Really, Officer Rumpza? What kind of a human would have the strength to pull another human through steel bars? That's crazy talk. This has to be an animal of some kind. A rabid one would be my guess."

"Listen, would you say these murders are somehow connected to the murder of Reverend Rump?"

"I certainly hope so. I wouldn't want two crazed, possibly rabid, animals running loose on the streets of Fremont."

"I found a footprint, a bloody footprint, a bloody human footprint in Rump's living room."

This bit of information threw Pendleton like a Frisbee. "Well, ah, yeah… It, it must have been left by Killion. He's an idiot. At least, that's what you keep writing in all your reports."

"While it's true that Killion's a moron, this was a footprint, not a boot print."

"I don't have an answer for that, Officer Rumpza, but I know the slaughter which occurred at the good reverend's and the carnage that happened here was performed by a wild beast. There is no other answer."

Rumpza persisted no further as the shade of crimson Pendleton's face had turned signaled this particular discussion was finished.

After clearing his throat, Pendleton said, "Tell me if you find any more clues as to what kind of animal this was, I'm heading home. It's been a long day."

Angered, Rumpza stuck out her tongue at his retreating Civil War back. Though childish, the act made her feel better.

Left alone, she went back to her sleuthing. Getting down on her hands and knees, she scoured the bloody floor for clues. She found Kennedy's mouth near the hat rack.

Picking it up, she said, "Oh, if only this mouth could talk."

She studied the mouth and, trapped in the corner of the lips, she spied a shiny and curled thread. She pulled the filament into the light, turned it over.

"Perhaps you can talk, Mr. Mouth," she said to herself.

It was a hair. A human hair. Long, it shined red, a brilliant red.

Watching the cute breather drift to the bottom of the swimming hole, Dearly considered leaving him there to fend for himself and heading off to find a new boyfriend. Some puny human who, although they would definitely have a smaller scrotum, wasn't so weak, so wan, so weird. Some guy who didn't make her chest hurt.

But, as she begun to swim away, the Other Girl raised her voice and scolded Dearly for her actions.

Not bothering to take a breath, Dearly dove down to the depths and retrieved Rusty, though she took her sweet time doing so.

Although he was out cold, she lifted him with ease and rose to the top. At the edge of the swimming hole, she floated out, landing butterfly-soft on the concrete where their clothes lay mingled. Though she could have let him drift to the pavement like a snowflake, she dropped him to teach the cute breather a lesson.

The only sign that he was even alive came when he shouted, "Mr. Toad, Mr. Toad, please come back! I need more clues!"

She rolled her eyes, dressed, and walked away without looking back.

Having a boyfriend, even a cute one, was quickly becoming a real pain in the ass.

Cuntlips McGoo sat in the gas station parking lot, his back against the tour bus, staring up at the early morning sun. This being Texas, the sun was only about ten feet off the ground. The star's heat pricked his skin and brought him great joy. Cuntlips smiled a rare smile.

"What the flock are you doing out here?" asked Sweaty Nips McGoo from a distance, ripping the fabric of Cuntlips' idyllic moment.

Turning toward his bandmate, Cuntlips saw exactly what he knew he'd see. A hungover Sweaty Nips standing in the doorway of the tour bus, his right arm pulling double duty as it clutched a half-empty bottle of Jack while draped over the scrawny shoulders of some SDT-laden groupie, emaciated and pierced, much like Sweaty Nips himself, whose other arm was slapped over his brow, attempting to block out the sweltering sun.

The groupie, incongruously, grasped a newspaper.

"I'm looking at the sun," explained Cuntlips, his voice low.

Grinning at his girlfriend du jour, Sweaty Nips said, "See, I told you, not only is he one facially deformed motherflocker, he's a complete retard."

Since joining Satan's Butt Buddies such verbal arrows had been slung Cuntlip's direction many times, but he'd never grown used to it.

In fact, even though he was the drummer for one of the most popular death metal bands in the world, there were still some nights, particularly after some hazing dished out by his bandmates, when Cuntlips fell into despair. When he was low, Cuntlips thought of his old teacher, the Buddhist monk ninja warrior assassin, and his bloody death. This never helped matters and many nights the rocker cried himself to sleep.

"Hey Cuntlips," called Sweaty Nips, not yet done with his fun, "I honestly can't remember, can you read or not?"

He could but he didn't care to. The drummer liked pictures. Pictures of pretty things, like sunsets over water, puppies romping, and baby sloths dressed in pajamas. These images helped him forget, for just a moment, that the world's a dark and dismal place, teeming with demons and other denizens of the netherworld.

"Of course I can," replied Cuntlips.

"Then you should take a gander at this. That minister, Rump, who's always protesting our shows, he was killed by a rabid animal." Sweaty Nips snatched the newspaper out of the skank's grasp and flung it toward Cuntlips. It landed ten feet away. For a moment, the drummer wondered if his bandmate was just messing with him. But curiosity got the better of him and he stood, retrieving the paper. Flapped it open.

The first thing to catch Cuntlips' eye was the photo splashed across the front page. It was not a pretty picture, not in the least. Though it was black and white, it was the most gruesome photo he'd ever seen and he'd spent a decade in a satanic death metal band.

It was of Rump's living room, blood everywhere, a decapitated head.

Cuntlips didn't have to read a word of the article, he knew exactly what was at work here.

"This wasn't any animal, rabid or no," he said.

"What?" asked the skank.

"This was a demon."

Sweaty Nips burst out with one of his trademark gut laughs that everyone seemed to enjoy except Cuntlips. Perhaps because these guffaws were usually aimed at him. "What the hell are you talking about?"

Staring into Sweaty Nips' bloodshot eyes, Cuntlips explained, "Reverend Rump was killed by a demon from hell."

Another gut laugh, louder than the first. The lead singer nearly fell from the bus. "Shit, boy, you do understand that all that satanic crap we pull – spitting up blood on stage, sacrificing virgins, building pagan altars – it's not real. It's just for show, you get that, right?"

"Oh no Sweaty Nips, it's real and I've got to stop it. I gotta get to Fremont, Ohio, right now, this very minute."

"But we got a show tonight in Denton."

"No, *you* have a show in Denton. I quit. But before I go, I think you should know that the last time we swung through Dallas, I had sexual congress with that woman who's currently hanging on your arm." Cuntlips didn't know if these words were true or not – there'd been so many women despite his mild case of craniodiaphyseal dysplasia – but it felt good saying them.

Dropping the newspaper in the dust, Cuntlips headed toward the horizon, toward the demon.

His eyes caked closed, his mouth dry as if his tongue were wearing a sweater, Rusty Slump awoke, naked, on the edge of the Rutherford B. Hayes Memorial Swimming Hole with a violent drug hangover. Wiping the crud from his eyes, he studied his blurry environs. It took a few moments before the events of the previous evening came rushing back, tackled him. Dearly Departed, those dope tits, and unfortunately, once again, passing out.

Then he remembered the drug trip itself. All those sepia-toned bathers, just as if he'd snorted some Purple Hayes. And that crazy toad, Mr. Frog. The amphibian had tried to tell him something important. Something important about Colorado but, for the life of him, Rusty couldn't recall what.

As his head felt like uncooked hamburger, he decided to think about that at a later date.

Climbing to his feet without grace, Rusty tried to concoct a believable a story to tell his father which would explain why he'd been out all night. Nothing came to mind. The idea of getting lost in a town the size of Fremont was preposterous, and he doubted whether the Judge would swallow a story that he'd fallen into a wormhole.

He was flocked and he knew it.

On instinct Rusty sniffed his strewn clothes to gauge their wearableness, as if he had an option. His Satan's Butt Buddies

T-shirt reeked of Dearly. He nearly passed out again.

What could that perfect beauty, that angel, think of him now that he'd passed out twice during foreplay? Surely she despised him.

After donning his clothes, he scaled the fence and took off for Rutherford B. Hayes Memorial High, as he feared being tardy and getting into more trouble than he was already in.

During his jog to school, he thought over the Dearly issue. She wasn't the only one who deserved to be angry about the previous evening. She'd left him by the side of the pool, naked and shivering. As if he were a piece of garbage. A nobody. He could get the same treatment from CoCo, had many times, and at least had received a boisterous but toothy blowjob in the bargain.

By the time he reached the doors of Rutherford B. Hayes Memorial High, Rusty had decided that he and Dearly were over.

Even if they hadn't really begun.

She had to get out of this town. Fremont was killing her, suffocating her with pillows stuffed with ennui. She feared if she didn't relocate soon, she'd simply cease breathing.

Daniella Locke had been trapped in this small Ohio town for nearly a decade, teaching gym at Rutherford B. Hayes Memorial High School. The kids sucked, the parents sucked, the other teachers sucked. Not to mention the indubitable dearth of hot lesbian sex to be found. In fact, the only other lesbian she'd come across in Fremont, Chrissy Rumpza, was no longer an option.

The couple had met while pumping gas into their respective Subaru Outbacks the previous summer. After a few furtive glances and sly smiles, they found themselves back at Daniella's place, knee deep in hot lesbian sex. For a few months, things were perfect. The gym teacher felt she'd found the love of her life, a person who could make Fremont bearable, a woman she wanted to come home to every night for the rest of her life.

Apparently, Rumpza didn't feel the same way. One night, after some stellar muff-noshing, Daniella proposed that they head over to the Rutherford B. Hayes Memorial Pizza Hut. Rumpza balked as they'd never been seen in public as a couple before. They'd spent their relationship staying in, ordering Chinese, watching HBO, and scissoring the flock out of each other. A fight ensued and Rumpza stormed out into the night, vowing to never return.

Daniella's life fell apart.

Unable to break her teaching contract, she'd had to wait out the remainder of the school year, dreaming of leaving this crap festival of a town and heading far, far away. Maybe Toledo, where, rumor had it, hot lesbian sex was like tainted water, it came out of the tap.

Now, as the school year drew to a close, it was the time to make this dream a reality.

As she sat at her desk deep in the bowels of the school, Daniella penned a nasty letter of resignation. She knew this was the perfect time to get the flock out of Dodge.

If she'd harbored any doubts about this, what she'd overheard in the teacher's lounge that morning had cemented her desire to clear out.

Usually Daniella, for her mental health, eschewed the teacher's lounge like a plague with bad coffee. She couldn't stomach all the squawking about which kids were having sexual congress with each other and which students had failed their Introduction to Rutherford B. Hayes' Beard Class. But that morning, as she was sneaking a much-needed Danish, she stumbled upon a different stripe of squawking. This bitchfest was desperate and heated and had nothing to do with sexual congress or beards. Apparently, the previous night, their former principal, the pisser Douglas Kennedy, had been brutally slain in the Rutherford B. Hayes Memorial Prison. The details were still a little sketchy but there were many rumors flying. Mrs. Carbureator, the Fashions of Rutherford B. Hayes teacher, had heard from a reliable source that Kennedy and some prison guard had not been killed by a rabid animal, as the Fremont Police Society were maintaining, but, instead, were the victims of a Satanic cult. The Favored Cheeses of Rutherford B. Hayes teacher, Mrs. Cumquat, said she'd overheard basically the same thing, that there was something extraordinarily terrible out there on the streets of Fremont, Ohio, something evil.

Many times Daniella had complained that nothing ever happened in their sleepy little berg, but this was not the kind of excitement she was hoping for. She was thinking about a miniature golf course opening or, perhaps, a new bowling alley. Not random disembowelment.

Signing her name at the bottom of her letter of resignation, the gym teacher fired up the antediluvian computer that rested on her desk. Going to Google, she began her job search in earnest. Typing in "female gym teacher" and "job openings" and "anywhere but Fremont," into the search engine, she was about to hit ENTER when she hesitated. After pausing for a moment, she added "hot lesbian sex" and "miniature golf" just to narrow her search and add a little excitement.

Again her finger hovered above the ENTER button but she stopped when she felt something move behind her. Petrified that she was about to be busted entering lesbian stuff on a school-owned computer by Rosalind Moorhead, the new, non-pissing, principal, Daniella turned while trying to formulate a plausible lie.

She needn't have bothered, as the person standing behind her was definitely not the elderly, medicinally-scented Mrs. Moorhead. This was a young woman, a student Daniella had never laid eyes on before.

Though she wished she had.

This young thing was the walking definition of hot. She had a great rack and fiery red hair. The Lynyrd Skynyrd T-shirt was a bit of a turn-off, but beggars in the world of hot lesbian sex couldn't be choosers.

Licking her lips, Daniella asked this young woman if there was anything she could help her with.

Without answering, the young woman smiled and closed the door behind her.

"Are you signing up for my class?"

The young woman giggled.

"Are you interested in joining the softball team?"

Though she could feel a flush spreading on the underside of her skin, Daniella knew that she had to proceed with caution. After the Connie Pendleton incident, when she'd blatantly come on to a student, she was certain she was going to be shit-canned. Then, fortunately, the Pendleton girl had bugged out of town.

If anything was going to happen with this hot young thing, Daniella would let it unfold but she wasn't going to force it.

Shaking her head, allowing her luscious locks to flip and furl, the young woman said, "I don't care to sign up for class or softball, but I would like to sign up for some hot lesbian sex."

Apparently, this was going to unfold the way Daniella hoped.

She tried not to show it, but Daniella was pleasantly shocked. Things like this never happened in the sexual cesspool that was Fremont, Ohio.

The hot young woman made her way toward the desk. Though the office was small, she took her time.

Watching this journey, Daniella found her voice and a modicum of morality. "This... this is probably a bad idea."

"It's the only idea," the hot young woman said through a thick smile.

When she arrived at Daniella's desk, the new student laid one tender hand on the teacher's shoulder, the other on her face. Daniella could hear her heart pound and she wanted to dance to its rhythm.

Leaning forward, the hot young woman's heinous Lynyrd Skynyrd T-shirt blossomed open, offering Daniella an unobstructed view of her bulbous breasts. The stunned gym teacher didn't even try to hide the fact she was gaping, taking it all in, just as one would the Sistine Chapel.

Daniella smiled as saliva gathered in the corners of her mouth.

Puckering her luscious lips, the hot young woman drew closer for a kiss. "I could just eat you up right now."

"And I'd let you."

Daniella closed her eyes and waited. Flock Chrissy Rumpza, flock Principal Moorhead, flock miniature golf, she'd found heaven and she was going to reside there for the rest of her life.

Unfortunately for the gym teacher, the rest of her life was measured in seconds.

The new student went past her lips and went straight for the throat.

And it wasn't a kiss so much as a rendering of flesh.

Daniella, still stunned, felt blood pouring down her front. Regardless of her love of menstrual coupling, this was not the type of bloody sex she found exciting. In fact, this wasn't sex at all, but death, which is very similar but very different.

With the surprisingly strong hot young woman holding her down, Daniella couldn't move, couldn't fight. And, seeing as her vocal cords had been ripped out, she couldn't even scream.

Daniella decided to sit still and just let this happen.

Her mouth a crimson mess, the hot young woman, who'd really lost her appeal, reared back, roared. Daniella smelled rotted meat and was displeased to discover it was her own flesh.

Dislocating her jaw, the girl opened her mouth impossibly wide. She put her lips atop the gym teacher's head and began to ingest.

The last depressing thought in Daniella Locke's depressing life was: *oh great, not only am I going to die, I'm going to die in flocking*

Fremont, Ohio.

It hit him in the middle of his the Geometry Of Rutherford B. Hayes Class.

While Mr. Braindeed stood at the front of the class, blathering about cubits, Rusty sat in the back, his feet up, staring out the window, letting his mind wander. Though it embarrassed him to recall the previous night's botched sexual congress, he couldn't stop thinking about that damned frog. There was something about that hallucination that pecked at the fringes of his mind.

Then he remembered something. A conversation he'd had with an elderly stoner during his week-long tenure as a drug dealer. The druggie told him a rather lengthy and rather boring story about hiking the Western United States in search of the elusive Colorado River Toad, an amphibian coated with a powerful hallucinogen.

"There's no greater high," related the elderly stoner, "than licking a Colorado River Toad."

Since Rusty, at the time, was sitting atop the world's largest (and only) supply of Purple Hayes and had no desire to wander the desert looking to tongue some stupid frog, he wasn't really listening to the tale and quickly forgot it.

But now it came screaming back from the underbelly of his mind.

The frog in his hallucination had referred to himself as a Colorado River Toad, and he'd compared himself to Dearly Departed's tits.

Dearly Departed's tits.

Every time Rusty had licked them, he'd been carried off to another land. An old-timey, sepia-toned, magical land, which was the exact same thing that happened when he'd ingested Purple Hayes.

"Sweet Baby G," exclaimed Rusty, "her tits really are dope!"

Only when he noticed the other students were staring at him did Rusty realized he'd spoken out loud. Mr. Braindeed folded his chicken arms across his pigeon chest and glared at the young man.

But Rusty didn't care, for he'd discovered a way to become the king of the vast and dangerous criminal underworld of Fremont, Ohio.

On feet of sunshine, Rusty ran from the classroom, disregarding Mr. Braindeed's entreaties to stop, to stay. Shiny dollar signs floating before his eyes, blinding him, making it hard for him to hear.

She felt sick.

There was certainly no good reason to have swallowed the lusty gym teacher whole; the demon was simply showing off.

She'd even devoured the woman's shoes. Those weren't going to be easy to pass.

Staggering through the streets of Fremont, holding her stomach, Dearly Departed had to make frequent stops to lean against something and consider hurling.

While she was leaning against a particularly rusty STOP sign, swearing off eating any more gym teachers in the future, the Other Girl made an appearance. Clomping into her brain.

Why did you kill Daniella Locke? the Other Girl demanded.

"Because it is what you wanted."

It most certainly was not.

"Oh, you poor puny humans, you don't even know what you desire. That's the reason you live lives of quiet desperation."

Well, yes, I suppose she was rather forward the last time we spoke, but I don't think people should be eaten for such behavior.

"Sure they should. People should die for lots of reasons and, thanks to me, they will."

The Other Girl drew in a sharp breath but didn't have time to continue her argument, for she cowered when she heard a loud sound coming from behind Dearly. Boots on pavement. Turning, Dearly saw a human, a cop to be precise, running toward her.

They were onto her, the living, and they'd finally followed her trail of dead to its logical conclusion.

She arched her back, bared her fangs, preparing for a battle but she stopped, relaxed, when she recognized the human running toward her.

It was that idiot Pendleton, the Other Girl's father, and he was beaming.

When he arrived, sweaty and sincere, he said, "I've been looking for you all day. Say, you don't look so hot."

"Something disagreed with me so I ate it."

"You mean you ate something and it disagreed with you."

"Yeah, something like that."

Putting his arm around her, "Let me take you home."

"So you can throw me out again?"

The breather pulled her close. "Listen, Dearly, that was a mistake, a big mistake, on my part. I was wrong and it will never happen again. This is my promise, this is my olive branch, this is my rainbow stretching across receding waters."

Dearly had no clue what this clown was babbling about but she really needed to lay down so she let him guide her to his patrol car, which was parked down the street.

After the cavalcade of bloody bodies, Officer Rumpza was bored by the simple, old-fashioned missing person report she was investigating. Gazing out the window and not taking notes while the principal of the high school droned on. That is until Mrs. Moorhead uttered the name of said missing person.

"Daniella Locke."

Dropping her pen, Rumpza felt as if she'd been socked in the solar plexus. "Did you say Daniella Locke, as in Daniella Locke the female gym teacher?"

"Yes, the carpet-muncher. She was there one moment, and the next… poof!" explained Mrs. Moorhead.

Staring across the elderly woman's desk, the cop studied the principal of Rutherford B. Hayes Memorial High School. The woman appeared to be about a hundred years old with wrinkled skin, Glaucoma-y eyes, and teeth that looked as if they'd been hammered into place by Helen Keller. Also, she smelled like a Walgreens farted.

Silently, Rumpza hoped her ex-girlfriend's disappearance was simply Daniella being lured away by the bright lights of Toledo, where, it was rumored, hot lesbian sex flowed like lava. During their time together Daniella had talked about doing such a thing, many times. Begged Rumpza to go with her. That was one of the reasons they'd broken up. Daniella was always pushing, always wanted to take their relationship to the next level. She talked about living together, adopting a baby, getting matching tattoos. It was all too much for Rumpza.

Silence owned the principal's office. Rumpza, her mind rampant with thought, could think of nothing to say. The old woman studied her with calculating eyes.

"Are you alright, Officer Rumpza?"

"Oh, yeah, sure. So, do you have any thoughts about what might have happened to Daniella?"

With pursed lips, Moorhead said, "None, save that Ms. Locke disappeared just like that Pendleton girl."

Another punch in Rumpza's gut. Though she felt like bawling, she knew she'd have to wait until she returned to the safety of her bedroom, wiping her tears away with Connie's much-sniffed panties.

Gathering her pen and her senses, the cop asked, "Has Ms. Locke been acting strange lately?"

The elderly principal thought for a moment. Her eyes sparked. "She was a dyke, does that count?"

Rumpza narrowed her eyes at Moorhead. "No, that doesn't count."

"Then no. Of course, Ms. Locke didn't say much to anyone about anything. She was kind of a loner, kept her distance from everyone. Everyone, that is, except pussy."

After pretending to scribble down the old woman's idiotic ramblings, Rumpza, headache flourishing, stood and headed down to Daniella's office to investigate, asking directions though she knew the way.

As she descended the staircase that led to the school's basement, Rumpza had wild thoughts that Daniella's office would be awash with blood, that there would be chunks of flesh everywhere.

But that, thankfully, was not the case.

Daniella's office was sparse and clean and smelled faintly of female sweat. Rumpza searched but found nothing out of place. Relieved, she sat at Daniella's desk, trying to escape the memory of the last time she'd been in this office, after a spirited pep rally. She and Daniella had engaged in hot lesbian sex on the desk. Rumpza had a stapler imprint on her ass for weeks.

When she leaned back in the chair, the cop noted that she could see straight into the girls' shower.

Had Daniella ever watched Connie lather up her small, perky breasts?

To chase that thought away, Rumpza shook her head. But something dark, something dangerous lingered: the last two women Rumpza had had sexual congress with were now both missing.

Lost in thought, Rumpza nearly didn't notice the three tiny dots on the linoleum floor.

Drops of blood.

One, two, three.

Daniella wasn't missing, Rumpza knew in her burning heart. She was gone.

"She has dope tits."

Rusty could tell CoCo did not share his enthusiasm for Dearly's dreamy funbags. She sat on the treehouse's fainting couch, arms crossed and a scowl cracking the breadth of her face.

"What in the hell are you talking about?" she asked.

"Okay, alright, let me start from the beginning. When you lick her boobs – which must have some kind of naturally occurring hallucinogen on them, like the well-known Colorado River Toad – you get high. Really high. Like a Purple Hayes kind of high."

"That's not the beginning."

"Excuse me, Sugar Glabella?"

"You said you were starting from the beginning, but that's not the beginning. For me, your girlfriend, the supposed love of your flocking life, the real beginning, the real question is HOW IN THE DO YOU EVEN KNOW WHAT HAPPENS WHEN YOU LICK HER FLOCKING TITTIES?"

The words shook the treehouse, his soul.

Her face aflame, CoCo stood and marched toward him like Nazi Germany.

This interaction was definitely not going as well as Rusty had hoped. In his mind, he imagined CoCo jumping to her feet, hugging him, kissing him, maybe giving him a blowjob that was boisterous but not so toothy, for having once again discovered a way to become the king of the vast and dangerous criminal underworld of Fremont, Ohio.

Before CoCo could carry out the evil that she was about to inflict, Rusty held up his hands in defense and screamed, "I overheard two guys putting up the decorations for Hayes Dayes talking about Dearly's knockers!"

As soon as the lie was out of his mouth, Rusty could taste how ridiculous it was.

Though she stopped advancing, CoCo still breathed like an asthmatic bull. Arms akimbo, she asked, "What two guys?"

"I don't know their names. In fact, I've never even seen them before. They must be new to town. They kind of looked like Bulgarians."

"And you're going to trust these two unknown Bulgarians about the magical properties of a woman's breasts?"

"Uh, well, they seemed super earnest when they talked about getting high off this girl's tits."

This seemed to placate CoCo. "Okay. So what? Her tits are magic. Maybe you haven't noticed lately, but mine aren't so bad themselves."

"Yes, yes, your tits are great, Sugar Trachea. But CoCo, I'm talking about monetizing Dearly's tits."

She furrowed her brow. "And how are you going to do that?"

Rusty had it all worked out, he'd been thinking about it all afternoon. "Easy. We go into business with her. We put the word out on the streets that for a hundred bucks, anyone can lick her breasts and be sent to a magical land."

Her scowl diminished as the machinery behind her face began to crank. "That's a flocking awesome idea."

"I know, right?"

"But it'll never work, not the way you have it sketched out."

Insulted, Rusty asked what was wrong with his plan in the voice of a wronged eight year old.

CoCo snorted. "Just that you don't understand human nature. I don't care how much of a slut this girl is – and she must be a whopping slut if she got it on with two Bulgarians – she's not going to allow every Tom, Dick, and Rutherford to lick her titties. And even if she did, how quickly would she realize that she didn't need the two of us around, hogging half the profits without doing any of the breast work? After a week, she'd set up shop herself. No, we have to tranquilize her, force her into doing this."

"What? Tranquilize? What are you talking about?"

"My father was an awesome zookeeper, remember? I still have his tranquilizer gun and tons of Azaperone, a drug strong enough to bring down an elephant. I say we shoot Dearly Departed full of the stuff and kidnap her. Then we strap her to a bed and let the games begin."

"No, no, no, CoCo. That wasn't at all what I was picturing."

"Everything you picture is dumb."

Rusty stood a little taller, the top of his head nearly reached CoCo's big mouth. "I am not going to help you kidnap Dearly."

Rushing forward, CoCo pressed her massive body into her boyfriend's scrawny one. Though he could feel her tits crowding him like a pair of pushy concert goers, there was nothing sexual about this move. It was a threat. Rusty's bones squirmed beneath his skin.

"Listen to me," she hissed. "I don't want you going soft on me. Keep in mind that you stole the body of a dead president and sawed off his dick off for me, right?"

"This is, this is different. Dearly is alive."

"Uh-oh. Do I hear a flocking lilt in your voice? It sounds as if my boyfriend has a crush on another girl, a girl with magical titties. Oh boy, that would certainly make me unhappy."

"No, no, no, no, it's nothing like that, Sugar Axilla. It's just, well, I don't know, kidnapping seems so serious."

"You're damn right it's serious. There's no way to climb the ladder of the vast and dangerous criminal underworld of Fremont, Ohio without stepping on a few toes or, in this case, titties."

With that she turned and stomped out of the luxury treehouse. He watched his supposed girlfriend's ass swish and sway but felt nothing but loathing for her.

Over her shoulder, "And if I hear of any hanky-panky between you and this Dearly bitch, I'll remove your balls and use them as giant bookends. And I don't even like to read."

Perhaps it was because of his long hair or the Satan's Butt Buddies T-shirt he sported - which featured the death metal band's notorious logo: a cartoon of an upside-down crucifix being shoved into a man's hairy ass - or the fact his face was mildly deformed, but Cuntlips McGoo and his outstretched thumb couldn't convince a solitary passing motorist to stop and give him a lift.

Though he was basically on a mission from God, Cuntlips was beginning to regret quitting the band and taking off in a huff. Certainly, he knew he had to get to Fremont and stop the demon who'd ripped apart Reverend Rump, but it would have been prudent to grab his wallet, his cell phone, and maybe a change of clothes.

Now he found himself just wandering north along a barren stretch of I-35 with his thumb stuck out, flat broke and a journey of over a thousand miles before him.

Sighing, he continued walking though night descended all around him. The stars came out of their hiding places. He had to get a ride and get one soon or the town of Fremont, Ohio, would be nothing but a ruin.

And the rest of the world would soon follow suit.

Headlights crested the hill, slowed.

On the drive home, Dearly Departed had fallen asleep in the passenger seat of Police Chief Pendleton's patrol car. Disobeying the rules of the road, he watched her. Intently. Hers was not an easy sleep, Dearly tossed and turned, the poor girl.

As he carried Dearly into his house, the cop felt the sting

of tears in his eyes. With no hesitation, Pendleton carried the slumbering teen up to Connie's bedroom.

Since his daughter had disappeared, the cop hadn't set foot in her room. He didn't have the heart to touch any of her stuff. But without a thought, he carried Dearly across the threshold. It was as if she belonged there.

As gingerly as he could – his long wool coat made bending over something of a chore – he laid the girl down upon Connie's bed. Stepping back, he studied her reposed form. She was just like an angel, that skin, that smile.

After killing Connie's mother and burying her in the basement, Pendleton had a series of nightmares featuring the garden-variety harlot clawing her way out of the grave and coming after him, all dead and vengeful. This made it somewhat difficult to sleep. Many nights, to calm himself, Pendleton had station himself in Connie's doorway and watched her slumber. Her tiny chest going up and down.

For a few moments, Pendleton did the same thing with Dearly. Watched her closely. But he didn't see her chest, which was the opposite of tiny, going up or down. It appeared as if the young woman wasn't breathing at all.

That's ridiculous, the cop thought, you just need some rest.

Rubbing his eyes, Pendleton figured it had been over forty hours since he'd slept. Suddenly, he was exhausted.

Retreating to his own bedroom, he fell asleep without even bothering to remove his uniform.

He never heard his cell phone ringing off the hook, even though cell phones don't have hooks.

"So… what's wrong with your face?"

Most people didn't ask. They pointed, gasped, shied away. But this woman, this housewife who'd picked him when he was about to throw in the hitchhiking towel, was different. She was direct, honest.

Cuntlips McGoo said, "I have a mild case of craniodiaphyseal dysplasia."

The housewife glared at him. "What the hell is that?"

"It's a disease of the bones that turns my face into a jumbled mess."

"Okay. And I take it you're on the run from something?"

"What makes you say that?"

"Cause we're all on the run from something." As if to emphasize her point, she glanced at the rearview mirror. "Say, I don't even know your name."

"It's Cuntlips. Cuntlips McGoo."

"That's a stupid name."

"I would have to agree with you there, ma'am."

"What kind of parents did you have? Stoners? Hippies? Cactus-fuckers?"

Cuntlips looked out the passenger window. "They didn't really get a chance to be parents. They died in a car crash when I was six weeks old."

The ex-rocker told her about growing up in the orphanage. He also told her the story of how he got his ludicrous name. It was just one of the many ridiculous things foisted upon him when he joined Satan's Butt Buddies. It had been Sweaty Nips McGoo, the lead singer, who'd had the idea that all members of the band would share a last name - just like the Ramones - and for their first names, they should have something sexually suggestive. Although he'd been repulsed by the idea – as he had been raised by a strict Buddhist monk ninja warrior assassin – Vince Kramer (Cuntlips McGoo's real name) didn't voice any opposition to the absurd conceit.

"Just call me Vince."

The former rocker went back to staring through the windshield of the station wagon. Through a thin patina of bug guts, the former rocker watched the horizon draw nearer, yet never arrive.

The housewife broke the silence. "I got a niece who likes Satan's Butt Buddies, but she also has an ear ring in her lady bits, so I don't got a ton of respect for her life choices."

"Well, don't fret, I quit being their drummer."

"Excellent career move, Vince. So I guess you're between gigs, as they say."

"Not exactly. I have a job."

"Which is?"

Cuntlips didn't wish to jeopardize their nascent relationship. Not only did he like the housewife, he didn't feel like getting tossed back onto the side of the road. So he didn't fill her in on the fact that he was traveling to kill a demon that had come to end the earth.

Instead, he said, "It's kind of complicated. Why don't you tell me a little bit about yourself?"

Never again, Dearly vowed as she threw up the gym teacher, never again would she devour a human. Maybe a hand now and again, or, if they really deserved it, a head, but, as her five minutes spent prostrate before the toilet had taught her, gluttony was truly one of the deadly sins.

Though it turned her stomach to do so, she checked the contents of the bowl. Chunks of Daniella Locke's face, tattered pieces of sweat pants, and, yes, that pair of running shoes.

Those babies had certainly stung coming back up.

Although her throat burned, Dearly had to admit she felt better. Ready to get back to her mission of ending mankind.

She spat and flushed.

The beautiful world of modern plumbing carried away a majority of the offal but those bothersome shoes and some of the larger chunks of face refused to go down, even after repeated attempts.

Dearly considered simply reaching in and removing the detritus but, every time her hand neared the bile-covered offerings, it shook. Sure, she could rip a human to shreds with glee, but touching something that had been in the toilet, no thanks.

Besides, what did it matter if some stupid breather stumbled upon pieces of the gym teacher? So far the idiotic police of this berg hadn't been able to trace the deaths of the preacher or the principal or the prison guard back to her. To boot, she had the Police Chief in the palm of her hand. This trip to earth, the demon had been smarter, more careful. No public slayings. No killing fifty people in a single rampage. This time she was going to succeed, had to succeed.

With a smile brimming, she quit the Pendleton bathroom. In the hallway, she heard snoring coming from behind one of the doors. She knew it was the cop. It would be so easy to walk in and kill him as he slept. But she was not going to as she couldn't stand the Other Girl's shrieks whenever she thought of such a thing.

Now she was sure this cop had been the Other Girl's father. Her certainty came from the fact that when she woke up in a bedroom in the Pendleton home, she knew instantly where she was. This was the bedroom of the Other Girl and it disgusted her. Every surface was covered by a Bible or a Bible quote or a framed photo of the Sweet Baby G.

She had hoped for better from a carpet-muncher.

Dearly had to get out into the world of puny humans to find someone with whom to mate. Though it pained her in her chest to think this, she'd decided the cute breather, Rusty, was too much trouble. All that pre-sexual congress fainting was a deal breaker. She needed a real man to impregnate her with the beast that would come and lay waste to everything mankind held dear.

As another wave of nausea washed over her, she decided the impregnating could wait until morning. She peeled off her clothing, rubbed her marvelous breasts for a moment, and climbed back into bed. Asleep in seconds.

"Dear brother, what strange ill has befallen you?" Rhombus Queerfolk asked as he lay a soothing hand upon the damp brow of his twin. Executor's flesh burned; Rhombus knew not whether to call a doctor or the fire department.

Executor was stretched out on one of the twin beds in the bedroom they shared in their small but tidy apartment, which was above the Rutherford B. Hayes Memorial Lawn and Garden Center. Everything smelled faintly of fertilizer.

With obvious strain, Executor smiled. It barely cracked the surface. "I am fine, brother, just a tad under the weather. But I fear I cannot go with you this eve and snuff out that little bastard Rusty Slump."

"I would suggest not. Nay, thee must remain in bed, rest, and await our next assigned ass kicking."

If the Queerfolks' parents, who'd been gunned down in a mugging gone awry many years before, could see their progeny at that moment, they would have been both greatly pleased and terribly disconcerted. Pleased with how caring and kind the brothers were toward one another and the fact that they employed overly correct English, just as they had been taught. Their disconcertedness would have stemmed from the twins' swearing and their chosen profession, working as muscle for the king of the vast and dangerous criminal underworld of Fremont, Ohio.

The Queerfolk twins' mother had been a professor of Algebra at Rutherford B. Hayes Memorial Community College, and their father had been a respected lawyer. When the boys were young, the elder Queerfolks wished for Executor to grow up to take over the reins of the law practice and for Rhombus to follow in his mother's footsteps. For the first fourteen years of the boys' lives, this plan had worked out perfectly – Rhombus was a whiz with a calculator and Executor could argue the most minute point – but then their parents were killed and the boys were placed in an orphanage that would have made Dickens crap his trousers. There, amongst the vile detritus of Fremont's detritus-filled society, the Queerfolk twins found they had many adversaries who cared little for fancy language, calculators, or arguments that didn't involve weaponry. The boys were often mocked or beaten when they tried reasoning with these ruffians in their antiquated fashion. For many years the twins lived in fear but, as they grew bigger and stronger, they found that, as soon as they shut their mouths and raised their fists, they garnered more respect. When they left the Rutherford B. Hayes Memorial Home For Children No One In Their Right Mind Would Want, their wicked rep proceeded them and they found work at the edges of the vast and dangerous criminal underworld of Fremont, Ohio, using their brawn to kick offending teeth down offending throats. At a fortuitous Kenny Loggins concert, they met Loco Lenny Labovitz who, after watching them successfully shake down a taffy vendor, hired them on the spot. Now fully realized goons, their parents would haven't have been able to pick them out of a line-up. Nothing was left of the old Queerfolk nature except for their impeccable manners and the frivolous fashion in which they spoke. Though this only happened at home. When amongst their fellow criminal element, they tended to grunt and shrug.

"Thank you, my dear Rhombus, and take great joy in turning Rusty Slump into humanburger." Again Executor attempted to smile, but it faded quickly.

Ruffling his brother's hair and returning the smile, Rhombus hid his deep concerns. Executor's skin had become waxen, his brow saturated with sweat, his lungs unsteady in their breathing. Rhombus feared that there was something seriously wrong with his brother, but Executor forbade all talk of hospitals and doctors.

"I'll bring you back a malted to ease your misery," promised Rhombus as he checked his Glock and headed for the bedroom door.

"That would be heaven," wheezed Executor, though, as Rhombus was already out the door, he wasn't sure his brother had heard him.

Parking before Police Chief Pendleton's home, Officer Rumpza climbed from her car. The Pendleton house was quiet, but as his patrol car was parked in the driveway, she knew her boss was home.

Rumpza tried his cell phone again. Though she could hear the phone ringing inside the darkened house, there was no answer.

A stab of fear cut into her. What if the superhuman serial killer had struck again, only this time his target was Police Chief Pendleton?

Drawing her Savage 1861 Navy revolver, Rumpza rushed the house. Flew up the porch steps and opened the door with a swift kick.

Inside, it was quiet, too quiet. The silence of the dead, even though it was only eight o'clock at night. The hairs on the back of Rumpza's neck stood up and demanded to be counted.

She didn't believe in God or saints or any of the other religious bullarkey collared men had shoved down her throat as a child. But standing in Pendleton's front room, she could sense something evil in this house. Felt it brush up against her, play with her hair, whisper her name.

Rumpza considered calling for back-up, but who would she call? Due to budget cuts, there were only three officers working for the Fremont Police Society: herself, the idiot Killion, and Police Chief Pendleton, who was, she feared, upstairs laying in a puddle of his own viscera.

Though she hated to admit it, Officer Rumpza missed Sergeant Snoopers, even with his haughty attitude.

This investigation, she knew, was all up to her.

It was not lost upon Rumpza that she was standing in the room where she'd failed Connie, allowing her to be taken from right beneath her naked nose. But she couldn't think of that right now. She had to stay focused. She had to find Pendleton, even if he were already lying in a pool of his own viscera.

Ready to light up the darkness with her Savage 1861 Navy revolver, the cop searched the first floor of the house. Front room, dining room, kitchen, den. Finding nothing out of the ordinary – no entrails strewn, no walls awash with blood – except way too many pictures of Sweet Baby G and his ilk.

She headed for the second floor.

Even though she treaded lightly, every step creaked. She swore under her breath, imagining the superhuman killer waiting for her in the shadows.

Bracing herself for lakes of blood and a jumble of body parts, Rumpza arrived on the second floor.

But no death scene awaited her, no screams rang out, no killer emerged from the darkness ready to tear her limb from shaking limb. Nothing.

Studying her environs, Rumpza found herself in a darkened hallway. There were three doors, all of them closed. She tiptoed to the first door, certain Death was waiting behind it, scythe sharpened.

As she had been trained to do, the cop threw open the door and leveled her weapon. But there was no need.

It was just an empty bathroom. Turning on the light, she did a cursory check of the vacant room, shook her head, and continued to the next closed door.

Death wasn't waiting for her in that room either, but a surprise was. Turning on the light, she saw that she was standing in the doorway of what was obviously Connie's bedroom, as it was decorated in Early American God.

But the most amazing thing was Connie herself was there! Back from the dead. Splayed across the bed, naked and asleep, snoring lightly as she had done that one golden night in Rumpza's arms.

But no, wait. This girl wasn't Connie. The hair was all wrong, and the face, and most definitely the boobs, which towered. Though there was something indefinable, something very Connie about this slumbering girl.

Rumpza felt a stirring in her heart, her stomach, her naughty bits. She wanted to touch this girl. Touch her deep, touch her soft, touch her often.

Just as she was about to enter the bedroom for some hot lesbian sex, the cop noticed something that gave her libido pause. The brassy red hair on the girl's head was exactly the same shade as the hair she'd discovered at the prison death scene.

Rumpza stopped, breathing and movement.

A voice boomed behind her, almost knocking her over. "Officer Rumpza, what are you doing here?"

She jumped, turned. Police Chief Pendleton was standing at the end of the hall, before the third door, which was now open. Clad in full military regalia, rubbing sleep from his eyes.

"I've… I've been calling and calling you but you, you never answered. I got worried, with a taint-twirling serial killer on the loose and all."

He held up his hands as if he were trying to stop the world from turning. "Now let's not go throwing around the S.K. label. Not on the eve of Hayes Dayes. Remember my motto: if there's no Hayes Dayes, there's no Fremont. And without Fremont, Officer Rumpza, would either you or I really exist?"

"But-."

"And I apologize that I didn't answer my phone. I've been in a deep sleep."

"So, who's this young woman..." The cop motioned toward the bed, but, to her surprise, she found the room was empty. No girl, just a pile of clothing in the middle of the floor.

Her mouth agape, Rumpza rushed to the bed. Felt the sheets. No heat. Unbelievable. She must have imagined the young woman. Some kind of mental breakdown, her mind's lame attempt at dealing with Connie's disappearance.

"I must..." She looked back at her boss, who now stood at the threshold of Connie's bedroom. "I must have been seeing things, some real ball-disorienting stuff."

"No, no, Officer Rumpza, there was a young woman here. At least, there was when I went to bed."

Out of the corner of her eye, Rumpza noticed the open window, the cold air rushing in. "She must have fled. Who was she? Is she a... love interest of yours?"

"Oh goodness no, she's but a child. Not much older than... not much older than Connie. She was afraid, alone. I let her sleep here."

That certainly didn't sound like the Police Chief Pendleton Rumpza knew but lately everything about Fremont had been a little screwy.

Crossing to the open window, Pendleton looked out, shook his head. "That's crazy. It's a twenty foot drop to the ground. And she didn't take her garments."

Officer Rumpza wasn't listening to her boss' bafflement. She was thinking dark and dismal thoughts which made her head hurt.

That flaming red hair.

No. No way. Not that innocent, beautiful girl who'd been sleeping, snoring softly. So much like Connie, except for those massive boobs. It couldn't be.

But why had she fled? And what was the hurry? Rumpza had only turned away for a moment and she was gone. So quickly, so quietly.

Rumpza felt her stomach lurch. The cop had always prided herself on being able to devour a bagel while surveying the most hideous car crashes or suicides or jaywalkers who'd been smashed pulpy by a freight truck. But there was something so searing about picturing that lovely creature ripping another human being to shreds that made the cop stumble out of the room and dash into the bathroom.

If she thought she was going to vomit before, what she found floating in the toilet bowl sealed the deal.

Growing up in an insignificant berg like Fremont, Rusty was well acquainted with driving around pointlessly for hours on end. Or, as the local teens referred to it, scooping the loop. Starting at the garbage-strewn McDonald's parking lot, rolling down the main boulevard that perforated the municipality, turning around at the town square, and returning to the garbage-strewn parking lot of McDonald's. Over and over and over again. It was a ritual Fremont kids performed every Friday and Saturday night to alleviate boredom, but it actually made them more bored. On the plus side, it did ready them for adult life, which is mind-numbingly tedious.

But that night, Rusty's scooping of said loop served a purpose.

He was searching for Dearly Departed for two opposing reasons, which caused him great conflict.

On one hand, he wanted to see her, needed to see her. Even though she'd deserted him at the pool, naked and shivering, and he'd vowed to have nothing to do with the lusty stranger ever again, he felt a comfortable pain in his chest whenever he thought of her, which was continuously.

In addition to his own desires, he was also doing CoCo's bidding.

Although her plan of kidnapping Dearly made his everything hurt, she'd bullied him into agreeing with her scheme. Spending an hour that afternoon berating him and once again rolling out her threat of turning him over to the police. Reminding him that the wise Machiavelli had said, "Whoever desires constant success much change his conduct with the times."

Though Rusty wasn't quite certain he fully understood this quote, he had to agree. Picturing himself behind the wheel of Loco Lenny Labovitz's mobile drug emporium brought a smile to the young demi-thug's face.

Though thinking of the things CoCo might do to Dearly made said smile come crashing down.

The mere thought of Dearly in danger turned his stomach a shade of sour he'd never experienced. But if he didn't return with Dearly in tow, CoCo would surely hurt him, hurt him good.

Driving the streets of Fremont in his safety-conscious Volvo, Rusty needed to find Dearly, but he didn't want to find her.

Passing by the Rutherford B. Hayes Memorial Courthouse parking lot, which was crowded with half-built floats the good people of Fremont would set ablaze during Hayes Dayes, the young man wished for lightning to crawl down from the heavens and fry him so that he didn't have to find Dearly or not find her.

On his fifth loop, he spied the beautiful girl walking down the street near the Rutherford B. Hayes Memorial Smelting Plant.

Fortunately, he'd found her. Unfortunately, he'd found her.

But tipping the scales toward the fortunate side of the equation was the fact Dearly was completely naked, those dope tits out and proud.

Imagining CoCo causing harm to those perfect gazongas made his heart sink. Though his erection stayed right where it was.

He considered driving past, driving away, and telling CoCo that, as with most of his endeavors, he'd failed miserably. Accept the beating, accept the blood.

But the young man couldn't do it.

With those tits singing a siren song he couldn't mute, Rusty swerved, applied the brakes, and came to a stop, blocking Dearly's path.

When he climbed from the safety-conscious Volvo, she smiled, said, "There you are."

"Have you been looking for me?"

"Yes. I regret to inform you, dear breather, that we should no longer date."

"We're dating?" Rusty asked, his teeth humming with hope.

"Not anymore."

"Are we breaking up because every time I get near your nipples, I faint? Cause I have an explanation for that. It's crazy but that doesn't make it any less of an explanation."

Gesturing toward the monumental dollop in his trousers, she said, "No. I don't want to date you anymore because, although you are obviously bursting with semen, I have grown weary of your many character flaws. They might hinder the child I hope to birth."

In an effort to make her see that his character flaws were no worse than the next guy, the young man considered wrapping his arms around Dearly, bundling her into his idling car, and driving until the horizon was but a distant memory.

But he never got a chance to move.

Right or Left – it's impossible to tell them apart – stepped from the shadows surrounding the smelting factory. Rusty knew this was no coincidence, Right or Left wasn't out taking the evening air. For one thing, he looked pissed. For another, he was gripping a gun.

"Hey Left," Rusty guessed, trying to keep things civil. Taking a step back and bumping into his car. Reminding himself to breathe, Rusty felt all his blood pool in the wrong parts of his body. Everyone in Fremont had heard stories about Right and Left. Their ruthlessness, their cruelty, their love of inflicting pain.

"I'm Right," Right said. "Now, who's this intoxicating and bewitching minx?"

Right's eyes, like little round elevators, traveled up and down Dearly's naked body.

Rusty had never heard either of Loco Lenny Labovitz's henchmen do anything but grunt and it was disconcerting. Those big words didn't sound right coming out of that big mouth.

"Her name is Dearly Departed. She's a friend of mine."

"Well, it's unfortunate that she happens to be here."

"Why's that?"

"For she must die."

Right raised his gun. Even it looked mean. Black, soulless. Rusty tried to take a step back but the car was still in his way.

Glancing over at Dearly, Rusty was surprised to see she didn't appear worried in the slightest. In fact, she was smiling and rolling her head back and forth, cracking her neck.

Odd, thought Rusty. But it didn't feel like the right time to comment on her behavior. Instead, he asked the henchman, "Why does she have to die?"

"Because you have to die and, in my line of work, witnesses are considered detrimental."

Upon hearing the news of immanent death, Rusty felt his insides turn to jam. If not for the support of the safety-conscious Volvo, he'd have crumpled onto the pavement and cried himself to death before Right got a shot off.

But then another thought hit him, a brighter thought.

Here was his chance, a golden opportunity to prove his metal. He could win Dearly back by rushing the thug, stealing his gun, and killing him.

It's what Machiavelli would have done in an Italian heartbeat.

Rusty knew the odds were against him, that he'd likely die if he rushed Right, but what a beautiful way to go, he reasoned, dying to save the woman he wanted to spend the rest of his life with.

Empowered, the young man took a giant step toward Right. He was going to kill this huge asshole, rip his throat out and stand there laughing as the world was painted red with his blood.

But Rusty didn't accomplished any world redecoration that night. Right, who'd been ready, who'd been waiting, trained his gun on the young man and pulled the trigger.

A sound akin to a thousand bursts of thunder shook the night.

The bullet, an unpleasant speck of gray, hurled itself through the air, straight at Rusty's face. He saw it streaking, growing larger. The boy, unable to move, accepted his fate, knew that chunks of his brain would soon be outside his skull, that he was going to die in the parking lot of a smelting plant.

At least it would be quick.

Rusty considered closing his eyes and going to his happy place, but he realized, regrettably, that he didn't have one.

Out of the corner of his eye, he saw something move. Well, not move, really, so much as change.

Dearly, who'd been standing about ten feet away, was suddenly positioned between him and Right, him and the bullet.

Typical. Life, once again, was turning the tables on poor Rusty Slump. He'd wanted to sacrifice himself for her, now she was doing it for him.

Great. Rusty couldn't win, even in death.

As Dearly had her back to him, Rusty didn't see where the bullet struck her. But it couldn't have been good, as she jerked and was thrown back, landing awkwardly on the pavement. Dead, still, silent.

Looking down on her body, that asshole Right chuckled. It was thick in his throat. Now Rusty not only wanted to kill him, he wanted to kill him, then resuscitate him just so he could kill him again.

The laughter in Right's throat died when Dearly jumped to her feet, dusted herself off.

She must not have been hit, Rusty told himself. But he knew this wasn't true.

The girl smiled and did that weird blurred movement thing again. She was one place, then, a moment later, she was somewhere else without moving.

This time her destination was Right. She landed atop his broad shoulders, perched there as if she were a bird of prey, and howled at the moon. Her teeth, long and knifey, glistened with saliva. Instead of thinking about how surreal this whole experience was, Rusty was seriously reconsidering his wish to receive a blowjob from Dearly, which might be boisterous, but definitely toothy. In fact, with that orthodontia, it could be downright deadly.

Not one to let the paranormal throw him, Right attempted to spin his substantial body, break loose, aim his weapon in the general direction of his attacker.

The thug didn't have time.

Dearly sank her fangs into Right's throat.

He screamed but not for long. Dropping his gun, which hit the pavement and did a little dance, Right grabbed the girl who'd clamped onto his throat. But he couldn't remove her, couldn't even make her budge. She found his jugular and crimson blood poured past her lips, drenching Right's suit.

Rusty thought how nice it would be to jump into his automobile and drive far, far away. Never think about Dearly's fangs or buckets of blood ever again.

But he couldn't move. Couldn't even look away.

Even when Right crumbled and became nothing but a pile of flesh, when he was surely dead and gone, Dearly didn't detach. Continued working and gnawing until the thug's bulbous head separated from his bulbous body and rolled away like a drunken bowling ball.

Though he felt as if every nerve, every cell in his body had imploded, Rusty managed to stumble toward Dearly's thin back, her spine poking through the skin.

Laying a trembling hand between her shoulder blades, he expected searing heat, but her skin was as cold as the grave.

She flinched, spun. Her eyes were burning, her mouth bloody.

For a moment, Rusty feared he was her next victim. But she simply stared at him. Smiling while licking blood from her chin with her disturbingly long tongue.

She stood and it was Rusty's turn to flinch as she leaned forward. Certain she was about to partake of his face, he said farewell to it, farewell to everything.

But she didn't lunge, she didn't bare her surprisingly large teeth. Dearly puckered, kissed his trembling lips. Soft, for a moment.

"You were trying to save me," she said, though Rusty couldn't say for certain there were words coming out of her mouth. "That was very brave of you. I recant my wish to break up with you. We can now have sexual congress."

Using her tongue, which was more like tentacle, she prized apart his lips to give the Frenchiest french kiss ever frenched. He felt her tongue tickle his uvula, travel south. Closing his eyes, he felt the intoxicating brew of saliva and blood flow into his mouth, didn't mind exactly.

When she finally pulled away, which could have been hours later for all Rusty knew, she leaned back and smiled. "Let us go find a soft spot for sexual congress. And, might I suggest, after we are finished, you should clear out of town as it is going to get mighty dangerous around here."

Stepping over Right's torso and its moat of blood, Dearly walked away. He wanted to call out to her, ask what she meant by her dire prediction about Fremont, but he couldn't speak. There was a foreign object in his mouth. Something large that wasn't there before the girl had forced her tongue into him.

Digging in his maw, Rusty pulled out the interloper.

It was the bullet, smashed.

Looking up at Dearly's retreating perfect form, he was on the verge of asking a thousand questions when he heard something whistling through the air.

The whistling sound stopped when Dearly dropped.

It's not always in the best interest of a crime lord to engage in reflection. Most of Loco's past actions were transgressions. It went with the territory. While climbing the ladder of the vast and dangerous criminal underworld of Fremont, Ohio, he'd stepped on many a finger.

It was astounding to recall that the first finger he stepped on belonged to a dog.

Sitting in his empty mobile drug emporium and waiting for his henchmen to return with the joyous news of Rusty Slump's demise, Loco thought back on that innocent summer afternoon not that long ago when his life of crime began.

He was sixteen and, having just finished mowing his father's lawn, walked to the local gas station to purchase a Dr. Pepper. As he approached the gas station, he spied the famous Oscar Mayer Wienermobile idling in the parking lot. The driver of the promotional vehicle climbed from the tubular vehicle and hustled inside, obviously in search of porcelain.

Studying the strange vehicle, Loco was floored. He'd never seen anything like it, certainly not in Fremont. It was long and orange and beautiful. He decided right then and there that he had to get inside that amazing hot dog.

Up to this point in his young life, Loco had never done anything wrong. He was a good boy with fair grades and a paper route. No one called him Loco, not yet. Back then, before he cut out Mike Bradley's tongue for simply pointing out that his mobile drug emporium was phallic, everyone knew him simply as Lenny. When the Labovitz family showed up at the Rutherford B. Hayes Memorial Synagogue, the boy was clean and nicely dressed. He'd never lied or cheated or stolen anything, not even a stick of gum.

But standing before the awesomeness of the Oscar Mayer Wienermobile, he decided it would be just fine if he bent the rules just a bit and climbed into the vehicular hot dog. That's all he planned to do. Sit behind the steering wheel for a moment, just to have a story to tell, then clear out before the driver returned from voiding his bladder.

But once he sat in the driver's seat and felt its power, he couldn't make himself vacate. He turned over the engine, as the driver, in his rush, had forgotten to take the keys. Putting the vehicle in reverse and thoroughly checking his mirrors, as he'd been taught in Driver's Ed, he backed out of the parking lot.

It was an action unaccompanied by thought.

Away he drove, laughing. He checked the rearview mirror and spied the Wienermobile driver standing in the parking lot, shaking his fist, his mouth flapping, probably swearing.

But Loco didn't care. He put the pedal to the metal, the wind in his hair.

The boy had no clue where he was going or why he was going there. A reasonable, calm voice in his head kept screaming for him to turn around, return the vehicle, and receive a well-deserved slap on the wrist for his sins.

Yet, he couldn't remove his foot from the accelerator. And he couldn't stop laughing. This was the most fun he'd ever had.

Which ended when he rounded the corner onto Rutherford B. Hayes Memorial Frontage Road and struck tragedy.

Before he could brake, before he could even think, a mangy mutt darted out into his path and simply stood there, staring at him, as if daring him.

Ever since that day, Loco had wondered if the simple beast was entranced by the giant tube of meat barreling toward him or if he was performing his sworn duty as an officer of the law.

It's impossible to know.

Either way, the dog didn't move and, although he slammed on the brakes, Loco couldn't stop in time.

The collision went the way all meetings between animals and vehicles do. The dog was smashed flat and the Oscar Mayer Wienermobile rolled to a stop.

Tears welling, Loco climbed from the cab and staggered toward the dark stain on the road that had once been a dog. Praying to Yahweh that he'd just grazed the mutt, that he would still be breathing, that everything was going to work out just fine, as everything had always worked out before. That he could return to his life of mowing lawns, reading comics, and lusting after girls like CoCo McArdle.

But none of that happened.

When he arrived at the stain, his knees gave out and he fell to the pavement. It was worse than he could have imagined. For not only was the dog dead, he recognized the body even in its squished state.

Sweet Baby G, it was Sergeant Snoopers, the greatest detective the Fremont Police Squad had ever seen.

Just the previous spring, Sergeant Snoopers had come to Rutherford B. Hayes Memorial High School and spoken with Loco's class about the dangers of drugs.

The dog spoke, through an interpreter of course, so eloquently that Loco, inspired, had penned a fan letter to the mutt.

Now his hero lay dead at his feet, killed by his own hand.

Closing his eyes, Loco saw his new future, an awful future,

stretch out before him. A long stint in jail for the combined crimes of novelty vehicular theft and killing a cop. He doubted he'd survive prison. He was young and pretty and he knew what happened to such boys behind bars. He'd be eaten alive and that prospect sickened him.

Wiping away his tears, which would be the last he'd ever shed, Loco knew exactly what he had to do.

Hardening his heart, he checked his environs. Though it was the middle of the day, he found, surprisingly, he had the frontage road to himself.

It was almost as if Yahweh wanted him to get away with this transgressions.

Scrambling back to the Wienermobile, he drove away from the scene of the crime. Staying well below the posted speed limit, keeping his hands at 2 and 10, Loco drove to his uncle's storage facility on the outskirts of town.

Over the next few weeks, Loco dropped out of school, painted the Wienermobile blue to confuse the local constabulary, and set out to become Fremont's next drug kingpin.

"That bitch," hissed CoCo McArdle.

After the little hussy had gnawed the head off of one of Loco Lenny Labovitz's henchmen – CoCo couldn't tell which one – she had, with malice aforethought, kissed CoCo's erstwhile boyfriend. With tongue.

Though she was on the roof of the Rutherford B. Hayes Memorial Recycling Center, which was a block away, CoCo had watched every detail of the kiss unfold through the scope of her father's tranquilizer gun. Every nerve in her body seethed with revenge.

Not that she loved Rusty or anything, but he was still technically her property, and no one trespassed on CoCo McArdle's property without a can of whoopass being taken down from the shelf.

"I'll show you who's up, you little hussy," she whispered, pressing the tranquilizer gun against her shoulder.

Not only had CoCo's father, Jinx, run the Rutherford B. Hayes Memorial Slightly Dangerous Petting Zoo, he was an accomplished big game hunter. Once a year he tromped off to Africa and returned with crates crammed with souvenirs that made CoCo's stomach flutter. Things like skulls and tusks and natives' fingers. He raised his daughter to respect guns, respect how awesome it was to blow something away. Every Sunday, save when he was in Africa murdering a handful of God's creatures, one could find the McArdles at the Rutherford B. Hayes Memorial Gun Range, firing away and giving each other copious high-fives.

Atop the Rutherford B. Hayes Memorial Recycling Center, CoCo lined up her shot, which was no easy feat as her target was on the move. CoCo knew she had to bring this little hussy down before she disappeared into the shadows of the smelting factory. Also, CoCo wanted to bring her down right in front of Rusty, who had - CoCo could plainly see the tent pitched in his pants - enjoyed the kiss immensely.

Breathing out slowly, just as she'd been taught, CoCo squeezed the trigger.

The dart, brimming with Azaperone, flew away. Twisting, it sailed through the night, striking the little hussy right in her neck.

As with so many things in this life, it happened near South Bend, Indiana.

Ever since he bared his soul about his mild case of craniodiaphyseal dysplasia and his life with Satan's Butt Buddies, the housewife had talked nonstop about her abusive husband, Keith. Pouring out her story, her soul, her tears. At first Cuntlips was only half-listening, his mind occupied with saving the world, but as she unwound her tale of woe, he found himself caught up in her story. Forgetting the demon bent on destroying mankind, he turned toward the housewife and studied her, as if seeing her for the first time.

She was an angel. Complete with blonde hair piled, blue eyes swimming, and pert lips pouted. Lithe and willowy, she was dressed in a billowing white housecoat. The former rocker wouldn't have been surprised if a pair of gossamer wings sprouted from her back.

He'd seen weirder shit in his life apprenticing with the Buddhist monk ninja warrior assassin.

"What's your name again?" he asked, not certain she'd ever given it.

"I'm Nicole, Nicole Clymer."

As she continued to speak, the woman's words wrapped around him like a blanket. Her honesty, her openness, made him feel safe. So secure was Cuntlips McGoo that, somewhere around South Bend, he opened up about his life with the Buddhist monk ninja warrior assassin. It was a tale he'd never told before, not to any of his band mates in Satan's Butt Buddies, not to any of the groupies he'd banged, no one.

After his parents died in a car crash, little Vince Kramer, as he was known then, was shipped off to an orphanage called God's Dirty Orphans, which was run by the Sisters of Perpetual Antagonism, in Plymouth Notch, Vermont. There he stayed for several years, unwanted, unloved. All around him other orphans were adopted, taken into warm homes. All he ever received from would-be parents, thanks to his mild case of craniodiaphyseal dysplasia, which gave his face a slightly melted look, were furtive glances of pity.

On his thirteenth birthday, Sister Mary Caliphate woke him, a smile brimming on her round face. There was a man, a religious man she said, who'd arrived in the middle of the night wishing to see Vince specifically.

The boy was dubious. This sounded like yet another nun trick (the Sisters of Perpetual Antagonism were legendary for their pranks, especially during the Inquisition). But when the young Doubting Thomas was led into the dayroom, he saw there was, in fact, a man waiting.

He looked like no man Vince had ever seen. He was very tall and very thin and was wearing what could only be described as a dress, which flowed all the way down his long body and pooled on the linoleum. There was not a drop of hair on top of his head but a lengthy ponytail erupted from the back of his skull.

"Leave me alone with the boy, Sister," said the man, his voice deep, dangerous.

Sister Mary Caliphate, who didn't like being pushed around on her home turf, made some noise about protocol, but was silenced with a piercing look from the man in the long black dress.

Nodding, she swept from the room as if it had been her idea.

When the sister was history, the man got down on his knees and looked Vince in the eye. He smiled, though it felt like an impersonation of happiness. "Do you know who I am?"

In the bunks, late at night, Vince had overheard the older boys whispering about men who wore dresses. "You're a gaywad."

"No, I'm not a gaywad, I'm a Buddhist monk ninja warrior assassin. I travel the earth defeating unimaginable evil. Three nights ago I was in Tunisia, sending a minor demon back to his home in the rocks. Exhausted, I spent that night in the desert, sleeping on the hard ground. I had a vivid dream. Can you guess what that dream was about?"

"Putting another dude's dick in your mouth?" Vince was nothing if not persistent.

The tall man's head dropped. "No, let me repeat, I'm not a gaywad in any way, shape, or form. I dreamt that it was time for me to acquire an apprentice. A boy who I could train to take my place as a Buddhist monk ninja warrior assassin, for I am growing older and fighting evil is a young man's game. In this dream, a name was spelled out in the sky with stars, it was your name, Vince Kramer. What do you think of that? Would you like to be my apprentice?"

"Sounds cool. As long as I don't have to lick a ton of nutsacks."

"No! For the final time, I'm a Buddhist monk ninja warrior assassin who travels the globe battling monsters, not a gaywad! So, I ask, do you wish to join me on my journey? It will be dangerous, deadly work and the only pay you'll ever receive is that you get to kill a multitude of bad guys."

That sounded totally doable to Vince, so he stuck out his small hand and a deal was struck.

For the next decade he did exactly as the man in a dress had promised. Training in the ancient ways of the Buddhist monk ninja warrior assassin, he learned every single martial art, from jiu jitsu to the Himalayan Art of Cordial Monkey Fighting. Also, he was taught how to use swords, dynamite, and incantations. For some reason, the Buddhist monk ninja warrior assassin, who never divulged his real name, also taught him how to play the drums, though that particular talent never came in particularly handy during demon combat. The pair traversed the globe, from Mozambique to Stanton, Iowa, vanquishing foes of the otherworldly variety. Over time, Vince grew strong, confident.

His world came crashing down one night in Southeast Asia. While he and the Buddhist monk ninja warrior assassin were vacationing on the beaches of Phuket, the cabana boy told them a rumor about a young female demon in Kuala Lumpur who had wiped out her entire village, which was called Quafftits. Chartering a private plane, the pair headed off without changing out of their swimming trunks.

Five hours later, when they landed in field near Quafftits, they found the rumor was true. There was no one left alive in the village, there were just badly battered bodies strewn all around. Everywhere Vince looked, there were limbs and blood and teeth.

Well, there was one person left alive, the demon herself.

Over the previous decade, Vince had seen his fair share of creatures spawned from hell. Usually they were red beasts, brutal things. Leathery skin, wiry tufts of hair, horns jutting.

But this demon was different. She looked just like a little girl. Black hair, big brown eyes, frilly white dress blotched with blood.

She couldn't have been more than twelve, squatting in a mud puddle, clasping a doll to her chest, bodies all around her, watching as the Buddhist monk ninja warrior assassin and his apprentice approached. Grinning, waiting for them.

"Don't be fooled by her innocence," instructed the Buddhist monk ninja warrior assassin. "This is the most dangerous of demons, this is Maude the Layer of Waste. Every decade she rises from the earth's bowels and inhabits the body of a recently expired female. Her only desires are to feed upon the flesh of the living and become pregnant. But not pregnant with child, but a demon so awful, so fierce, it could easily overrun the world of the living."

During his apprenticeship, Vince had learned that everything the man in the dress said was gospel, but this seemed a little hard to swallow. The girl in the puddle looked as if she'd just skipped off a school bus.

Drawing his katana, which was made from a space age polymer, the Buddhist monk ninja warrior assassin ordered Vince to stay back and advanced on the girl. The young man was surprised to see something in his master that he'd never seen before: fear. The Buddhist monk ninja warrior assassin's hands were shaking, his gait unsteady. As he drew near, the girl stood, dropping her doll into the mud.

"You're too late, assassin," she hissed. "I have my baby."

Vince noticed her stomach bulging beneath her bloodied dress.

"It's my job to send you and the child you're carrying back to the netherworld," promised the Buddhist monk ninja warrior assassin, though his voice quivered.

Bearing her teeth, the girl growled. She jumped or ran – it was hard to tell which, as she moved so quickly – and was suddenly all over the Buddhist monk ninja warrior assassin.

The girl ripped open the man's throat with her teeth, and the space age polymer katana, unswung, clattered to the ground. The Buddhist monk ninja assassin tried to escape death by dancing around and flailing his arms but the demon held fast. The dying man yelped in pain, a sound that chilled Vince to his marrow. Fortunately, his screams didn't last long as the demon continued to gnaw and claw, drawing blood which soaked the already bloody ground. The Buddhist monk ninja warrior assassin collapsed.

Without thinking, Vince rushed forward. The Buddhist monk ninja warrior assassin had always preached heading into every altercation with a battle plan, but Vince didn't have a solitary thought in his head, he only had rage and revenge. Bellowing nonsense, he picked up the katana while the demon was distracted with devouring his master. As he raised the weapon high into the air, the thing that he'd mistaken for a girl turned.

She was still wearing her smile but it was now frosted with blood. And her teeth, they were impossibly large in her small mouth, jutting and jagged.

Filled with fear, Vince froze. The space age polymer katana dropped to his side. The girl stood, advanced. Not a blur this time, but a girl, out for a stroll.

An odd thought struck the young man as he was about to be killed. He'd never known the caress of a woman. This probably had something to do with his face looking like an old candle, but also the Buddhist monk ninja warrior assassin preached a life of austerity. No booze, no cigarettes, no tail.

As the demon drew close, the young man vowed that if he ever got out of this village alive he'd eat a steady diet of pussy for the rest of his life.

This thought, this bolt of positivity, gave Vince the push he needed. Swinging his arms, yelling wildly, Vince brought the katana up with all his might.

The space age polymer sliced through the air until it reached the demon, then it sliced through flesh. Letting out a hellish howl, the creature collapsed to the ground, basically cut in half, blood flowing freely. Something that looked like a wolf with scales slid out of the demon's stomach. Her devil child. Vince continued to attack, chopping up the demon and its spawn until they resembled nothing more than a heap of hamburger.

Exhausted, his arms burning, his heart about to blow a gasket, he dropped the weapon and rushed to the Buddhist monk ninja warrior assassin, who lay on the ground without moving. Cradling the older man's bloodied head in his hands, Vince hoped for a few last words of wisdom, but when the Buddhist monk ninja warrior assassin opened his mouth for the last time, all he said was, "My name is Tim."

And then he died.

The young man, now an apprentice to no one, stood amongst the dead. He was more alone than he'd ever been, even when he ran around the backyard of God's Dirty Orphans, playing tag by himself.

It was alarming how quiet it was. No birds, no insects, no breeze, nothing.

Turning his back, Vince walked away from the village of death and his life as a demon slayer without looking back. He continued walking through the jungles of Kuala Lumpur, across its dusty deserts, fording rivers. Looking for a sign, any sign telling him what to do with his life.

Eventually, he made it to Kuala Lumpur City. He happened to arrive on the same day as Satan's Butt Buddies, who, on a world tour, were playing a sold out show at the Kaptain Yap Ah Loy Memorial Auditorium. As if it were a beacon, Vince followed the sound of the heavy metal to the venue. The woman taking tickets didn't even try to stop him as he walked past her. Perhaps because he was wearing only a tattered pair of swim trunks, maybe because he was deathly gaunt and wan, possibly because she was frightened by his mild case of craniodiaphyseal dysplasia. However it happened, Vince ended up in the back of the smokey auditorium as Satan's Butt Buddies headbanged away. The former apprentice let the sonic waves wash him clean. This music tortured his ears but made him forget all about little girl demons, the village of the dead, and the demise of Tim, the Buddhist monk ninja warrior assassin. Sure, this band was all about Satanism but it was a cartoon version of Satanism. They had it all wrong. Horns, pentagrams, backward messages. Childish tripe.

About halfway through the show, Satan's Butt Buddies' drummer (who was named Cuntlips McGoo) collapsed onto his kit. The heat, the booze, the drugs had taken their toll. He couldn't be revived, even by the nervous paramedics who flooded the stage. Sweaty Nipples McGoo approached the microphone and jokingly asked if there were a drummer in the house.

This was the sign Vince had been waiting for. The reason the Buddhist monk ninja warrior assassin had trained him on the skins.

Throwing the occasional elbow, Vince made his way forward through the tightly packed crowd. The band members watched with a mixture of amusement and horror as this terribly ugly, terribly haggard, nearly naked specter climbed onto the stage and took his place behind the drums as if he belonged there.

When the band came out of their stupor, they launched into

their most recent hit "After the Rape Comes the Kill," expecting the worst from the untested drummer. The worst never arrived. Although he'd never laid ears on the song, Vince kept perfect time, even through the emotional bridge of the number. During the guitar solo, Sweaty Nipples McGoo looked back at him and grinned.

Vince, now burdened with the mindless moniker Cuntlips McGoo, knew he was where he was supposed to be, playing stupid music with ridiculous people.

Until something better came along.

When Cuntlips finished the story of his checkered past, which had taken hours to tell, he glanced over at Nicole Clymer, the angelic housewife. She was glaring at him with a look of either shock or amazement; it was hard to tell which.

For a moment, the former rocker feared being ostracized from the vehicle, being left on the side of the road now that he was close to the Ohio demon. Also having to part from Nicole, of whom he'd grown fond.

Instead, the housewife smiled.

"Wow," she said, "I've never heard anything like that."

Putting his hand to his heart, Cuntlips swore it was all true, every word.

"Oh, I believe it," she said, pulling her necklace out from beneath her housecoat. A shining silver cross.

Feeling freer than he had since the Buddhist monk ninja warrior assassin's death, Cuntlips filled Nicole in on quitting the band and the reasons behind that decision.

"It's Maude the Layer of Waste, I can feel it in my slightly misshapen bones," he said, his words so full of gravity they barely made it out of his mouth.

Looking out the window at the fields sliding past, Cuntlips' mind filled with bloody images of the demon girl and her grotesque offspring.

He was surprised when a warm hand wormed its way into his closed fist. Startled, he looked over at Nicole. She was smiling, squeezing. Even though he'd spent the last decade making true on his promise of eating as much pussy as humanly possible, no woman had ever looked at Cuntlips with such emotion in her eyes.

"I'm coming with you," she said.

"What? Why?"

"I want to help you slay this demon. I done some bad things in my life, real bad things, and I feel I gotta make up for them."

"Grab her ankles, will ya? We gotta load this bitch into the back of your Volvo before the fuzz gets here. Or worse, Loco."

"You seem particularly mad about something, Sugar Purlicue."

"Don't 'Sugar Purlicue' me, flocknuts. You deviated from the plan. You were supposed to pick up this little hussy and bring her to the treehouse where I was waiting with my trusty load of Azaperone."

"Well, sorry I didn't follow your orders to a T, but I got a little freaked out when Dearly chewed Right's head off."

"And then what happened?"

"What do you mean?"

"After the head thing, what happened next in the story?"

"She… she walked away and you shot her. Say, that reminds me, I wasn't the only one who deviated from the plan. What were you doing in this part of town anyway? You were supposed to be waiting for us in the treehouse."

"I didn't trust you to do the right thing, so I followed you."

"You didn't trust me? But I'm your boyfriend."

"And I was right not to. This little hussy and her magic titties would have waltzed off into the sunset if it hadn't been for me. And, if you recall, the real question was what happened between the time she gnawed Right's head off and I shot her full of tranquilizer."

Rusty turned a rust color, looked down, kicked at the loose gravel and chips of broken glass in the Rutherford B. Hayes Memorial Smelting Plant parking lot.

CoCo said, "I thought so. Now, grab her ankles and help me load her into the car."

When one thinks of romantic fumblings, of spit swapped, of hands coaxing flesh, of moans of pleasure and groans of surprise, of sweet sweat drenching, of furtive pelvic thrusts, and of the beautifully symphonic *fwap, fwap, fwap* of sloppy sex, one does not usually imagine a lonely interstate rest area bathroom as the backdrop. But now and forevermore, Cuntlips McGoo would think of only that, for he first banged the true love of his life, Nicole Clymer, in a toilet stall.

During their lovely boinking, Cuntlips tried to reason out how the two participants had arrived at this magical moment and time in the universe.

After Cuntlips had spilled the beans about his secret Buddhist monk ninja warrior assassin past and Nicole begged to join him on his hopeless quest, they were quiet, smiling at one another, a million words passing between them in the silence of the car.

Swerving, Nicole said something about a bathroom break, cutting across three lanes of traffic and barreling up the offramp toward the Rutherford B. Hayes Memorial Rest Stop.

"Hurry, please," begged Cuntlips as Nicole climbed from the car. "The sooner we get to Fremont, the more likely we are to prevent all life as we know it from ending."

"Come with me," she said. There was something in her voice which hadn't been there before. Something dark, something dangerous, something fun.

Cuntlips sat up straight. "What?"

"I need a hand in the bathroom."

Without further explanation, Nicole turned and sashayed away, her ass swerving across three lanes of traffic and disappearing into the women's restroom.

Although, over the last decade, he'd had buttloads of groupie sex, Cuntlips completely misinterpreted Nicole's innuendo. His imagination ran wild with ugly possibilities of what manner of assistance his new acquaintance might need in the bathroom. Trembling, his mind flashed to the image of Sister Mary Caliphate's colostomy bag. Though he'd never had any direct dealings with the plastic pouch of waste the nun kept secreted beneath her cassock, he did catch a regrettable glimpse of it during a particularly raucous game of ping-pong.

Setting his jaw, Cuntlips decided that if it were colostomy bag maintenance that Nicole needed help with, he would be there for her, as he found his heart stirring for this kind, nurturing woman.

With a deep sigh, he headed for the women's restroom.

Expecting a plastic bag brimming with dross, Cuntlips was pleasantly surprised when he discovered Nicole standing in the middle of the bathroom, completely bereft of clothing.

"When I said I needed a hand, I meant I needed a hand getting off."

She said these words slowly, giving each their own area code. With every syllable she took a leggy step forward, that patch of thatch between her legs growing closer, growing larger. Her journey ended with her naked body pressed firmly into Cuntlips' trembling one.

Pulling him close, she kissed him long, hard. He closed his eyes and saw everything in the universe. With a gentle hand and a firm smile, Nicole guided him toward a stall, toward his death, toward his new life.

Putting up the mildest of protests, Cuntlips said, "But we have to get to Fremont."

"You've told me how dangerous this demon is, we might not live through this encounter. We should spend some of our last moments on earth banging the ones we care about."

Safe from the outside world in their cramped metal room, they made out as she tore away his clothing. When his erection sprang forward, Cuntlips momentarily considered Nicole's husband, the abuser, back in California.

But all thoughts of Keith vanished when Nicole took said erection into her mouth.

In fact, Cuntlip's mind went completely blank, a beautiful *tabula rasa* that stretched to the horizon of his brain and back. No nagging thoughts of irate husbands or world-ending demons or dead Buddhist monk ninja warrior assassins occurred as Nicole's dishwater blonde head went up and down, up and down.

When he blew a hellacious wad of steaming hot cum into the housewife's waiting maw, he knew that he'd found the woman of his dreams. The perfect mate, someone with whom he could share his life, regardless of how short that life was going to be.

"I love you," he said. A phrase he'd never uttered before. Not to any of the groupies or the Buddhist monk ninja warrior assassin or Sister Mary Caliphate.

After swallowing with some difficulty, Nicole looked up at him with the biggest eyes humanly possible and said, "I love you, too."

They had sexual congress four more times that night in the stall of the bathroom. Missionary, the Trump Twister, double sideways camel, and anal.

Wrapping their arms around one another, professing their undying love, they collapsed to the tile floor and fell asleep.

"I must apologize Junior Officer Killion, I fear I didn't hear your question. As you can easily understand, this entire devastating event has had a rather discombobulating effect on my entire psyche. Pulled from my sick bed to discover that the only family I have left in this dark and dismal world has been gruesomely murdered. My head still spins."

Junior Officer Jeff Killion studied Left, the thug who worked for Loco Lenny Labovitz. He was a foot taller than Killion and outweighed him by at least a hundred pounds of meaty muscle.

The big man sneezed again, shaking the parking lot of the Rutherford B. Hayes Memorial Smelting Factory.

Clearing his throat, Killion reasked, "Do you know of anyone… or anything, rabid or no, who would do… *this*… to your brother?"

Left gazed down upon the mangled body at his feet, then over at Right's head, which lay twenty feet away. "Regrettably, I have no earthly idea."

"Did your brother have any enemies?"

"Life is long and difficult, Junior Officer. Anyone who travels through it and doesn't acquire his fair share of enemies has not really lived."

Left looked down on Killion. Sure that the thug was giving him the business, the Junior Officer felt sillier than usual. It didn't help he was straddling a pink bike. The Fremont Police Society had only two patrol cars, another attempt to save some coin, and if all three officers were on duty, Killion was on two wheels.

He'd taken the original call about the body discovered in the parking lot of the Rutherford B. Hayes Memorial Smelting Factory while cleaning toilets at Police Headquarters and biked straight over. Killion identified Right right away. Though fatigued, he biked to Left and Right's apartment and retrieved the other Queerfolk, bringing him to the scene of the crime, which was a difficult endeavor as Left was quite massive and they barely both fit on the bike's sparkly banana seat.

But seeing as both the cop and the thug were on Loco Lenny

Labovitz's payroll, it felt like the right thing to do.

"Okay," said the cop. "Can you give me a few names on the list of enemies your brother acquired in his long and difficult life?"

"Sweet Baby G, swing a cat. Everyone in this depressing berg was jealous of my brother's prowess. His strength, his superior fashion sense, his dominance in the world of Pong. Search all those faces that have turned green with envy and among them you will find the rouge who committed this unspeakable act upon my dear, departed brother."

A muscular tear slid down the thug's face. Left didn't bother to wipe it away, but let it run its course and fall to the pavement.

Deciding that he was going to get nothing more out of the thug, Killion said, with a measure of disgust, "If you'll excuse me, I have to peddle to the hospital to get an ambulance. This stupid bike isn't equipped with a radio and I can't afford a cell phone. Can you wait here until I get back?"

"Certainly, officer."

With a tip of his hat, Killion peddled off into the night.

As he stood over his brother's body, more tears came Left's way. For a moment, he was confused about which part of his dead brother, the head or the torso, to make his vow to. The torso had the heart, but the head held the brain. As his brother had always been proud of his mental agility, Left decided to go with the head. He walked over and, kneeling, looked into Right's dead eyes.

"Dear brother, I swear to track down who did this and make them regret the moment they were conceived."

Again, he sneezed.

Intent on tendering her Savage 1861 Navy revolver and badge, then retiring to the all-female dude ranch that she'd read about in the pages of *Lesbian Today*, Officer Chrissy Rumpza sat on the back porch of Police Chief Pendleton's home and stared at nothing. She was empty, hollow. There was no more food remaining in her stomach, no tears left to cry, no more hope in her heart.

She'd done her job and done it well, discovering the identity of the serial killer who'd been plaguing her town. The person who'd slaughtered four people was a young woman, Dearly Departed, whose innocent face reminded her so much of her lost lover, Connie Pendleton.

What was this dark and dismal world coming to? Beautiful teenage girls ripping people limb from limb? It was too much to consider, too much to believe, too much to live with.

Hearing the back door open behind her, Rumpza didn't even have the energy to turn and see who was joining her. It could have been the murderous Dearly Departed for all she cared.

It was Pendleton, out of his Civil War garb and back in his police uniform. Shaved and showered. Taking a seat beside her, he rested his hand on her shoulder.

"Well, you were right, Chrissy. I dug that tennis shoe out of the drink and it had LOCKE written on the tongue. So, we've found some of our missing gym teacher."

Knowing she'd correctly identified her former lover did nothing to raise Rumpza's spirits.

"And that's not the only thing you were right about. I have to admit, Hayes Dayes or no, we have a serial killer roaming the streets of Fremont and the people have to know that."

Again, she felt nothing. She was beginning to wonder if she'd ever feel anything again.

"The silver lining to this awful situation," continued the Police Chief, "is that we know the identity of this fiend, as unbelievable as it is. Add to that that she's apparently not wearing any clothes presently, it can't be too hard to find her in a town of 16,000 souls. Now, that's not saying bringing Dearly Departed in is going to be a walk in the park, we've both witnessed the damage she can inflict. That little girl is a killing machine. It's time to get serious about this. I need to stop playing dress up and be a real cop. My war isn't on some far flung battlefield of yesteryear, it's right here and now on the streets of my town. We've got to catch that killer."

"*You've* got to catch her."

"Excuse me?"

Rumpza sighed. "I wish you luck on this case, Chief, you're going to need it, but I will not be beside you. I'm tendering my badge. I'm no cock-chugging good at police work."

Surprisingly, Pendleton scoffed. "No good at police work? Who in tarnation is made for police work? Hades, Sergeant Snoopers was born a gosh dang dog! He should have been digging holes and chasing his tail instead of solving crimes."

"Yeah, well I'm no Sergeant Snoopers."

"Okay, you're right on that account. Cause you're better than Sergeant Snoopers."

She looked her boss in the eye. Her voice soft, she asked, "Are you serious?"

"Have you ever known me not to be serious? Sergeant Snoopers was a great media invention but he was also a pain in the posterior. I'd take you over him any day. For one thing, I don't have to walk you and pick up your droppings. For another, Sergeant Snoopers was terrible at paperwork. You're a great cop, Chrissy, and don't let anyone ever tell you different."

A burst of joy traveled through her system. Her heart sailed to the sun and returned tanned. Apparently she could feel again.

Pendleton continued, "And since we're being honest and all, I got to admit that I've always had feelings for--."

Rumpza interrupted him by jumping to her feet. She barked, "You take your patrol car and start combing the town. Send Killion out too. On the bike, of course. I'll search your house for any clues, see if there's anything we overlooked."

It was ridiculous, her shouting orders at her superior, but she was simply too excited to think.

"But I was about to tell you about my heart, Chrissy-."

"We don't have time for that now, Chief, we have a serial killer to stop."

Looking a little dejected, Pendleton nodded and scrambled toward his patrol car. Rumpza hurried inside to search the house.

First, she rifled through Dearly's clothes heaped on the floor of Connie's bedroom. There were no labels to identify them and nothing in the pockets except a little dirt.

Unable to stay her hand, she guided Dearly's frilly red panties toward her nose. She inhaled like nobody's business.

Lollipop pussy, whispered the whiff, *lollipop pussy...*

Rumpza dropped the panties before she fainted.

Part III:
Hayes Dayes

It was the long line that made Rusty nervous, chew his fingernails down to the quick.

The queue of horny males stretched down the luxurious treehouse's mother of pearl ladder, snaked along the side of the judge's house, and nearly reached Rutherford B. Hayes Memorial Court before petering out. Comprised completely of deranged looking men, their eyes untamed, their tongues lolling, their grubby hands clutching their grubby money. They neither looked at one other nor engaged in conversation, they only stared into space, each lost in their personal wicked dreams, waiting for their chance with Dearly Departed.

They'd all heard the rumors, seen the flyers posted in alley and sex shoppes. A smoking hot girl endowed with magical tits that could ferry you far away from your pain and woe.

The perfect way to kick off the Hayes Dayes weekend.

Gazing out the window of the treehouse served two purposes for Rusty. One, he could keep an eye on the line, which, thanks to a preponderance of volatile male hormones, he feared might to erupt into a riot at any moment and, two, it meant that he didn't have to look at Dearly, who was strapped down to Thomas Jefferson's four-poster bed in the middle of the treehouse.

Coco was feeding her a steady diet of Azaperone, which she insisted on shooting from the tranquilizer gun instead of simply injecting. Each and every time she pulled the trigger, she laughed manically.

None of the men minded Dearly being comatose, some even got a charge out of it.

Pedro Proença, the town's problematic postmaster, said, while rubbing his small, enveloped-stained hands together, "Oh wow, this is great, it'll be just like flocking Cinderella."

"I think you're thinking of Sleeping Beauty," said CoCo, "and you read the contract, Mr. Proença, there's no intercourse allowed. You get to lick her titties, that's it."

"Sure, sure, we all know that a contract is a binding agreement between two or more persons or parties; esp: one legally enforceable." That's how he talked, Proença. Like a walking dictionary. Just one of the many reasons he was problematic.

Even though the postmaster had given the Webster's definition of a contract, his eyes were still pregnant with trouble. And he wouldn't stop licking his stamp-scented lips.

Fortunately, when it was Pedro's turn with Dearly, he played by the rules, licking her nipples and wandering off in a fog.

With marginal help from Rusty, CoCo had cleared a majority of the antique furniture out of the treehouse, freeing up room for the men, who were too messed up to climb back down the mother of pearl ladder, to find the nearest available space to lay down and drift away. After being open for only an hour, there was quite a stack of men piled about. Rusty thought the treehouse was beginning to resemble an opium den, with an unconscious naked woman as its centerpiece.

With a tremulous hand, Rusty waved CoCo over to the window.

His girlfriend, if she was still his girlfriend, didn't even attempt to hide the exaggerated eye roll that swept over her face. Rusty knew that CoCo had witnessed Dearly kissing him in the parking lot of the smelting factory, which had soured their relationship considerably. Gone were the days of the boisterous but toothy blowjobs.

But still, he had to speak his mind even if his voice was shaking.

With a grunted sigh, CoCo joined him at the window. "What now?"

"Well, it's just that there's an awful lot of screwed up men laying around here."

She glanced, with a sly smile, at the bodyscape of prone men. "Yeah? So? That means business is booming. A ton of semi-catatonic men means money, just as it does for a majority of American industries."

"But… but… well, I'm sure we're breaking some pretty serious fire code regulations here."

She laughed. It was short and mean like CoCo herself. "Rusty, we've kidnapped a woman, drugged her, tied her down, and are allowing strange men, for a hundred dollars a pop, to lick her titties to get high, and you're worried about getting a citation from the flocking fire department?"

"No, no, it's just this has gotten out of hand. There's like a hundred dudes sprawled on the floor, and even more waiting to get in. What if my father comes home?"

She patted his cheek, which felt like blows. "Let me worry about the flow of men. And as far as your father goes, you know he's booked solid today with judging the Rutherford B. Hayes Memorial Rutherford B. Hayes Dayes' Rutherford B. Hayes Look-Alike Contest. He won't return home until long after dark. So, stop worrying."

Rushing to pull Aaron Mellott, the town drunk and mayor, off Dearly's breasts before he OD'ed, CoCo left Rusty behind to worry.

"Well, I'm not requesting vacation time, I'm simply informing you that, in no uncertain terms, I'm taking the vacation time due to me, which, when tallied, is three weeks, starting immediately."

Though he should have been beating his henchman about the face and neck for such insubordination, Loco Lenny Labovitz could only stare at Left, his mouth agape. He'd only ever heard the thug grunt semi-phrases but now, suddenly, sentences were flowing from him like wordy rivers.

Employing a soft, conciliatory tone, Loco said, "I'm terribly sorry about Right, he was a good man, a good goon. I feel as if I've also lost a brother. But we both gotta put those feelings aside and concentrate on the fact that it's Hayes Dayes and we've got a ton of Hayes Methmatch just sitting around gathering dust cause we got a big problem. When I showed up this morning and there wasn't a single soul waiting outside the mobile drug emporium, I got a little curious. So, I went for a walk, a little fact-finding mission. Down by the river, I ran into Rob Allen, you know, the cactus fucker. Sure, he's a creep, but when he doesn't have his prick in some prickly pear, he has his hand on the pulse of the wrist that is Fremont. So, I struck up a conversation with old Rob and, after striking him a few times, he told me who's up. Once-a-flocking-gain there's a new killer drug on the streets of Fremont and it ain't mine. The cactus fucker's a little light on details but, from what he's heard, this drug has something to do with a lady's magical boobies, which, when licked, transports the licker to the wondrous world of yesteryear. You can see how I'm in something of a real bind here. Not only have I lost one of my most beloved henchmen, I have a bunch of product that isn't moving and I'm facing some fairly stiff magical booby competition."

The sick goon sniffled, wiped away some snot. "I feel for you and your distribution predicament but I made a vow to Right's head that I would hunt down his killer. Hence, my vacation time."

Groaning, Loco looked at the pile of Methmatch on the floor

of the mobile drug emporium, then back at Left.

Left said, "I can tell that you are vexed by this news. Let me relieve you to some degree. My guess is that whoever killed Right and whoever is selling this new drug might be the same person. Therefore, our wants dovetail. I could be killing the proverbial pair of birds with one stone."

Although he had a hard time following what his henchman was saying, Loco felt it was good. He smiled. "If I was you, I'd start by finding that Slump asshole."

Left sneezed thunderously. "My thoughts exactly. I'm going to locate Rusty Slump and ask him a few questions. If he gives me the wrong answers, I will remove his head. If he gives me the right answers, I will also remove his head."

Although he was watching clown after clown miraculously emerge from a miniature car, Police Chief Pendleton held no joy in his heart. There was a teenage girl who was tearing his town apart, murdering people willy-nilly, and, although he had Junior Officer Killion out posting alarming flyers in every alley and sex shoppe warning the general populace there was a distinct possibility they could be ripped limb from limb if they ventured out, he had largely been ignored. The people of Fremont loved their Hayes Dayes – the horse trough races, the beard burning contests, the clown-only Rutherford B. Hayes Memorial parade, where Pendleton was now, scanning the crowd for the adolescent serial killer.

One of the clowns slipped on a staged banana, Pendleton's favorite gag, and he couldn't even bring himself to smile. Instead, he thought of chunks of lesbian gym teacher floating in his very own toilet bowl. Sure, carpet-munching was a sin against God, but that was no way to solve the problem.

With a shake of his head, he returned to scouring the crowd, thousands of people enjoying Hayes Dayes, all of them without a care in the world, as if there wasn't a more-bloodthirsty-than-average teen in their midst.

Pendleton spied Junior Officer Killion across the town's square. Looking peaked, the young cop ducked into Barbra Berlovitz's Donut Yurt.

Stomping toward the yurt, ready to reprimand Killion for dereliction of duty, Pendleton was stopped when his walkie-talkie blistered to life, tossing a tinny version of Officer Rumpza's voice out into the world. "Police Chief, are you there?"

"I am," he informed the walkie-talkie.

"I'm reporting in. I've checked every inch of this town, no Dearly Departed. We're never going to find her before she strikes again!"

The Police Chief could hear fear in his sexy subordinate's voice. He had to keep her grounded. "Tarnation, Chrissy! Don't sound so negative! Now, I'm at the parade and there's nothing suspicious here except for the outrageous number of clowns that can fit into a single tiny car. But we can't give up now, keep looking. I know that little murderess is here somewhere, I can feel it in my bones!"

"You do realize that we're not talking about your average teenage serial killer here, right Chief?"

His voice ashen, he said, "I'm aware of that."

"She ate Daniella Locke, ate her whole, even devoured her gym shoes."

Rumpza made a gulping noise that Pendleton couldn't quite discern. "Chrissy, are you crying?"

"No, no, it's just been, well, it's been the worst Hayes Dayes ever."

"I would have to agree with that sentiment."

She blurted, "I don't think we have a serial killer in Fremont, I think we're dealing with some kind of monster here."

Pendleton had been thinking the same thing but he'd never dare voice it. "Now listen here, Officer Rumpza, you got to keep a lid on your emotions. We already got Junior Officer

Killion riding around on the police bike, putting up flyers about a serial killer, let's not get the people too riled up."

"Okay, okay, you're right, Chief. But what if we can't find her? What if someone has taken her in? Offered her shelter? Is protecting her?"

"If some fool did that, they're probably dead by now."

Rusty wished he were dead. Considered jumping from the window of the luxurious treehouse, ending it all, his body broken upon his father's azaleas.

But that sounded painful.

Though it was not quite noon – Rusty could hear the first barrage from the pie shooting contest wafting from the town square, blocks away – the line leading up to the treehouse had dwindled down to nothing, all the ne'er-do-wells of Fremont had had their fill of Dearly Departed's dope tits and were sprawled on the floor of the treehouse, dreaming their creepy dreams.

Using her father's old iguana trap as a cash drawer, CoCo sat amongst the unconscious, within tranquilizer gun range of Dearly, counting mounds of money, a smirk fixed on her face.

"How'd we do?" Rusty asked, though his voice held no enthusiasm. He didn't really care; he just couldn't stand the silence any longer.

"Over five grand. And when these slumbering flocks awake, I think we can count on some return business and a lot of positive word of mouth. A week or two of this kind of business and you, my friend, will definitely be the new king of the vast and dangerous underworld of Fremont, Ohio."

He blurted, "With you on my arm, whispering in my ear, controlling every move I make."

She looked at him as if he were a talking turd. "Is there anything wrong with that scenario?"

"No, no, Sugar Philtrum," he replied post haste. Took a step back though there was no step to take.

But there was something wrong with that scenario, something terribly wrong. Through the course of the morning, Rusty had arrived at the realization that not only did he have no love for CoCo, he found that he loathed her, despised every look she cast, rued every breath she took. She was a heinous individual, the way she bossed him around, the brusque way she dealt with the customers, the awful smile she got when she picked up the tranquilizer gun and aimed it at Dearly's prone body. Not only did he wish for a CoCo-less future, he was ashamed of sharing a past with her. Regretting every single one of those boisterous but toothy blowjobs, seeing them, for the first time, for what they truly were, just a way to wrap him around her little finger via his dick.

Niccolo Machiavelli would never have put up with that shit.

During his time of introspection at the window, Rusty dreamed of escaping CoCo's grasp and taking Dearly with him. But watching his demi-girlfriend's prowess with the tranquilizer gun, he came to the conclusion he'd never escape her. That he would die beneath her thumb.

That's when his thoughts turned to snuffing himself.

Stuffing the money back into the iguana trap and snapping it shut, CoCo stood. "I'm going to go put this money in the bank, you stay here and do some general maintenance."

"General maintenance?"

She sighed, defeated. "When these flocks wake up, stuff a flyer in their pockets and help them get down the ladder, we don't need any lawsuits. And keep this little hussy drugged, you've seen the damage she can do when she's awake. Those teeth, those lips, that tongue."

Rusty felt the jab of those words land as his erstwhile girlfriend exited the treehouse.

A smile forming, Rusty watched her stridently stride right through the azaleas. Her ass perfect and mean.

He was alone, unguarded. Rusty knew this would be his only chance to unbind Dearly, carry her down the ladder like a bride, climb into his safety-conscious Volvo and drive far, far away.

Maybe Toledo. Where they could live happily ever after, even if he had to take a job in a dog park, which were well-known battlegrounds in the bloody turf wars of Toledo.

Legs tingling with excitement, the young man crossed to the four-poster bed. Some of the men stirred as he trod upon them, but he paid them no heed.

Standing over Dearly, Rusty could barely control his breathing. His eyes brimmed with tears as he imagined the perfect life with this perfect woman.

A noise interrupted his reverie. All around him, there was movement. The prone ne'er-do-wells were stirring and he could tell by their lusty moans that they needed another hit of tit. Rusty had to hurry.

Feeling like Machiavelli from his head down to the balls of his balls, Rusty picked up the sleeping girl.

Dearly was surprisingly light, like a ghost, like a dream, like the ghost of a dream.

Rusty couldn't help but smile with Dearly's body pressed into his. This was perfect, this was everything.

That smile evaporated when he saw, standing between himself and the door of the treehouse a figure. A hulking figure. Pedro Proença, Fremont's problematic postmaster.

And he appeared even more problematic than usual as he was holding a gleaming machete in his hand.

"Where are you going with her, the girl with the magic dubbies?" asked Pedro, his voice as husky as a dog.

"Away."

"No you're not, bro. You and me, we're gonna dance. And by dance, I don't mean to move one's feet or body, or both, rhythmically in a pattern of steps, especially to the accompaniment of music."

The news that they had a teen serial killer killing serially in little old Fremont rattled Junior Officer Killion. With trembling hands and shaking legs, he'd biked all over town, putting up flyers that read: HAVE A GREAT HAYES DAYES BY STAYING INSIDE AND AVOIDING THE SERIAL KILLER TEARING PEOPLE APART. ALSO, NO PARKING ON THE ODD SIDE OF THE STREET. Printed on red, white, and blue paper, keeping with the presidential theme. That had been Killion's idea.

In desperate need of pastry-based solace, the young cop had, when he'd run out of flyers - some of which, admittedly, he'd tossed in a Dumpster behind the Rutherford B. Hayes Memorial Tan 'N Touch - pushed his way through the throng of parade revelers and entered Barbra Berlovitz's Donut Yurt. Taking a seat in the back with a comforting cruller in hand.

As he'd been blessed since birth with a complete lack of moral fortitude, Leigham Shardlow had a tough decision to make when it came time for him to choose a career. There were so many options in modern America for someone soulless. He could have been a pharmaceutical salesman or a professional jaywalker or a Republican Senator. As his only passion in life, outside of non-consensual anal sex, was large amounts of cash, he decided to become a banker.

But after a decade of employment at the Rutherford B. Hayes Memorial Savings and Loan, he began to feel restless, unsatisfied. Certainly he was well compensated for forcing farmers off their land and talking the poor into getting loans they could never repay, but whenever he sneaked a peak at the accounts of the truly rich and powerful of Fremont, his guts conflagrated with jealousy. People like Prestley Jones-Prestly, owner of the Rutherford B. Hayes Memorial Methadone Clinic, who raked in millions every year. Or Shirley Twatmiser-LeStrange, who inherited all twenty-three Rutherford B. Hayes Memorial Sex Shoppes in Sandusky County from her grandfather; she had several chunks of gold in her safety deposit box that were as big as Shardlow's fists. And, thanks to a rather rigorous masturbation schedule, the banker's fists were nothing to shake a stick at.

Every night, Shardlow lay awake in his bed, playing with himself and dreaming of joining the ranks of the rich and powerful of Fremont. Owning a stupidly large yacht and a stupidly small dog. He longed for Belgian chocolates, Cuban cigars, and Toldeoan whores. Those few, simple things would make his life complete.

That's why he started stealing. It was easy at first. Skimming a few dollars from the accounts of people like Prestley Jones-Prestly, who'd never miss it. But these performances of petty pilfering didn't balm his wanting soul. He needed more. The amounts he stole ballooned to several digits and, just the previous week, he'd opened Shirley Twatmiser-LeStrange's safety deposit box and shoved one of her golden fists down his pants, kept it there all day. Even after returning home, he didn't remove the fist as if felt so good, so gold against his junk.

The first twinge of regret he'd ever felt in his life came when he noticed, not long after the theft of the gold, that the bank's head of security, Gary Frutkoff, began to stare at him out of the corner of his eye as he sat in the break room.

Shardlow suspected that the hammer was about to drop and he was the nail, that he was on the verge of being arrested. He needed to divert attention away from himself. Someone or something else had to soak up Frutkoff's heat.

That's when he devised the killer toaster plan.

One of the careers that he'd spoken about with his alarmed high school guidance counselor was that of terrorist. Not working for one of those chuckleheaded Islamic organizations, the zealoty flocks who believed that if they martyred themselves, they'd find seventy-two virgins waiting for them in Paradise. That's not what the boy was talking about. First off, young Shardlow didn't fancy the thought of martyrdom and, secondly, when he got to heaven, he wanted to find seventy-two sluts lounging on his cloud. No, he was more of the old school mercenary type, working for the highest bidder. Blackwater type stuff. Gunning innocents down in the streets, blowing shit up, which he was good at. In shop class, he'd assembled a pipe bomb when the teacher, Mr. Lumbload, had his back turned. The boy used the pipe bomb to destroy the mailbox outside the Rutherford B. Hayes Memorial Post Office.

Although the guidance counselor tried to poo-poo the terrorist career path, Shardlow stuck with it until he scanned the local want ads and found there was very little need for mercenaries in the Fremont area.

Though he suspected that his bomb-making skills might come in handy in the future.

One day, when Frutkoff was out with gastric distress due to his hot dog addiction, Shardlow snuck his toolbox into the closet where the bank kept the stash of toasters it doled out to new customers. Working his magic fingers while whistling, the vile banker wired a handful of the small appliances to explode when plugged in and hid them in the back. This bit of sabotage would bring vitriol aplenty down upon the crispy shoulders of Natty Thatcher, the little old lady who was in charge of promotions at the bank, especially after Shardlow started spreading rumors that Natty had been trying to save money by ordering cut-rate toasters from Mexico. This act of negligence would cost some poor housewife an arm or maybe even her life and Gary-flocking-Frutkoff would be off his trail long enough for him to gather his booty and get his booty out of town.

It was the perfect plan, it simply needed the perfect victim.

On the first morning of Hayes Dayes, Shardlow was feeling low as he was forced to work, which meant he'd miss the turtle carving contest. But his mood lightened considerably when a young woman approached his desk and said sharply, "I'd like to open an account. Make it snappy."

Immediately, Shardlow knew that he'd stumbled upon the perfect victim for his first toaster attack. For one thing, this young woman was a bitch and he wouldn't miss any sleep over blowing her to smithereens and, two, she was pretty to a point and everyone cares more when an aesthetically pleasing person is pulled, charred, from the hulk of a burning appliance.

"Certainly, certainly," Shardlow said, trying to keep the creamy glee-filled center out of his voice.

He stood, offered his hand to shake. She pretended not to see it as she dropped a large metal box on his desk.

"Hey," said Shardlow, lowering his hand, "is that an iguana trap?"

"Yeah."

He studied her closer.

Back in high school, Shardlow had a part-time job at the Rutherford B. Hayes Memorial Slightly Dangerous Petting Zoo. Taking tickets, selling popcorn, forcing the injured to sign falsified affidavits. His boss was Jinx McArdle, a complete asshole and gun nut, who reeked of cordite and bestiality. At that time McArdle had a little daughter. Dark hair, dark eyes. Always scowling, always bitching.

"Are you… are you… do you happen to be Jinx McArdle's daughter?" Shardlow asked. He was so excited he could taste his words.

For the first time, she looked him in the eye, tensed.

"Yeah. Who wants to know?"

"I'm Leigham Shardlow. I worked for your father when I was young. Great man. I was so sorry when I heard about the rabid ocelot incident."

He wasn't sorry at all. In fact, he'd been overjoyed when he'd heard about Jinx McArdle's death, certain the creepy zookeeper had gotten exactly what he deserved. Although the official report read that McArdle had been sexual assaulted to death while feeding the ocelot, Shardlow knew of the petting zookeeper's strange sexual proclivities and guessed that McArdle had been having sexual congress with the beast when it turned on him.

"Yeah," this woman said with a shrug. "Shit happens."

"So, you wanted to open an account? Checking? Savings? Both?"

"I don't flocking care. I just need a place to plant this cabbage."

From the depths of the iguana trap, the McArdle girl pulled a stack of cash that made Shardlow's eyes waltz.

"If some fool did that, they're probably dead by now."

With those words, Police Chief Pendleton ended their walkie-talkie conversation, and Officer Rumpza was allowed to return to her sobbing.

It felt as if her whole world had crumbled. After waking up on the floor of Connie's bedroom, still grasping the pungent panties, the scent of her former lover wafting, a thought struck the cop that would have knocked her over had she not already been prone.

She knew it was impossible, but the person - or whatever it was that they were dealing with - who'd last worn those panties not only smelled like Connie, it was Connie. Had to be. Rumpza had a hell of a nose for snatch and every one was different, just like a hairy snowflake.

Not that she could have explained any of this to her boss.

But she did voice her suspicion that the person that they were tracking wasn't a person, and her boss reacted in the way she feared he would react. He shut her down.

After their conversation ended, instead of continuing to search Fremont for Dearly Departed, who was, in her mind, also Connie Pendleton, she searched for a place to hide. Although Fremont was choked with revelers, Rumpza found sanctuary behind the Rutherford B. Hayes Memorial Pilates Center. She parked her patrol car and cried her eyes out. She didn't have the heart to continue her hunt for this murderous girl that somehow was and wasn't her former lover.

Perhaps she would just sit there until she died of old age. Or Dearly found her and ripped her throat open.

Of course, he found Killion in Barbra Berlovitz's Donut Yurt. A more jocular goon would have made light of the cop/donut paradigm, but he wasn't in the mood.

Grimacing, Left approached the table in the back occupied by the Junior Officer. He noticed that the young man tensed as he drew near; he loved when that happened.

Left took a seat without asking permission, let his weight shift the table, spill the cop's coffee. "I'm looking for a judge. Ironic, seeing as I'm a goon."

"Huh?" croaked Killion.

"I'm looking for Judge Slump. Rumor placed him at the Rutherford B. Hayes Memorial Rutherford B. Hayes Dayes' Rutherford B. Hayes Look-Alike Contest, but that rumor bore no meat. In fact, it turns out that there is no Rutherford B. Hayes Memorial Rutherford B. Hayes Dayes' Rutherford B. Hayes Look-Alike Contest. Seeing that you, just like myself, are on Loco's payroll, I thought you might help me out with this quandary."

The cop studied him. "Why would a thug want a judge?"

"It's not the judge I'm really looking for, he's simply a conduit. I'm looking for his son, Rusty Slump."

"The floorshitter?"

"Precisely. Know his whereabouts?"

"Why do you need to find Rusty Slump?"

"I'm fairly convinced he had something to do with Right's passing."

Killion burst out laughing. "Rusty didn't kill your brother. I probably shouldn't tell you this, but, as you pointed out, you and me are on the same team."

"We're not on the same team."

"Well, whatever, according to my superiors, your brother was murdered by our local serial killer."

Eyebrows knitted, Left asked, "Serial killer?"

"Yeah, a young woman named Dearly Departed. Have you not seen the flyers I posted all over town? Has all my work been for naught?"

"So, you're trying to tell me that Right was killed by some random act of senseless violence."

Nodding, Killion took a knowing bite from his cruller.

Watching the idiot chew, Left said, "I bet those two, Slump and Dearly, are working in tandem. When he was murdered, Right was following Rusty."

Killion couldn't respond as his mouth was filled with cruller.

Continued Left, "I bet if I find Rusty Slump, I'll find Dearly Departed."

Killion continued chewing.

Left, "So, is that everything you know?"

Again with the idiotic exaggerated nodding.

"Then you won't be needing this," said Left, reaching forward with surprising speed and agility. The thug's punch cracked Killion's forehead in two. Blood everywhere. The cop, already dead, dropped his cruller and fell forward. Before his head hit the table, Left pushed his hand inside it and, with a sickening *fwap* noise, freed Killion's brain from its moorings.

Holding the organ at arm's length, the thug walked slowly from Barbra Berlovitz's Donut Yurt.

Every eye on him, every eye terrified.

Waking up in the arms of a woman was a new experience for

Cuntlips McGoo. Usually heavy metal groupies slunk off after a bout or two of sexual congress, wanting neither cuddling nor compassion. This arrangement was fine with Cuntlips, who believed love to be an illusion.

Not anymore. Waking up entangled with Nicole Clymer on the floor of an interstate restroom was heaven on earth.

That was, until he realized that he'd woken up because a strange woman was pounding on the door of their stall, making demands, her voice shrill with anger. "What in the name of the Sweet Baby G is going on here? I count two pairs of legs in there and one of them is hairy. If you two don't vacate this stall in the next thirty seconds to let me do my business, I'm calling the Highway Patrol or… or… whatever governmental agency is equipped to handle such a disgusting situation!"

Stifling embarrassed laughter, Cuntlips and Nicole looked deep into one another's eyes, kissed. They pulled on their clothes as if the stall were burning down and cleared out, ducking their heads to avoid the scowl of the irate woman.

Out into the early morning sunlight they stumbled. The world was just waking up. Birds on branches, tweeting away. For a few moments, Cuntlips, still shrugging off sleep, nibbled on his lover's ears.

Then an unpleasant dash of lightning bolted across his brain.

"Oh my God," he shouted. "I forgot all about the demon! We have to get to Fremont!"

Being a staunch member of the legal community, Judge Slump was not accustomed to fibbing. But that's exactly what he'd done when he told his son that he'd be tied up all day judging the Rutherford B. Hayes Memorial Rutherford B. Hayes Dayes' Rutherford B. Hayes Look-Alike Contest. The judge simply wanted to spend some time alone, away from the hustle and bustle of Hayes Dayes, away from his son, away from his past.

For this holiday brought with it a deluge of memories of his beloved Buhltulha, Rusty's sainted mother.

The elder Slump met the love of his life many Hayes Dayes prior, at the hot dog polishing contest. He was a contestant and she was the celebrity judge, having recently been crowned the Quasi-Queen of Hayes Dayes. He'd never seen such a vision of beauty. Everything about Buhltulha was bubbly: her blonde hair, her broad smile, her big boobs. For Slump it was love at first sight. They soon married and lived happily ever after.

Well, they lived happily until the tragic Pancake Collapse of Ought-6.

In that fated year, the mayor of Fremont, Aaron Mellott, a drunkard, had a dream and that dream concerned planting the town of Fremont squarely in the pages of the Guinness Book of World Records. The mayor saw a clear path for this achievement: the world's largest pancake. For a year, he secretly siphoned funds away from public works, schools, and civic safety, and diverted them into a slush fund to buy ten tons of flour, four hundred gallons of canola oil, and a frying pan the size of a Winnebago. A hundred volunteers were rounded up to help with this endeavor. One of those volunteers was Buhltulha Slump, who loved both pancakes and records. Unfortunately, on that terrible first day of Hayes Dayes in 2006, the unthinkable happened. During the first flip of the massive pancake the crane handling the mega-spatula - which was being operated by the soused mayor - malfunctioned and the giant pancake fell to earth from a great height. Poor Buhltulha was crushed, the only fatality of the incident, if one doesn't count Fremont not making it into the Guinness World Book of Records.

These days Judge Slump spends every Hayes Dayes in splendid isolation, locked away in his third floor office in the courthouse.

Sitting in solitude and reflection, eating bologna sandwiches and masturbating.

As luck would have it, he was in non-masturbation mode when the door of his office crashed open and in strode well-known miscreant, Left Queerfolk. Slump knew it wasn't Right Queerfolk, as he'd heard that Right had met an unpleasant end the previous eve. It was distressing news that Right had his head removed, but, on the bright side, the judge would now be able to tell the brothers apart more readily.

As the big man lumbered with purpose toward his desk, sweating profusely, the judge stood, his face blistering. "You know the deal, Left! I take my bribe monies down behind the Rutherford B. Hayes Memorial Sex Shoppe #9, not in my office!"

"Of your bribery proclivities I am well aware, but that is not the reason for my visit. I brought you a present."

The big man held out his massive paw. Nestled in it was a gray gelatinous botchery that bore a strong resemblance to a mushed human brain.

"Is that a brain?" asked the judge, who was a big fan of clarification.

"Sorry it got mushed on the walk over."

The thug slammed the brain down on the judge's desk, which was loaded with sandwich fixings. It exploded, sounding like a wet fart, sending gray gunk everywhere.

"What's the meaning of this?" demanded Slump, who was daintily picking slugs of brain off his robe.

"It means that I'm flocking serious. I don't know if you're aware or not, but my beloved brother was murdered last night and I'm going to track down his killer if it's the last thing I do."

"Well, I am truly sorry about your brother's passing, but I'm a tad confused about what Right's death has to do with me."

"I think your son was involved with his untimely demise."

Despite the threatening look sprawled across Left's face, the judge laughed. "Rusty? That little idiot couldn't find his nutsack with his dick. Do you honestly believe he possesses the fortitude to gnaw the head off another human being, especially if said human being was three times his size?"

"I realize it sounds ridiculous, but Right was following Rusty when he was killed."

Frowning, the judge asked why.

"It appears as if Rusty has once again stumbled upon a killer drug. This time it has something to do with magical nugs, if I'm understanding correctly."

Slumping down in his chair, the judge murmured, "Sweet Baby G, not again."

"I have it on good authority that the actual murderer of my brother is a young woman with whom your progeny has been known to associate. She has red hair, Herculean nugs, and travels by the unlikely handle Dearly Departed. Does that ring any bells in your belfry?"

Slump's mind flashed back to the young woman who'd been waiting on his porch the previous evening. She had red hair, remarkable fleshy bagpipes, and a forward air. "I don't know her but I believe I've seen her around."

A step forward. "Do you have any idea where she and Rusty might be laying low?"

The judge straightened in his seat. "I don't … I don't know. Listen, Left, Rusty isn't a bad kid. At worst he's a floorshitter led astray by that awful McArdle girl. I don't want him hurt."

"I have no desire to harm your son, I am only looking for his female associate."

The judge sighed. "He… he seems to spend a lot of time in his treehouse, in my backyard."

"Thanks for the info. Now you must die."

Standing, Slump stumbled backward, coming to rest against the wood paneled wall. "But... but, you can't kill me! When you kill this Dearly girl, you'll need friends in high places!"

"You'd be right, your Honor, if I gave a damn what happened to me. But since Right is dead, I have nothing to live for."

"But... but... but..." said the judge as he pissed his robe.

Laughing, the thug advanced, eyeing the spreading stain. He loved it when they urinated right before.

With his massive hands, Left wiped away some snot before picking Slump up and carrying him to the nearest window. Before he tossed him, Left whispered in his ear, "And just for the fun of it, I'm also going to kill your son."

After the tossing and the screaming and the breaking glass, Left returned to the judge's desk, staring down at the sandwich fixing. Fearing his blood sugar was dangerously low, he wiped brain from a loaf of bread and tucked it beneath his arm.

"It appears to be some kind of crazed civic celebration centered around a dead president, drinking, and destroying things," said Nicole Clymer as she sidled up behind Cuntlips McGoo, who was studying a flyer about a local serial killer stapled, upside down, to a telephone pole.

As his mind was occupied, he didn't really hear his recently acquired sexual partner. With an anxious hand, he tapped the flyer repeatedly. "This town doesn't have a serial killer, they have a demon in their midst and they don't even know it."

"Well, how would they know that?" said Nicole, defending the tiny town of Fremont, which people so rarely do. "Demons aren't an every day occurrence in America like serial killers."

Cuntlips spun on her. "Actually, demons *are* an every day occurrence, people are just too blind to see them!"

"Okay, okay," she said, holding up her hands in a defensive

position. "So what's our next move?"

"Well, Maude the Layer of Waste usually doesn't keep her presence much of a secret. If we simply stroll down the street, I'm sure this possessed being will reveal herself."

As they simply strolled down the street, Nicole took her lover's hand. When they had made sweet, sweet love on that filthy restroom floor, his hands had felt so good against her skin. Warm, confident, strong. But now they were clammy and weak, shaking. This disturbed Nicole but she kept her mouth shut and discreetly dropped his hand.

Though it was morning, it appeared as if a vast majority of the locals were shit-faced. Walking crooked, laughing loudly. They passed a woman perfecting her goulash juggling, a child painting a cat with toothpaste, and a man manicuring his eyebrows with a pair of garden shears and an unsteady hand.

"This whole place seems populated by demons," observed Nicole.

But Cuntlips wasn't listening. He'd stopped in his tracks and was glaring at the horizon.

"There!" he spat, raising a finger.

The former rocker was pointing at Barbra's Berlovitz's Donut Yurt, which sat across the square. Its façade was criss-crossed by yellow police tape.

Taking off, Cuntlips yelled over his shoulder, "This simply reeks of demon!"

Shaking her head over her boyfriend's peculiar behavior, Nicole followed him across the square. The silver lining, she tried to convince herself, was that as long as she stayed with Cuntlips McGoo, she would never want for adventure.

Although the tape warned him specifically not to do so, Cuntlips crossed the police line. In fact, he did so with gusto, leaping through the cobweb of tape as if finishing a marathon.

Nicole followed suit, but at a much more non-athletic pace. She felt guilty, demon or no.

When she entered the DonutYurt, she nearly lost her breakfast although she hadn't eaten anything.

In the back of the restaurant, there was a dead man slumped over a table. His head, at least what was left of it, was a pulpy mess of goo and there was about seventy gallons of blood drying on the table, walls, and floor.

Looking away, Nicole fingered her cross necklace and said a short prayer, as Cuntlips continued into the restaurant, toward the two people who were standing as close to the crime scene as the lake of blood would allow. One was a cop, the other a woman who looked as stricken as Nicole.

"You're not supposed to be here," the cop warned the former rocker. "The tape outside should have told you."

"Sorry to sully your crime scene, officer, but I have some pertinent information about the dangerous young woman who did this."

The cop's anger evaporated. "You know Dearly Departed?"

"In a way."

"Well, the one thing I know about her is that she didn't kill Junior Officer Killion here, that was done by Left Queerfolk, there were a dozen witnesses to this fact."

The woman, presumably Barbra Berlovitz, nodded severely.

Silence ruled the day as Cuntlips looked at the cop and licked his slightly misshapen lips. "Okay, but I bet you've had other mysterious deaths in the area."

Narrowing his eyes, the cop said, "Why don't you tell me everything you know about our little serial killer, Dearly Departed?"

"Well, first off, she's not human, she's a demon."

The cop turned red and reached out, clasping his hands

around Cuntlips' throat. "Listen, you freak, this town, my town, is in enough of a panic without you, a stranger, showing up and spouting a bunch of bullarkey about demons."

"Officer, I know it sounds crazy but you have to believe me."

"I don't got to believe nothing. Now if I weren't so busy with multiple murder investigations, I'd take you out back and show you a thing or two about Ohio justice! But I'll just have to settle for tossing you out on your rusty teakettle and promising you that if I ever see your dag-nabbed ugly mug around these parts again, I'll remove it!"

With an ease that surprised Nicole, the cop hoisted her boyfriend above his head, carried him past her, and tossed him through the flaps of the yurt. With steely eyes, the cop turned on Nicole. "Now do you wish to join your dad-blamed friend under your own power or do I got to toss you too?"

Lowering her head, not saying a word, she headed for the street. Although it was a short journey, it was filled with contemplation. Certainly she had her own idiosyncrasies – such as the fact that she'd murdered her abusive husband, buried him in his pot patch, and fled, a secret that she'd told no one, not even Cuntlips – but how well did she really know her new lover? She'd found him by the side of the highway, spinning outrageous stories of heavy metal bands and demons and a Buddhist monk ninja warrior assassin. It did sound a little crazy when one thought about it.

What if Cuntlips McGoo was cut from the same cloth as her deceitful husband Keith? What if he was just another sack of yak shit?

Perhaps it would be best if she simply cut bait. Walked out that yurt, got in her car, drove home, and turned herself in. Lead the cops to the plot where she'd buried Keith. It was California, how harsh could the punishment for killing your mate be? Picking up trash on the side of the interstate for a few months? She could handle that, as long as they didn't make her wear orange. As she was a winter, orange simply wasn't her color.

When she stepped out into the sunlight, she spied a bruised Cuntlips sitting on the curb, cradling his head in his hands. Crying a little.

All doubt fled. Instantly, she knew that her initial instincts about this man had been right. Cuntlips McGoo was a good man on a holy mission. He wasn't crazy, he simply saw things other people didn't see. He definitely had nothing to do with yak shit.

She made a vow to tell him that she'd beaten her husband to death with a bag of lentil beans and buried his body behind their property.

Later. Right now she had to comfort this righteous man.

Taking a seat beside him, Nicole said softly, "That cop sure is a major douche."

Cuntlips didn't look up. "Nicole, I'm sorry that I dragged you into this whole demon mess. I have no idea what I'm doing here. I wasn't the Buddhist monk ninja warrior assassin, that was Tim. I was only an apprentice Buddhist monk ninja warrior assassin. If Tim were here, he'd have known what to say to the irate cop, what path to take, which mountains to climb and which ones to walk around, but not me. I'm lost."

Gently putting her hand on his shoulder, Nicole leaned into him and said, "You know exactly what you have to do and you're going to do it. I don't know this Tim fellow, but I know Vince Whateveryourlastnameis and I have faith in him. And just so you know, there's no one on earth that I'd rather be battling demons with than you."

Uncradling his slightly misshapen head, the former rocker wiped away his tears and looked at her with a wan smile. "You're right. We're going to send that demon straight back to hell."

"That's the spirit! Straight back to hell! Right after a little bathroom break." She woggled her eyebrows.

Nicole stared deeply into Cuntlips' slightly misshapen eyes as he stared deeply into hers.

"Are we talking about more public bathroom sex?" he asked, his voice small.

She exploded, a flesh-colored firework. "It's called baleophilia and it affects one in every five million Americans! I'm not proud of it but the only way I can achieve orgasm is by having sex in a public bathroom. The dirtier, the better. I've always been this way and I don't know why but I'm not changing any time soon. Although we never talked about it, I'm pretty sure it's why Keith grew cold toward me. He found public bathroom copulation, even if we did it at new Macy's in Stockton, to be dirty and degrading."

When she started talking about Keith, she broke down. Tears flowing like the mighty Sandusky, it was Nicole's turn to drop her head into her hands.

Luckily, Cuntlips was there to break her fall. He hugged her so tight their two heartbeats became one. "Hey, just so you know, I'd have sex in the most disgusting bathroom in America, as long as that disgusting bathroom contained you."

"Yes, Señor Proença, I'm well aware that you're not talking about moving one's feet or body, or both, rhythmically in a pattern of steps, especially to the accompaniment of music. I know you are, in fact, going to try and kill me. But, does it seem fair that you're armed with a machete while my hands are full of girl?" Rusty Slump asked.

"By 'fair' do you mean 'marked by favorable conditions' or do you mean 'an exhibition, usually competitive, of farm products, livestock, etc., often combined in the US with entertainment and held annually by a county or state'?"

Rusty stared at the problematic postmaster with his mouth ajar but no words forming.

"I'm just messing with you, *muchacho*. One is an adjective and the other is a noun, which wouldn't make any sense in your sentence. So, the answer is yes, I do find this situation marked by favorable conditions, thanks to the Armed Mail Carrier Act of 1920."

1919 was a shit year for the United States postal carriers. In April and June, socialists mailed several bombs to prominent politicians and businessmen across America. In Fremont, the socialists weren't so mechanically inclined, so they resorted to mailing out postcards with really sharp edges. Several mail carriers in Sandusky County received nasty paper cuts and the mayor of Fremont, Aaron Mellott, drunkard, sliced his entire thumb off. The Great Sharp Postcard Scare of 1919 resulted in the Armed Mail Carrier Act of 1920 which stated that all deliverers of mail and their families were not only permitted to carry weapons of their choosing, but obligated to do so. Also, they could employ said weapons to defend their wellbeing, their property, the property of others, or "just 'cause."

Pedro Proença flipped the machete into the air, where it seized the light and flickered, and caught it in the opposite hand. "And there's another thing you should know about your local postmaster, I'm problematic."

"That's what everyone says."

"Well… they're right. And yet another thing you should know about me, I'm *muy loco*. Remember about ten years ago, the mailbox outside the Rutherford B. Hayes Memorial Post Office exploded? Well, I was there, *muchacho*, ground zero. I caught a dictionary right in the forehead. Sure, now I have a gargantuan vocabulary, but it also scrambled my brains. So, *adios amigo*."

He charged.

Rusty considered flight but knew he couldn't evade the blade. He was going to have to stand his ground and fight.

As the young man's arms were preoccupied with a limp Dearly Departed, he did the best he could and kicked at the advancing postmaster.

Thankfully, the kick landed right where it matters most: the nut region. Of course, the fact that Pedro Proença had balls like pomegranates, much like Rusty himself, might have helped.

The postmaster screamed as if in the throes of childbirth and stumbled backward, tripping over Aaron Mellott, the mayor.

Spewing foul language, as he often did, Mellott jumped to his feet, knocking Pedro Proença to the floor with a bone-altering thud.

Like a cursing alarm clock, the mayor's yelps woke the other dopers.

"That motherflocker," bellowed Mellott, pointing at Rusty, "is flocking stealing the flocking girl and her flocking magic funlamps! Let's get him!"

The crowd of oversexed men rose and moved toward Rusty as one. They were drooling, shuffling their feet, and making guttural noises. Once again in America, a group of men had been turned into lust zombies.

Rusty was painfully aware that there was no way that he could nail all these dudes in the nuts at once. Of course he could have simply dropped Dearly - that's all these fiends wanted – and flown the coop with his life. Shuffled off to Toledo by his lonesome, started his new life walking dogs and dodging bullets.

But there was no way he was going to leave Dearly to these monsters. He was either going to save her or die trying.

As the men drew closer, it certainly seemed as if the later was going to be the case. There was an army of men heading his way with death shining in their dead eyes. To make matters worse, Pedro Proença had regained his footing. Walking funny thanks to his nut injury, he looked wildly displeased. Twirling his machete like a baton, he joined the death march toward Rusty.

Though he'd promised himself to stand his ground, Rusty took a step back. Catching his foot on the corner of an antique wash basin, he fell. Landing on his ass with a yelp of fear, he managed to keep his hold on Dearly.

With their quarry on the ground, defenseless, the horny horde picked up the pace. Shuffled faster, groaned louder.

When the men arrived at Rusty, they leaned forward, their arms reaching. The young man kissed Dearly ever so sweetly on the forehead, saying goodbye forever.

The last thing Rusty saw before he shut his eyes was the problematic postmaster raising his machete, his teeth white and wide.

Despite the pleasing orthodonture, not a pretty picture.

Interrupting everything, shots rang out. *One, two, three.*

In the confined space of the luxury treehouse, it sounded like a canon roaring. Everyone, even those still slumbering, jumped to their feet. Well, everyone except Pedro Proença. He didn't jump as he was too occupied dropping his machete and grabbing his massive chest. Trying to staunch the flow of blood from the trio of wounds he'd received. Staunching was not to be had that day as blood poured through his sausagey fingers. Color ran from his face like passengers fleeing a burning zeppelin. His eyes rolling back in his head as he collapsed to the floor, dead.

Realizing that he himself wasn't dead, Rusty opened his eyes. Spied CoCo standing in the doorway of the treehouse, her father's smoking .38 gripped firmly in one hand, in the other a toaster. On her face: a scowl.

"Everyone back away from my investment," she said between clenched teeth.

She took two steps forward and the men took five steps back. Holding up their hands as if this were a robbery.

"Okay, whatever tragedies have transpired here in the treehouse are in the past and there's nothing we can do about that. We must all move forward from this point. So, you men clear out and never breath a word about this. Everything, on both sides, will be forgiven and forgotten. Is that a deal?"

CoCo's commanding tone and commanding gun worked their magic. Without another grunt or threatening move, all the men filed out of the treehouse one by one, stepping over the bloodied corpse of Pedro Proença, but not daring to look down upon him. This exodus unfolded under the watchful eye of CoCo, who lowered her weapon but made sure it stayed in sight, black and smoking.

Though Rusty knew the gun's secret: it was bereft of bullets. The .38 was as empty as a Republican senator's heart.

With the men gone, CoCo turned her focus and her anger toward Rusty, who hadn't even bothered to get up from the floor, hadn't bothered to release his grip on Dearly.

CoCo looked back and forth between her boyfriend and his girlfriend. "Now look what you've gone and done! The word of mouth about our new business is gonna be shit."

"I… I'm sorry." Rusty couldn't bring himself to look at her and her bruising eyes.

"But that's not the worst of it. Obviously you were attempting to escape with that little hussy, weren't you?"

Rusty, defeated, nodded. There was no use lying now, he didn't have the energy. He could feel hot tears of hate welling but he refused to let them escape. There was no way he was going to allow CoCo to bring him to tears.

Stepping forward, his ex-girlfriend continued to press. "And what was your plan, big man? Were you gonna haul your new girlfriend far, far away from your mean, old girlfriend? You want to know the truth, Rusty, if that happened I wouldn't shed a single tear over losing you, I don't give two yak dicks what happens to you and your public-shitting ass. But I would be terribly sad if I lost the best drug to hit the streets of Fremont since Purple Hayes."

Still, he wouldn't look up. With one final stomp, she reached him and, using the barrel of the blistering .38, pushed his head back so that he had to look her in the eye.

She smiled her rictus smile. "You and me, we're through."

"I'm sure you two are well aware of what the great Dorothy Parker said about the minefield that is love," said a voice, deep and wide, from the doorway.

CoCo turned. Rusty turned.

Left Queerfolk stood at the threshold of the treehouse, blocking out the sun, blocking out the air, blocking out all hope. His face sweaty, flushed.

Incongruously, he had a loaf of broad tucked beneath his arm like an edible football.

"Ms. Parker said, 'Ah clear they see and true they say/That one shall weep, and one shall stray'. That verse should be carved into the tombstone of every young love affair."

"What the flock do you want?" CoCo spat.

"Just dropped by to offer up a memorable quote about the crooked road we call love. What's up with the toaster?"

Looking down at the small appliance as if it had just magically appeared in her hands, CoCo said, "I opened a savings account."

"Bright girl. 'Too many people spend the money they earn on things that they don't want to impress people they don't like'."

"Dorothy Parker again?"

"The Dorothy Parker with a dick, Will Rogers. Funny, you and me, on different sides of this conflict, one of us with bread, the other with a toaster. In another world, we could make beautiful music together."

"I'll ask again, what do you want, Left?"

"I want the doped girl, who I assume is Dearly Departed. Also, I want the boy holding the doped girl. But I got a bad feeling you're not just going to let them go and I'm going to have to fight you and it's going to be a whole thing."

"For all I care you can have the boy, but the girl stays with me."

Pulling in an acre of breath, Left sighed. Then coughed. "Well, I guess we'll have to discuss who's leaving this treehouse alive."

Looking back and forth between the two verbal combatants, Rusty realized he didn't really have a dog in this fight. It seemed that whoever won, things were going to go badly for for him. And Dearly.

"Well," CoCo pointed out, "I'm the one with a gun."

"And a toaster."

"So I assume I'll be the one who leaves this treehouse alive."

"Again I am struck by the irony that we can find no common ground though one of us is toting a loaf of bread and the other is in possession of a toaster."

"If that's how you feel, you can have the toaster and the boy and I'll keep the girl."

She flipped the toaster at the thug. It flew through the air like a silver, square bird. Left caught it in his free hand.

He smiled. It looked like a crack in his face.

Just one of the many cool things about the luxurious treehouse was it was wired for electricity. There were crystal sconces and outlets all over the place.

Still smiling, Left strode to the nearest available outlet. "Looks like, before I kill all of you, I'll have myself some toast, which is really a slice of dry, crunchy heaven."

"Will Rogers again?"

"No, that was just me."

Getting down on one knee, as if he were proposing to the wall, Left uncoiled the electric cord from the toaster and plugged it in.

He was still smiling when his sweaty face was blown clean off his head by the explosion.

To Rusty, it seemed as if a neutron bomb detonated right before his eyes. A white flash, deafening and searing, filled the treehouse, filled all space and time.

Left, hovering over the toaster-bomb, took the brunt of the explosion. He was lifted off his feet and thrown across the room, landing in several meaty chunks that would have made all the king's men throw up their hands in defeat.

CoCo dropped the gun and Rusty dropped the girl and everyone and everything flew far and wide. Dearly, who remained unconscious, ended up near the fainting couch. Rusty and CoCo landed against the back wall in heaps, their clothes rent, their bodies bruised and scratched.

Rusty's ears rang like church bells. He tried to scream but nothing of interest came out.

Even when the explosion had run its course, things continued to fall apart.

The luxurious treehouse, once the envy of every youth in Fremont, was now nothing but a smoldering disaster. All the antique furniture was broken, the windows shattered, all the art ruined. Great stretches of the walls were simply missing and the sun would have shown through the gaps if everything weren't smoke and fire.

Even though his ears were shot, Rusty heard something groaning as the treehouse shifted and swayed. It sounded like wood, old wood, giving up the ghost, cracking.

The main branch supporting the treehouse snapped and again the world was thrown into the dryer.

For over a decade, the treehouse had been nestled securely in the oak's arms behind 3131 Rutherford B. Hayes Terrace but all good things come to an end. Like the cradle in the famed nursery rhyme, the treehouse fell to the ground, complaining all the way.

With all the turmoil in her head, she had no idea how she dozed off in her patrol car, but she had.

Unfortunately, her nap was the opposite of restful. Crammed

with dreams that surged and grabbed. In one, she stood near the altar in a giant church where dear, sweet, innocent Connie was being devoured by an enormous beast with red eyes, horns, and way too many teeth. Trapped in the beast's massive maw, Connie, crying, reached out to Rumpza, called her name. Though she wanted to, the cop couldn't move, as if her feet were glued to the floor. Rumpza hid her face so she wouldn't see the slaughter. But she could not block out the sound of Connie's screams, the crunch of her bones.

Awaking with a start, Rumpza quickly checked her environs. Surprised to find herself in the patrol car, parked behind the Rutherford B. Hayes Memorial Pilates Club.

With a shiver, she relived the nightmare. Rumpza knew it was too vivid for a simple dream. This was a vision, a communication from the world of the dead.

The cop had a hard time breathing. Her heart hung in her chest like a condemned man. And she felt, right behind her eyes, a torrent of tears ready to take the stage.

But no. She wouldn't cry. She wouldn't give into emotion. Not now. She had a job to do. Revenge.

For she knew who'd taken Connie from her. Dearly Departed, whatever she was, girl or monster, had devoured Rumpza's lover and she (or it) had to be stopped. No time for crying, no time for sleeping or hiding. She had to find Dearly Departed. Kill her.

But first she had to pee.

Climbing from the patrol car, she rushed into the Rutherford B. Hayes Memorial Pilates Club, where she happened to be a member, though she never went.

She walked through a class – they were working on the Egg Dodge, Rumpza's favorite exercise – she waved at the instructor, signaling she had to use the facilities.

Scurrying down the back hallway, she threw open the door of

the restroom.

Rumpza had witnessed some pretty weird shit over the last few days, but stumbling upon the couple fucking with impunity in the restroom of the pilates club while a demonic serial killer plagued her town, blew the cop's mind.

With a nervous cough, she closed the door. Rumpza told herself she should just walk away, find another place to empty her bladder, as Dearly Departed was still out there and the clock was ticking.

But something stopped her. Maybe it was the guy's creepy misshapen face or the fact the woman wouldn't stop thrusting her hips even when the cop looked her straight in the eye. Or maybe it was because they were having so much fun exchanging bodily fluids and Rumpza knew that she would never find true love again.

The cop ducked back into the restroom, drawing her Savage 1861 Navy revolver, which she aimed squarely at the guy's erection.

"You're under arrest for lewd conduct in a public restroom."

And yet, the couple continued humping.

There was a word or two in the Holy Bible about burning bushes but there was no mention of a burning oak.

"This dratted day," swore Police Chief Pendleton as he watched the tree burn to the ground.

Without a doubt, it had certainly been a dratted day.

Just an hour before, he'd been standing over the body of Junior Officer Killion. Then a disfigured freak who was asking too many questions had to be tossed into the street. Then Rob Allen, well-known cactus-fucker, dashed into Berlovitz's Donut Yurt to inform him that Judge Slump's broken body had been found on the lawn of the Rutherford B. Hayes Memorial Courthouse.

Pendleton assumed the judge had committed suicide, grieved

over his wife who'd been squished by a giant pancake a few Hayes Dayes back. The cop knew how hard it was to lose a wife. Even if you were the one who killed her.

But when he interviewed the handful of county employees unfortunate enough to be working on Hayes Dayes, he discovered they all had seen the same mysterious man duck into Judge Slump's office right before the judge left via the window. The mystery man they saw was universally described as "huge" and "sweaty" and "a mouth breather of the first degree."

Left Queerfolk.

First Junior Officer Killion's de-braining and now the judge's unplanned flight. Left had obviously been driven mad by the death of his brother and was exacting revenge on the people of Fremont sworn to uphold the law.

This thought caused a chill to run up the cop's sworn-to-uphold-the-law spine.

As Pendleton stood over Slump's body, a woman who worked at the courthouse informed him she'd received a call that there was a fire raging out of control behind the judge's house.

His gut told him the conflagration was somehow connected with Left's rampage. Pendleton ran back to the square, found his patrol car, and cranked the siren to clear the streets of revelers. Most of the said revelers ignored him or flipped him off, which made it slow going as he drove over to the nice side of town.

There he found the burning tree and treehouse. And, nearby, a body. Well, chunks of a body. Based on the size of the chunks, he determined it was the man he was seeking, Left Queerfolk.

"This blasted day," he said to no one. "Someone's killed the man who's been killing everyone."

Obviously Dearly Departed, who had a penchant for ripping people apart, was the killer's killer.

Rumpza's words concerning her fear they were dealing with

something inhuman came back to him. He knew his officer was right but he didn't want to say it, didn't even want to think it.

This was the work of Beelzebub, pure and simple.

Fearing he might faint, the cop plopped down amongst the body chunks. It weighed on him to know the devil himself was right here in Fremont, reeking havoc, and, Pendleton feared, this was all because of him and the sins of his past. Namely, killing his Satanic wife and her lawn-mowing lover. Then lying about it. Sin on top of sin.

Old Scratch had come to claim his due and his due was Pendleton's soul. Satan was going to kill all those around him – his daughter, Reverend Rump, Junior Officer Killion, the judge – then he was going to kill Pendleton himself in some gruesome way.

Talk about a blasted day.

It was all too much for a simple small-town police chief.

Curling into a ball like a spider bereft of life, Pendleton collapsed to the ground and waited for the mighty fire to consume him.

Heaven's weird.

That thought pranced through Rusty's mind as his eyes fluttered opened after dying luxuriously in the luxury treehouse explosion.

When he was young and his brain was tender and his mother had yet to be squashed by a non-record breaking pancake, she'd given him a copy of *Heaven Is For Realsies*. This book was the story of a boy, about Rusty's age, who, as a consequence of careless bicycle riding, had "died" and gone to heaven. When the paramedics arrived, they revived him, so he was only in paradise for a few short minutes. But what a few short minutes those were. According to the boy, heaven was an awesome place.

For months after reading *Heaven Is For Realsies*, Rusty got down on his knees nightly and looked up at the ceiling with a plaintive eye and chatted away with an invisible dude who resided in the clouds. The boy asked that the little black kids stop starving in Africa and that China stop being so Communist and that his dick would grow to be the size of the other boys in his class.

After a few months of this questionable behavior, Rusty realized praying was for the birds. The little black kids in Africa kept starving, China carried on their Communist ways, and his dick remained shrimpy and the source of merriment for the other boys in gym class. Not to mention, Rusty's knees began to scab and, injury to insult, a giant pancake fell from the sky and squished the only human on the planet who cared for him.

Rusty came to the conclusion that if this God person really did exist, he was a douchebag.

But, as the old saying goes, there are no atheists in burning treehouses, and Rusty, as his world crashed around him, made a pact with God. If the Good Lord did not send him down to the flames of hell - which seemed repetitive as he was already engulfed in flame - he would never again refer to him as a douchebag.

Though the heaven the young man found himself in when he awoke varied greatly from the rocking afterlife described in the pages of Heaven Is For Realsies. There were no skateboarding angels, no touch football games with Ronald Reagan, no rock music blaring at the Pearly Gates. Rusty's heaven was not, as promised, built out of strawberry-flavored clouds, but metal. It was long, tubular, and filled with laboratory equipment.

As being dead was too much to ponder, the young man closed his eyes and went back to sleep.

Disparaging cops is as American as apple pie.

That said, Cuntlips McGoo could feel his face burning bright with shame as he listened to the beautiful but foul-mouthed Nicole Clymer berate the female cop who'd busted them making sweet love in the lavatory of the crazy pilates place. Even though he'd spent a decade in the most decadent heavy metal band in world, who'd experienced more than their fair share of run-ins with the law, the former rocker had never heard a more brutal tongue-lashing than the one being doled out in the patrol car where he and Nicole were crammed into the backseat, naked.

"And for your edification, the proper name of the affliction is baleophilia, and one in every fifty million Americans suffer from it! So get used to us, copper, we're here, we're proud, and we're probably going to have lots of sex in public bathrooms! Just because your sexual proclivities, I'm sure, are missionary position, once a month, lights out, doesn't mean other, more adventurous expressions of love aren't valid! I love this man and love having nasty sex with him in filthy bathrooms! That's not a crime, pig!"

Leaning over with great difficulty, as his hands were cuffed behind his back, Cuntlips whispered in his lover's ear that she might want to calm down a bit.

That was a a bad idea.

Armed with a new enemy, Nicole swung her bound body around to face Cuntlips. Well aware that he was about to be laid into, Cuntlips couldn't help but notice his lover's pendulous breasts beautifully sway as if they were fleshy zeppelins that had not been tied down correctly.

Back in the bathroom of the weird pilates place, after he'd finished blowing his sweet wad into Nicole's sweet love canal, the angry cop didn't even allow them to don their clothes before cuffing them and dragging them through the astonished pilates class, who all stopped whatever they were doing with a spatula and a series of numbered ping-pong balls to watch. Though he was embarrassed at the time, now, staring at his lover's lovely lugs, he was glad for their nakedness.

For this could, boob-wise, be his last hurrah for quite a while. They were under arrest, soon they'd arrive at the police station and be thrown into separate cells. Cuntlips feared he wouldn't see his love for months, perhaps years.

The worst part of this somber scenario, of course, wasn't the absence of Nicole's beautiful baps, but the fact that Maude the Layer of Waste and her evil spawn would probably destroy the world while Cuntlips was incarcerated.

A sobering thought that took the joy out of Nicole's breasts.

Her face only inches from his, she shouted, "Shut up, you assbutt! Instead of telling me how to handle myself, you should stand up for me! You and your malformed cock are well acquainted with my baleophilia! Hell, getting nailed in the can seems to appeal to you too! But now you've turned on me, you sexual Judas! Well, flock you! I wouldn't be in this mess if I hadn't joined you in your quest to stop that demon possessing the dead girl!"

Though they weren't traveling very quickly, thanks to the drunken revelers blocking the patrol car, the cop slammed on her brakes. Turning, she glared at Cuntlips, her eyes bulging, burning. "What's she talking about?"

One of the things Cuntlips had learned from the Buddhist monk ninja warrior assassin was the beauty of silence. Many times in this life people speak when they should hold their tongue. He knew he was already in deep dutch for being caught fornicating in a public restroom, there was no need to get tossed into the nuthouse for telling tales of demons to representatives of the law.

"Tell me who's what," demanded the cop. She leaned over the seat. "This lady said something about a demon possessing a dead girl! Spill the taint-crunching beans, bathroom flocker!"

Looking into the cop's eyes, the former rocker saw something that surprised him. This woman wasn't asking to hear about the demon because she thought he was crazy, she was asking because she genuinely wanted to know.

He took a deep breath. "I… I'm something of a demon hunter

and, although I'm still technically a novice, I do possess a wealth of experience on the subject. A few days ago I was down in Texas when I read about your local minister who'd been brutally murdered."

"Reverend Rump."

"Yeah, that one. I could tell from the gruesome photo that accompanied the newspaper article that he had been killed not by a human, but a demon known as Maude the Layer of Waste."

"Maude the what?"

"Maude the Layer of Waste is a monster born of hell who occupies the body of one recently buried. She comes back to kill and copulate with the local males in hopes of getting pregnant."

Cuntlips stopped talking when he realized the cop had stopped listening. Turning around, she slumped down behind the steering wheel, stared out the window at the parade of wasted humanity.

Softly, he said, "You… you know the girl who was… who was.. used?"

"She was my lover."

The inside of the patrol car grew solid, silent, until Nicole piped up. "Listen, Madame Police Officer, I'm… I'm sorry I said all that shit about your sex life. I was wrong, it isn't boring."

Wiping away a tear, the cop said, "Thanks for that."

"And Cuntlips, I'm sorry I called you a sexual Judas. You're not. You're a sexual dynamo."

"Thanks."

Clearing her throat, the cop said, "Okay, so how do we stop this teat-emulsifying demon?"

"Well, the first step is to uncuff."

"Look at me, you blasted coward!" commanded the ghost or drug hallucination or whatever he was.

"I thought the only time you showed up was when I was polluting myself with self-love."

"Well, thankfully, now I'm here during your non-polluting time to tell you that you have a life and death decision to make and you must make it fairly soon."

Police Chief Pendleton opened his eyes and looked up at Rutherford B. Hayes. The ghost or drug hallucination or whatever was towering over him in the judge's backyard, fire swirling all around them.

"Yes, I can see, this fire is about to extinguish me."

"That is a fairly obvious observation, you worthless cur. I'm addressing what happens after you burn. You see, if you expire then this whole town will also expire."

"I know, this devil has come for me."

"Dear Sweet Baby G, you are a dramatic self-centered taint-sniffing scoundrel. This creature of the damned isn't here for you, she's here for everyone. But it is within your power to stop her. If only you were brave enough to stand."

"I ain't yellow."

"You, sir, are as yellow as a Chinaman's piss. To prove this, I have brought along an old friend today from the afterlife."

To the cop's amazement, a frayed gray form appeared beside the phantom president. Slowly, it took shape. It was a canine, but not just any canine. It was Sergeant Snoopers, the greatest detective the Fremont Police Society had ever known, and he was back from the dead.

Although there was a murderous teenage demon lose in his hamlet, the Police Chief couldn't help but smile. "Hey boy, how are you doing?"

Sergeant Snoopers shook his head, cast his eyes down.

"See, you cussed cockchafer, he's as disappointed in you as I am. Get to your feet, man, and save this town that means so much to both of us and, in doing so, save the woman you love."

"You… you know about about my love for Chrissy Rumpza?"

"Are you kidding? She's all you talk during the act of self-pollution. And I completely understand as she has a mighty fine posterior. Just like my own dear Lucy, I loved her so, and I so loved pounding her pelt."

"Excuse me?"

"My earthly wife. So dear do I hold the hours that I spent burrowing deep into her fur burger with my love brisket."

"But... but how can you talk so? You're a man of God."

"Who do you think invented the beaver? Our Dear Lord. He equipped Eve with a moist snatch and instructed all men to bury their knoblocks as deep into that beautiful quiffy quagmire as humanly possible. So, you must slough off your scared skin, go save Chrissy, and then pound the holy hell out of her!"

"Yes... yes!" screamed Pendleton. "I will save her and tell her that I have always harbored carnal intentions toward her!"

By the time Pendleton got to his feet, both the president and the ghost dog were history. If they'd ever been.

With a start, Rusty awoke. Looking around, he got his mental feet beneath him.

He'd been mistaken earlier. This wasn't heaven. Far from it. He'd been here before, several times. Buying weed, being nervous. He was in Loco Lenny Labovitz's mobile drug emporium, strapped down to a cot.

There was just a touch of silver lining. Dearly Departed had also apparently survived the fiery treehouse crash. The dark lining to that silver cloud was that she was still unconscious and also strapped down to a cot.

And that was just the tip of the shit iceberg.

No, Rusty Slump wasn't in heaven. He was in hell.

CoCo McArdle – with whom he was fairly certain he was no longer an item – and Loco Lenny Labovitz stood over him. They were both smiling and Rusty had a sour feeling that he was the punchline of the joke.

"I was afraid you'd never wake up," said CoCo. This made the young man feel a bit better. Perhaps she wasn't so mad at him, time heals all wounds and that rot. "If you never woke up, I couldn't watch you die."

Apparently, not enough time had passed.

"You've been asleep for some pretty neat developments, so let me quickly fill you in. When I came to after Left blew himself up, I dragged you and your little hussy here and struck a deal with my new best friend Loco. We're going to be business partners and I'm gonna assist him in securing his place at the top of the vast and dangerous criminal underworld of Fremont, Ohio, by eliminating the competition. That's you, by the bye. So, I'm gonna kill you. Then I'm going to get every ne'er-do-well in town hooked on your girlfriend's dope titties, and Loco and I will become millionaires. Of course, all the while I'll be sucking his cock and never thinking of you. How does that sound?"

Loco giggled as CoCo reached into a leather scabbard hanging at her side and pulled out a knife that was laughably long. She explained, "This was my father's knife. He used it to gut unruly pygmies when he was down in Borneo to capture poisonous tree frogs for the Rutherford B. Hayes Memorial Slightly Dangerous Petting Zoo."

Even in the swallowing darkness of the mobile drug emporium, the knife shined and winked. A pitiful noise started in Rusty's gut but didn't live long enough to make it to his lips. After all the tough jams that he'd gotten out of over the last few days, he was finally going to die. That was most certainly a certainty. He was going to die at the hand of his ex-girlfriend and it was going to be messy and painful and awful. Just like her blowjobs.

Like most people, Rusty wasn't thrilled with the idea of his own passing and, if it had to happen, he wanted to say something witty or memorable so that CoCo would feel like a real turd later when she thought back on the experience.

Unfortunately, nothing witty or memorable came to mind.

Putting both hands on the hilt of the knife, CoCo raised it up into the air. A look of maniacal joy flamed over her face.

Finally, Rusty blurted, "Your father was a lying turd whistle."

She dropped the knife to her side and looked, if that was possible, even more pissed. "What?!?"

"He used to always brag that he was heading off to Borneo or Walla Walla or some other unchartered place, hunting down poisonous this or deadly that. But that was all just a scam." As CoCo's face turned redder and redder, Rusty felt himself gaining strength, gaining control. "He never went to Borneo, hell, he never even left the state. All his supposedly dangerous animals came through the mail from some place in Florida."

"You have no idea what you're talking about, Rusty, you're the lying turd whistle!"

Out of the corner of his eye, the young man saw Loco take a step back. He'd never seen the drug kingpin scared before. This was fun. Deadly but fun.

"Sure I do. Last year my father went down to Cincinnati for a gavel convention. One day he was walking down the street and he spotted your father eating at a Spaghetti and Company. My father thought this was odd, as Jinx had told everyone he was going to Bora Bora to collect tse-tse flies. Well, my father marched up to your father, who was gulping down a pile of linguini. My father didn't say a word before Jinx broke down crying. He confessed that he was afraid of all forms of travel. He couldn't get on a plane or a boat, and hovercrafts were right out of the question. Through tears, he told the judge that he'd never even traveled out of the state of Ohio his entire life. He got all his animals through the mail and, when none were available, he'd shave a squirrel, paint it some weird color and give it an exotic name. Sorry, CoCo, but your father was a scaredy cat and a big, fat liar."

Growling so loudly she shook the mobile drug emporium, CoCo raised the supposed pygmy-gutting knife high. Rusty, having had his say and feeling surprisingly at peace, closed his eyes.

"Oh no," murmured Loco, interrupting Rusty's murder, "look who's stirring."

The knife didn't come down, Rusty wasn't disemboweled. After a few moments of non-deadness, the young man opened his eyes. On the other cot, Dearly was rousing. Loco and CoCo stood over her, watching her the way one would watch a fast-approaching tornado.

"If she's as dangerous as you say," said Loco, "you'd better dose her again."

"Sure thing, partner," said Coco, sliding the ludicrously long knife back into the scabbard and picking up the tranquilizer gun.

Inspecting the weapon, CoCo said, "Uh-oh."

"Uh-oh? Why uh-oh?"

"I'm fresh out of tranquilizer."

Cocking his head, Loco thought about their situation. "Well, we can't kill her."

"Of course not. She's the goose who laid the golden titties."

"Huh, isn't this a pickle? Well, if the shit is going to go down," said Loco, an odd smile screwing up his face, "I best sample the product first."

Though CoCo screamed a warning, the leader of the vast and dangerous criminal underworld of Fremont, Ohio, bowed and licked Dearly's breasts as if they were scoops of ice cream, making a childish slurping noise.

The psychotropic effect of her dope tits was instantaneous. Mumbling something about soldiers coming to get him, Loco stumbled back against the curved metal wall.

"Sweet Baby G," hissed CoCo. "I don't need this shit right now."

Looking down at Dearly, who was becoming more and more animated, CoCo let out a cry of anguish that made the entirety of the mobile drug emporium shudder.

She stopped screaming when the first bullet struck the outside of the vehicle.

PING, it said brightly.

Though he was still naked, he was, at least, free of the handcuffs and riding in the front seat of the patrol car as the trio of demon hunters combed the town. While the female cop drove, Cuntlips explained everything he knew about Maude the Layer of Waste.

When he finished, the cop said, "So, she's dangerous."

"Dangerous doesn't even begin to cover it. This demon killed the man who taught me how to be a Buddhist monk ninja warrior assassin and he was the Buddhist monk ninja warrior assassin's Buddhist monk ninja warrior assassin. If we don't stop her, she'll destroy all mankind."

"But you did defeat her, right, my restroom Romeo?" said Nicole from the beak seat. Though she was using a cute pet name for him, her voice was flooded with fear.

"Yeah," he shrugged, "but that was just beginner's luck. I don't think that will happen again. Hey, stop! Look!"

Hitting the brakes, the cop turned on him. Her eyes wide, her eyes wild. "What? Where do you see her?"

"No, sorry," he said, pointing, "but there's the Oscar Mayer Wienermobile!"

Shaking her head in frustration, the cop, "What the hell are you talking about?"

"That vehicle right over there. The giant one parked beneath the sign for the Rutherford B. Hayes Memorial Sex Shoppe #11."

She followed his gaze. "You idiot, the vehicle in question belongs to Loco Lenny Labovitz, local ne'er-do-well. It's his hideout."

"I'm pretty sure that's the Oscar Mayer Wienermobile just painted blue," he replied.

As if he were trapped in a trance, Cuntlips climbed from the cruiser.

"Where are you going?" demanded the cop.

Over his shoulder, he said, "It's on my bucket list."

"Mind your pretty pecker out there in the wild," chimed Nicole from the back seat.

Cuntlips and his pretty pecker made their way to the middle of the road. There, he stopped. Something hit him. Something heavy but invisible. A scent. Raising his head, he sniffed the air.

"Sweet Baby G, we don't have time for this cervex-chidding bullarky," cried the cop as she crawled from the cruiser. Nicole followed.

But Cuntlips didn't even notice them approach him. He was too busy sniffing. Too busy worrying.

Arms akimbo, the cop watched Cuntlips work his nose. "What in the hell are you doing?"

"There's something… a weird smell coming from that blue Wienermobile."

"That's probably just meth."

Cuntlips closed his eyes and took a strong sniff. It was undeniable. He'd been up close and personal with Maude the Layer of Waste before. She smelled as if a pile of shit had taken a shit. The smell roiling off the Wienermobile was nearly powerful enough to topple him.

"There's death in there," he said to himself.

Opening his eyes, he saw the lady cop glaring at him like he had misplaced a few of his marbles. "How do you know that?"

"Tim the Buddhist monk ninja warrior assassin taught me to

be one with the universe and how to use all eighteen of my senses. Evil has a scent and that Wienermobile reeks of evil."

She didn't look particularly convinced.

"Okay," she said, "we'll take a look but all we're gonna find is a buttload of drugs."

Brushing past the naked man, the cop started across the street with quick, coppy steps.

Cuntlips blurted, "Wait, wait, wait!"

She spun on him. "What?"

"This isn't some drunk redneck who slapped his wife around or a methhead who stole a porno mag from the local Kum & Go. This is evil incarnate."

"So?"

"So we can't just go knocking on the door."

"What do you want me to do? Draw my regulation Savage 1861 Navy revolver and go in shooting?"

"That's exactly what I want you to do. Unless you happen to have a rocket launcher."

When the cop spun on him, he was surprised to find tears filing out of her eyes. "But what if you're right. That's my Connie in there!"

Rushing forward, Cuntlips wrapped his arms around her, pulled her tight, whispered in her ear. "That's not your girlfriend, it's a demon occupying her corporal body, making it more overtly sexual to get what she wants. Although it may look like Connie, it's not. It's just her shell. If you go in there firing away, you can't hurt Connie because Connie's already dead."

"But what if she isn't? What if she's alive in there somewhere?"

"Then she's a prisoner in her own body, unable to control her own actions. Does that thing act like your girlfriend? If Connie could speak, she'd tell you to kill that damned demon."

The parade of tears continued down the cop's cheeks. "I don't know if I can do it. I don't know if I can put a bullet in that beautiful body."

She collapsed as if all the bones in her body had been washed away by the tears. Cuntlips propped her up.

"This is no longer about what you want to do, this is about what you have to do. You have sworn to uphold the law. That monster, who is not your lover, is going to mate with the most ejaculate-filled men around, then she's going to give birth to a hellbeast that will destroy the world. Do you want that on your conscience? Sure, we're just two people with the odds stacked against us, but that doesn't mean that we can't go down swinging."

The cop stared into the former rocker's eyes. He saw something moving behind her pupils. Something made of guts and steel. Her bones re-fused and she stood up straight. In one swift motion, she wiped off her tears and pushed him away. Without preamble, she drew her Savage 1861 Navy revolver from her raw-hide holster and spun. Marching toward the repainted Oscar Mayer Wienermobile, with determination.

Cuntlips had trouble keeping up.

They both stopped dead in their tracks when they heard a scream issuing from the tubular vehicle. It was a woman, a woman in great distress.

Raising her arm, the cop fired helter-skelter, the bullet striking the skin of the hot dog vehicle.

PING, it said.

The fire had spread dramatically.

Driving his patrol car through the neighborhoods of Fremont, Police Chief Pendleton found the conflagration, no longer satisfied with simply consuming the judge's property, was now devouring houses on several blocks. The streets were clogged with fire trucks and emergency personnel who, thanks to the infamous Hayes Dayes two dollar boots o' beer, were drunker than usual and too consumed with fighting each other to fight the fire. Regrettably, Pendleton didn't have time to pull over and put a end to this tomfoolery with his Savage 1861 Navy revolver, for he had to save his town and the woman of his dreams.

Although he had no idea where to start his search, he soon happened upon a fairly serious shoot out unfolding in the parking lot of the Rutherford B. Hayes Memorial Sex Shoppe #11. Pendleton spied Officer Rumpza, the light of his life, sprawled on the ground, wounded but still firing her weapon. With pride Pendleton beamed at the sight, his heart burning bright for this ferocious little minx. On the other side of the fire fight was Loco Lenny Labovitz, dancing around the parking lot, his Uzi blazing, like a man possessed. On the ground behind Rumpza were two naked people that Pendleton didn't recognize. One was kneeling over the other, who was obviously injured.

Slamming on his brakes, Pendleton jumped from his vehicle and squealed, "What in tarnation is going on here?"

In answer, he was promptly shot in the chest by Loco Lenny Labovitz. He felt one, two, three bullets rip into him. As it seemed silly to remain standing with such injuries, the cop collapsed to the pavement.

It was only in that moment, as death sauntered his way, that the police chief noticed how beautiful of a day it was. Blue sky, only slightly obscured by the haze by the fire consuming Fremont, a few white fluffy clouds hanging around as if waiting for a tip. He smiled as he didn't feel the blood pumping out of his wounds so much as the sun shining into them.

Harp music began. Distant but sharp. And high above him, a beam of light so crisp. In the light appeared two figures. A man and a dog racing toward Pendleton from the heavens. Recognizing Rutherford B. Hayes and Sergeant Snoopers, the dying cop attempted a wave.

When he drew close enough, the ghost or drug hallucination or whatever he was, let loose with a volley of swears. "What in the dickens are you doing, you inveterate lick-finger! This is all ass-backwards. You're not meant to perish, you're to vanquish that bell-fire demon!"

For his part, Sergeant Snoopers barked angrily.

At this point the ghosts or drug hallucinations or whatever they were, were upon him. Kneeling beside Pendleton, tears in his eyes, Hayes took Pendleton's hand. "I'm sorry, private, but it looks as if you're coming to join me and Sergeant Snoopers in the afterlife."

The dead president bent and with great civility kissed the cop on his mouth. Pendleton would have found this moment more pleasing if Hayes hadn't slipped him a little tongue.

"Now, private, it is up to me to send this dad-blamed whore of a demon back to blazes!"

Standing, Hayes took the form of a living, breathing human but was immediately torn asunder by a bevy of bullets fired by Loco Lenny Labovitz. Essentially cut in half, the dying president fell to the pavement right beside the dying cop.

Barking ferociously, Sergeant Snoopers took off toward the source of the gunfire.

"I know that I am going where Lucy is," proclaimed Hayes as he breathed his last yet again.

Thinking about his own wife, Pendleton sincerely hoped that he didn't end up anywhere near that garden-variety harlot.

All thoughts of his dead wife disappeared when Officer Rumpza appeared above him. Seemingly floating. She laid a hand upon his face. It felt as cold as the grave. Perhaps it was his face that was growing colder.

After coughing up a comma of blood, Pendleton managed, "Chrissy, there is something I must confess before I go. I have loved you from afar these many years and I greatly regret not informing you earlier as I have always harbored carnal intentions toward you."

Knitting her perfect brow, the love of his life said, "Oh, well, that's not going to happen."

"Is that because," he said, hoping his smile wasn't too much of a bloody mess, "I am not long for this world?"

"No. Sorry, but as you are obviously dying, I think you should know something. I have feelings for Connie. In fact, I love her."

"What?!?"

"And she loved me too. Right before she went missing, I had my face so deep in her tangy vag, I feared I would never find my way out. If there's one thing I will remember about your lovely daughter it is the taste of her sweet lollipop pussy."

A solid tear slid down Rumpza's lesbian face.

Although he'd never sworn in his forty-four years, not even when he caught his strumpet wife *in flagrante delicto* with the satanic lawnboy, Pendleton said, as he died, "Oh, flock this crud!"

PING, said the first shot, striking the metal skin of Loco Lenny Labovitz's mobile drug emporium.

Rusty jumped, everyone did.

CoCo, the first to regain her footing, reached into a cabinet and pulled out an Uzi. Shouting his name, she tossed the automatic weapon to Loco, who was so messed up on the nectar of Dearly's tits that he was walking in circles and babbling about soldiers coming for him. Having been the shortstop on the Rutherford B. Hayes Memorial High School baseball team before he switched to crime lording, instinct took over and Loco caught the Uzi in one hand. Stared down at it with a mixture of surprise and awe.

Pointing toward the door, CoCo barked, "Get out there, Loco. Those soldiers are right outside!"

"Damn Rebs," bellowed the king of the vast and dangerous

criminal underworld of Fremont, Ohio, as he hurled himself out the door, into the sunlight, his finger caressing the trigger of the automatic weapon.

A shitload of shots were fired outside the tubular vehicle.

Groaning as if she were waking up with the world's worst hangover, Dearly opened her eyes and, ripping her restraints away as if they were fashioned from wet paper, sat up.

"Oh flock," said CoCo. "I don't need this aggravation right now!"

Once again she reached into the cabinet of death and pulled out the Uzi's twin. Which she aimed right at Rusty's head.

He held her in his arms as she died. Watched the light drain from her eyes, just as he'd done with the Buddhist monk ninja warrior assassin.

When that idiot, who wasn't a demon but a crazed asshole, high on something, came charging out of the Wienermobile, guns blazing, Nicole took a pair of the first bullets fired. Both in the gut.

With a yelp of surprise, she crumpled.

Forgetting the demon, forgetting about saving mankind, forgetting the gun battle which raged around him, Cuntlips McGoo rushed to her side, knelt.

Held her as she died, cried copious tears.

"I'm sorry," he said. "I'm sorry for getting you involved with all this demon hunting shit. Please forgive me." The former rocker so wanted to hear some final words, something he could carry with him for the rest of his days, which he feared were few.

"That's okay," she said with her final breath. "Tell the cops they'll find Keith buried beneath his pot patch."

"What?" he asked. But it was too late for an answer.

Flocking Southern soldiers. Flocking Johnny Reb.

Outside the mobile drug emporium, Loco Lenny Labovitz found himself surrounded by a flocking forest of Rebel soldiers. Some more real than others. All ready to come down on him with their minute balls and shit, ready to assume control of the vast and dangerous criminal underworld of Fremont, Ohio. Flock them. This was his turf, his town, his everyflockingthing.

These soldiers had to be the ones who killed Right by ripping off his stupid head and they'd probably killed poor Left too, as Loco hadn't seen him for hours. Flock them solid. For he was about to kill them all with his gun and his trigger and his finger.

When his feet hit the pavement – which was flavored with a dash of cinnamon, funny he hadn't noticed that before – he started shooting, fanning the Uzi, and down they went. One, two, three. A hundred. It was as easy as shooting soldiers in a barrel.

But then, he noted with alarm, that one of the more real looking soldiers was firing back at him.

In his hands the Uzi danced and sang its throaty dirge. Bullets like tiny metal butterflies. Another of the soldiers fell. The one with the gun who, although wounded, kept firing in Loco's general direction.

Loco returned fire, filling the air with more and more tiny metal butterflies. Another of the soldiers went down and Loco could tell this one was staying down as there was a giant splash of blood.

A car pulled up, flashing lights. Another Reb climbed from the vehicle. *Sweet Baby G, where were all these soldiers coming from?*

The new soldier shouted something but Loco didn't hear him as he was too busy sending more bullets off to do their job. The new soldier went down.

Loco started laughing, inside his head and out. This was the most fun he'd had in a long time. The Rebs were being repelled, beaten back from the shores of his mobile drug emporium.

More good news: the one returning fire ran out of bullets. Loco was about to walk up to her and put one in the old brain pan when he stopped.

He stopped because he heard music from on high. Harp music, if his ears weren't deceiving him. Looking up, he saw a man and a dog, both transparent, descend from the clouds.

There was no way this gun battle could get any weirder.

The heaven man reached earth and kneeled down beside the recently downed soldier and kissed him.

Okay, the gun battle just got a little weirder.

When the heaven man stood, Loco filled him with lead. He had a sneaking suspicion you can't kill a dead man but this particular one went down. Dead again.

The heaven dog began barking like mad. It charged Loco, yapping. The laughter issuing from the leader of the vast and dangerous criminal underworld of Fremont, Ohio, went away as the ghost dog grew nearer, more recognizable.

It was Sergeant Snoopers, the dog he'd accidentally run over to start his life of crime, returning to haunt the shit out of him.

Tears of anger, tears of rage welled up in Loco's eyes. Flock that dog, that dog ruined his flocking life.

By the time he'd raised the Uzi to kill Sergeant Snoopers a second time, the dog was upon him. Loco had to fire the automatic weapon straight down. The tiny metal butterflies tore through the phantom beast, perforating the pooch from bark to ass, and struck the cinnamon-scented pavement below. Some ricocheted.

Bullets that ricochet are funny things. Given a second chance to kill, they usually just fly off willy-nilly and embed themselves somewhere useless, a fence or a senator. Those are the kind of ricocheted bullets that people never discuss around the dinner table or in novels.

It's the ones that ricochet and cause damage, strike gold, that get all the attention.

Like the one that came right back up at Loco.

Still spinning, still searing, it tore into Loco's taint. As four out of five doctors will tell you, taint injuries are the worst, and Loco howled in pain. But the bullet didn't stop there, it was on a roll. It ripped through his stomach and continued its journey upward. During its trip through Loco's body, the bullet ripped open his heart, a lung or two, and finally came to rest in his brain. Which would have informed him that he was dead if he weren't so dead already.

Outside the world was scarred by gunfire. It sounded as if World War III had landed upon the shores of the Sandusky River.

But inside the mobile drug emporium, Rusty couldn't have cared less about all the death happening outside.

He had eyes for only one gun, and that was the Uzi CoCo had cradled in her arms like a deadly baby. "One thing you should know before I plug you and your girlfriend is that I never really loved you. It was all an act. At first, given your history of fecal-related lawlessness, I thought, with a little work, I could mold you into the next king of the vast and dangerous criminal underworld of Fremont, Ohio, but that, as we can both plainly see, didn't pan out. All along, I was just using you. All those blowjobs were faked."

"I don't think you can really fake a blowjob."

"You know what I mean. Despite where my mouth was, my heart wasn't in it. Now you must die."

She raised her deadly baby.

As he was closing his eyes – as no one likes to see themselves being eaten alive by bullets – Rusty spied, on the cot next to his, a blur of flesh, a mention of time, a schmear of air.

Suddenly, the cot was empty. Nothing, no Dearly.

Then the screaming commenced. Loud enough to obliterate the pitched battle unfolding just yards away.

Turning, Rusty saw that Dearly had CoCo in some complicated wrestling hold. It appeared as if the love of his life had more arms than the average human and all of them were wrapped around his ex-girlfriend, squeezing her from behind. Rusty heard bones snap. As CoCo dropped the Uzi and screamed in surprise, Dearly's neck elongated so that she could look her prey in the eye.

Getting right in CoCo's face, Dearly hissed, "Back off, this particular human is mine!"

Dearly's arms stretched and stretched until all eight of them were swathed around CoCo's body several times. Rusty continued to watch but stopped thinking.

Out of breath and out of time, CoCo stopped screaming. Though her face turned crimson, then purple, then a color that Benjamin Moore had yet to name, Dearly continued to squeeze. CoCo's eyes, which were already bulging to an unhealthy degree, popped out of her head and shot across the tubular room. One struck Rusty square in the forehead with a *fwap* sound that could only be described as sickening.

That brought the young man to his senses. Wiggling out of his restraints, he stood and took a step toward the death scene. But only one. He didn't wish to draw too close as the floor was now slick with all the blood gushing out of CoCo's multiple ruptured orifices.

"Okay, sweetheart, I think you've made your point. I'm pretty sure she's dead."

Turning her tubular neck, Dearly glared at Rusty as if she'd forgotten of his existence. "Whatever you say, dear human."

She unfurled like a flag and the strip of flesh that was CoCo's once voluptuous body fluttered to the floor.

In a blink, Dearly's body was back to normal. Well, she was still naked and as exciting as a zeppelin crash, but she was no longer an elongated spiderish woman with multiple arms.

Shaking his head, Rusty convinced himself he'd just been seeing things. The strain of having his life constantly threatened was beginning to wear on him.

"I guess I should thank you," he said.

"For what?"

"Saving my life. Just then. From CoCo. Also, I need to apologize."

"For helping those nasty humans drug me and allowing a bevy of local ne'er-do-wells have their way with my teats?"

"Yeah, that."

Taking a step forward, Dearly said, "I should kill you where you stand."

He shied. "I'd rather you didn't."

She laid a hand, which was somehow so hot it burned and so cold it burned, on his shoulder. He was pretty sure it was going to leave a mark. "Don't worry, the Other Girl has feelings for you, strong feelings and, as I cannot kill her, I cannot kill you."

"That's good news. But who's this Other Girl that you're talking about?"

"I do not have time to explain right now for I feel compelled to have sexual congress with you, right here, right now."

Despite the gun battle going on outside, despite the fact his ex-girlfriend had been turned into a human flatworm and was laying at his feet, despite the fact he feared this girl as much as he was drawn to her, Rusty felt a murmuring in his pants when she mentioned sexual congress.

He only hoped that he remained conscious this time. He made a mental note to not lick her tits regardless of how dope they were.

"So, drop your pants, insert your penis into my vagina, and fill me with your seed."

Rusty wasn't big on foreplay either. Just as he was reaching for his belt, Dearly spun, looked at the door of Loco's mobile drug emporium. Sniffed the air.

To herself, she said, "I smell demon hunter!"

"You smell what, sugar tits?"

She turned back on him. "Pull up your pants, dear puny

human. We must leave this place as my life is in danger."

Dearly hoisted him upon her shoulder and dodged out of the mobile drug emporium.

Into the gun battle.

When the cop laid her hand upon his shoulder, he jumped like a man who'd taken a seat in the electric chair. Looking away from his shredded girlfriend, Cuntlips McGoo stared at Chrissy Rumpza as if he'd never seen her before.

"She's dead," he said, his voice hollow.

"I gathered that."

"We have to bury her, say prayers."

"We will, later. Right now we have work to do. Listen, I'm really sorry your bathroom-loving paramour is no more but we've all lost people today. I just held my boss' hand while he died. His death makes me the last officer of the law standing in Fremont. And you, I'm fairly certain, are the only demon hunter in Sandusky County. We have to act quickly before that… that thing destroys the world."

The sad, naked man once again looked down at the corpse that had once been his lover. "But she's dead."

"Yeah, I got that part. If it's any consolation, my girlfriend is dead too. Only she's not resting, she's not at peace. Her body is out of the grave, occupied by a force of evil."

Cuntlips stared at the cop with eyes waxed with confusion. It was as if she were speaking Canadian to him.

Officer Rumpza was terrified that the former rocker was too far gone, too fried to act. If that were the case, she'd simply have to leave him here with his dead girlfriend and go off in search of the demon by herself. Knowing that she would fail, that she was going to die, but she was going to die trying.

She was mostly dead already. Having taken a handful of Loco's bullets to her torso. Bleeding profusely.

Giving him one last chance, she grabbed Cuntlips by the shoulders harshly, shook him, pulled him close. "Listen, buddy, right now it's just you and me. We're it. We're all that stands between baseball, snatch, and apple pie, and world destruction. Sure, we're just two people with the odds stacked against us, but that doesn't mean that we can't go down swinging."

His eyes focused on hers and she felt a twinge of hope. "I've heard that somewhere before."

"You certainly have. You said those same words to me not ten minutes ago."

"And now they mean nothing to me. Nothing means nothing to me."

With that he sank down and down, coming to rest beside his girlfriend and looking just as dead.

Sure, being toted around town by a hot chick certainly sounded awesome but Rusty also found it to be embarrassing.

When he and Dearly emerged from the safety of Loco's mobile drug emporium, the scene that awaited them was pretty gross. Right outside the door, Loco lay spread-eagle on the pavement, the top of his head AWOL. About twenty feet away there was a female cop kneeling over Police Chief Pendleton, who was beyond dead. There was another bloody corpse out in the road. Hovering over her and crying like a baby was a dude who totally looked like the drummer from Rusty's favorite band, Satan's Butt Buddies.

But that didn't make any sense. What would Cuntlips McGoo be doing in little old Fremont? But it certainly looked like him, messed up face and all. Rusty didn't get a chance to find out for sure, as Dearly bolted from the scene.

She ran really weird. Loping, like a deer, hurtling over anything that got in her path: pets, people, the occasional small building. While crossing Rutherford B. Hayes Memorial Boulevard, she landed atop a moving car. Crushed it flat and carried on without looking back.

Once again, Rusty had a sneaking suspicion that this girl wasn't normal. During their flight, he had plenty of time to think as he didn't have to concentrate on walking. He thought about the weird way Dearly smelled, like turned earth. He thought about the ease with which she screwed off Right's head, as if she were opening an already open jar of pickles. He thought about the way she moved, when motivated, traveling through space and time like a blur wearing a jetpack. He thought about the fact that she may possibly have grown extra arms when crushing CoCo to death.

None of that was normal, not even for a teenage girl.

While he considered this disturbing thought, Dearly continued traveling through the streets of Fremont. At some point, Rusty realized that there was more smoke in the air than usual. During a normal Hayes Dayes, the celebrants routinely torched a handful of random things: cars, trash barrels, the occasional stray cat. One particularly rowdy year, Fremontonians set the public library ablaze. Seeing as the library was housed in an abandoned phone booth and their collection consisted mainly of old phone books, even that wasn't much of a big deal.

But this, this was different.

The air was so choked with smoke and particulate matter, it seemed as if the whole town was ablaze. In the distance, Rusty heard sirens. He could feel heat all around him.

Their jostling journey ended in front of the Other Other One True Way Church. As Dearly took in the massive structure, she laughed. A disturbing, throaty laugh that sounded as if she swallowed children whole. Rusty was beginning to have some reservations about allowing this girl, who may or may not have been a girl, anywhere near his naughty bits.

"You know, Dearly, I think I better head home. The town is burning down and I bet my father's worried about me."

"Your father is dead, dear puny human. Is this building we stand before a church?"

"Wait, what? Did you say my father's dead?!?"

"Yes, but do not fret, soon everyone will be," she hissed, looking down at him. Her eyes filled with blood, her skin glowing red. And, Rusty noted, she'd grown a pair of horns.

With this, the young man became fairly certain that Dearly was not a normal girl. He'd seen some weird shit on the Internet in his day. Even, once, on a dare, checking out some Canadian porn, a film called "*Mounting Mounties*" which disturbed his dreams for days. But this chick, the chick with the dope tits and the red skin and the horns, this was something else. Something he didn't wish to mess with.

"Ah, you know, Dearly, I think I might have left the bathtub running, and I--."

"Answer me, puny human, is this ridiculous building a church?"

Despite his agitated mental state – the fire, the news of his father's death, the possibility that his next sexual act might be with a devil of some sort – Rusty nearly laughed at Dearly's question. The Other Other One True Way Church, which was the largest building in all of Sandusky County, had buttloads of crosses adorning every surface and had hundreds of stained glass windows, all of which featured Reverend Stevie G. Jones and the Sweet Baby G walking through Fremont, pointing out various scenes of vice and shaking their stained glass heads. The goal of every miscreant in the vast and dangerous criminal underworld of Fremont, Ohio was to end up immortalized in the stained glass of the Other Other One True Way Church.

Even though his voice quivered with fear, Rusty answered

Dearly's question. "Duh."

She, or it, ignored the sarcasm. "Then this will be the perfect place to have sexual congress and become pregnant with a hellbeast that will lay waste to all mankind."

Smiling, Dearly licked her lips with what appeared to be a forked tongue. Against his better judgement, Rusty considered all the marvelous things she could do with such a tongue.

"You know, Dearly, although the thought of sexual congress with you is pretty cool I don't-."

The very unhorny young man was not allowed to finish this thought, as Dearly leapt up the thirty-nine steps of the Other Other One True Way Church in a single bound.

By simply looking at the doors, Dearly made them explode off their hinges.

He had it made in the shade.

Well, admittedly, there was no shade in Fremont that day, as the whole place was on fire, but Leigham Shardlow, former banker, current fugitive, believed he was going to get away scot-free.

Once he heard the multiple sirens wailing outside of the bank, he saw his opportunity to bolt. While the rest of Fremont panicked, Shardlow calmly loaded the remained explosive toasters into his red Camaro - red was his absolute favorite color - and drove to his apartment on Rutherford B. Hayes Memorial Parkway, and packed all the money he'd stolen, Shirley Twatmiser-LeStrange's fist of gold, and his collection of Precious Moments figurines.

Pointing his Camaro for the horizon, he took off. This entire burg was about to burn to the ground and no one, not even God, would take the time to sort through the ashes to see who'd been incinerated. Everyone would assume that poor Leigham Shardlow had simply perished in the conflagration while, actually, he'd be in Bangkok with all the lady boys a fist of gold could buy.

Smiling to himself, picturing a line of male prostitutes stretching to the horizon, Shardlow drove down the center of Rutherford B. Hayes Memorial Boulevard and was about to turn on the Rutherford B. Hayes Memorial Expressway when something landed on the top of his car, something big, smashing it.

Climbing from the smoldering wreckage, Shardlow saw, with dazed eyes, that his bitching red Camaro was dead. Smashed flat. He was lucky to survive.

Reaching into the heap of twisted metal, he found that every single one of his Precious Moments figurines was now nothing but powder. What was really surprising was the fist of Shirley Twatmiser-LeStrange's gold had suffered the same fate. Nothing but a pile of sparkling powder. Obviously the fist of gold wasn't really a fist of gold but a fist of plaster spray painted gold. Flocking rich people.

Cursing a god he no longer banked on, Shardlow pulled the only thing that survived the weird crash besides himself from the wreckage. An explosive toaster.

With the appliance tucked beneath his arm, he took off. Angry, in search of another way to get the hell out of Fremont.

The thing that was most definitely not a girl screwed Rusty so hard that he shat himself. He would have crapped his pants if he'd been wearing any, but this thing, this creature, this abomination had ripped them off right after they entered the gold-plated narthex of the Other Other One True Way Church and stumbled upon Reverend Stevie G. Jones himself.

The oily-haired preacher was running for the exit, toting a fortune in gold. Golden chalices, golden crosses, golden idols of himself and the Sweet Baby G.

"Out of my way," shouted the minister. "I have to save God's most precious commodities, this gold and my soul."

It was only when he got a few steps away from Dearly that

Jones stopped and noted who - or, rather, what - he was addressing.

Dropping the gold, a cacophony of clatter. Pointed a shaking hand at the large red horned creature blocking his path.

"You... you're the devil."

"Close enough, preacher man."

The minister took a step back and stumbled over a golden diorama of himself and the Sweet Baby G kicking a drunk into the gutter. Jones fell on his holy ass. Tears streaming down his face.

As the demon advanced upon him, the sniveling minister said, "Listen, I... I'm sorry. I know I've made a few mistakes stealing-from-the-poor-wise and having-sex-with-disturbed-parishioners-wise, but I think I deserve a second chance. I did build this giant church and-."

The creature that Rusty had once mistook for a hot chick leaned down and bit Jones' head off. Swallowed it whole.

What was left of Jones, blood spurting, toppled to the travertine and the thing that was once Dearly continued further into the church, ripping away Rusty's clothes with claws and glee.

As she galloped up the aisle toward the altar of the Other Other One True Way Church, Dearly changed dramatically with every step. She no longer resembled a human in any way, shape, or form. She grew in size exponentially and, as she grew, tufts of hair appeared all over her body. Out of her back emerged a giant gray dorsal fin. Wings, black and course like a raven's, sprouted out her sides. Her arms turned into legs and she sprouted six more. Her head elongated, and lost all of its human softness until it more resembled an ibex, snorting as it loped up the aisle, crushing pews.

His eyes wild, Rusty, still in Dearly's grasp, stared at what she'd become. The creature that he'd recently lusted after had the body of a spider, the fin of a shark, the wings of a raven, the head of an ibex, and the genitalia of a porn star. Shorn and shiny.

Rusty cursed himself for getting hard.

Reaching the altar, she threw the young man down, mounted him without pretext, and commenced flocking him as if she were trying to whittle his dick down to a toothpick. Bouncing up and down on his bulbous balls.

He harbored doubts about making it out of this sex act alive.

That's when his bowels gave up the ghost.

Not that the introduction of a steaming pile of feces in any way stymied the creature flocking him. The beast continued to bounce up and down on his crotch. He could feel his bones cracking.

Knowing that his demise was nigh freed Rusty's tongue. "Listen, whatever you are, I know you're punishing me for killing that girl, the girl that I actually liked, and I know I totally deserve it."

The thing stopped flocking him, stared at him with its big ibex eyes. It still spoke English, the language of the damned. "What girl do you speak of?"

"Connie Pendleton."

Rearing back, the thing roared and Rusty witnessed yet another miraculous transformation in the beast. And this one was the most unsettling of all. Its face morphed. Now it was half-ibex, half-Connie. Rusty's eyes nearly popped out of his head.

He managed, "Connie, I, I-."

"You were the one who killed me?!? Man, what Ms. Locke said about men was right, they are awful. I can't believe I ever had a crush on you."

"You had a crush on me?"

"Yes. But then, just out of curiosity, I had hot lesbian sex with Chrissy Rumpza. Granted, I still held feelings for you but now I can safely say that the only feeling I have for you is hate. I love Chrissy Rumpza and I'm glad I went full-on lesbian."

"Listen, Connie, I'm sorry but I had to shoot you was that you were going to shoot me, so-."

But he was too late for reasoning now. Connie was gone. The beast was full ibex again. "Be still, puny human, for I must have sexual congress with you until completion!"

The monster returned to literally flocking the shit out of the young man.

Tears in his eyes from the pain, Rusty could barely make out the crucifix that hung above him on the altar. Sweet Baby G nailed to the cross and looking, as one would imagine, distressed about the whole situation. But there was a ray of hope for the Son of God, as the statue also featured the Reverend Stevie G. Jones, who'd scaled the cross and was employing a crowbar to pry loose those pesky nails.

No one, thought Rusty, *is on their way to save me.*

"Stop that sexual congress in the name of the law and dismount that human, you hellbeast!"

Turning, Rusty saw the female cop from the Fremont Police Squad rushing up the aisle. She had her gun drawn and a serious look on her face.

So relieved was the young man that he ejaculated greats heaps of semen out of his large love apples and cried out, "I'm saved, I'm--."

Then the creature that was most definitely not a girl finished his sentence for him by ripping his head from his shoulders.

Cuntlips McGoo barely recognized Tim, the former Buddhist monk ninja warrior assassin. In death, he'd packed on a few pounds, grown a beard, and, for some reason, was dressed in old fashioned military garb.

But the eyes, the eyes were the same. A cold blue, fierce, fiery.

Though he was busy waiting for death to come and take him, Cuntlips tried to focus on the phantom who floated fifteen feet above the former rocker and his dearly departed girlfriend.

"Tim?" asked Cuntlips, his voice clogged with wonderment.

"Sure, whatever," said Tim. "I have come from the Great Beyond with a message for you, you great cussed scalawag."

"Wait... Tim, are you cursing me?"

"I wouldn't have to if you weren't such a blamed bollocks."

Unable to believe his ears, Cuntlips sat up. Though strict, the Buddhist monk ninja warrior assassin had never spoken to him so harshly. "I don't... I don't understand what's going on here."

"I've traveled from the land of the dead to inform you that A, you're a dad blamed cockchafer, and B, that you should rise and go help the police lady with the fine keister battle that demon."

Although his curses were antiquated, Cuntlips knew Tim's condemnation was merited. He felt a sear of shame in his stomach. "You're right, Tim, you're right. You spent a decade teaching me how to fight the forces of hell."

"I did?"

"Don't be coy. I can see how you think you wasted your time. Here I am, wallowing in sorrow just because the only human who ever loved me has been cut to ribbons."

"That's the spirit."

"I should be fighting, not dying."

Standing, Cuntlips bade a quick farewell to his beloved, dead girlfriend. Glancing up at Tim, who was fading away, the ex-rocker asked, "Hey, do you smell smoke?"

Had Rumpza heard right?

Had she seen right?

Did this beast, this creature, this demon wear the face of sweet, innocent Connie for just a moment? Did it speak of loving her?

These questions were pushed aside when the giant spider shark raven ibex thing got its ibex face back, continued to flock Rusty and, after a bit more of hiding the sausage, ripped the poor boy's head off and flung it over its shoulder. As if aimed, poor Rusty's head struck the statue of Reverend Stevie G. Jones feeding a gaggle of children homemade soup right in the face. It made a *fwap* noise that could be described as sickening. Blood splattered.

Officer Rumpza bent over and threw up all over the travertine floor. She knew, if she lived, which she wouldn't, she'd never feel normal again.

Before he'd gone nuts over his dead girlfriend, Cuntlips had warned Rumpza of this demon's ultimate goal: to conceive a child with a human male. That child would be a thousand times more dangerous, more destructive than the demon herself, and would bring about the end of mankind.

Call it female intuition or a cop's gut, but Rumpza was fairly certain that this beast was now with child.

During a rough patch of confused sexual orientation in her early 20's, Rumpza believed herself straight her senior year in college. Thanks to this misstep, she'd seen her fair share of the horrible face men make when ejaculating. That awful cringing grin and fluttering eyes. That look had passed over Rusty's face right before the giant spider shark raven ibex thing ripped his head off.

The demon had gotten what she came for.

After her foray into the world of puking, Rumpza straightened and noticed two things that were equally alarming: the spider shark raven ibex thing was no longer in sight and knives of flame were cutting around the edges of the building. The Other Other One True Way Church was ablaze, much like the rest of Fremont.

After leaving Cuntlips and making her way through town in search of the demon, Rumpza was horrified to see that everything and everyone was on fire. She'd nearly given up hope on living long enough to find the demon when she spied the doors of the Other Other One True Way Church blown off in a suspicious fashion.

But after seeing the demon in its true form, she wished that she hadn't been so lucky, that she'd simply perished in the fire along with all the other Fremontonians.

Looking about, Rumpza spied the spider shark raven ibex thing climbing up the wall of the church, heading toward a gaping hole in the ceiling created by the raging fire.

Rumpza knew that if the demon made it out of that hole and escaped into the wide world, it would be bad news for the wide world.

Not on Rumpza's watch.

Surprised to find that she was still gripping her weapon, Rumpza aimed the 1861 Savage Navy revolver at the escaping creature, attempting to steady her hand. Pulled the triggers.

Click, said the first trigger.

Click, said the second trigger.

Of course, she was out of bullets. She'd used them all in her battle with Loco Lenny Labovitz.

Like any action movie star worth their salt, Rumpza tossed the empty gun at the fleeing demon. Missed her. The cop searched for another weapon with which to dispatch the creature.

This being a church, there was a real dearth of weapons. She would have to kill this thing with her bare hands. Although Rumpza was terrified of heights, she was going to have to climb after the spider shark raven ibex thing.

Sandwiched between a stained glass window depicting Reverend Stevie G. Jones and Sweet Baby G kicking the recently-departed Loco Lenny Labovitz for all they were worth and a stained glass window featuring the reverend and Sweet Baby G pulling a bearded man from his vehicle for not wearing his seat belt and working him over pretty good with a baseball bat was a statue of Stevie G. Jones that nearly scraped the ceiling of the church. The statue featured Jones soaring toward a waiting heaven wearing a jetpack and carrying something that certainly looked like a bag stuffed with toys.

Jumping pews and dodging chunks of falling, burning debris, Rumpza raced for the statue. She kept one eye on the spider shark raven ibex thing and one eye on her perilous path.

Grabbing a hold of the jetpack's marble vapor trail, the cop pulled herself up the statue slowly. Though every muscle in her body burned, though she was still bleeding from her collection of bullet wounds and though she knew that her own death was imminent, the cop continued to climb.

When, at last, she reached the marble heaven, Rumpza looked over at the spider shark raven ibex thing, alarmed to see that its front two legs were already through the hole in the ceiling.

Without weapons, without a plan, without hope, Rumpza let go of heaven and jumped. She sailed through the smoky air and burning embers, reaching out for the fleeing creature.

Rumpza was well aware that she didn't stand a virgin's chance in Toledo. She was going to miss her mark and fall to her death. In a church, of all places. Though she wanted to close her eyes so she didn't have to witness her own death, the cop kept them open just in case something accidentally went right on this day from hell.

Something accidentally went right.

Just as she was losing momentum and about to tumble a hundred feet, the spider shark rave ibex thing kicked out one of its back legs to find purchase on the ceiling and Rumpza grabbed onto it.

Once, desperate and drunk, Rumpza had hot lesbian sex with a truck stop whore from Toledo whose bush fanned out from her vagina like a search party, covering a shocking percentage of her torso. That was now the second most disgusting thing she'd ever touched. The spider shark's leg was covered with course hairs and had the consistency of a rolled booger.

Sensing that something was amiss, the beast whipped its head around to face its attacker. The thing roared and Rumpza could smell the rotting corpses of a million souls on its hot breath. And just a hint of lollipop pussy, a hint of Connie.

To dislodge the interloper, the spider shark raven ibex thing shook its leg furiously, battering it against the burning ceiling of the church. Though she felt her hair singe and her flesh blister, the cop held on.

Trying to shut off her taste buds, Rumpza bit into the leg of the spider shark raven ibex thing, broke skin. Green blood oozed as the beast cried out in pain.

In desperation, the thing lunged at Rumpza, snapping its massive jaws. She saw rows and rows of twisted teeth coming at her but the creature couldn't get its terrifyingly large ibex head close enough to do any damage.

Swearing and sweating, the cop kicked at the beast's head. None of her blows landed but it gave her a small measure of satisfaction to simply be fighting back. "Let go of my girlfriend, you demon bitch!"

Shoving her hand deep into the bite wound, Rumpza rent the flesh of the demon, widening the wound, deepening it. Green blood gushed. Bellowing in pain, the spider shark raven ibex thing leapt at Rumpza. In doing so, the thing lost its purchase on the ceiling and the demon and the cop fell toward earth.

Screaming, Rumpza continued to hold onto the leg, which was difficult as it was now slick with blood. Together, they tumbled ass over tea kettle. Rumpza faced the ceiling, the floor, the ceiling. Certain she was going to die at the completion of the ride, Rumpza took some solace in the fact that the creature was going to die with her.

She hoped this meant sweet Connie would finally find some peace. Maybe – if any Fremontonians survived their hometown inferno – they might take pity on the young, hot lesbian couple and bury the lovers side-by-side in the Rutherford B. Hayes Memorial Cemetery, if it too hadn't burned to the ground.

When they landed on the floor, shattering pews and smashing hymnals – which featured a gold embossed picture of Reverend Stevie G. Jones and Sweet Baby G breaking up a poker game by clubbing the contestants with crosses – Rumpza was surprised and, admittedly, a little disappointed, to find that not only was she not dead, she hadn't even suffered a scratch. Sure, she hurt like hell, but she'd felt that way ever since taking a bevy of bullets.

She looked around to find that she had landed on the giant spider shark raven ibex thing which had cushioned her blow.

But it hadn't cushion its own blow. The beast lay motionless on the floor, its legs curled, an ocean of green blood pooling.

Standing, Rumpza backed away from the thing. She tried to catch her breath, but it remained at large. Stumbling, she sat down on the steps of the altar. Unable to move or think or care, Rumpza decided to sit there and wait for the flaming building to collapse upon her.

But, at least, the nightmare was over. The demon was dead, Connie was free.

The first bit of movement she noticed was a little twitching at the end of one of the spider shark raven ibex thing's legs. Rumpza sat up straighter and tried to convince herself this was just muscles convulsing after death. But then all eight legs began moving. Slowly finding their way back to life.

"Flock," whispered the cop, standing and once again casting about for a weapon. This time she was in luck, discovering a sharp shard of pew wood in the rubble.

Wielding it like a sword, she advanced on the stirring creature. Noticing that the legs were now moving and not just twitching, she picked up the pace, raising her weapon high, ready to plunge it into the soft underbelly of the demon.

But before she could do any plunging, the demon jumped, flipping over on its legs with a speed and agility that would have brought tears to the eyes of the most hardened figure skater.

Rumpza finally lost her shit. She screamed and dropped her weapon when those beady red ibex eyes focused on her, searched her soul.

The creature took a step toward her, licking its ibex lips with its ibex tongue.

"Hey yoo-hoo, demon, remember me?" called a voice from the destroyed entrance of the church. It was hard to hear over the fire that was now devouring the building.

The spider shark raven ibex thing spun and, in doing so, its tail, a whip, knocked Rumpza to the floor, forgotten.

From her vantage point amongst the rubble, the cop spied the crazy demon hunter that she'd left behind, standing at the back of the church. Predictably, he was without the benefit of clothing but he was, unpredictably, wielding a sword which was fashioned from some kind of space age polymer.

The nude dude's whole demeanor had changed since she'd last seen him, weeping beside his shredded girlfriend.

He now looked like a complete and utter motherflocker.

With every step he took through the burning city, his confidence flourished.

When he parted ways with the ghost of Tim, the Buddhist monk ninja warrior assassin, Cuntlips McGoo still harbored doubts about whether he could defeat this mighty demon. It had been years since he faced anything more deadly than a crabs-addled groupie, and this wasn't just any demon, it was Maude the Layer of Waste, the mightiest of all demons, and it had ripped the town of Fremont a new one.

But, as he combed the berg, death and destruction raining down all around him, he felt Tim's steady hand guiding him, he heard the former Buddhist monk ninja warrior assassin whispering encouraging words in his ear. Under Tim's guidance, the former rocker stumbled upon a massive katana store – Katana's 'R Us – that was being looted during the deadly conflagration.

Even before he'd slain Maude the Layer of Waste with one, katanas had been Cuntlips weapon of choice. Light, versatile, deadly.

Pushing his way through the throng of folks grabbing katanas off the shelves by the dozens, Cuntlips wandered through the store, which was curiously large for an establishment that dealt solely in ancient Japanese swords. There were katanas of every shape and size. Some were made from teak, some from ash, and, for reasons Cuntlips couldn't understand, there were some made from balsa wood. Maybe for the little ones.

At the back of the ransacked store, right beside the katana target range, the former rocker came across a cache of katanas made from a space age polymer that were virtually untouched.

Even looters are surprisingly traditional.

There was a red one that had Cuntlips' name written all over it. The sword was just like Tim's, the one he'd employed to kill Maude the Layer of Waste last time.

Picking it up, stroking the shaft, Cuntlips nearly ejaculated with pleasure. Tucking the rod into his pants, he rationalized it wasn't stealing, as he was doing the Lord's work.

Smiling – an act he thought he'd never engage in again after watching his girlfriend slip away into the Sweet Hereafter – Cuntlips turned to go.

But blocking his path was a man with wild eyes, jittery muscles, and a face that couldn't be mistaken for a welcome mat. So sweaty he looked as if he were melting.

Also, incongruously, he was toting a toaster.

Reaching out with his un-toastered hand, the man said, "Give me that katana."

Motioning, Cuntlips, "There's a whole rack of them right here, dude."

"I want the red one. Red is my favorite color."

"Let's not be ridiculous here, take an orange one. Orange is a cousin to red."

"Red one!"

"Listen, we don't have time to fight over this katana. I've got a demon to slay and you've got a fire to survive."

"Listen, buddy, don't mess with me. I've had a bad day."

"Look around, dude, we've all had a bad day."

"But I lost my collection of Precious Moments figurines! Even the one with the boy and girl flying a kite and kissing! That's a flocking classic!"

The jittery dude took a jittery step forward. Apparently, there was no reasoning with this guy and his crazy mind. Cuntlips drew the katana out of his pants. "Please don't make me go all Buddhist monk ninja assassin warrior on your ass, you won't like me when I'm all Buddhist monk ninja assassin warrior."

Holding out the toaster, the crazed man smiled a crazy smile. "I plug this baby in and this whole place goes BOOM."

"That's one rad toaster, dude."

"You know it."

"I see only one minor problem."

"Which is?"

"Where you gonna plug it in?"

Looking around, the man's smile dried up but the sweat continued.

He lurched, the crazed man. Or, at least, he tried to. Cuntlips didn't have time for this shit. Not now. With one lightningish move, he cut off the non-toastered arm of his attacker. Said limb landed on the linoleum with what could only be described as a sickening *fwap*!

Staring down at his severed arm, the man's eyes dazzled with disbelief. His voice became very small, very distant. "That's a katana.You're not supposed to be able to chop people's appendages off with a flocking katana."

"Then you're not doing it right. Now clear out of my way before you lose the other one."

Not taking his eyes away from his severed limb and all the blood rivering from his body, the crazed dude stepped aside, his deadly toaster tucked.

Aware that the man would bleed to death before help arrived, as there was no help that day, Cuntlips hustled out of the bustling store.

Now armed, he practically danced through the fiery streets, looking for any sign of the demon.

He stopped when he spied the suspiciously destroyed doors of a ridiculously large church. Cuntlips became certain when he heard unearthly bellowing coming from inside the building.

Drawing his space age polymer katana, Cuntlips bounded up the stairs.

He got inside just in time to see the cop, who he assumed was dead, advancing on a spider shark raven ibex thing, with her own rustic version of a katana.Though the demon was prone on the floor, Cuntlips could tell it was still alive, still breathing. He admired the cop. She was brave and crazy and determined. But there was no way in hell she could kill the most powerful demon in the netherworld alone.

This was his job, he was the last hope for humanity.

Unfortunately, he was proven right. The beast came to life before the cop could finish her off and leapt to its feet.Advancing on the cop – who dropped her weapon and made no attempt to flee – moving in for the kill.

Cuntlips had to put the brakes on the carnage that was about to go down.

Clearing his throat, he called out to the demon. "Hey yoo-hoo, Maude the Layer of Waste, remember me?"

The evil beast whipped around to face him. Cuntlips continued, "You might recall, I killed you in the wilds of Kuala Lumpur a decade ago. Although you totally snuffed out my only friend in the world, I ended you. I'm gonna do the exact same thing today. Coincidentally, I'm brandishing a katana made out of space age polymer just like-."

Cuntlips wasn't allowed to finish the overly detailed description of his weaponry before the beast attacked. Though he knew such an event was inevitable, the demon hunter was not prepared for it. The poor man didn't even have time to raise his much discussed weapon before the spider shark raven ibex thing barreled into him in the gold-plated narthex of the Other Other One True Way Church. Sending him into the air.

During this trip, Cuntlips dropped his katana. With a sickening *fwap*, he landed in a pile on the travertine floor.

Shaking his head, which was bleeding profusely, the demon hunter got to his feet and stumbled toward his fallen katana, retrieving it.

When he stood, he found that the demon was circling him, taking up most of the room in the narthex. Flicking its tail with bad intent.

Cuntlips could feel Tim's hot breath on his shoulder, whispering instructions into his ear. Reminding him to keep up his guard and never look away from the beast regardless of how repulsive it was.

While the hellbeast circled him, he circled it.

Ready to send this beast back to the flames, Cuntlips leapt forward with a rebel yell that rattled everything inside and outside of his head.

As she watched the demon and the demon hunter circle one

another, Officer Rumpza stood on shaking feet, dusted off her uniform. Though she hadn't muttered a single prayer since her youth, the cop was surprised to find herself having the usual one-sided conversation with the Lord. Made sense, as she was in a church. Or what was left of a church.

Rumpza prayed that the nude dude, despite his odd bathroom sexual proclivities, would win this epic battle of good versus evil. Although it seemed a long shot, she really wanted to see him plunge his weapon deep into the belly of the beast and punch its one-way ticket back to hell.

Apparently the Lord was on a break, for that didn't happen.

Raising his wooden sword thing, Cuntlips lunged toward the spider shark raven ibex thing.

Over the last forty-eight hours, Rumpza had run across a nauseating number of icky deaths, but there was something about the manner in which the demon hunter was snuffed out that was particularly demoralizing. Maybe it was because just seconds before his death he'd seemed so sure, so brimming with confidence. Perhaps it was due to the fact that she knew once the demon dispatched the demon hunter, it was coming after her. Or it could have simply been because his death was so blatantly awful.

When the demon hunter charged, the spider shark raven ibex thing didn't even flinch. It simply flicked its tail, which came around like a telephone pole and knocked the nude dude off his nude feet.

He flew through the narthex like a fleshy kite, traveling at an unhealthy speed. He probably would have broken every bone in his body if he'd struck the gold-plated walls, but instead, he hit a statue first.

This particular statue, standing twenty feet tall, was of Reverend Stevie G. Jones and the Sweet Baby G tearing a sodomite limb from limb. Though the reverend and the Savior were dressed in business casual, the sodomite, much like the demon hunter himself, was buck naked and his top-shelf schlong was fully erect.

The nude dude was impaled on the erection with a *fwap* sound that could only be described as sickening. Full penetration. Thirty inches of marble cock sticking through his chest. Although copious amounts of blood poured from his body, the demon hunter didn't die immediately. He hung around for an embarrassingly long time, crying out in great agony, staring down at the massive kidney-buster protruding from chest, his eyes twigged with jealousy and despair, watching the life drain from his body.

Rumpza, realizing its futility, stopped praying.

As a trained law enforcement officer, she was well aware it was her job to do something, anything. But she couldn't move, couldn't even blink. For there was no way to help, all hope was lost. She simply stood there, watching the demon hunter's tragedy unfold and waiting for her turn to die.

The beast sauntered toward the dying man with a triumphant smile on its ibex lips. When it arrived at the sodomite statue, the demon and the demon hunter locked eyes. The light was fading in one, absorbed by the other.

The screaming that the nude dude was partaking in turned to whimpering, then tears, then, finally, after what felt like hours, nothing. Closing his eyes on this dark and dismal world, the demon hunter's head slumped forward, forever.

The shark spider ibex thing laughed and lowered its head to lick a slathering of blood off the dead man's chest.

"Hey, demon, flock you!"

As she assumed she could no longer speak, Rumpza was surprised to find that these words had sprung from her own throat. They traveled across the burning church and made the demon turn. Glare at the cop.

Everything in Rumpza's body turned to liquid, except the liquid, which froze.

The spider shark raven ibex thing smiled its thousand and one teeth. They were filched in blood.

Forming fists, Rumpza took a defensive stance. Yes, she was going down but she wished to appear to give a damn.

Its smile turning into a roar, the demon squeezed through the gold-plated narthex's door and came charging down the church's main aisle, barreling toward Rumpza, wings flapping. The cop stood her ground, lowered her center of gravity, and prepared to die.

But death didn't come. The ceiling of the Other Other One True Way Church chose that moment to finally collapse. Flaming debris rained down. As this was the end of everything, Rumpza didn't even bother to cover her head.

But she escaped the fiery deluge unscathed.

The creature was not so lucky.

A massive chunk of the fresco that adorned the ceiling of the church – featuring Reverend Stevie G. Jones and the Sweet Baby G slitting the throat of a man stumbling out of bar – landed squarely on the demon, pinning it to the ground.

The thing cried out in pain, which woke Rumpza down to her marrow. What was she doing just standing there? This was a perfect opportunity for her to escape. Leave this demon to burn and get the hell out.

Maybe, just maybe, she might live.

Turning, the cop ran. She made it about ten feet before she heard Connie's sweet voice. Like a song, like a dream. Filled with distress.

"Chrissy, Chrissy, please help me! I'm trapped!"

Rumpza stopped and turned, though she knew it was the wrong move, knew it was a trap. But she couldn't help herself. What was pinned beneath the burning roof was no longer the shark spider raven ibex thing, it was Connie, sweet Connie. Naked, bloodied, and in great pain.

Though there was a very logical voice screaming in the back of her head to not do so, Rumpza walked back to the scene of the accident. The reek of charred flesh filled the smokey air. She couldn't look away from Connie's eyes. Filled with hurt and remorse and... and love.

A warning voice continued to harp as she dug down into her battered body and found the strength to push the flaming fresco off the girl.

The cop wondered if she and Connie and Connie's lollipop pussy could have a bout of hot lesbian sex right then and there as the church burned down all around them.

Or, at least, a hug.

But a hug was not in the offing. And certainly there wouldn't be any hot lesbian sex.

For once the thing was freed, it shed its Connie-ness and turned back into the shark spider ibex thing. Before it was even done changing back, the cop felt something wrap around her waist, squeeze the air, the life, right out of her. It was the demon's tail and it was intent on internal injuries.

Rumpza felt so stupid.

With a victorious roar, the thing flew to the wall above the altar and began to climb. Rumpza was carried along for the ride.

Unable to breath, unable to think straight, the cop lost her will to fight, to live. It was all over except for the part where the demon decapitated her, which she hoped would happen soon. She couldn't stand to see any more death, any more destruction.

The shark spider raven ibex thing burst through the last section of ceiling that was still intact and suddenly, they were outside. Standing on the walls of the church. Though the air was choked with smoke, Rumpza could see a majority her hometown. She saw that everything, everyone, was either burning or burnt.

Even more than usual, Fremont was a hell on earth.

Rumpza knew that this was what was going to happen all over the globe when this creature pooped out its hell baby. As the end of the world was too bleak to comprehend, Rumpza broke down.

Molten tears scalded her face. She cried for all the dead: the demon hunter, his girlfriend, Junior Officer Killion, the Police Chief. But her biggest tears, her brightest, were reserved for Connie. Ever since that night a lifetime ago when Connie walked out of the Pendleton home and disappeared, Rumpza had allowed herself to keep the smallest glimmer of hope for her safe return. She wished that Connie would come home unscathed and they could spend the rest of their existences together, knee-deep in hot lesbian sex. Even when Rumpza came to realize that the killer lose in Fremont was a demon using Connie's body, she still held out hope that the demon would flee and let the poor girl live.

But now, standing atop the crumbling walls of the Other Other One True Way Church, all those hopes became gossamer, ripped easily and were scattered by the wind.

When the beast whipped its tail around, Rumpsza found herself face-to-ibex-face with the snorting demon.

"Go ahead," said Rumpza, her voice small.

"What?" demanded the beast. It no longer sounded like Connie, but like something which dwelled in darkness.

"Decapitate me, rip me limb from limb, bite me in half, whatever. I don't care anymore. Just let me talk to Connie one last time."

"Who's Connie?"

"The beautiful girl whose body you're using. I loved her and I want to say goodbye to her before you kill me."

"The Other Girl is gone. She died long ago."

"No she's not. She's inside you somewhere. I just saw her in the church when the ceiling caved in on you. It was her I saved, not you. She's alive, breathing, inside of you. And you know that. You would have killed me right after I freed you, but you didn't. I'm still alive for a reason, and that reason is Connie, her goodness still burns bright inside of you. At times, it even overrides your evil nature. In fact, I can see her right now, there's a flicker in your eye. Whether you like it or not, my girlfriend is inside of you as much as you are inside of her."

"No, no, no! None of that is true, you lie puny human!"

"It's true and you know it and that's why you're so mad. Connie is inside you and she's bursting to get out. She wants to live and love and smile and dance and swim and partake in hot lesbian sex and you can't stomach that spark of goodness in your blackened heart."

The thing looked up at the smoky sky and cried out. When it looked back down, Connie was no longer in its eyes. It pulled Rumpza so close she was nearly asphyxiated by the smell of rot on the creature's breath. It roared, blowing back Rumpza's hair. The cop closed her eyes, expecting to be devoured.

But the world stilled and nothing happened.

Opening her eyes, Rumpza stared at the spider shark raven ibex thing and, although its face was still that of an ibex, all across its snout there appeared constellations of freckles.

"Oh Connie, sweet Connie, there you are," whispered Rumpza.

"It's so dark in here," said the Connie thing. "So dark and so cold. Yet I'm burning up."

"I know, sweetheart. But you can get out. You can win this battle. Keep fighting, I believe in you. Think of me, think of all the hot lesbian sex we'll have."

Suddenly, the creature sprouted a tuft of red hair above its dead eyes. The thing shook its head violently.

The creature's gaping maw turned into a winning smile and it grew a pair of small, pert breasts. It began to attack itself, bite at its own haunches. It was a sight to behold.

Officer Rumpza, tossed about in the attack, continued to shout encouragement to her lover though she didn't know if Connie could hear her over the violent snapping of jaws.

The creature spun round and round as if dancing with fire. The next time the cop saw its face, it had completely changed. No longer did it look like a creature, it was Connie. 100% Connie. Beautiful young Connie who held her heart and her labia.

She wanted to reach out and touch her, kiss her but there wasn't time.

The walls of the church caved in.

Together they fell, the half-girl, half-thing and the cop. Screaming, flipping over and over.

Right before they hit the ground, the demon wrapped its wings around Rumpza.

Though they felt a lot like arms.

Part Four:
Lesbian Heaven

A splitting headache. That's the feeling she awoke with, her brain being cleaved by a very dull but very persistent axe. She opened her eyes just a bit, as much as her hammering head would allow.

Rumpza was in a glen or a glade, it was hard to tell which with her head hurting so. But the bullet wounds no longer burned. In fact, there were no bullet wounds. She felt her torso. No blood, no holes.

For a moment, she believed she was in heaven. Then she recalled that any human who'd put even a millisecond of thought into it knew there was no such location.

She was simply lost.

But she was lost in a beautiful place.

Everything was green, verdant, and there was no fire, no smoke to choke on. No demons. Throwing caution to the gentle breeze, she sat up and opened her eyes all the way.

She was definitely in a glen.

Just as she was about to attempt to rise, Connie came out of the trees. In one hand she was carrying a clutch of dead squirrels, the other hand was waving manically. She was dressed in the tight Lynyrd Skynyrd T-shirt and short skirt Dearly Departed had made famous. Her long legs long, her flowing red hair flowing.

Wiping away a pond of drool, Rumpza realized she was, in fact, in heaven. Lesbian heaven.

Rushing to Rumpza's side, Connie knelt and ran her non-squirreled hand through her hair. "Oh good, you're finally awake. I caught us some lunch."

"So we're not dead?" Rumpza wanted to make absolutely sure.

"No, silly."

"Then where are we?"

Looking around, Connie bunched her eyebrows. "I can't say for sure. I'd guess we are a few miles east of Toledo, I've been carrying you for hours."

"Carrying me?"

"Yeah. We were both knocked unconscious when the church caved in. When I came to, I couldn't wake you, so I had to carry you out of that burning building, out of that burning town. Oh Chrissy, can you believe I'm me again? And that' s all thanks to you. Your love set me free and sent that demon back to the pit it crawled out of."

For the first time in a long time Rumpza smiled. It was too good to be true. Or maybe it was too true to be good. She didn't care. "And you're safe? You're fine?"

"I'm better than fine, sweetness, I feel strong. I feel vital. I feel like I've never lived before. And I've got some great news. Well, at least, I hope you think it's great news."

A cloud passed over Rumpza's everything, darkening. "What is it?"

"I'm pregnant. I'm going to have a baby, our baby, Chrissy! I can feel him kicking inside of me already. He's a strong one, my love, he's powerful!"

Connie smiled. She had more teeth than a person had a right to. All of them were sharp and jagged and coated with squirrel innards.

Though she felt like recoiling, wanted to run away, fast and far, Rumpza didn't, couldn't. She tried to look on the bright side, overlook her lover's flaws, which is what anyone has to do to make relationships work.

A baby would be good for them, cement the couple together for life.

The cop – she supposed she was an ex-cop now that her city was gone – didn't need a crystal ball to gaze into their shared future. The three of them living in a small house on a tree-lined street, playing with their boy in his cage, engaging in hour after hour of hot lesbian sex in a Jacuzzi filled with bubbling champagne.

Everything she ever wanted.

Well, nearly.

(Photo by Seana McCroddan Photography)

Bix Skahill starred in the movie Fargo.
That's the truth.
Look that shit up.

CPSIA information can be obtained
at www.ICGtesting.com
Printed in the USA
BVOW08s1823140217
476184BV00001B/57/P